THE DISGRACED MARTYR TRILOGY

BOOK I

THE HIEROPHANT'S DAUGHTER

THE
HIEROPHANT'S
DAUGHTER

M. F. SULLIVAN

The Hierophant's Daughter
© 2019 M. F. Sullivan
ISBN: 978-0-9965395-7-9

Text: M. F. Sullivan
Editing: Michelle Hope
Cover Design: Nuno Moreira
Typesetting: Jennifer Cant

www.paintedblindpublishing.com
publicity@paintedblindpublishing.com

FIRST EDITION

Ah, not Cassandra! Wake not her
Whom God hath maddened, lest the foe
Mock at her dreaming. Leave me clear
From that one edge of woe.
O Troy, my Troy, thou diest here
Most lonely; and most lonely we
The living wander forth from thee,
And the dead leave thee wailing!

—Euripides, *The Trojan Women*

I

The Flight of the Governess

The Disgraced Governess of the United Front was blind in her right eye. Was that blood in the left, or was it damaged, too? The crash ringing in her ears kept her from thinking straight. Of course her left eye still worked: it worked well enough to prevent her from careening into the trees through which she plunged. Yet, for the tinted flecks of reality sometimes twinkling between crimson streaks, she could only imagine her total blindness with existential horror. Would the protein heal the damage? How severely was her left eye wounded? What about the one she knew to be blind—was it salvageable? Ichigawa could check, if she ever made it to the shore.

She couldn't afford to think that way. It was a matter of "when," not of "if." She would never succumb. Neither could car accident, nor baying hounds, nor the Hierophant himself keep her from her goal. She had fourteen miles to the ship that would whisk her across the Pacific and deliver her to the relative safety of the Risen Sun. Then the Lazarene ceremony would be less than a week away. Cassandra's diamond beat against her heart to pump it into double time, and with each double beat, she thought of her wife (smiling, laughing, weeping when she thought herself alone) and ran faster. A lucky thing the Governess wasn't human! Though, had she remained human, she'd have died three centuries ago in some ghetto if she'd lived past twenty without becoming supper. Might have been the easier fate, or so she lamented each time her mind replayed the crash of the passenger-laden *tanque* at fifth gear against the side of their small car. How much she might have avoided!

Of course—then she never would have known Cassandra. That made all this a reasonable trade. Cold rain softened the black earth to the greedy consistency of clay, but her body served where her eyes failed. The darkness was normally no trouble, but now she squinted while she ran and, under sway of a dangerous adrenaline high, was side-swiped by more than one twisting branch. The old road that was her immediate goal, Highway 128, would lead her to the coast of her favorite Jurisdiction, but she now had to rediscover that golden path after the crash's diversion. In an effort to evade her pursuers, she had torn into a pear orchard without thought of their canine companions. Not that the soldiers of the Americas kept companions like Europa's nobles. These dogs were tools. Well-honed, organic death machines with a cultivated taste for living flesh, whether martyr or human. The dogs understood something that most had forgotten: the difference between the two was untenable. Martyrs could tell themselves they were superior for an eternity, but it wouldn't change the fact that the so-called master race and the humans they consumed were the same species.

That was not why Cassandra had died, but it hadn't contributed to their marital bliss. And now, knowing what she did of the Hierophant's intentions—thinking, always, what Cassandra would have said—the Governess pretended she was driven by that ghost, and not by her own hopelessness. Without the self-delusion, she was a victim to a great many ugly thoughts, foremost among them being: Was the fear of life after her wife's death worth such disgrace? A death sentence? Few appreciated what little difference there was between human and martyr, and fewer cared, because caring was fatal. But she was a part of the Holy Family. Shouldn't that have been all that mattered? Stunning how, after three centuries, she deserved to be treated no better than a human. Then again, there was nothing quite like resignation from one's post to fall in her Father's estimate. Partly, he was upset by her poor timing—she did stand him up at some stupid press event, but only because she hoped it would keep everybody occupied while she got away. In that moment, she couldn't even remember what it was. Dedicating a bridge? Probably. Her poor head, what did the nature of the event matter when she was close to death?

That lapse in social graces was not the reason for this hunt. He understood that more lay behind her resignation than a keening for country life. Even before he called her while she and the others took the *tanque* to the coast, he must have known. Just like he must have known the crash was seconds from happening while he chatted away, and that the humans in her company, already nervous to be within a foot of the fleeing Governess, were doomed.

Of the many people remaining on Earth, those lumped into the group of "human" were at constant risk of death, mutilation, or—far worse—unwilling martyrdom. This meant those humans lucky enough to avoid city-living segregation went to great lengths to keep their private properties secure. Not only houses but stables. The Disgraced Governess found this to be true of the stables into which she might have stumbled and electrocuted herself were it not for the bug zaps of rain against the threshold's surface. Her mind made an instinctive turn toward prayer for the friendliness of the humans in the nearby farmhouse—an operation she was quick to abort. In those seconds (minutes?) since the crash, she'd succeeded in reconstructing the tinted windows of the *tanque* and a glimpse of silver ram's horns: the Lamb lurked close enough to hear her like she spoke into his ear. It was too much to ask that he be on her side tonight.

Granted, the dogs of the Lamb were far closer, and far more decisive about where their loyalties stood. One hound sank its teeth into her ankle, and she, crying out, kicked the beast into its closest partner with a crunch. Slower dogs snarled outrage in the distance while the Disgraced Governess ran to the farmhouse caught in her left periphery. The prudent owners, to her frustration, shuttered their windows at night. Nevertheless, she smashed her fist against the one part of the house that protruded: the doorbell required by the Hierophant's "fair play" dictatum allowing the use of electronic barriers. As the humans inside stumbled out of bed in response to her buzzing, the Disgraced Governess unholstered her antique revolver and unloaded two rounds into the recovered canines before they were upon her. The discharge wasn't a tip-off she wanted to give to the Lamb and her other pursuers, but it hastened the response of the sleeping farmers as the intercom crackled to life.

"Who is it?" A woman's voice, quivering with an edge of panic.

"My name is Dominia di Mephitoli: I'm the former Governess of the United Front, and I need to borrow a horse. Please. Don't let me in. Just drop the threshold on your stables."

"The Governess? I'm sorry, I don't understand. *The* Dominia di Mephitoli, really? The martyr?"

"Yes, yes, please. I need a horse now." Another dog careened around the corner and leapt over the bodies of his comrades with such grace that she wasted her third round in the corpses. Two more put it down as she shouted into the receiver. "I can't transfer you any credits because they've frozen my Halcyon account, but I'll leave you twenty pieces of silver if you drop the threshold and loan me a horse. You can reclaim it at the docks off Bay Street, in the township of Sienna. Please! He'll kill me."

"And he'll be sure to kill us for helping you."

"Tell him I threatened you. Tell him I tricked you! Anything. Just help me get away!"

"He'll never believe what we say. He'll kill me, my husband, our children. We can't."

"Oh, please. An act of mercy for a dying woman. Please, help me leave. I can give you the name of a man in San Valentino who can shelter you and give you passage abroad."

"There's no time to go so far south. Not as long as it takes to get across the city."

It had been ten seconds since she'd heard the last dog. That worried her. With her revolver at the ready, she scanned the area for something more than the quivering roulette blotches swelling in her right eye. Nothing but the dead animals. "He'll kill you either way. For talking to me, and not keeping me occupied until his arrival. For knowing that there's disarray in his perfect land. He'll find a reason, even if it only makes sense to him."

The steady beat of rain pattered out a passive answer. On the verge of giving up, Dominia stepped back to ready herself for a fight—and the house's threshold dropped with an electric pop. The absent mauve shimmer left the façade bare. How rare to see a country place without its barrier! A strange thing. Stranger for the front door to open; she'd only expected them to do away with the threshold on the stables.

But, rather than the housewife she'd anticipated, there stood the Hierophant. Several bleak notions clicked into place.

One immaculate gray brow arched. "Now, Dominia, that's hardly fair. Knowledge of your disgrace isn't why I'll kill them. The whole world will know of it tomorrow morning. You embarrassed me by sending your resignation, rather than making the appearance I asked of you, so it is only fair I embarrass you by rejecting your resignation and firing you publicly. No, my dear. I will kill these fine people to upset you. In fact, Mr. McLintock is already dead in the attic. A mite too brave. Of course"—he winked, and whispered in conspiracy—"don't tell them that."

"How did you know I'd come here?"

"Such an odd spurt of rain tonight. Of all your Jurisdictions, this one is usually so dry this time of year! Won't you come in for tea? Mrs. McLintock brews a fine pot. But put that gun away. You're humiliating yourself. And me."

Dominia, with some delay for her trembling, slid the gun into its holster, then entered a building that gleamed with history. Such a nice ranch house, with generations of pictures on walls that had themselves been carefully preserved, or identically restored. People were meticulous with homes like these. They lived. This one had been around a long time. Two millennia, based on the style. Centuries of love and care, about to be disrupted by a terrible bath of blood.

A friendlier dog than the ones outside greeted her at the door, and the Hierophant bent to ruffle its floppy black ears. "A new friend for the Lamb, perhaps, after you've cruelly killed three."

"As poor a guard dog as he's proved tonight, I don't think he's the hunting sort."

"Of course not. But we can always use more pets, can't we?"

Wasn't that the use of courtiers? She kept the joke to herself. In an intimate, doily-filled drawing room, the Hierophant drew an antique oak chair from the matching table and patted its scroll-carved back. Dominia lowered into the place set in anticipation of her coming, wherefrom she, scowling, studied him with she had already begun to consider her "good eye." The Hierophant, that eerie smile never leaving his pale lips, poured the tea as he spoke.

"I remember when you were first martyred. You'd pout at every supper, refuse to eat your food. I ought to have seen this night arriving."

"You did. You only pretended not to."

"True! I always like to think I've some small say in destiny. That if I ignore inevitability hard enough, it shall not rear its head. But that never seems to be the case. These tedious things all end the same."

"This is drugged, I suppose."

"It's as if you don't know me. How passé! No, my dear, I only wish to speak to you and—Carol?"

Now the berobed, befuddled woman Dominia had expected made her belated appearance. The Hierophant flashed her a smile stupid men cherished and wiser men feared. "I don't suppose you've a few spare pastries?"

"Some donuts for the children," she mumbled automatically, paling to have reminded herself, and the Hierophant, of their existence.

"Well, far be it from me to take food from the mouths of babes. Why not bring them to share with us! Rouse the tykes from bed. I love to see sweet, sleepy faces."

"Please," said the woman.

"No," said Dominia.

The Hierophant's black eyes danced between them. "I suppose it is rather late for sugar, but you ladies are taking this much too seriously. Carol, dear: go get the children. Or would you rather I fetch them?"

That suggestion chased her right up the stairs. The Holy Father smiled as he plucked with huge hands a delicate teacup adorned with painted roses; the gesture resembled that of a better father, playing tea with his daughter's tiny plastic saucers. "What a hostess. Up at two in the morning with such moxie!"

"Why are you doing this?"

"Don't you wish for a bit of civility amid all the violence and terror? You looked like you could use a sit-down. Please, drink the tea."

With a sniff that detected nothing but jasmine, she did, and broke up the heretofore uninterrupted taste of blood to which she had adjusted. Meanwhile, the flow of blood had stopped above her left eye, and a little shard of glass was pushed out by the work of the sacred protein. That good protein, her one friend. While she blinked the shard away in relief to know she was not fully blind, she finished her tea and tried to calculate a way out of the house before he got his hands on her.

No chance of that. A bonny pair of children soon tumbled down the stairs, wired from their mother's angst and promises of midnight donuts. The Hierophant laughed in delight and clapped his hands, and the girl gasped in wonder.

"Isn't that the Holo Man?"

"It's the Hierophant, Betty." Exclaiming this, the boy froze at the entrance of the room. Their mother whisked past, her anxious stare trained on the Hierophant to whom the girl, brash with innocence, giddily darted. Wiser with his eight years of dread, the boy licked his lips. "Has our family done something wrong?"

"No, no. There will be donuts." Pleased, the Hierophant turned his attention to the girl, whose golden locks fell in disarray while he whisked her up to bounce upon his knee. "I do love children," sang the martyr, far taller in the presence of the doll-like girl. Dominia gripped the table to remind herself of her own size. "They take joy in such simple things. Their courageous connection to the moment, that *joie de vivre*, has yet to be deadened by social laws."

The Governess couldn't hold her tongue. "By your laws."

"God's laws. There are men, and there are martyrs. That is a fact about which nothing can be done—no more than anything can be done about the martyr's inherent superiority. Thank you, Carol." He turned his smile to the tense woman who deposited plates of donuts before her unwelcome guests. On eye contact, her pupils shrank to pinpoints. With a lingering stare for her daughter, she hustled her son to the corner of the sofa and sat with him, one iron hand clamped to the base of his neck.

"You always had a problem accepting that," resumed the Hierophant, breaking up the powdered pastry and offering half to the bright-eyed girl. "Our superiority, I mean. Oh, you tucked your ideals away with enough years' worth of tutors, and enough time spent in the proper culture, but I admit that I saw your regression the instant you took up governance of the Front. Even after your sordid military career, your heart is too soft for these more difficult matters. Will you continue to let Cassandra's unraveling destroy your future?"

"She didn't 'unravel.' You drove her insane. She died because of you. She—"

"Is this a topic for young ears? Please, dear. I must apologize, Carol: despite my best efforts, my duckling never grew into a swan as did her younger sister. There are always kinks worked out with older models. Your name was 'Betty,' wasn't it, princess?" At the oblivious girl's happy nod from behind her powder-coated fingers, the Hierophant offered her the other half of his donut. "Well, Betty, you remind me an awful lot of my Lavinia. Do you know who Lavinia is?"

At the name, the girl's eyes widened, and she preened as any small child would when compared to royalty so high. "She's the real princess! The best princess in the whole world, and the prettiest!"

"She certainly is. What do you think of Lavinia, darling girl?"

"That she's pretty," emphasized the child again. How old was she? Three, going on four? How old had Dominia been when the Hierophant martyred her? Seven, or eight. He preferred that humans did the bulk of early raising; bed-wetting increased the transition's already unbearable difficulty. She had to lean on her notion of his preference and hope that he had only bluffed about his killing mood. There was no moving faster than him. No wasting a bullet on him. At the slightest provocation, or none, he would snap the girl's neck and be on the mother and her son two seconds later. Dominia already saw it happening and willed the images away as the child continued rattling off that Lavinia, "Gets to live in a castle with a lot of horses and doggies and all her friends. And she sings pretty, too."

"Ah, doesn't she." The Hierophant smiled with fondness, then pointed across the table at Dominia. "Do you know who that is?" he asked in a half whisper. The girl, who had been glad to have the donuts but reluctant to look at the bloodied Governess, now followed his finger and shook her head.

"What's wrong with her eye?"

"I know who she is," called the boy, to his mother's visible anguish. "She's the Governess of the whole United Front, all North America."

"'Was' the Governess, lad. Come here." The Hierophant waved a regal hand, and over came the boy, in danger far graver than his sister by virtue of age. As Dominia's breath stilled, the Holy Father reached across the table to pluck up her donut in offering to the boy. "What's your name?"

"Murph McLintock." Donut acquired, the breathless child edged toward the Governess as much as manners allowed.

"Do you see the Disgraced Governess's eye, Murphy?" asked the Hierophant. The boy turned to regard the (slightly) less notoriously evil martyr.

"It's all full of blood."

"Let's play a game. What do you reckon the odds that the Disgraced Governess's eye will stay intact 'til morning?"

The grim boy regarded the jelly extruding from the edge of the donut. "What happened to her?"

"Dominia? Would you tell Murphy what happened?"

With a resentful glance at her Father, Dominia turned her good eye toward the boy. "I was in a car accident. On the way to the shore."

Her Father pressed. "To do what?"

"To…leave."

"To run away," corrected the Hierophant, his solemn expression still aimed at Murph. "To abandon her post and deliver information to the enemy. This woman is a criminal."

Face writ with anxiety, the boy stepped back from the table. The Hierophant's smile never wavered.

"Have you ever met a martyr before, lad?"

The boy shook his head.

"What do you think? Is a martyr different from a human?"

"Dad says—"

"I don't care what 'Dad' says. I want to know what Murphy says."

Between the Hierophant and the Governess, the boy swallowed like his saliva had been replaced by sand.

"Yes. Martyrs are different from humans."

"And how are we different?"

"Well, humans are born, and then we die. But martyrs are born human, and then they die, and then they're born again as martyrs."

"And what happens when they're born again? What makes a martyr superior to a human?"

The boy's face tightened, and Dominia thought, that's right, we're not superior, there's nothing that makes a martyr superior, nothing that merits his treatment of humans, and you don't have to say it; but, of course, she didn't vocalize this thought. Instead, she sat frozen as she'd been in the instant of Cassandra's death. She was back in that dark and bloody room until Murph said, "Well, they're fast, and strong. Some are geniuses—magical, almost, like you. They don't have to worry about anything, even if they get into an accident and need a wheelchair like my aunt Hilda. 'Cause they get better so fast. My aunt doesn't live here," added the child, chin raised in a defensive posture. The Hierophant chuckled to himself.

"And what does a martyr need, my boy, to sustain that second life?"

"Human flesh." The boy spared a reluctant glance for his sister in the Hierophant's lap. "Or blood."

"That's right: although, flesh is better. And how is a martyr made?"

"By eating," whispered Murphy.

"Yes, dear boy. By eating the flesh or drinking the blood of a martyr. And other means, of course, not suited for young ears." The Hierophant winked at pale Carol, who rested her elbow upon the back of the couch and cradled her forehead in that worried hand. "What other things are passed that way, lad? Outside of martyrdom?"

"Well, sicknesses. But it's a sickness, isn't it? Martyrdom? It's a kind of sickness, and that's why all the rich people left in—when was it, Mom? I saw on the history program one day, but I don't remember. After Mars was good enough for people to start living there."

"1744 Anno Lucis," his mother answered from behind closed eyes. "My ancestor wasn't quite seventeen, too young to go with her fiancé, so they forged her documents and pretended she was eighteen. They had to leave their baby behind, and that's why we're still here."

"To think, Carol, you begged before to know why I was here— coming as you do from a family of criminals! Martyrdom is not a sickness, my boy. It is the cure to sickness—all sickness. But it is more than mere earthly cure. It is a mission. A privilege. It is an honor in which one becomes part of something grander than oneself. Grander than one might ever comprehend. One becomes a gift to the world. To reject that, and see that as anything but a privilege…do you suppose that is right, Murphy? Do you think it is *fair* that a martyr should reject the role chosen for them? Should they deny the importance of their task, and the importance of the tasks being done by their brethren?"

Caught in a trap by the sensibilities of his age, the reluctant boy shook his head. The Hierophant's hands spread in Dominia's direction. "There you are, my girl! I have no choice."

He snatched her right eye from her skull in a motion so quick Dominia could only scream in tandem with the children before propelling from the table to writhe upon the floor. Blood oozed through her fingers while her legs kicked to fend off the pain; meanwhile, the girl's panicked feet carried her cries to her mother. With his most feline expression of amusement, the Hierophant dipped the much-abused sac into his tea.

"We never did place a proper bet, lad, so I'll count that as a 'win' on my part, if you don't mind. Do you like your life the way it is?"

"No!" Dominia arched her back against the pain and gnashed her teeth, unable to lift her hand away to view the unfolding scene. "Don't do it! Don't do it, you bastard!"

"I will deal with you at an opportune juncture," said the Hierophant. "Come here, Murphy. Answer the Holy Father."

Again, obligated by well-instilled values, the boy neared with but a flicker of attention for the crying mother who cradled her second child and prayed for her first. Amid all her screaming pain, Dominia thought to herself how praying would only make the situation worse, but she had no strength to say it as her free hand fumbled around her belt.

"I love my parents."

"And your sister?"

With more reluctance: "Yes."

As the boy answered, the Hierophant lifted the lid of the sugar bowl and scooped a few generous teaspoons into the cup. "What if I told you that you could keep your family safe from me forever? All you'd need do is trade your life for them."

"No," cried Dominia again, a word useless to him.

The wise child asked, "You don't mean really die, do you?"

The Hierophant smiled in that mockery of patriarchal tenderness which was his trademark. "No, I don't. It has been a long time since I've been a new grandparent."

"Murphy, don't." His mother made one futile plea, but the boy looked in her eyes and saw her fear, saw her neck wet with the tears of his sister. Strangled with grief, Murph turned back to the Hierophant.

"I'd do it for them."

"You'll come with me and grow into a man who will never age beyond his apex. Never sicken. Never die. You'll have wealth beyond measure, more friends than you could count; I'll make you a duke, or an earl. Not so bad a trade for your old human life? For your family's lives?"

Mute, the boy shook his head. The smiling Hierophant offered the cup of tea and blood. That nauseating admixture stood poised millimeters from the boy's lips when Dominia managed to lift the gun and, half blind, pull the trigger.

She would wish for the rest of her life that she had gotten the shot off sooner, and that Murphy's last memory of life before the bullet ended his suffering wasn't the tea of ocular matter nearing his lips for the sake of his cowering family. She would wish and wish and it would never change, that second of realization that she had killed a child to save him from martyrdom. Nothing about it would change, neither that cry from his mother, which pierced the air for miles around, nor that cold, dead-faced look from the Hierophant, who regarded the corpse, then his daughter, with disappointment.

"That was a stupid thing to do."

"Well, you know me." Dominia took a haggard breath while the Hierophant, in a petty rage, stormed across the room to snap the necks of both mother and daughter. It was the most painless death possible for either of them after the night's direction. "I've never been your favorite."

"You could have been, had you ever tried to adapt. Nothing you could have done for me, for the Family, ever could have made you my favorite child until you accepted my love into your heart! Yet you have always refused it, that love. All the things I gave you—all the sacrifice, the attention and education. The land. Your governance! Oh, Dominia, what an awful shame!"

Feeling pathetic, Dominia endeavored to turn her last bullet on herself, but recalled as she pulled the trigger that her last had been spent on Murph. The Hierophant swept the gun out of her hand, as angry as if she'd been successful. "No, no, no. You ridiculous woman. Shall I take both your eyes? Eager as you are to destroy your world, I would do you a favor by blinding you to it."

"Fuck you," she said, and was whipped across the face with the handle of the gun.

"I have never been as humiliated by your mouth as I was tonight. What a pitiful waste."

He drew back his leg and kicked Dominia once, hard, in the stomach. As her hand shifted protection from her eye socket to her winded gut, the Holy Father clutched her by the throat to fling her against the table. Precious more than a rag doll, she lay upon the broken shards of a porcelain vase and its half-dead posies. The Hierophant regarded her with a heavy sigh.

"Oh, Dominia, my dear. How sad I am to leave you thus. Should I tear out your tongue to let you drown in your blood? That would be easiest, perhaps. Instead, I'll take these." He bent and, with one great hand, forced open her jaw. With the other, he reached into her mouth. After a sickening snap-crunch-pop, first came one silver fang, then came the next. Dominia kicked and screamed, and the family's border collie crawled into the room to bark in an effort it knew was fruitless. The Hierophant was careful his fingers were free of her teeth before allowing her to shut her mouth again. Then he slipped the cuspids into the pocket of his waistcoat, wiped his hands clean of blood on Dominia's leather breeches, and smiled at the dog.

"Hello, hello! How are you? Aren't you a lovely boy."

As the towering man approached it, hand outstretched, the dog's ears pinned back. It edged away with a growl.

"So upset. Wouldn't you like a new friend?"

Once, twice, the dog barked, and Dominia, when she turned her head, caught a glimpse of white tooth. Please, go hide! But the Hierophant chuckled over his shoulder at the Disgraced Governess.

"Perhaps I'll leave him to keep you company while you die." With a lamp from an end table, the Hierophant shattered the most modern object in the room—the holo-center and its attached phone, all tucked in the corner by the couch. Too woozy to protest as he shattered the projector and tore wires from the installation within the wall, Dominia let her head roll back against the floor. "Call some friends on your watch if you'd like us to trace their numbers, assuming you haven't excised yourself of friends as you've tried to excise yourself of family. It's a few hours until dawn. When it comes, why not crawl to meet it? A few minutes after, you'll have nothing to worry about. Oh, but—leave the door open behind you. Wouldn't want the dog to starve once his family is down to bones."

As her Father's back receded along with her gun, her teeth, and her sense of reality, existence faded into the whine of the dog. How funny: after all this time, all this luck, all one thousand battles, Dominia felt certain she'd die in her sleep.

Fate, of course, would never be so kind.

II

Adrift

René Ichigawa seemed a resourceful man, so Dominia wasn't surprised when she jolted half upright to find herself enclosed in a casket that was, in its turn, enwombed within the sound of waves. No, the surprise came when she tried to lift that casket's lid and discovered her enclosure had no lid at all. As her nostrils were assailed by the smell of wet dog, she turned to make visible the McLintock border collie, once hidden in her new blind spot. The delighted dog barked, and while Dominia struggled to regain her bearings, footsteps hurried across the deck. A shaft of light belched into the lazaretto where she'd been stowed alongside other odds and ends with no place topside.

"It's still hours before dark, Dominia. You'll need your rest; go to sleep." René's face appeared, the Franco Japanese professor's foxy features softened by what looked to be gunpowder (or mud) that contoured his face and ears. "The fishing boat is still on schedule to pick us up, and the wind is with us, so we may make it to them by tonight's scheduled rendezvous."

"And if we don't?"

"Then we'll sail all the way to Japan!"

Dry-mouthed, Dominia regarded him, then the dog. "All the way to Japan, with me and some mutt sharing a storage locker?"

"Purebred, I thought. He's not yours? He insisted on following us and wouldn't get off the boat."

"The Hierophant killed his family." Her mouth felt wronger with each word, and as she remembered her missing incisors, she rubbed her upper lip and grimaced at the bare gum. As her hand moved up and encountered fabric around her forehead, René reached into the lazaretto to slap at her fingers.

"Leave that alone! Martyr or not, infections are real. Count yourself lucky he left you alive, and with that." He pointed at the diamond resting on her heart; her hand lowered to Cassandra's smooth facets. Oh, Cassandra! Dominia pushed the image of her wife's lost body away with a tight swallow while René carried on. "I made a bandage out of my tie—you're welcome—but when we get to Japan, we'll have to get you a new one."

"A new bandage?"

"A new eye." He glanced between Dominia and the dog, certain he'd get his answer from one of them. "What happened?"

"There was a mole. There must have been. Someone who knew we left tonight. The escorts you arranged had me almost to the coast when Elijah and his cronies crashed into us. Without Cicero, no less, which means they're serious. I don't think I've seen them apart since 1994."

"The Lamb! What a nut. The fang trend, I suppose I get, but ram-horn implants?"

"Don't laugh. He needs them to filter all the pleas if he's going to focus on one prayer at a time."

The human did laugh, of course. "Like a tinfoil helmet! So he's just a schizophrenic?"

She didn't feel like arguing. That the Lamb's miracles had physical effects were a given. Not believing in him was like not believing in gravity; but so was believing in him, because nobody could fully explain gravity, either. "I don't understand how any of it works—hardly anybody does but my Father—but it does. Without those implants, he hears all prayers, all the time. Of course he'd seem insane without them. When you can make anything that's possible happen with surety, you're going to be the focus of a lot of attention."

"Like he'd waste his time helping a non-martyr…or even a martyr, most of the time."

She wasn't yet inclined enough against her Family to trash the Lamb along with the rest of them, and said, "He saves martyrs every week, every time they get dragged in to Mass to taste his blood—that's one whole week of not having to eat human flesh. Not if the martyr doesn't want it."

"And how is this different from the Lazarenes?"

No reason to get annoyed; she hadn't believed the tenants of the Holy Martyr Church in years, shouldn't be getting sensitive about it. Better to keep it about her Family. "I wasn't sure I'd made the right choice in leaving. Not until I saw the Lamb in the *tanque* that hit us. Now, I realize this is my only option."

Irritation marred René's face. "I thought you were committed to this."

"I am now, aren't I?" When his features didn't relax, she scoffed. "It's ridiculous, isn't it? Throwing away my governance on some crazy hope that—"

"The Hunters know where Lazarus is," insisted the professor. Back into religion they slipped again, despite the Governess's best efforts. Or—well, not a Governess now, was she? Back to a General again. Debatably. She struggled to reframe her own perception of herself as the human carried on, "Whether resurrection is possible—I'm skeptical, myself. But everybody seems certain Lazarus is a real guy, and I'd give an awful lot to see if he can make a miracle. Prove it or disprove it. Who wouldn't? Since my idiot cousin is so convinced of it, I might as well see for myself."

The dog watched with an occasional wag of its curled tail. She turned from it and asked René, "What happened to you?"

"We were ambushed right while I took a pee break—the reason I survived! The Lamb must have come for us after attacking you."

"I'm sorry."

"It doesn't matter. As long as we have you—and as long as I'm alive, of course!—we'll be in perfect shape."

"Even if you die, don't worry. I'm staking my life that resurrection is real, right?"

Weakly, she returned René's laughter as he once more sealed her into the lazaretto. The border collie turned big blue eyes on her, spicing it up with a hopeful tail wag that carried on until she ruffled its ears.

"I still might eat you, you know." As she spoke, her tongue wiggled into one of the gaps of her stolen cuspids. The replacement, a furry canine, responded with a knowing whine as she lay her head against the ropes that formed her pillow. "Yes," she agreed, "pretty pathetic."

By now, the Internet brimmed with rumors about her. The cracked face of her smartwatch, even with its location functions long disabled, perceived enough to indicate it was 1300 hours in their time zone. More proof to Dominia that the thing's functions were never capable of being disabled. If it was accurate, she had hours before the sun would relieve her from her prison. Most of Europa's highest citizens—certainly those around the Hierophant's preferred castle of Kronborg—had already seen news broadcasts (with subtitles, even) uploaded to every livestream Internet site in which the Hierophant had his fingers: that being, of course, most of them. With a few taps of the watch's digital screen, she picked her own primary source, San-5 News, and found its stream featured an angry, spray-tanned martyr hostess already shouting at the camera with the odd wild gesticulation and, once, the tossing of her pencil.

"It is my personal pleasure to announce the traitor, Governess Dominia di Mephitoli, has been killed by Our Lord the Hierophant while attempting to flee her own municipality of the United Front. I'll remind you that, a mere four months ago, on May Night, Cassandra di Mephitoli had her martyring completed. I think we've all heard enough of the official line by now—but perhaps there's a more sinister story at work." As the General's jaw tightened, the idiot ranted on. "The truth will never be known—rest her soul, the poor woman—but I say, good riddance to the worthless Governess, who let her post corrupt her past the point of no return." There went the pencil. "There's no room among martyrs for traitors, apostates, and liars who intended to bring secret military intelligence to the enemy. Our leader, however, is more generous than I am."

The clip cut to a press conference in what she recognized by the scarlet leather chair and goldenrod drapes to be her own office. Not more than two hours after he'd left her near death, she'd wager. With his beetle eyes the picture of mournful calm, the Hierophant lifted a hand to smooth back his gray-blond hair. He opened his mouth, lost the will, and began to weep.

"My children—" He covered his lips with his fingers, then let those same deft digits dip into his breast pocket for the folded cloth square with which he dabbed those tears. "My children"—he began again— "I apologize. This morning has been one of great emotion for me. It is with profound sorrow that I announce my eldest daughter, Governess Dominia di Mephitoli, had her martyring completed in a confrontation early this morning—owed to an anonymous tip that the Governess intended to flee the United Front for the Empire of the Risen Sun. When we spoke, she remained unreasonable, and I had no choice—though I wish she had given me one. I wish she had given me a choice, my children; oh, my children, my daughter is dead! Sweet Dominia."

His face disappeared behind his hand and his handkerchief. As a camera-decapitated figure rushed to comfort him with a touch upon his shoulder, the Hierophant rose. This forced the camera to pan up and reveal the snot-nosed face of Dominia's baby brother, smug as a pig in shit.

"But, as we all know: in every death, there lies an opportunity for rebirth. Therefore, amid this tragedy, I award stewardship of the United Front to my son, Theodore del Medico. Governor Theodore, please."

The Hierophant swept away with a microsecond's bleak stare into the camera, a look that Dominia sensed to be for her, whenever she would watch the feed repeated in cuts and recuts, news and talk shows, for nights or weeks. Unless something worse happened, anyway. Events unraveled so fast that it was possible for something to steal her unwanted spotlight within hours. She started to zone out into the pain of her eye socket as her tedious brother failed to keep the gloating from his voice. "We will all mourn with heavy hearts the loss of my sister. But I swear, citizens of the United Front: I will do you proud."

Yeah. Proud. Most of the citizens of the Front were human: Europa, especially in the Baltic region and New Scandinavian region, was the area most populated with martyrs. Therefore, martyrs living in the United Front were better off—at least, less likely to know their neighbors, and given to higher odds of success and social advancement. The humans were better off, too, and with much open land made available by migration in and out of cities as the times changed, hopeful mortals struggling to breathe in cramped Eastern countries made the mistake of immigrating, through legal means or otherwise, to the Front. This meant that there was a proliferation of bounty hunters and terrorists hidden among the human population, but it also meant that there were far, far more good, honest, hardworking people who happily withstood the danger of living in proximity to martyr territory if it meant they got ahead. Governance of the region belonged to somebody responsible, somebody who'd govern with compassion for the latter group of humans, which needed looking after if they, and the planet (and, consequently, the martyrs), were to survive. The Hierophant knew that, which was why he'd put Dominia in charge to begin with, and why he put Theodore in charge now. It would agonize her to see. He knew perfectly well that she lived.

"He said he thinks you're dead," observed Ichigawa when she showed him the feed above deck eight hours later. The professor lit a Sterno can with the electric arc of his lighter.

"He's lying so he gets to say later that whoever abetted my escape will merit death."

"Don't you suppose he'll be made a fool of?"

"No. He'll make me look like a cunning terrorist. Not so hard, now that I'll need an eye patch."

"Not necessarily. Your new eye can appear identical to your old one, depending on the features you're after. The fangs, though—those'll be harder. Nobody does fangs in the Risen Sun, for obvious reasons."

"I'd like something more reasonable, anyway. Those surgical fashions…they're practical so long as you're a predator. I'd started to regret mine."

"Trading in your fangs for teeth?"

"For Cassandra. I've given up everything for her. My whole Family, my whole world."

"You still have to give up one more thing before we're able to resurrect your wife."

"Sell my Father and my nations to the Hunters, you mean."

"What does he want?" asked Ichigawa. Dominia lifted her head to the white face of the winsome moon; beyond, semi-terraformed Mars glowed with starry promise. It had been so bright in the sky the night of the meeting—mere weeks after Cassandra's funeral—wherein the Hierophant announced to a room of military geniuses the implementation of a multiphase plan. A lunatic's plan. Project Black Sun, which had, after Cassandra's death, pushed Dominia into final, foolish action.

"He wants to give martyrs the ability to walk in the sun."

"How will he do it?"

"He never said. Only that it's a multiphase effort relying on an assault on Jerusalem. There won't be anyone who knows more if he's not one hundred percent sure they can be trusted."

"How does he know that they can be trusted?"

"How does he know anything? How does he evade bullets, how does he seem capable of traveling vast distances in impossible spans of time? Why does he seem to know everything I do? He'll tell you it's because he's close to God, but I suspect it's the Lamb. He affects probability; he must know something about the future. All he needs to do is say the word to the Hierophant, and your whole plan is kaput. Once a person is equipped with information and therefore has a high probability of betraying them with that information, the Lamb is able to rectify the situation. But there's one person that the Hierophant would trust with anything. Cicero."

With a sickle smile, René lifted his eyebrows. "El Sacerdote. His eldest child, yes?"

"By a hair, though it's said he and the Lamb were martyred at once. And he's not just the eldest: they're the only survivors out of…countless generations. The Hierophant has ruled for two thousand years, and Cicero has been his highest priest and right hand the whole time. My

Father acts like I'm the first kid he's ever killed for disobeying him after the age of a hundred, but there have been plenty more. At least six generations I can name. He's taking advantage of short memory spans: the median age for active martyrs is something like three hundred and sixty right now. Martyrs who were alive for his older generations of children are few and far between."

"So Cicero is almost two thousand years old. How old is the Hierophant?"

"Ageless, he says."

"How is it he's so much older?"

"Time lived before his reign, of course, on his planet of origin, where he was the high priest in the way that Cicero is here. The martyr planet, from which he brought his blood and the ways of martyrs. That's the official line, anyway."

Here, Dominia lost the professor, as all martyrs lost any human with whom they discussed the subject of the exoteric trinity and the origins of the Hierophant. It was touchy for them, as it was for René, who shook his head. "That's fine, if goofy, but mixing it up with a bunch of religious nonsense is where I get prickly about it. The last great barrier to sensible living."

Her lip gave the instinctive twitch of someone too long in the practice of suppressing their smirks. "It's one he's tried his best to eliminate. Any religion but his, anyway. Always hard to stamp that spirit out, though."

Lowering his head over the canned stove, Ichigawa probed the roasting potted meat. Hard to digest as what she had told him, that stuff; but the professor took both in stride. "Mankind has, in all fairness, been unified by the martyrs and the Hierophant. Old prejudices of race, language, gender, disability, sexuality—none of it matters now. There are the poor and the rich, but so it will always be, I think. Perhaps one day, religions will be unified. The final prejudice to be destroyed is the prejudice between the living and the dead."

Dominia regarded her hand. Was it really her hand? What once was animated and controlled by cells was now animated and controlled by the sacred protein that had edited those zombie cells, dead but still alive. Preserved for eternity in their ideal physical state by a protein that never

ceased its editing. To support the body's state of constant high maintenance, martyrs kept their proteins educated with DNA samples from
healthy blood and flesh; otherwise, the protein was liable to overedit, as
it was when exposed to the sun. The result of this starvation long-term
was not death, but something closer to epilepsy, or, in certain unlucky
martyrs, cancer. Ergo, their diets were incompatible with peaceful existence, much as they were incompatible with an average level of vitamin
D. Exposure to sunlight resulted in a hyperefficient state wherein the
martyr's immune system destroyed itself and the body it inhabited in a
matter of ten to twenty minutes, depending on age. If that were to happen to the General, would the sun kill her, or reveal her?

His mind along a similar track, René split the potted meat between
himself and the dog head poking out from the lazaretto. "I didn't
manage to save any rations more than the Spam in the locker. When
was the last time you ate?"

"Twelve hours ago."

"The tremors will start soon."

Yes, the tremors. Then the insomnia. Then the dysarthria. "There's
nothing to be done."

"Nothing, yet—but we'll be picked up soon. I hope."

"A fishing vessel out to sea isn't going to have a steady supply of
blood." At Ichigawa's blank look, Dominia sucked the gaps in her teeth.
"No, René."

"I'm just trying to make suggestions!"

"They're helping us!"

"They're not helping us so you can starve."

"I'm not going to starve." Over the edge of the boat, she stretched
her fingers toward the water. Her reflection, disrupted by the churning
water and the brooding dark, recalled Cassandra. "I'm not an animal.
I can wait."

As if on cue, a ship began to peel itself from the invisible horizon
that blended water and sky. "We'll see about that."

Dominia drew her collar high around her face. "How much do
they know?"

"As much as you'd tell a cab company. 'One woman, one man, a
little luggage.' Didn't mention the dog."

"Or the martyrdom."

"No, didn't mention that, either. Would have been much harder to secure transportation, even with Tenchi's help. These fishermen are used to helping whole families of humans escape martyrs, not helping martyrs escape to East Asia. At any rate, they won't ask many questions when they see—well."

The wind nipped up to splash salt water across her lips. As Dominia's remaining eye trained on the ship, she refused to allow herself to feel trepidation, or pain. Certainly not grief over her eye, the eye that had been with her since her first, human birth and before—the eye whose companion now looked on with agitated acuity, presenting a world that began to her left and ended at the crescent of a nose she noticed more than ever. Another brisk slap of the water licked her mouth, and she allowed this one to conjure the spray of foam that had produced her first look of naked Cassandra while the human emerged, laughing, from the sea. Dominia had taken shelter from the sun in one of a great many coves around the dramatic Pacific beach, and lo! was visited by an angel.

She would forever remember Cassandra's eyes: those fair twin moons rendered crescents as she looked around herself with one hand across her breasts and the other planted between her long legs, bared by the kind ocean for (then mere General) Dominia's astonished scrutiny. Four hours had the General remained in the cove, praising the low tide and waiting for some break in the sun. Now she saw why she had come, why she had been drawn to the ocean and to what hint of light her body could stand. A run seemed it would do well for her distracted mind. That was why she'd come to the shady seaside town in the Pacific Northwest, after all: distraction. It had been as different from Mexico as one might imagine, and a fine place to get lost in thought.

But the dawn that called her to her senses had found her miles from her cabana. The Pacific northwest and its sullen coastlines were known for their morning haze, so where had it gone? She'd felt so stupid, sitting with her coat spread beneath her, hidden in the darkest, driest place she'd managed to find. That foolish feeling remained until sweet

Cassandra appeared, her rich honey hair wet to a dark-taupe tangle of curls that streamed over her shoulders and clung to her breasts like the seaweed of a mermaid's fabled locks. Then, this woman with her tumbling hair and her big eyes saw the martyr hidden in the cove and, likewise amazed, let her brassy limbs fall free from her body. In the sun, she almost glowed.

"You're that martyr general." Without a trace of fear. "I know you. Dominia, right?"

Yes, yes, Dominia, yes, general, yes, martyr, yes, yes, many things. Oh, agony! What to say? What trouble, words! "I feel like I'm interrupting something by being here."

"Interrupting? Oh!" Those hands began to move, and so did seated Dominia's, until she conquered instinct—but there was no stopping her voice, which pleaded, "You don't have to," before tapering off in a sad note of embarrassment. At the exquisite stranger's smile and the way her body relaxed, the General's self-consciousness faded.

"It's so hard to get morning sunshine here! I was sunbathing, and just... My name's Cassandra." The human stepped with nimble feet across the rocks, and Dominia sat straighter, heart hammering. "What are you doing here? I thought martyrs couldn't go outside in day."

"We can't, strictly speaking. I went out late for a walk, and I— I thought it would be cloudy."

"Do you live near here?"

"Sort of wish I did." Both laughed, and as the naked woman embanked near Dominia's shelter, the General bit her lip. "You strike me as a local."

"How'd you guess? I love the sea. The soft sound of the waves. They put me to sleep every night." She hovered at the edge of the shade. "Can I— Am I bothering you?"

"No, please." Dominia's voice was as hoarse as her lips were dry; but, oh, how she smiled in that moment. "Please come in, Cassandra. Sit with me."

"Dominia."

René's voice called her back to the present, where salt water heralded only the looming trawler. A flashlight poured into her sensitive eye, and the sound of a barking animal rose over those of waves as the professor shouted, "Are you okay? Did you hear me?"

"What did you say?"

"I asked you, 'How do we move the dog?'"

"I'll take him," she said, shaking herself free of her one moment of joy. "Don't worry."

III

Aboard the Jun'yō

If a refugee wanted to avoid questions when boarding the fishing vessel set to smuggle them to freedom, all they needed do was lose an eye. That, or bring a dog. The McLintock border collie so stole the proverbial show from either Dominia or René that they barely had to do a thing but accept a coarse pair of blankets and watch the comfort-starved men fawn over Fido, who tried his best to pay all sailors equal attention while he pranced around the mess hall. "I'm going to have to come up with a name for that dog," she said as the first mate, a portly, tanned fellow— the Tenchi who was Ichigawa's paternal cousin—came with the ship's doctor. René barely looked up from the lab-grown leather shoes he'd begun to polish the second it was polite. This doctor, a strange and squat fellow who looked less Japanese and more like some sort of gnome, lifted his eyebrows as he examined her socket.

"He says it's a clean job," supplied Tenchi at the doctor's muttered Japanese. "He says if it wasn't for a few bits of glass, it would look like a soft-boiled egg had popped, whole, from its shell."

She asked René, "Whose bedside manner is worse?" The professor laughed while the doctor rifled through the contents of his medical bag. "It's hard to tell with a translator. Is it the doctor, or is it your cousin?"

"Don't blame me," said Tenchi. As the doctor hurried away to wet a sponge and clean the tweezers, he waved a hand at his back. "This guy's used to working with sailors."

Dominia snorted. "What's your excuse?" The doctor, now gloved, returned to wipe the sponge over her nose, cheek, and brow, uncomfortably close to what she'd begun to intellectualize as a depression in her face. Still, she felt her eye like it was there, and feeling her eye made her think of losing her eye. The doctor was right. It had been a tidy job, outside the expected blood. It made her sick to think about, that egg thing, but now it was all she thought—eggs and grapes and her eyeball dipping in and out of the Hierophant's fucking teacup. She shoved the doctor away and ran to the big mess hall sink where she vomited, full of clots and tissue she rushed to rinse away before anyone noticed. "Sorry, I'm sorry."

"You're in shock," said the doctor, aided by his temporary translator, as both men guided her into the nearest seat. René watched, arms crossed while Dominia rested her head against the cool surface of the counter behind her. The bun into which her hair had been placed for the doctor's easier scrutiny had slipped; the inky strands that tumbled down didn't seem like her own, but Cassandra's wet from the ocean, and made her cry.

"Now, try not to do that." The doctor continued plucking splinters of glass from her eyelid without fuss or flinch. "Try not to move."

"I'm sorry; I'm shaking. I'm diabetic." As she lied, she watched the doctor's mouth. Would a fleck of her blood fly in? Would it be enough? Was there a cut on him somewhere? "Have you ever dealt with someone who's lost an eye before?"

"Not for years and years. But it'll be fine. We just have to get you ashore as soon as possible— you'll need eye drops to prevent infection, and a steroid to help your recovery. A conformer, too, for a few weeks while it heals."

She didn't have a few weeks, nor did she need the steroids, but the eye drops would be nice. As the sponge became cotton balls and the motions more delicate and careful, he clicked his tongue, saying in Japanese, "Surgical, surgical," while Tenchi asked, "Who did this to you?"

"Some martyrs," said René, his flat lie the elegant combination of truth and fiction one would expect of a literature professor. "Dominique and I wandered off to take a pee. At the same time, our group was attacked."

"Take a pee, huh," repeated skeptical Tenchi, looking between them with an eye of wry ignorance that must have seemed from within a stroke of genius. "Yeah, I'll bet."

"We're definitely not like that," said Dominia. The doctor understood that English well enough, for he laughed. "René and I are—associates."

"Business partners," supplied René, springing from where he'd sat on the edge of the table with legs swinging to and fro. As his back stretched and his hips gave an audible pop, the professor sighed, then moseyed over to clap his cousin's shoulder. "No need for jealousy, Ten-chan. She's gay."

"What! But she looks so girlie."

"I'll pretend that was a compliment," said Dominia.

The first mate went on with a playful stroke of his multiple chins as his cousin might his beard, "She does have a pretty strong jaw, huh."

"I miss the United Front already."

René jostled his cousin. "Have respect, would you! Dominique is a widow."

"Oh, *gomen!*" The blanching sailor hastened a bow; the doctor, after taking his meaning, sighed and shook his head. "Very sad," said the old fellow in marbled English, throwing away the cotton balls before retrieving bandages. Tenchi went on, his ruddy face further reddened by shame.

"I didn't know."

"It's fine. You never know if you don't try, right?"

The redness now in the tips of his ears, Tenchi nodded again, and the nod turned into a brisk bow. From this bent position, he muttered some excuse and was gone, having so humiliated himself that the only choice was a breezy escape. Despite herself, Dominia smirked, and then, when René also smirked, she laughed, trying not to show the gaps that would betray her in a second. With a twinkle in his eye, René shook his head.

"Man, that guy. He's never been able to keep it together."

"Keep what together?"

"Anything. Life." After dragging over a plastic chair, René flipped it around and sat in it backward; because, Dominia supposed, he felt this made him cool, or edgy, or because it was what Camus did two thousand years before. "How are you feeling?"

"I'm okay."

"I can see. But how are you *feeling*?"

While tightening her trembling hands into better-controlled fists, Dominia licked her lips. "I'm fine. Tired. Dehydrated. How long is it until we reach land?" The doctor answered René's translation of the question.

"Five more days," said the professor, "though our friend here says when he was our age, this journey would take about seven from here. Thanks, modernity."

"When I was his age," Dominia murmured with a hint of a smile and humor hidden in her eye, "it would have taken nine."

René laughed as the serene and oblivious doctor stepped back to assess his work. After showing her a depressing glimpse of her bandaged reflection in the nearest hand mirror, the doctor took up a cotton ball and emphatically mimed the pattern of wiping on his own eye. "He wants you to clean nose to ear, and never the actual socket. Only around it."

"I'll try not to cram it with cotton balls." The doctor passed her the bag of them, then bowed. As she bowed back, she asked René, "Does he expect me to pay?"

"It's part of his job," said Ichigawa. The old man hurried off with his bag, following portly Tenchi the way he'd hustled off. "You're not the only refugee this ship plucked from the ocean. It's no wonder the Hierophant's navy seems so dead set on destroying even the most innocuous Japanese vessel they encounter. The last number I heard Tenchi throw out was a thousand people have been rescued over the life of the operation. Just *this* ship, I mean."

As the dog, tired of affection, extricated itself from the adoring longshoremen, Dominia held out her hand. It lay its massive head in her palm. "That's pretty miraculous, considering how the border is controlled."

"No operation is perfect. If anyone is going to get people out of this place, it's the Empire."

True. Much as, in ancient times, the Japanese had resisted with violence the emergence of Christianity within their culture, so, too, did they resist the (initially spiritual, later forceful) entreaties of the Hierophant, who soon after decided to leave the Empire and most of Asia to their business. As a result, the Asian nations thrived as a bastion of liberty while most of the rest of the world succumbed to the centuries-long power campaign of the Hierophant. The endless fight to maintain existing order while increasing what he already possessed. His greatest ambition was all but impossible: uncontested ownership of the entire Earth. Then, his eye would land on Mars—assuming it had not already, for he spoke of the mistletoe planet often enough, and had contributed enough to the technological developments that allowed its blossoming to feel undue possessiveness. It was natural that, after Earth was in hand, the next step was for martyrs to pack into rockets to explore the vast reaches of space. The thought made Dominia shudder; but maybe that was hunger. Her teeth chattered so viciously she feared she'd off her tongue, and she rose with the support of the dog and René.

"You look pale, even considering."

"I feel exhausted."

"I'm sure. Come on, let's get some sleep."

The prospect sounded wonderful—cool, delicious sleep, soft on her aching, itching eyelid—but was impossible. Sleep would not come. Not on her sad little fisherman's cot, with its wafer-thin mattress pad, and the stained pillow whose stuffing was unknown (rocks? plastic?) but whose exterior was the worn, smooth fabric of something into which years of foreign dirt, sweat, and face oils had been mashed. Eventually she threw the pillow aside and rolled her coat behind her head, a hard support stuffed under the nape of her neck. Ichigawa snored in the bunk above her, her every shift and twist and turn of discomfort lost on the man who had lured her to sleep to steal it all for himself. That was what he seemed like, Ichigawa. A thief. A thief, or a con artist, hands wet with snake oil. It was even hard to discern his age—and not just because it was hard to tell a human's age once they'd gotten into the standard panel of antiaging genetic engineering procedures. He looked thirty, but it was clear to Dominia he was a forty-plus who aged well. If you asked, he'd say twenty-seven, and that was obvious bullshit. Sometimes she got the sense that he lied for lying's sake. That it was a game for him, or a compulsion, or perhaps a result of his identity as a failed writer. Not that she'd known him long: mere weeks. Yet, he had worked from inside the United Front, risked his life as a pivotal doorway by which humans were liberated from the Hierophant, and she believed him when he said he was tired of shuttling people out while putting himself at risk. For all the risk he endured, it was a surprise he looked so young. Maybe it was the lying; he lied himself youthful. Where no one could see it, Dominia cracked a smile.

It wasn't so bad, being awake all night and all day, the rough wool blanket around her body the only source of warmth, her stomach eating itself while her hands shook. Being awake meant that she couldn't awaken further into crushing disappointment. It meant she wouldn't sleep in that deep, deathlike way, plagued with awful dreams: petty, stressful dreams where Cassandra had gone for a walk and wouldn't come back for a long time, or any of the other uncountable images reflecting Dominia's heartache at being left behind. But the dreams were preferable to that second she awoke saying, "No, please," halfway out of bed, expecting Cassandra to sit up with her. To be there, murmuring, "It's okay, you're with me, you're safe." That wouldn't happen anymore. Instead, the memory of her absence and terrible death always flooded back into Dominia's brain, an imitation of the painful moment lived anew each waking.

All that was avoidable if the General never slept. Insomnia wasn't so bad. This tiny room wasn't so bad. She might live here. Starve to death here. How long ago had she last eaten? The day before yesterday, she guessed. The longest she'd gone in ninety years. Since the Battle for the Reclamation of Mexico from the South American Resistance Army, when she'd spent six days and nights as a prisoner of war in a Nogales cell. She still tasted the dirt, sensed its granules up in her gums, all the grit and filth in the air having settled in to make her suffocate. To grind her down. But it didn't. She survived, and she would survive this, too.

Her growing concern, however, was that this could not be said of everyone aboard. On the main deck, the night crew worked their twelve-hour shift. She, wrapped in her blanket, wandered to watch them. Like a woman's cry, the winch squealed the trawl aboard and revealed to the flooding lights of the boat a pulsing tumor of fish bodies, which, quivering with slime, gasped for impossible breath. What were they? She'd never been good at identifying fish. Pollack and flat fish, Tenchi would tell her, later, once the crew was no more. For now, a few of their number working together split open the great net and, after loosening the bundle by pushing a few fish down into the grate to the processing deck, shoved them all in a gross, living pile to mechanical deaths.

IV

The Massacre

Ensuring the crew's survival meant avoiding them. This wasn't because she was some savage animal. Nor was the issue one of self-restraint. She could restrain herself. Starving humans didn't walk around taking bites out of living cows, did they? When a starving man killed an animal, there was butchery involved. Steps were taken between the moment of death and the act of consumption. Thus, Dominia's hesitance to spend time around the crew of the *Jun'yō* was not motivated by insatiable craving. Rather, it arose from the implicit understanding that humans and martyrs had built over the centuries: martyrs were predators, and, like most predators, were considered by most humans a threat worth eliminating. There were humans who had, like the McLintocks, managed to eke out a living by keeping their heads down, and contributing to society in a tangible way; there were also those who, like Ichigawa, took the risk to mingle with martyrs in the name of education, art, and daring social advancement; but then there were those humans who took a dim view of martyrs, their appetites, and what the two had done to the human race.

The men on that powder keg of a ship were the third sort of human. All it would take was one spark to send the whole thing up in flames. She wasn't sure what that spark would be, but she somehow wasn't surprised when it proved the fault of her Family member, Cicero.

Cicero—or the Hierophant, anyway. Both, she supposed, had hands in the speedy orchestration of her funeral, which must have been in the planning since at least Cassandra's death to so hastily tail the incident at McLintock farm. Not surprising. The surprising part of it was that the sailors' network of choice was livestreaming the event. She knew that, for the sake of the intelligence, the Empire of the Risen Sun kept tabs on martyr media, but she didn't expect livestreams of anything but theater: actual broadcasts by the Hierophant, she'd assumed to be kept for political or military use. Had she known otherwise, she would have disabled their televisions while they slept, and done her best to wreck their Internet. Things could have stayed peaceful.

They were peaceful to start with. She had read somewhere once—several somewheres, several times—that real sailors thought it bad luck to bring women aboard, but these men, she assumed, were used to it with all their rescue work. They kept to their own devices, maintaining the ship and attending to their duties as though she were not there. For the most part, she was indeed not there: rather, she was in her bunk. The dog—trauma-bonded, she supposed—stayed with her, which meant René had to return to feed it sometime midday.

"Have you thought of a name, yet?"

"Bentley?" The dog snorted over its food, a big bowl of dried jerky and rice flavored with some foul-smelling gravy made from the stored grease of many meals. "No?"

"God no. What is he, the member of a country club? 'Bentley,' please. You need a real dog's name. 'Basil,'" suggested Ichigawa. The collie's tail wagged. "You like that?"

"Fine, 'Basil.' What do I know about naming things? If I wanted to name something, Cassandra and I would have had a kid." Lifting her head to regard the canine, which scoffed, eyes toward her, she noted, "Pretty sapient dog."

"It does seem that way." The animal, licking the bottom of the bowl, then stuck its hind leg in the air and contorted to lick its privates. Ichigawa smirked. "Sometimes."

As Dominia's head lowered upon her bunched coat, the professor asked, "So you'll stay inside the whole time? Right here? They'll get suspicious, you know."

"They'll be even more suspicious when they see the way I'm shaking."

"Keep telling them you have low blood sugar. You'll get free sweets."

"The last thing I want is unproductive food."

"Well, I can't help you, I'm afraid."

"Strictly speaking, you could."

"Yeah, so they can notice Chekhov's puncture wound? I won't do it." His arms crossed, and his back went rigid like a woman ill-propositioned in a seedy bar, so Dominia dropped the subject and folded her hands over her ribs.

"We'll have to think of a long-term solution," he admitted while staring off into space. "We still have to take the Light Rail from Kyoto to Shanghai and all the way into Afghanistan. And that's the easy part. When we're bumbling around Kabul trying to find this guy…"

"I thought your Hunters knew where he's preaching."

"Sure, but that doesn't mean he'll be easy to find, or working on a convenient schedule. You're going to need rations, and protection from the sun, if we're going to make concrete progress in a reasonable amount of time."

"You think this guy is real? Lazarus? They're not conflating old biblical stories about Lazarus and Jesus with facts about the Lamb? I always thought it sounded crazy." To say the least. What she had done to the Lazarenes during her two-hundred-year tenure as one of the top generals in the martyr military—and, during rare bouts of peacetime before her governance, head of secret police—was enough to gray the faces of even the most irreligious humans. But, as she told herself, she had done this with cause. Dangerous cults had to be broken up before they corrupted the masses.

"There's at least a guy calling himself 'Lazarus.' I think he named himself after the famous human. He can't be that biblical Lazarus; martyrs didn't exist until 2045 CE— at least, not officially. Cicero and His Ass-Holiness and your beloved Lamb had to be operating for at least a few decades prior to that, since they didn't come out with news about the protein until they made sure they had every big-name politician and tabloid beauty queen in their cannibalistic pockets. Imagine being alive back then! Weird to think about—but the point I'm trying to make is that, based on all the texts I've studied over the past few years, *this* Lazarus starts showing up around that time. As far as the static, historical record is concerned, I mean. The Lady's prophecies kept by the religious higher-ups of the Red Market have predicted his coming since before the Jews predicted a Messiah. Maybe they're one in the same."

Speaking of dangerous cults whose groups she'd many times interrupted over the course of her career. The Lady and the Red Market were a whole other can of Pagan worms; she didn't even want to get into it. "So we know there's a verifiable martyr masquerading as this guy. But why would the Hunters let him live? Abrahamians despise martyrs."

"He's an exception to the rule, because he's valuable to them."

"That immortalizing blood he has, right?" She laughed and rubbed her forehead while contemplating the notion. "The one that makes people live forever without martyring them, or damns them to hell, depending on who you ask."

"I don't think the Hunters are worried about your Father's hell."

"Then why aren't all Hunters immortal?"

"Same reason they're able to track his location but not get him. He won't let them. I've heard he's as fast as your Father, or faster, and disappears in the blink of an eye the same way." At her skeptical look, René lifted his eyebrows and added, "I've also heard that he doesn't partake of meat or blood."

"Then he looks and sounds like a stroke victim." A knock resounded at the door as she added, "If he's even real."

Tenchi's head appeared in the gap, ready with a smile for the dog, his cousin, and then, shyly, for Dominia. "Sorry again about earlier. Won't you join us for lunch? You didn't eat anything when you came aboard, you must be starving!"

"Let me think about it," she said, but to her irritation, René slapped the edge of the bunk.

"That sounds like a great idea. Maybe fresh air, after?"

"It's a bit cloudy," cautioned Tenchi. René, still smiling, nodded.

"All the better, cousin! A spritz of rain is good for the soul. Come along, Dominique." Hand on her elbow, René whisked her out past Tenchi, and the dog followed after, tail wagging with each step to indicate him as the most relaxed member of their group. Outside the cabin, the wet smell of metallic fish grew all the more pungent, and from the decks above and below resounded the shouts and grunts and thumps of men processing the catches to be frozen.

"How large is the crew?" she asked, and Tenchi answered, "Twenty-five, including the doctor and me. Would you believe this thing started life as a fishing trawler, then turned to a battleship? It's a trawler again, obviously, but to have survived that long! Amazing."

"That long?" Now it was René's turn to be skeptical. "You told me this thing was a trawler even before the year 2000! You can't tell me it's the same ship."

"It's been *repaired* through the years," protested Tenchi. "But it's still the same ship."

"Remind me to tell you sometime about the ship of Theseus."

"It's quite a vessel," said Dominia, too tired to suffer their bickering. As they emerged in the mess hall, the General shuffled through every corner of her mind in search of a memory: any sign of whether she had encountered this ship before, during her eastern campaign. She hadn't, she was sure, because most human ships she'd encountered now rested at the bottom of the ocean, although her service in the navy was neither as fulfilling nor as prolific as her time on land. Even so, one might never be too careful, and if she was keen on avoiding the crew before, now she couldn't afford anything more than a millisecond of eye contact and a polite nod of her head before they resumed their variety show. The program, which required live interaction from home audience members' digital devices, had the six crew members on break tapping their watches in hopes of helping their preferred contestant (or victim) reach the other side of a tightrope suspended above a pool of raspberry jelly. From what she discerned, every tap widened the tightrope of the chosen contestant, while diminishing the tightrope of their opponent; thus, it was in the contestants' best interests to appeal to audience members before setting out on their journey, to make themselves seem as personable and beloved as possible. With enough followers, a player won by default. This was one competition of a near-infinite number of them, officiated by a cute young woman, a stern-looking old man, and a well-trained Shiba Inu that sat in a chair with its paws upon the table: the most impassive and least-invested of any of them, yet, the obvious star. Basil gave a bark of excitement.

"He sees his friend." Tenchi placed pair of soup bowls before Dominia and René. "Eat up! You'll need your strength."

She would if she could, and she did sip enough to ease the snarling of her stomach, but in the end, it was a nasty trick to temporarily settle the martyr gut: energy spent on needless digestion would beget no new energy for her to use, so eating food without human components was a surefire way to cause malnutrition. It was the kind of illusory fullness experienced by humans so impoverished they were forced to eat dirt. Yes, her stomach was full. But she was still famished. She felt as she would have after experiencing a full day's sleep of bad dreams, plagued by that bone-deep ache of dread that pushed her nerves against the underside of her skin so that even the leather of her breeches and the fabric of her once-white shirt scratched her into discomfort. She wanted to tear them off, along with her skin, and scream; she remembered in sudden, sharp relief feeling this way when she was first martyred. She would sit at the table, distantly aware of the conversations of others while she, trembling, wanted to fling her plate and blink her life out in a painless instant. Of course, had she flung away a meal at her Father's table, the following instant would have been anything but painless; so, in childhood, she had learned to stay measured, contained, and observant. Those lessons served her long into adulthood, even when her teeth ached and her right eye (socket) itched with phantom pangs. She had learned to swallow her food, to think of it as medicine. To avoid thinking about it. A great many martyrs were selected because they took the same perverse joy in their diet as the Hierophant. Dominia was not one of them.

It still, over three hundred years later, came to her in flashes: rousing from bed at a noise downstairs and hearing, like the sounds of a tahgmahr, a distant voice. The Hierophant. What a different person she was at that time, even with a different name—Morgan—but, no matter how far she plunged into memory, history, and myth, her Father was always the same. That first night she met him, he wasn't her Father. He wasn't anything more than any other boogieman. On awakening, she'd thought her parents had the television up too loud, but soon recognized that, whatever the muffled contents of his speech, her parents responded to him. The cold fear of that instant would never—could never—leave her. She watched the news. She was young, but she was old enough to understand what happened when children woke up to a visit from the Hierophant, or any martyr. Worse than the Krampus.

Tiny heart pounding in her throat, Morgan had crept on bare feet into the bedroom of her parents, and found it empty. From their bath, she took her father's straight razor; then, with this dangerous object folded shut and held between her lips, she wiggled into the closet crawlspace which emerged in their attic. The room's real entrance was the kitchen, and many times she'd taken joy in hiding above the sounds of her mother's cooking, her parents' conversations. Now, her heart pounded. How would she open the trapdoor without being heard? She hadn't thought this far ahead. Or perhaps it was best to wait here, hidden, and hope that he would leave—

The trapdoor opened, and Morgan quite literally fell into the arms of the laughing Hierophant. While her mother cried out in dismay, and the girl, catlike, thrashed to free herself from his grasp, the tall, black-suited man adjusted his hold. "Hello, my doll— Here I thought a raccoon had gotten into your parents' roof. Now, what need has a girl your age of a thing like this?" He plucked the razor from her mouth and showed it to her parents, who hovered at the edge of the kitchen. "Never too young to start getting at that five-o'clock shadow, I suppose."

Then he'd put her down, and when she darted to her parents, he bent to ask questions that seemed strange non sequiturs. "Do you know much about taxes, dear? No? How interesting. Neither do your parents. I intended to make examples of them."

Intended?

"Now knowing that you're here, that changes things! They weren't reporting you on their census, or their taxes, or even their immigration paperwork. I wonder why?" In that terrifyingly bland way, he smiled up at them. "They are *very lucky* to have a daughter like you. A brave and clever girl— What is your name? 'Morgan.'" He repeated it on her speaking and stared into her face as if seeing through her skin, through her skull—into the substance of her thoughts. "Well, Morgan, I have a question for you: What do you think of me?"

"I think," said the eight-year-old, "that you're a real bastard."

While her parents gasped in stereo horror and scrambled to explain she hadn't meant it (and had never, ever heard anything like that from either one of her parents), the Hierophant burst into a spell of laughter so great it left him on the verge of tears. With a few claps of his hands, the Holy Father exclaimed, "How I love children! Not a churchgoing family, are we." At the reluctant admission of her parents, he said, "That is a pity. But I find myself interested in Morgan's religious education. Perhaps we might discuss it over hot chocolate? My cocoa is top-notch."

The illness came on her much slower than the so-called industry standard one-week-ill/one-week-dying formula that cured martyrs of all ailments in exchange for their humanity. In Morgan's unfortunate case, it wasn't until three weeks later she started shaking; four weeks later, she couldn't write, could barely speak, and her parents couldn't stop crying; five weeks in, and she was sleepless, day and night. No one explained what was wrong. It was the flu, her family repeated— the flu, and pneumonia. Then, one day, she fell asleep in bed, her crying mother holding her hand. She did not dream as one would expect from a fever so severe. Instead, it seemed to her as though she awoke the next instant in a bed four times as large, hidden away in a windowless room while the Hierophant read from some book. For the first time in weeks, she wasn't shaking, or sweating, or in terrible, clattering pain.

"You've come back to the world!" Smiling, he shut his book to take her hand. "My sweet girl. What a tiger you are to have so fought your virus! You will let nothing conquer you, my Dominia."

"Is it the soup?" asked Tenchi. Dominia lifted her hand to hide her tears as she laughed.

"No! It's great, thank you, Tenchi. My compliments to the chef." She lifted the bowl to prove she enjoyed it with a big gulp of the hot liquid. While her mouth and vision were obscured, one of the crew members made an annoyed request in Japanese; amid protestations, the channel was changed to Sun Empire News. This was fine for the first few seconds. The peppy Japanese rambling of the woman on the screen meant nothing to Dominia, and was much less grating than the sound effect–riddled chaos of the variety show. It was also less distracting, until, amid all the foreign words, she recognized her own name, pronounced as though it were a series of musical notes: "Doh-mi-ni-ah."

The trick was not moving too fast, she told herself as she stood. "I think I'm going to go take a nap," she said to Tenchi, trying to modulate her volume so as not to let her words attract attention by the universally suspicious susurrus of whispers. "I'm more exhausted than I am hungry."

"You're exhausted *because* you're hungry," chided the first mate, oblivious to the program that changed to live footage of an ostentatious cathedral in Elsinore. The Church of the Sacred Ram was stuffed with weeping mourners, Cicero already at the altar. Spitting image of the Hierophant, that man—so much so that it was easy to (sometimes) believe the story that the Holy Father was an alien who had, cell by cell, replicated the looks of the man to whom he first appeared with news of the protein. From black eyes to high cheekbones to towering frame, the most notable distinctions between the two, outside El Sacerdote's general preference of the cassock, was age. The Hierophant, clean-shaven, was a far older-looking man than devil-bearded Cicero, and claimed it was because he had already been so long-lived on his own planet, Acetia.

What did the General believe? The simplest explanation: that they had been relations while human: father and son or brothers much older and younger. But this nonbelief was one of the reasons why she had been forced to flee from the Front, and why she was eager for a life outside her Father's influence. It was important she survive long enough to enjoy said life.

As Dominia lowered her bowl into the sink, she made good use of her roving consciousness by trying to detect what hymn Lavinia sang. In a dress that, to the General, was little more than a wild mess of jet gauze and lace, the girl made her way up the aisle toward the high priest. "Be Washed in Blood," she recognized as, ten feet from the door, three more fishermen bustled into the mess. From the sink, she grabbed a knife and hid it by her thigh. Well, if nothing else, that put nine—ten, including Tenchi—in the room with her. If his math was right, she'd have a mere fifteen more to go. The trick was keeping René alive, and sailing the ship, and all at once there was no time to think, for a great murmur arose among the men. She turned, hand on the door, escape almost good, to see the camera had panned across an array of memorial photographs. Foremost among them stood her and Cassandra's wedding painting, with the General's face, in full view, recognizable no matter the number of eyes.

The air was still on the screen and in the mess hall. As Lavinia stopped before the altar to kiss her brother's hand, then curtsy to the pews of mourners, the sailors vacated their seats. After jamming the nearest mop through the handles of the mess hall doors, Dominia turned in time to see René stuff Tenchi beneath the table. Sweet relief. She wouldn't have to kill him. With the brittle steak knife in her hand, the General faced one of the three late arrivals already arming themselves while repeating the various Japanese appellations for "demon."

The Disgraced Governess was not a monster. She was a ballerina of death, as the Hierophant had taught her to be. He never got her to believe in the Family, or the Faith, or the alleged Freedom in which martyrs told themselves they lived; but he did teach her to believe in herself. Thus, it was not a lack of confidence that made her regard this battle with unease; it was simply that such a battle was the least desirable outcome, and that disappointed her. But it wasn't as though they could talk about it. "*Konnichiwa, watashi wa* Dominia," was all the Japanese she remembered in the heat of that moment. The furthest thing from helpful. Even if she spoke a language they understood, they wouldn't listen.

As a country, the Empire of the Risen Sun had long since decided that beheading was the way to deal with martyrs. Interpreting with the help of Tenchi and René was out of the question. Time slowed as her body took over for her mind, her motions tumbling with the grace of a river down its ageless path. One thousand battles she had fought, and the first man to charge her, a sink-wet boning knife clutched in his hand, caught the weight of each of those one thousand in the quick in and out of her knife into his lungs while her free hand bent him into the blow. As he cried, she tossed him aside and greeted the next with his comrade's knife: first to gut him like a fish, then to shove him so hard into the stove that the great pot of soup scalded his screaming face. A bare-fisted moron came after her before she descended into regret; from her right, three more rushed over. She was able, with a quick hand, to drop the solitary comer, and was left with only the group.

"Only." It didn't feel like "only" when one of them grabbed her by the hair to smash her face, hard, into the metal of the refrigerator door—the blind spot was already making itself known. Nor did it feel like "only" when she twisted around and got her hand up in time so, thanks to its tremors, it was "only" half impaled. Better than having her throat cut or, somehow, a vertebra severed, though the latter seemed unlikely, given the quality of the kitchen knives. On the rest of the ship, though, where fish were processed day and night, who knew? The men did, like the remaining three television watchers who had lingered behind during the start of the fight. Now, on seeing Dominia occupied, they took their chance to snap the useless broom and burst, screaming, through the mess hall doors. Teeth clenched, the General used her knee to wind one of the men, but thought herself mere seconds from losing her good eye as the most tenacious of the trio, still clutching that knife, pushed it farther through her hand, up toward her face. Martyrs were stronger than humans, but this one was nearly the exception when poised against her hunger-weakened body: this was a sailor carved by years of manual labor, baked hard by the eye of the sun. Knife fights, fistfights, gunfights. The man was ready for anything, except for a dog to run up and bite him on the ass, and, when he wheeled with a howl of pain, the groin.

"Where were you when your family was murdered?" she asked the dog before catching sight, with a snort, of René's shiny shoe as he disappeared through the door with wheezing Tenchi. After yanking the serrated blade from her hand, the Disgraced Governess crammed the tool into the smaller man's eye, impaled the heart of the weedy guy who'd been smart enough to let her go at Basil's approach, then focused on the unlucky muscle head who had thought the next minute would see him a hero instead of a corpse with a slit throat. After a second's consideration for her growling stomach, she grabbed the great man around the neck and hauled him to the half-emptied pot of soup; while he refilled it, gurgling like a caught fish, she attended to the death of the one-eyed man with an apology. Basil watched her drop the body with a wag of his tail and the happy eyes of a dog who knew himself to be a good boy.

"Do dogs like soup?" she asked. When, despite the light of understanding in its eyes, the dog tilted its head, she fetched a pair of fresh bowls, pushed aside the dead sailor, and filled them both with something more suitable to the needs of the quivering martyr. With Basil on the floor beside her, and chaos growing outside the mess hall, Dominia cured her weakness with a meal and watched her own funeral. There was no point in rewinding: she had heard bits and pieces of it, though was distracted by the fight. It hadn't been worth listening to, anyway. All conventional drivel about martyrs being already chosen and saved and having no need to fear death— and about the forgiveness of the Hierophant and the Lamb, the latter being depicted with great, upturned eyes and prayer-clasped hands in the stained-glass window towering behind Cicero. For his part, El Sacerdote watched as the parishioners rose from their kneeling stance for a prayer being spoken in the name of Dominia's soul, that it might find its way home to the bosom of God and not be lost in purgatory. The beard and mustache he wore in the fashion of the fictional devil who provided his name to Dominia's home country did not even wiggle with amusement. He stayed solemn, still. He took no joy in this at all, the goodly priest, but instead delivered up another soul to God. People stood and knelt and sat and he took no relish in it. All standard, until Lavinia rose again from her seat to the side of the altar, then joined Cicero at the pulpit.

"This being, under normal circumstances, the point at which I would refer to thoughts given us by the family of the deceased, I will unconventionally use this moment to give myself a few seconds of grief. She was, after all, my sister. And I—"

Cicero looked askance, his eyes flat with what was, to the General, a sorry attempt at emotion, then shook his head and crossed himself. "She will be missed."

As El Sacerdote claimed Lavinia's seat, she took his place at the pulpit. Dominia was forced to turn up the volume to combat the emergency alert that filled every room of the ship with panicked Japanese. In Elsinore, the youngest of the Hierophant's daughters looked over the crowd, her golden hair pinned in place with a brass tiara, her features warped in sorrow. The Duchess of Florence, Princess of Europa, and Merciful Miracle of the Holy Father lifted her gloved hand to wipe away the only tears Dominia trusted. She, like everyone else, loved Lavinia. In the Princess's case, the official word was that she had been martyred as an infant, most likely by tainted breast milk, and left to die; unlike all other martyrs, the infant did not rise but remained clinically dead, as was to be expected—an additional reason martyrdom was held off until prepubescence. The body seemed best equipped to adapt to the change then, but Dominia knew the primary reason the Hierophant martyred the young came down to psychological malleability. Martyred adults had too many emotions, were too often hampered by human taboos. Children could be more readily indoctrinated in the busy comings and goings of society. Simple as flipping a switch. Most basic preparation for human society was applicable to martyr society; it was a small matter of reorienting the moral and mental compass of the child so that, when they came out the other side, they saw themselves as a species distinct from humankind. Oh, he had tried the occasional experiment, slipping violent or depraved content into otherwise wholesome children's programs as a form of conditioning humans to accept the martyr way of life, for instance. But there was no replication for the change in a child when they were liberated from petty things like human morals. Nothing could prepare them for it.

Lavinia, however, had never had that problem. Lavinia was a miracle because her body grew while she was dead, her cells manipulated by the undead protein inside, each mimicking, say, the antibodies of a living martyr; no human cells muddied the waters. It was not so much that the Princess was being edited as were all the other martyrs. Rather, one could argue her body *was* the sacred protein.

Lavinia had never not been a martyr, because when she gained consciousness in 1930 Anno Lucis, it was the first time since infancy that she had been alive at all. Everyone had expected her to be dead, but the Hierophant had hidden her away to grow, and up she sprang one day, a beautiful golden flower: his Miracle. Proof of faith. Faith in him, faith in martyrdom, all represented by one sweet, innocent girl who now watched the people with sadness. Somehow, at sixty-six, she had lost none of her girlish charm, though she usually composed herself with the grace of her station.

"I intended to read today from the Gospel of Elijah, but I can't. Oh, I can't. I'm so sorry, I—" Her fingers fluttered across her lips, and Dominia fought not to internalize Lavinia's genuine pain at losing her sister. For those long seconds, she wished to send a message: "I'm here! I'm alive! Don't cry." Instead, she had to watch her sister collect herself as Cicero rushed to support her arm. When a look into his stoic face emboldened her, she returned to the microphone.

"This might be wrong of me, but I don't care what she did, or what she tried to do. Of all the people in the world, nobody treated me better than Dominia. I wasn't a curiosity to her, or strange, or even a miracle. I was her little sister. 'Was.'" Lavinia half laughed through her pain. "'Is.' Dead or no, she's still my sister. Please—please don't think of her as dead. She lives on with God, and with her wife. Oh, Dominia—I hope you're happy."

Squeezing shut her good eye, the General pounded back the contents of her bowl, then rose to turn the television off before

Lavinia began her reading. There was no time to sit around listening to Bible verses.

"Stay," she told the dog as she rose. It wagged its tail to communicate that it had never possessed any intention of leaving this room for the foreseeable future.

Outside the mess, the ship was eerily quiet. Her focus narrowed for the lightest sound, she crept through the corridor and back to her room. Inside, Tenchi released a squeal of terror before René silenced him with a penknife poked near his face.

"What did I tell you!"

"Don't terrorize him." Dominia waved René away, then took his cousin's pudgy face in her hands. After brief scrutiny in which she found pinpoint pupils of terror and the moist scent of adrenaline but no sign of treachery, she asked, "Can you sail this ship?"

"What?"

"Can you sail this ship? Think hard, Tenchi, because your life depends on the answer, and so does mine, and so does your cousin's. If everyone else on this trawler ends up dead, can you sail the ship?"

"I— Yes. It would be hard with just one person but—maybe."

"'Maybe,' or 'yes'?"

"Yes," he decided, nodding his face out of her hands, then bowing. "Yes! I will sail, I'll do it, anything you ask. Just please, don't kill me. Don't eat me!"

"I don't think I'm at risk of running out of food anytime soon." She turned away and took a deep breath. "What was that announcement before? What's the plan in this scenario?"

"The men have gone below, to the processing areas. Where the fish are gutted and...prepared for freezing." He turned a queasy artichoke shade. "You're not going to— I mean—"

"It's not as if they'll be interested in talking."

Ah, the brief spark of hope in his eyes. "Maybe I could come with you? I could translate!"

René laughed at that, rather cruelly; Dominia pitied Tenchi while his cousin, in routine chastisement, said, "Yes—and slow her down, assuming you don't get killed by one of your own crew members."

"Just stay here, and be quiet." She tried to be gentle as she patted Tenchi's hand but nonetheless elicited a wince. "I'll be back soon; then we can get through the next five nights as painlessly as possible. All right?"

"All right." The first mate looked as reluctant as he surely felt.

As she began for the door, René asked, "Do you have a weapon?"

"It's the processing floor, isn't it?" Somehow, she restrained a spate of dark laughter. "I'm not sure I'll need one."

V

El Sacerdote

TERROR AT SEA!
Fishing ship Jun'yō docks with crew dead, security footage destroyed

KYOTO—Terror and tragedy struck more than twenty families Thursday when the fishing trawler Jun'yō docked in the Port of Kyoto with its entire crew dead, save for its first mate and its doctor. First Mate Ichigawa Tenchi was uninjured aside from psychological damage, but was unable to explain what happened. Police have refused to share Dr. Miku's testimony and have no details to add, except to say that the original security footage seems to have been destroyed in the attack along with all its backups. The men appear to have been dead five days prior to docking. No further facts have been released to the media at this time. Those with information are encouraged to contact their local police.

For such a horrible event, the article was a footnote in a neglected corner of the *Morning Sun*'s third page. More so the better: the less the people knew, the less the Pontifex knew.

"Soon"—finished reading the article to her, René slapped the paper upon the table of her Kyoto hospital bed—"you'll be able to read this yourself. Damn robot eyes keep us from having to challenge our brains.

Why learn any languages when machines will translate our grunts and gestures?"

"Have to learn something to understand the machines, won't we? Anyway, however lazy it makes me: I'm lucky. Thank you, René."

"Don't thank me! Thank the hospital."

"But you called them. Set it up before we'd even left."

"I knew you'd need a checkup; I didn't know you'd need a new eye. As many refugees as they get, it's a miracle they'll be able to perform the operation so soon."

No kidding; but, then, cyborgans were as commonplace and easy to acquire as contact lenses. Easier, when the hospital in question was run by DIOX, the corporation responsible for most of the artificial components on the market. Sure, there was customization to be done—everything had to be built or printed for the individual when you talked body parts, especially for bigger items like hands or limbs—but that was easy as tolerating a couple of doctors who probed and measured and muttered in Japanese before flipping to English to ask what color she wanted. The same as her other eye?

In retrospect, the question had begun to disturb her. "The same, of course," had been her answer at the time. However, it now occurred to her that she could have picked any color. Indigo, chrome, rainbow, cat's. That was a weird fashion among humans: ocular replacements designed to mimic animal or cartoon eyes. The idea had bothered her when she'd read about it years ago in some magazine, but now, having decided "the same color as before," she was forced to live with the decision and ponder what that said about her. She had to talk about something else.

"Did you get our tickets for the Light Rail?"

"So anxious! Don't you trust me?"

"If I'm honest?"

"And after you just thanked me for this appointment! Dominia. You'd better get to the root of that problem. Trust is all we have, you and I. Without it, there's nothing to bind us together, alive, until we complete our task." After stretching to his feet, René moseyed to the window, which he cranked open with a glance for security cameras, holo or otherwise. For the sake of legal liability, the hospital, which primarily serviced refugees, shied away from them. The professor removed from his breast pocket a pack of cigarettes, illegal in Europa and the UF, and Dominia rolled her eye.

Through the cracked window and the inch to which he'd pushed aside the curtain yawned the international orange lightning bolt of Kyoto Tower, a structure built in honor of the Tokyo forebear ruined in a battle, which, centuries ago, had made Dominia's bloody name. Its peaked shape, like an alien mountain, recalled the Eiffel Tower, and how Cassandra couldn't stop eating croissants. How cute she'd looked with crumbs on her cheeks and her eyes brighter than all the lamps of those fair streets! Two weeks they'd been dating, and already, the General had whisked her off to Paris in a jet. A hopeless case from the start.

"This city is so beautiful," her lover had marveled. "Like nothing else."

"Most humans are very afraid to be here." They did get a strange look now and then, but Cassandra's new wardrobe, furnished by Dominia, helped her pass in the chic, shimmering dresses her lover keened to strip; and if that was not enough to shield the human from the occasional bit of unwelcome attention, the identity of Cassandra's companion most certainly did. If anything, since their arrival to Europa a week before, bubbling rumor transformed Cassandra into a whispered extension of the Bitch of Europa. That evening, when the odd daring passerby stopped to beg her (less-sought) Family blessing and she told them the usual "*pax vobiscum*," one in particular stood out. A little old woman, some mother martyred by a sentimental child when faced with their former parent's death by age. She had not wanted the blessing of the General, which was regarded in some circles as an ill omen to the self and, in others, a powerful curse upon one's enemies. Instead, this woman had studied Cassandra with difficulty, then, deciding she was a member of the Holy Family, took the human's hand and kissed its back thrice. The shriveled martyr held this soft hand to her forehead, and said in poor English, "This is how you will give blessings, when you are a Mother of the Church," in a way which made

Dominia laugh but which touched (or in retrospect, rattled) gentle Cassandra, who smiled in awkward thanks.

Dominia, moved, said to Cassandra, "See? Everybody already likes you." As if the human had been one-quarter as concerned as Dominia. What a fool she was! She never should have doubted that he would let her have Cassandra, human or no. She never should have doubted that he would let her love, just so he'd have something with which to crush her down the line. Easy as plucking an eye from her socket—or putting one back in.

The primary reason for her hospital stay, the doctors had explained in crisply practiced English, was mental: to her refugee status, and her missing eye. Her refusal to open windows or go outside was seen as evidence of depression, not at all uncommon with her sort of trauma; as for food, René would sneak in packaged rations of human jerky made far too long ago, during the hottest years of the Pacific War. Where he got them, she didn't know, and didn't ask, but it kept her from going hungry. It didn't keep her active, and her lethargy was attributed to grief over her physical condition. Every time the cutest of the nurses came by, her round cheeks glowing with the light of compassion, she would pat the General's hand and say "*Ganbatte, ganbatte*," before helping clean her eye. Three days, this had gone on, and twice in René's presence; the nurse, taking him for Dominia's spouse, would nod and say in Japanese what a brave wife he had.

It wasn't so much that Dominia was brave. It was that she had long since realized she had no choice in where she found herself at any given moment. If she didn't like it, she had the options of waiting for it to change, or changing it herself; and if neither option were possible, there was no point in wasting emotional energy over it. Most patients in her situation were still absorbing the traumatic loss of their eye, but, numb even five months after Cassandra's death, the diamond of ashes cool against her breast, it seemed nothing.

But, ah, how deluded she sometimes felt. Would Dominia see her wife again? She had to believe, had to hang on to hope. After her wealth and station and Family had been taken from her—after she had chosen to take them from herself to better pursue an impossible dream—hope was all she had left. Hope, and a weasel who tossed his cigarette butt out the window while he asked, "Did they prep you on the procedure?"

From the eerie blind spot to her right bloomed occasional sheets of phantom color: blotches of phosphorescent viridian, or a trailing speck of light that quivered around as if consciousness sought for a pupil no longer there and thus perceived itself. Out of this hallucinatory cavern, Dominia's right hand produced a folder from her invisible bedside table, and René strode over to take it. Though it did contain paperwork, the most immediate feature on its opening was the hologram that it projected from its upper edge: upon the folder there stood a convincingly three-dimensional, turquoise-haired cartoon nurse who stood six inches high and spoke in over-enunciated robot English. Its accent was indistinguishable from a human's English, save for a tone best described as "dreamy." While René laughed, the petite hologram clapped, produced a party cracker, and pulled its string with a hop of delight for the excited bang.

"Congratulations, patient, on your ocular replacement surgery! We are so happy to have you with us, and to give you the opportunity to see anew. My name is Mimi Shin, and I am here to explain your procedure! Regardless of whether you will receive a full pair, we will install"—both snorted at the choice of verb—"one eye at a time: the process of receiving an ocular replacement can be traumatic for the body, and though our patented Install Tech is designed to intelligently combat rejection, studies have indicated that receiving two implants at once increases the odds of a problem."

From nowhere, Mimi produced a blackboard and telescoping pointer; she tapped the dark surface as it chalked itself with a drawing of an eye. "The precise nature of the procedure will depend on your condition. Your file tells me you have already experienced a surgical removal!" It was close enough to the truth, anyway; while René pulled paperwork out of the file to skim along, the artificial nurse adjusted her slipping cap in a programmed show of thoughtless habit designed to humanize her. Dominia found this effect alarming as the chalk eye was erased in its illustrative socket while Mimi continued, "This means the procedure will be shorter, and easier!

"Because of the discomfort experienced during the procedure, as well as the psychological trauma experienced by some patients, you will be lightly anesthetized. Just like being at the dentist's office! You will be put under by our caring team of experts, and while you are unconscious, the area around your eye socket will receive topical anesthetic, which helps the muscles to relax. Then"—Mimi stepped "out of camera," and the chalkboard blew to the size of the whole projection, then turned into a cartoony, three-dimensional rendering of a face and the muscles of an empty socket with lid held open—"our on-staff surgeon will place the implant so its connective nerve can find its new home."

Then came the horrible part, played out in holographic cartoons: gloved fingers dangled a vine of wire "nerves" and the realistic eye down into the empty socket. The skin of the face became translucent so viewers might observe that, as the surgeon pressed a tiny button inset in the side of the eye, the cyborgan came to life. First it quivered; then it stretched; then it jammed its tendrils into the brain of the cartoon patient. René grimaced at cheerful Mimi's disembodied voice explaining, "Our artificially intelligent body parts not only consciously soothe the tissues during the post-surgery adjustment phase, but, in most cases, install themselves! This is true of your ocular implant. The procedure is so simple, it could be outpatient! However, as explained, some patients find the process—and the recovery—challenging. For reasons of mental health and emotional adjustment, we at DIOX insist patients remain in the hospital for at least three days to learn all the exciting features of their new implant!"

Again, Mimi reappeared. "Some patients may experience physical discomfort while adapting to their new eye, which is normal. Prolonged swelling may be sign of an infection, in which case—"

"I can't take it." With a heavy sigh, René shut the folder and dissipated the peppy mirage. "She goes on and on."

"You have no idea. I watched the whole thing: it's at least two more minutes."

"Then why'd you let me open it!"

Dominia shrugged. "'Misery loves company,' I guess."

"Well, Misery's going to have to be disappointed"—he checked his watch—"because it's almost time for your procedure, and I have to go."

"You have to go? What do you have planned? We're incognito."

"Of course! I'm not going around waving a banner with a name tag stuck to my chest. 'My name is René Ichigawa, and I am on the run along with Dominia di Mephitoli. Please report me to the nearest Hunter and/or call the Hierophant to arrange my extradition...'"

"I'm not questioning your intelligence, René. I'm paranoid."

"Like I said, you've got to get to the root of that issue. I threw away my life for you, you know."

"You came to *me*, telling *me* stories about this guy."

"To do you a favor! To help you!"

"To help yourself, and your organization. Don't lay responsibility on me. If it weren't for you, I'd be—"

"Struggling to pretend you're still the person you were before Cassandra came into your life, instead of embracing who you've become since her death." The philosopher came out in him and shut her up. His urge for literal finger-wagging satisfied, René left it at, "I'll chalk your ingratitude up to stress."

"Thank you, René," she remembered to say, wondering if she had said it before.

"You're welcome."

The door slid shut behind him to leave Dominia in what resembled a prison. She reached into her dark right side and found the shape of a remote control, which manifested in her vision while she flipped through the stations of the hanging 3-D TV. Without her other eye, the effect was somewhat lost; the old-fashioned 2-D set on the ship had appeared a higher resolution than this one. She paused on the hospital's private channel, and a soft-spoken woman narrated something in placid Japanese that soothed beyond language. The camera panned across beautiful grounds blossoming full of cherry trees, and spent loving time on a knee-height hedge labyrinth for the pleasure of strolling patients. Agony clutched Dominia, not just at that most desirous image of the sun but at the beauty of the grounds. It had been by then at least a week since she had gone for a walk. If she had any idea how much she'd soon be walking, she might not have pined so much. Melancholy, she flipped away, right into the unpleasant smile of Theodore during a speech from her San Valentino office. He said something about how the people needed to "band together in a divisive time such as this, and reach across community boundaries between rich and poor, human and martyr. It is time for martyrs to take a more thorough, compassionate interest in their short-lived friends. I intend to use my new position to reduce within human populations the scourges of poverty and pestilence. Every human being in the United Front will be fed and housed. Every human being will be given work, and the medical support to maintain it. As martyrs, it is our duty to protect our human brethren. None shall be left behind."

Theodore del Medico was prone to bullshit, but this was laying it on thick, even for him. A speech written by the Hierophant? Probably. She'd be surprised if he let Theodore open his mouth in private without scripting it, stupid as her younger brother could be. Or, if not stupid, then so caught up in the euphoric whirlwind of his own ego that he couldn't stop saying stupid things. The problem was that he deluded himself into thinking the stupid things sounded intelligent. This carefully worded mission statement said nothing and everything, and left Dominia with a queasy concern for the humans in her former domain. Pieces of a boy's skull, scattering wetly across the floor. The first death of many during this sabbatical. There was little compassion in her Family for humans. Whenever they pretended they possessed some, it meant something was wrong.

"Dominique?" She hadn't heard the door slide open and jolted at the nurse's voice, to which she turned and nodded and laughed. The girl hurried over to take her blood pressure, then hear her racing heart. With a few short nods, she hit the buttons on Dominia's bedside, and the entire unit detached itself like an electric stretcher; the whole thing, magnetically suspended, she supposed, floated down the hall to the operating theater.

Like all operating theaters, this room resembled less a place in a hospital and more some strange spaceship control room. Try as she might, Dominia could not regard the masked staff members milling about as anything other than alien. Not the best thing for a mind about to undergo anesthesia. She tried to focus on Cassandra: lips, hair, eyelashes, the way she snored sometimes. Especially after drinking. Oh, how the General could have used a drink of her own!

The masked surgeon on the other side of the room inspected the silver tray of tools, particularly a thing that looked like a scoop or a shoehorn. The bed clicked into place upon a silver stand that allowed it to rise and fall at the behest of the surgical team, but he did not turn at the noise. While he picked up the black box containing her new eye, the cute nurse, with smiling eyes above her mask, strapped the martyr down. This bothered her; the nurse's smooth brow furrowed as she worked out Dominia's English concern, and then, with a nod, the girl tapped her own head and said, "In case—ah, sei-zure. Very rare!"

Oh, right. A mild concern. That was what cartoon Mimi had said, too, during her long spiel on side effects aborted by impatient René: seizure and, in some cases, complete blindness that was temporary and regarded as the psyche's adaptation to the product. It was one thing, after all, when one received a robotic limb. Still eerie, but somehow less confrontational than seeing through a new eye. A robotic eye. Dominia's stomach lurched. Sure, she'd had her teeth done. But this was a bigger deal. In some ways, a virgin territory about to lose its sheen; but, if the untouched state of her body was the qualifier of that, it had not been virgin territory since her proteins refolded, died, and then reanimated as a kind of horrific, cannibalistic parody of antibodies, collagen, keratin. The Hierophant and his servants preached that the proteins—hardly better than prions—were individually intelligent gifts from God, cells inhabited with choosy consciousness. Ironic, in light of the unconsciousness of many martyrs.

With careful hands, her head was lifted and the bandages unwrapped from her socket. The area was cleaned, and, with a syringe missing its needle, an ointment was applied around the surface. When the nurse nodded in satisfaction and said something in Japanese to the surgeon, another woman—the anesthesiologist—hurried over some great cart unseen in the right side of Dominia's world. As a plastic mask was fit over her face, the surgeon bent over her, black eyes a-twinkle so that even before he said in English, "Sister, dear, what are we to do with as wily a woman as you," a white chill of horror paralyzed her limbs with recognition. Cicero tugged down his surgical mask to reveal that immaculate facial hair and explained, "Tragic that no matter what we try to stop you, your rampage continues."

Before Dominia cried out—if she even could, for her tongue was already thick in her mouth and her lungs tasted cotton-tinny with the drug she was forced to inhale—her older brother drew her gun from beneath his scrubs and shot dead all four humans in the room. While she squeezed out a few silent tears and half a squeal, Cicero regarded the gun in his gloved hand, then allowed it to clatter onto the floor. "Fine way to repay your rescuers; but what can they expect? A farmer who rescues a snake had ought to have insurance."

She couldn't move, barely breathed as the mask was lifted away. "I took the liberty of replacing Tomoko-san's cocktail with one of my own, designed for a combination of lucidity and paralysis. Effective, no?"

With a doting hand, which reminded her too much of the Hierophant's, he swept a tear from beneath her eye, then turned back to the table of implements. "I thought it was important you be awake to see what you've done, that you may better grasp what is happening when you awaken—because I do not think you will prove capable of maintaining consciousness throughout the entire procedure. But we shall see! Not every computer program requires the machine to reboot prior to its use. Either way, when you're free, you'll want to take that gun. There aren't many between here and Kabul."

Panic: hot and cold, cold from the sweat and hot from the drug, or from the depth of his knowledge. Dominia tried to focus on her breathing while her brother returned with the miniature silver shoehorn poised between thumb and forefinger. The box rested in his other hand. "Father and I had a long conversation about whether to allow you to have this. We decided it would be unfair not to allow you what you'd spent a voyage anticipating. Not that being down an eye seems to have handicapped your prowess, much to the chagrin of the families of the *Jun'yō*. But it would seem most unsporting if you met your end because of a lost eye. That wouldn't be a victory for us at all!"

Cicero opened the lid of the box and removed the eye, which dangled from his fingers much as Dominia's original had dangled from those of the Hierophant. Though it was gory in naught but implication, missing as it was a coating of blood or tangled ropes of tissue, it was as vile—if not more so—to see a white orb on the end of black and silver wires. These swinging wires, he positioned over their new home.

"Inquisitive a mind as you have, you may wonder why I don't kill you. After all, you're more helpless now than you've ever been, or may ever be again. The answer is twofold. First"—he used the implement to lift the lid of her empty socket—"Father says there is more that you will do for us, whether you mean to, or not. And, second"—with the orb held between his fingers, he used the back of the implement to press the tiny button inset on the eye, which made a noise so subtle it seemed more an adjustment to the air—"well, it would be far less cruel to kill you *now*, wouldn't it?"

The eye was the least culpable of any party involved in this situation and yet, somehow, the one who seemed the most malicious. As the cyborgan booted up, the cords activated, wiggled, and began to burrow into her socket. Paralyzed though she was, her lips parted to allow an exhalation that longed to be a scream, that would have otherwise been a scream, as wires tunneled into tissue that had filled her socket in the absence of an eye. It dug into her brain and found the pathways once used by her optic nerve to reach her visual cortex; there, to her horror, it encountered a wormlike scrap of tissue leftover from the removal by the Hierophant. The DIOX-I reacted to this by using its wires to clutch the leftover nerve and yank it from its place in a way so horrible that, along with the skull-splitting agony, a collection of wavering colors and shapes and lights exploded in her right side. Somewhere above her, Cicero watched, saying, "Fascinating, beautiful," while the cords plunged back to work, sank into the tissue of her brain, and activated. As those hallucinatory blotches began to resolve into a new, crisper world, Dominia proved her brother right, and lost her grip on consciousness.

VI

Escape from Japan

Meadows. Lips. A long-running wave that peaked in a crash of consciousness-by-sound and Dominia running from hounds, the midnight velvet of the womb long gone but never really, the universe expanding out of it like a great balloon, a great breath taken in and let back out. A man who loved her like a daughter and whose face she couldn't see walked her out of paradise, told her something she forgot. Yet, she felt his sentiments in a profound way beyond the grasp of words, so when she awoke with the leather straps loosened around her wrists and a room full of dead bodies, she was somehow euphoric, left with great unconscious catharsis. That euphoria didn't fade as she saw the body of the cute nurse poised in a pool of blood beside Dominia's bed, though it did soften to sorrow, and blacken into the unnamed when the default settings of the new eye—about which she'd forgotten—recognized the object before it as a face, looked up that face's social media profile, and, with a helpful bubble, tagged the cute (now dead) nurse as one Sakaki Kurosawa.

Murph and Carol and Betty McLintock; Sakaki Kurosawa. Dominia didn't like getting to know all these names. When she learned a name, she had to remember it. She thought in shame of Sakaki and the life she might have led in the future; the eye interpreted this as a command to pull up the social media profile of the woman in question. The window filled the right half of Dominia's vision and made her blind with nausea as it flipped full tilt through an entire lifetime of photos, achievements, goals, sound bites, and even short videos. Her relationship status, her favorite foods, her—

Dominia hurried outside the theater to wash her face and clear her head, more rattled by the intangible ruminations of a digital conscience than by the bloody footprints she left behind. While she steadied herself with her grip on the sink, Dominia squinted through the window of the theater: the eye zoomed in, darting hither and thither in her lack of focus. It raked across all the bodies—Tomoko Ito, Yoshimaru Suzuki, and Kyōka Watanabe. In quiet, postwar times, her preferred tradition was to memorize the names of those deceased by her hand. But now wasn't the time for such a thing, and at that observation, her eye prompted her with the question, "Shall I make a list?" Before she responded, it presented her with a notepad application, its beige window already arranged with the names in helpful bullet points. As she absorbed this, trying to still her mind to keep the eye from reacting in a manner so hypersensitive, another prompt appeared.

"To save this list, DIOX-I requires access to your Halcyon Network Account. Set up now? Y/N."

"Yes." She sighed, rubbed her aching forehead, and then, fighting through her brain fog, located the gun she'd left floating in Sakaki's blood. "Yes, go on."

She'd been given a dummy account to use for the trip, but the dummy account would only work with a device whose data entry was manual. Automatic, reality-augmenting cyborgans couldn't be stopped from information harvesting without practice, of which the General had none. What happened next happened in an invasive eye flash: When prompted, Dominia could not stop her brain from releasing the information in automation, used as it was to privacy in its own space. Username? "LADYDOMINIA_CONFIRMED." Password? "3119191144181." Would she like to receive notifications from— No, God no. She wished the thing had a tutorial.

"Would you like DIOX-I to run the customization wizard," it prompted while she used her hospital gown to towel off her gun. Blearily, she looked toward the clock, then realized there was now always a clock floating in the lower right-hand corner of her vision. Ten past ten. Her procedure had been scheduled for nine: by now, everyone in the hospital was dead, and half the population of Japan knew or was soon to know. This also meant the Special Assault Team was on its way. She would be lucky if she had the opportunity to dress to greet them, and it was hard to focus with her new eye flipping through prompts to her right.

First came the calibration, where the eye asked her to look at a few virtual targets that augmented the hallway before her. Then, it asked her to picture a few basic shapes and think a few basic words. By the time she was near her room, it was asking her whether she wanted it to function by eye blink or by mental commands, the latter being more sensitive and consequently more useful despite its invasion of privacy, decency, and mental health. To this, the General reluctantly consented, though she willed the device to dampen its sensitivity so that only focused, conscious commands would activate its more annoying features.

"Your DIOX-I comes equipped with a wide array of special modes, each calibrated to a specific situation." Outside, a few vans screeched to a halt along with at least one grinding "Tiger" T1-63 Reticulated Vehicle, which became known during the Reclamation as one of many *tanque* varieties—an old model, she suspected, claimed after the Pacific War or delivered as part of the Hierophant's reparations for the ruin of Tokyo. Dominia scrambled into her room and found her armor and clothing arranged upon her bed, the footlocker having been emptied by the same person who'd left a fresh box of bullets. There was even a shirt: crisp, white, and not yet bloodstained. Incredible, how it felt like a slap in the face. All the while, the stupid eye went on. "Your custom settings have been saved under PERSONAL MODE, but be sure to explore other preprogrammed modes as the situation requires."

Stripping away her bloodied hospital gown in favor of her clothes, Dominia asked aloud, "Do you have a battle mode?" and the eye responded with the prompt that, "As a pacifist corporation, DIOX abhors violence."

With another few seconds' consideration and the sound of doors being smashed open three floors below, Dominia yanked on her leather jacket, then loaded the .44 Magnum she thought she'd never see again. So familiar in her hand, that single artifact of normalcy's dead empire, she might have wept over it, had she the time. Instead, she held its cool metal upright against the dexterous side of her face, specifically the puffy temple of her forehead, which was, indeed, aggravated by the foreign eye that had burrowed like a parasite into her brain. "Do you have a hunting mode?" she asked, and the prompt changed faster than she could blink: "HUNTING MODE ACTIVATED."

She expected change in the world, but nothing altered. Not until, back in the hallway, a few bodies were circled and tagged with the word "NEUTRALIZED" in an imperious shade of red. As she marveled, the lights were cut by the team in the basement; the eye responded by adding a neon-green circle next to her clock to indicate it had flipped on its night vision. This effect of night vision in one eye and regular vision in the other was so disconcerting that Dominia, with a shake of her head for the irony, squeezed shut her left eye, her good eye, the eye leftover from the tatters of her humanity, and relied on the invader to do its work.

Many floors below, the team gained ground and confirmed the loss was total. That they thought Dominia was capable of such a thing proved her reputation had survived the march of time. Many, many generations of humans had been born and died since she had last been to Japan; but they never forgot what the Bitch of Europa—the Bitch of the Hierophant—had done to their ancestors, or country. Likewise, no matter how she tried to maintain a moral compass, no matter how she tried to advocate for the humans in the Front, she was forever the General whose bloody banner had portended the deaths of thousands at the heights of multiple wars. It was a banner she forever trailed, no matter how she tried to shake it off. But it was also a banner not without its uses as Dominia tipped carts, arranged tables, and scattered chairs, then picked the southeast corner to crouch in the dark and wait for the first unfortunate cop to pass her by.

The laser sights of guns flashing across the hall, the chartreuse beams of night-vision glasses marking positions: she would have had an easy time locating her quarry without electronic help. Still, the DIOX-I proved its utility—not with its night vision, but with its twelve targets, which encircled each man's head like ill-starred halos. A video game, she thought with rueful humor, rueful humor being the thing with which she maintained her cool as she pressed tighter against the wall. The men split their group in half to begin the sweep. Two slowed behind each party of fellows marching down the hall, and these began clearing rooms. She stilled her breath. Once she moved, her position would be given up, and she'd need to deal with the consequences. So would the men, who, in an attentive group of four, crept past an overturned table. The DIOX-I highlighted their weapons to reveal the positions of a few hidden knives, and she waited, waited, squeezed shut her eyes as an officer neared, sure to blow her cover. But he was not observant enough, and she was protected by the veil of impossibility and rumor, and when the man passed, she raised her gun and took one, two, three, four, five, six shots, and the four men dropped while she, in a movement too quick for a human to emulate, reloaded her revolver to greet the four others who emerged from the rooms, shouting, guns at the ready. These unfortunates died with their fingers on triggers which jerked as consciousness absented itself from four more brains.

Footfalls approached from the distance. Dominia tucked her gun back into its too-long empty holster and swept up the nearest assault rifle, then emitted a disgusted sigh: identity locked. The so-called security only succeeded in promoting tastelessness in battle, as when Dominia dropped to the floor beneath the body with her hand upon its gloved one. As soon as the other units appeared, she squeezed the dead man's finger. The rifle was a powerful one and, from the awkward angle, almost impossible to hold. It took too long for two of the four targets to fall, the other pair having been pelted haphazardly in armor and helmets rendered bullet resistant by an admixture of graphene that didn't seem like a bad idea at a moment like this. Meanwhile, more charged from the hospital's other wings, with other officers surging up floor after floor, or waiting outside with rifles. Then, of course, there was the sun. Glittering bright and hot.

She had to do something stupid.

The bullet-bloodied body draped in her arms until the gun clicked empty, Dominia darted into the nearest cleared room and barred shut the door with the life-support machine of a dead man killed by Cicero and whatever team he'd brought. But what Cicero often failed to take into consideration was that he was unmanageable, and, unlike the calm Hierophant, prone to unpredictable bouts of temper. This was never truer than when he was separated by business or ill fortune from the Lamb, who was more beloved by Cicero than even the populace. El Sacerdote had been in too good a mood to be there alone; surely, that bringer of miracles, that parent who loved her for who she was and not what she could do, was also there. That parent who, at times, looked into the future, and who had, at some point, no doubt foreseen the person Dominia would become. Knowing that, he stopped neither his lifelong partner, Cicero, nor his Holy Father, from bringing her into the Family. She could not understand it now. Dominia had never the faintest idea what a troublemaker she would become: not until Cassandra stood before her. After that, conflict with the Hierophant and the apple of his eye was inevitable. But her quarrel had never been with the Lamb. Never had he been anything to her but gentle and kind: no matter what the Church of the Hierophant had done to him, or forced him to do to others. It was the propensity of the Hierophant to render the Lamb complicit in his crimes, and this propensity was why praying to the Lamb, given her intent at that specific moment, seemed stupid. But there was a reason she had survived so many battles, beyond natural cunning.

As behind the locked door she fell to her knees to pray, Dominia stretched out the limbs of her mind and cried, "Help," as a child for her gentler father. That gentler father responded in immediate kind: the distant roars of men and the thuds of the door slowed, slowed, fell off, and Dominia was inside of herself. Inside and behind her body, a conscious spark: a mere rider of her form, as a body might ride a horse, camel, or elephant. His spirit entered her and she eased her troubled mind. She imagined she glimpsed him standing before her in some formless Void within her mind, the ram's horns around his head—installed to reduce and channel the directions whence he received otherwise-unmanageable psychic input—glowing the soft moonshine silver of stained glass.

"You still answered me. But I guess you don't have a choice. Oh, Rabbi"—the word meant "teacher," but to her it meant "Daddy" and it made her cry all the harder as he took her in his arms—"I think I'm afraid. Maybe it's because I'm so sad. But, please, I need your help."

"There will be consequences," he said. "Greater than those already faced."

"You let me live. You saw this path and let me live, knowing what I'd do. Would you let me come this far and allow me delivered into death's cold hands? Please." Outside the room, the team was close to bursting through the door. She felt numb as she begged, "This once on my journey. Please, lend me your grace. I'll take the consequences that must come, as long as you don't let me meet my end. Not now."

The silent Lamb regarded her face, then bent to kiss a tear from her cheek. It was as though she felt the coarseness of his beard. "My child," he said, and she was in fact a child, standing upon the big feet of her father back in that lost Mephitolian cottage. Outside of herself, Dominia rose on feet commanded by a spirit that was not hers, that was not bounded by time in the way of her own. Though she had but half sense of what happened, being as she was a child learning to dance upon her father's feet, she watched in awe as that good father made her throw open the door so a few unready squad members tumbled in. The trip left them disoriented enough for her to shoot them dead through the throats. She did not know where all the soldiers would be; yet, with the Lamb in her, somehow she did know, and moved all the faster, as if her muscles pounded at their maximum capacity even given a martyr's endurance. The Lamb, like some organic quantum computer ever-calculating at nontemporal rates the amplitudes of an infinity of possibilities, knew in a way beyond knowing the exact position, at every second, of every being on Earth, because he was within all beings, was all beings, as much as he was also himself. As much as he was a slave to the Hierophant. A slave who could only take what petty opportunities he could to rebel, such as this: this fleeting moment when Dominia, bouncing a grenade back to the senders, looked into the face of the Lamb and wondered, "Why are you helping me?"

"Because I believe in you."

"Believe I can do what?"

He didn't say. He just kept dancing, danced her right out into the hall so that she was faced with a pair of specialists holding vibroblades; swords whose high-vibrating frequencies made them as dangerous as they were useful. They required a great deal of experimental armor to operate, but the armor was only a delaying tactic to give the user a second or two in which to cut the blade's power and keep it from sawing through their own flesh. While bullets flew from a distant handful of cinnabar-outlined targets, Dominia focused on the blade wielders, dodged a swiping sword, and was moved by the Lamb to the left. Thus, she narrowly avoided a blade and caused a too-enthusiastic squad member to shoot one of the swordsmen between the eyes. Dominia caught up his sword before he was on the ground. The rest was quick, and clean: in through the gut of the other swordsman, back out, then off, her boots pounding a trail of blood down the hall as she dodged, through sheer providence, the hail of bullets whizzing every way. One snagged her coat as she dove down the stairs and pinned a hapless man to the ground like a butterfly to a display board. His partner's cry of fury was soon silenced by the last bullet in a gun she loaded yet again.

As she snatched up a no-longer-required helmet, it struck her as possible that the Hierophant was aware the Lamb helped her. Maybe even supported the idea. But it didn't matter, in the end, who helped her, or why; even if it was all a scheme to make her look worse than she already did (and it was, she felt in her heart). All that mattered was that she got out alive.

The first-floor lobby was a mess of people when she arrived, and a mess of bodies when she exited. At the Lamb's urging, she dug in her proverbial heels and ran into the sun with the sword still in her hands; sadly, the weapon was quick to slip away from her, as she had to leave it lodged in some poor fellow's chest to dodge roof-mounted snipers. Bullets rained across the pavement while militarized officers screamed orders in Japanese. It didn't matter what they said: the *tanque* was her goal, and no one poised near it was fast enough or stupid enough to stop her as she tore open its door, yanked the driver from his seat, and sent the passenger stumbling out with a gun in his face. She didn't worry about closing the doors before she took off, though she grimaced as the windshield shuddered with a few deflected bullets, then hissed as one lucky shot sliced the edge of her neck. The *tanque* snarled into the closed road and took out the roadblock like it was a wall of hay. At last, she was released into the freedom of a road where all drivers hastened to pull aside for her. "Thank you," she said to the Lamb, out loud, in her head, the white knuckles bared by her driving gloves already pinkened from those seconds under the sun, "thank you, thank you, oh, thank you."

"Please be careful," he said in her heart. "Please be safe. Please, don't pray to me again. Not for a while. I can't keep him from knowing forever."

"I know. I'm sorry I had to ask this of you."

"You don't ever need to apologize: not to me. Go in peace, my daughter."

"And you, Rabbi. Please, stay safe."

Then, her mind was still, and around her, rising traffic noises gripped her consciousness. She felt so alone she almost missed René. With some irritation for the circles that kept indicating pigeons and other potential hunting quarry, Dominia dismissed hunting mode for the "personal" set of features, then used her wristwatch to call Ichigawa.

"You and Basil need to be ready to leave." With a few mental pleas on her part, the DIOX-I pulled up the address of the hotel, which René had given her during his visits. As her new feature mapped it out in a translucent pane that floated in the lower right-hand corner of her vision, she told him, "I'm three minutes away."

"Huh? What's the matter? What have you done?"

"Turn on the news while you pack your bag. Just trust me when I say we needed to be at the LRS half an hour ago."

"*Yare, yare…* What kind of car are you driving?"

"You'll figure it out."

The radio station on which the *tanque* landed played classical music from before even the Hierophant's time, some ancient Japanese artist now dead for almost two thousand years. It struck her as better than the recent stuff, which was all heavy electronic and grinding metal that reminded her too much of the gunfire she'd just evaded. As she rounded the corner before the hotel, a police chopper—or news helicopter, she couldn't be sure—hovered above, but she was undaunted. Beneath the overhang of the hotel's entrance, Basil wagged his tail and barked a few times as he recognized the driver of the massive vehicle that bounced into the parking lot, honked its way past a few short-stopping autos, then screeched to a halt in front of a startled René.

"You weren't kidding about the car," he said, flinging open the door and hustling the dog into the back seat. "This is a European model! Nice, too. They didn't identity-lock it? Pft! The suckers." As he slammed the door shut and Dominia hit the electric, the wail of police sirens encroached on their position. "But how do you expect to make it onto the Light Rail now?"

She hadn't thought that far ahead, living as she was in a minute-to-minute frame of mind. Looking too far ahead would get her into trouble. Thinking too much about the precious gem around her neck, more precious than any diamond anywhere, in this or any world, more precious than the diamonds rained on Jupiter—that would get her into the most trouble of all, because she would think about how easily lost that diamond was, and how she needed to protect it. The more she thought about her duties and the consequences of not completing them while in the line of fire, the clumsier she became, like a person becoming aware of their tongue and no longer finding it suited to their mouth. She tried to focus her consciousness elsewhere, on something productive. She looked into the rearview to see the face of the dog, then asked René, "What's the deal with the tickets?"

"They're universal LR Tickets: good for any one-way ride."

"Under whose names?"

"Your fake one, Dominique LeBlanc. I don't need to hide if I'm not coming back." From his breast pocket, he presented a new watch, cheaper but newer than hers. It was preloaded with information belonging to Dominique LeBlanc, who might even have been a real person: Dominia, for her part, had acquired a few stolen identities for the odd espionage mission over the years, each used once and discarded for some purpose like a mask made of a human (or martyr) life. After programming the vehicle to take the shortest route to the Light Rail, she accepted the watch with skepticism.

"And there's no tracing the tickets back to us?"

"No, no. They're donated. Our organization has many wealthy donors who subsidize or fully fund the Light Rail tickets of refugees who will not be staying in Japan. Far faster and less risky crossing the sea by train than by ship. You're not the only person the Hierophant has gone to great lengths to reacquire."

"I'm not so sure it's an acquisition he's after."

"Then, what?"

"I don't know."

"Well what do you know? You're being tight-lipped about this Black Sun thing." While the dog whined, René slithered into the passenger's seat to admire the thick Kyoto traffic and the glowing skyscrapers enclosing it. Great billboards all around them showed advertisements, but Dominia found to her displeasure that her DIOX-I overlaid existing ads with new, targeted marketing. Normal commercials for toothpaste featuring smiling women through Dominia's left eye became, upon slipping into her right side as they rounded a corner, a Red Market advertisement, which disturbed Dominia because it implied the device had already divined she was a lesbian—perhaps through her Halcyon information, she consoled herself, and not through its access to her literal brain—for purposes of advertisement. It was also rather distasteful, seeing as she was married: but, then, she wasn't now, was she? The recognition came upon her once again with a sad twist while the lingerie model parted her lips and winked at Dominia as if her prerecorded body had been produced just for the former Governess.

"Earth to Dominia," snapped René, his irritation keeping her from projecting Cassandra all over the model. "Come in, come in, I'm talking to you, here."

"Sorry! It's this eye, it's really—" A champagne advertisement, golden fluid showering down, became a tumbling leadfall of bullets asking her to buy from a military surplus website. A blue jean advertisement transmogrified into one for graphene-based armor, which she'd just been admiring. (The one for Lavinia's livestreamed performance in *La Traviata*, however, stayed the same.) "Distracting, showing me all these ads."

"Then turn it off." He stroked his goatee with irritation as he fell against the window. "Didn't you ask the doctor how to use the damn thing before you shot him?"

"You can't think I did that! I tried to keep from discussing it with you until we were on the train— Cicero's in town."

"Cicero," repeated René, his eyebrows lifting high. "What could he want?"

"He was my surgeon"—the glittering gold of the distant rail, visible for a length before it eased down into the Earth, shimmered into sight while they crested the hill—"and he wanted me to know how easily he could have killed me."

"So why didn't he?"

In answer to René's question, advertising on all passing billboards was interrupted, and the radio flipped from music to an emergency news broadcast. While a frantic Japanese man spoke over the radio, a woman paled by urgency introduced on the billboards a clip Dominia struggled to ignore. Camera footage from the masks of the swordsman: her body, steered by the Lamb but herself all the same, slaughtering the unlucky men sent to kill her. Dead, all in a gambit by Cicero to leave her looking—well, like a terrorist, as she said before. One eye, two eyes. It didn't matter, and she grimaced to see her old two-eyed POW mugshot shown as René, sighing, shielded his eyes with his hand to the sound of some woman's scream. As though to add to the clamor, the footage switched to an aerial view of the T1-63 R thundering through hastily parting but still too-thick traffic. So it had been a news helicopter, then. That meant that it didn't have guns like the encroaching sirens, whose noises were now naked amid the news anchor spitting out rapid warnings to the denizens of whatever shopping district through which they plowed. Dozens of people began speeding and worsening the traffic in effort to flee the area, and dozens more, seeing how close they were to the General, opted to abandon their vehicles in the street and run screaming.

"How would you feel about leaving the dog behind?" asked Dominia, looking at Basil in the rearview. While his ears pinned in displeasure at undisguised comprehension of these words, René shrugged. "It was inevitable, right? That, or we would have to portion him between us when we started starving in the desert."

"Right. I'll ask how you plan to keep me alive through that when we get there."

"Yeah, and focus instead on how you're going to keep me alive right now." René lifted his head toward other *tanques*, which, under the control of their proper owners and equipped with gunners, fired down the street of the shopping district. The guns did more to tear up the pavement than penetrate the armor of a machine: most models of *tanques* were designed to survive this scenario under the reasoning that any misappropriated vehicles were better waylaid than destroyed. After all, drivers had to emerge at some point. So did passengers, which was a worrying detail when she considered René. Studying the chaos of the crowd nearby, and how racks of courtesy bicycles offered by the city were emptied in droves, the General careened in that direction. "Grab a bike and get lost in the crowd as fast as you can."

"Ride away," he cried, "with my bags? But we're not even to the station yet!"

"It's five blocks! You can get there from bike paths faster than I can from this mess of a street. Ride away like these people are doing, like you're terrified of me, and do whatever you have to do to get in on the tail of the passenger line."

"What if they're already closed?"

"It would be inhumane of them to turn passengers away from safety with someone like me on the loose. Tell them that."

"And then?"

"And then I'll drive into the station, as near to the train as possible."

"And what happens when I get hit with a bullet? Or when I'm seen and recognized?"

"Then you keep running, or I leave you behind and find Lazarus without you."

"You couldn't manage that on your own!"

"If my only option is to try, then that's what I'll do. I'll draw the gunfire away from you as much as I can, but ultimately"—she shifted the vehicle into its highest gear and allowed it to grind over the sea of vacated cars lining a street that had become decorated by faces pressed against every pane of glass in the flanking buildings—"it's up to you to keep yourself from getting killed."

Scoffing, René pulled his bag into the front seat and threw open his door as Dominia broke to a screeching halt before the packed crowd still fighting for bikes. "You don't have many friends, do you."

"I don't think I have even one," she admitted, but it was with none of the sorrow or pain that had come with the notion when first it arrived in her life. Ichigawa decided to feel that pain for her and shook his head while clambering out. Above the din, he shouted, "That's very sad! If you make it out of this and start treating me decently, I'll be your friend."

"I'll have to think about it."

The door slammed shut; he bolted into the crowd. Sure enough, one or two people winced out of his way for having noticed his association. This gave an advantage, and he was soon on a bike. Meanwhile, in the distant station, passengers crammed their way into the doors. According to history books, Kyoto's Light Rail had been a global wonder when it was opened in 1564. Martyrs across Europa requested special travel visas so they could risk their lives to experience a piece of technology the Hierophant had deemed "a vain and useless show of technical capabilities, though impressive," which was the most cumbersome way to pronounce, "those grapes are sour," Dominia had ever heard.

His sourness arose from the fact that the Light Rail was the finest work of technological art mankind had ever devised, and the world's greatest art collector could never add it to his many claimed museums. Linking Japan, China, India, and the Middle States, the Light Rail's establishment was a process that outlived its initial developers but which would have made them proud. Using the trails upon which far earlier humans had traded silk, tea, and philosophy, tireless engineers had made it possible to get from Kyoto to Istanbul in fourteen hours, with stops in between and quite a few subsidiary lines going far south as Cairo. Istanbul, being as it was one of the most contested cities in the globe and given to a heavy martyr presence, was not a popular destination despite being the end of the line for the primary Light Rail, nor was it Dominia's destination.

Today, they were headed to the center of the Middle States. In its heart awaited the primary cells of the cabal known as the Hunters: René and Tenchi's masters, and the organization behind not only the evacuation of refugees from the UF, but the funding and outfitting of human soldiers in South America, the Middle States, and South Africa. The Hunters had certain standards designed to prevent a martyr from reaching them, and they were not often willing to make exceptions, even for the price of information. Dominia would have no help without René. She had to gamble he'd get on that train.

Kyoto Station, the grandest of the stations and a neighborhood unto itself, was designed for ultra-wealthy humans to make a comfortable life among high-rise town houses. Said town houses were situated overtop a sprawling mall that opened, after many a brick road lain for its quaint European feel, to the station, proper. The Light Rail Station was always closed without a ticket, and in the event of an emergency like this, it was on lockdown. As she and Basil barreled around a corner where the city of technology ended in favor of the city of wealth, Dominia discovered a barred security gate had been pulled across the street to render the glittering wall impassible. Lucky for her, the T1-63 Reticulated was designed for just this situation.

While, elsewhere, René bullied his way onto the train, Dominia pounded the electric. The vehicle slammed into the gate in one, two, three, belligerent attempts to ram it down; after the great machine's onboard computer realized it wasn't going anywhere, it adjusted itself like an enraged predator fixing its posture to fight its way against, through, and over the fence that held it. The vehicle lifted itself from its wheels and, with audible metallic strain, jumped, its front tires used like limbs to drag its bulk over the fence in a series of sharp undulations. In the untrained, this provoked a nasty combo sea- and carsickness. Dominia had long since gotten used to the experience of being shaken around in a *tanque* and neither blinked nor winced as it landed within the station and resumed its forward motion, then brought itself back to speed to tear through the palatial ghost town. Its citizens had managed to move their expensive cars off the road and their expensive selves into their businesses, apartments, and train cars long before Dominia's arrival. This was good: this meant that it was mere seconds and a few blocks until she skidded to a halt before the ticket booth.

The other side of the actual station was, to Dominia's relief, sheer madness, the economy section of the train a lower priority and thus still being filled: here a mother with screaming children, there a few harried businessmen shouting and trying to squeeze on, here the peaked-cap conductors demanding order along with tickets. Their eyes fell on her vehicle, and the shouts began in earnest, all pretense of tickets-taking dropped. Dominia checked her gun, her bullets, then programmed the vehicle to auto-defend the area against assailants, which the other *tanques* had made of themselves in a constant hail of gunfire. Unsure if René had made it, Dominia hoped that he did, told the dog, "Sorry," and scrambled from the vehicle while it wheeled itself around to face its pursuers. A twinge of guilt crossed her mind as she watched it go, and yet—no dog sat in the window, now. Basil should have stood, paws against the glass, pathetic. Perhaps it was a mercy she could not see: she assumed the beast cowered beneath a seat in much the way the passengers, visible in the golden train's temporarily translucent windows, ducked their heads from Dominia's view. As she hopped a turnstile, the conductors cried in panic, and the one within shut the car before his comrades joined him. No doubt they were relieved when she passed them without a second glance, not stupid enough to force her way onto the train through a passenger car. Better to make for the back of the train, where passenger cars disappeared and were replaced with shipping cars. After all, along that ancient path, the Light Rail was as much a mode of commerce as of transportation.

Four, five, six, long cars down, with gunfire rattling behind her, the train began moving and was already entering the tunnel which would propel it faster. Gritting her teeth, the General allowed two cars to roll past before she came to one that, windowless, seemed good a choice as any—and with the massive train picking up speed, no wheels to hamper it and reduced air resistance thanks to its bullet design, the choice slipped further from her hands every nanosecond. Desperate to get out of the sun that burned her forehead, Dominia caught the handle of the great door along the side of a shipping car and forced herself to hang on. She had seconds until the train hit the tunnel: as ever, it was good she was not human, but better that, by some miracle, some oversight (or, she would wonder later, some conspiracy), that great door from which she flapped in the breeze was unlocked. Her foot, braced against the body of the car, pushed the massive thing open with a terrible grind. A second before the shipping cars were in the tunnel, she yanked her leg inside, down upon the floor with her, then forced the groaning door shut.

Miraculous. But she'd expected to be alone. A female porter, her hand upon the door that led to the enclosed gangway from the ship-ping to the passenger cars, emitted a cry of surprise. The General silenced it with a firm hand upon her mouth. With a warning look, she put away her gun. Then, it was a matter of trying to retrieve Japanese lessons from three hundred years ago.

"*Watashi wa* Dominia—uh, *watashi wa tom*—no, uh...*anata no tomodachi.* Okay? Uh... *Iie himei,* okay?"

The porter, having overcome her surprise, assessed Dominia through a tight pair of dark, cold eyes. The General had to wonder if either were a DIOX-I, now that she was equipped with one of her own. She took for granted the assumption that most people opted to keep their organic eyes. The daring and Internet addicted would immediately see the benefit of replacing their organic models with new ones. She'd begun to, herself. The DIOX-I explained that this girl's name was Romanized as "Miki Soto," which she repeated out loud.

"Yeah," said Miki, in a tone so flat that Dominia flushed, "that's me. What of it?"

"You could have told me you spoke English while I fumbled around."

"Well, I'm telling you now. And?"

"And—and I'm not going to hurt you."

"Congratulations."

The girl moved quick—not as quick as a martyr, but quick all the same, and Dominia reached for her gun until the second plump lips contacted hers. Having foregone any flirting since Cassandra, let alone a kiss, Dominia's brain flicked at rapid-fire pace through available options before accepting the touch, the breath, that soft, wet tongue. Sweet distraction! A kiss every bit as lewd as Cassandra's were sweet and chaste. She was so startled that she didn't feel the electrical baton poised against her ribs: not until the kiss ended and Miki giggled. "But I'm still going to hurt you."

How many times was Dominia going to lose consciousness on the way to Afghanistan? She'd have asked herself that if unconsciousness hadn't come over her like a pop in the back of her skull: a hiccup that left her, on awakening, without Cassandra's diamond.

VII

The Light Rail

Cassandra's absence was not her first discovery. That was her (officially) broken watch, whose blank face reflected her own bleary one. Then came the porter's uniform, folded beside her unconscious body with such tight creases it looked as if it had been ironed: it smelled like the lavender of the woman who had pinned her against the cool metal of the train car to multiply the current's kick. That, plus the ache in her stiff muscles, meant the woman was no hallucination. Dominia had escaped Japan, and now had a whole new level of problems. Who was she? Miki Soto. A card sat atop the uniform, its front embossed with a black-petaled, red-outlined lotus. Familiar symbol, but one she couldn't place in her post-electric haze. She sat up to rub her head and neck with a pained sigh that turned into suffocation as her hand found the necklace gone from her throat.

Her palms were wet with sweat beneath her gloves. She stripped them off to feel around on her chest, then cried out to confirm Cassandra gone. Up the General sprang, then back down on hands and knees in search of her beloved's remains. No trace.

Dominia knew where she was: with that same woman who had left the uniform. A disguise for the train, in exchange for her wife's body. Cassandra! Oh, poor Cassandra, forever dying in Dominia's mind, much as she forever stood in her flowing black dress, whose lace she smoothed while they waited outside the throne room of the

Hierophant. Telling her, "You look beautiful, don't worry; you're so smart and funny, everyone will love you."

She had been emboldened by that, all the way into the absurdly long and courtier-filled throne room of Kronborg. The Hierophant, from his great gilded throne modeled after the seats of ancient, greedy Popes, sat forward. "So this is Cassandra!"

"Yes," Dominia had said, "this is Cassandra."

He descended the stairs two at a time to circle like a shark. Dominia, on edge, made panicked eye contact with the Lamb, who stood silent by the empty seat. In truth, she'd been every bit as frightened as she had urged Cassandra not to be.

"You do move fast," he said. Though Dominia had the urge to reply, the comment was for Cassandra, who blushed.

"Excuse me, sir?"

"'Sir.'" He chuckled warmly and shared a glance with the courtiers as for a precocious child. "Please, dear: 'Your Grace' will do." Before Cassandra became embarrassed, he carried on. "I mean to say that you, my girl, have courted our fair General for all of..." At his question, Dominia surrendered the (yes, humiliating) number, "Five weeks." This elicited a few tuts from the audience. The Hierophant made no comment; he lifted his eyebrows at Cassandra.

"A menstrual cycle's worth of romance—plus a few nights—and you would shed your human life to spend eternity with this woman? You know how many she has killed."

Embarrassed (or, in retrospect, threatened) to have it put that way, the human said with an evasive glance at Dominia's shoes, "I love her, Your Grace."

"Oh, and I am quite sure she loves you. Every now and then I find someone I love quite a lot, myself; however, do you see any of them with me now?"

Glancing around a room empty but for sycophants, Cassandra said, "You have the Lamb and Cicero, sir. Your Grace." Dominia sensed that slip was intentional, and strained her ribs trying not to smile. The Hierophant never bothered preventing his.

"Yes. Two thousand years. We are Family, that is why. Do you see these paintings, my dear? Here, here." After taking her arm with a look for Dominia's permission (or to gauge her reaction), the Holy Father guided Cassandra toward a crowd of martyrs who hustled out of the way in an awkward clamor of strange gauzy dresses and the plunging-neckline, techno-chic suits that would, to the General's relief, go out of fashion around the time Lavinia awoke. On their redistribution, they revealed a painting against the obscured wall: "The Martyring of Regulus," depicting the third-generation Family child in question, naked and screaming beside the red waistcoat and merry disposition of the fictional executioner about to toss him into the maw of a great, spiked centrifuge.

"If I wish to avoid tragedy, perhaps I should stop naming my children after tragic figures. But I suppose I cannot help that I see their substance when I martyr them; the Lamb's eternal eye always confirms it. Dear Regulus, he was not as noble a general as his namesake. Instead, he began to think himself a holy man. Of course, he was part of the Holy Family, responsible for blessings, and so forth, but he thought himself holy as me. Holy as the Lamb. And so, he needed putting down, and received a fate appropriate in light of his name. Of course"—he winked—"we did better than a barrel. Here's a fun fact for you: in reality, it was Cicero who did the tossing. The painting was commissioned many years after the event, when we acquired Kronborg in…oh, 1472, I recall…"

As he began to ramble about the castle's history for the forty thousandth time in Dominia's life, the General had relaxed. Hundreds of years and hundreds of girlfriends, short- and long-term, and she had never dared bring anybody home. She had never wanted his opinion about her love life; but for Cassandra, even had she been a martyr from the start, it seemed somehow important that the Holy Father agree Dominia's choice was splendid. This moment, therefore, broke over two hundred years of vague anxiety. He was almost like a real father giving approval to his daughter's girlfriend and taking her on a tour of the house. Oh, sure, there was always a degree of threat implicit in speaking with him. That was the way he was. He didn't do anything violent without telegraphing it in ways increasingly unsubtle until it was too late to turn back; the Regulus thing was boilerplate intimidation for anybody interested in becoming a martyr as an adult. Had his intention been refusal, Dominia would have sensed it right off. There would be one last, standard question, which came as he explained the fire in 416 BL, from which nothing but the chapel was saved. After lulling her into a state of intense boredom, he asked Cassandra, "Have you ever been a Lazarene, my girl?"

Cassandra, who had assessed the painting—which featured a crowd of figures and the Hierophant watching over the proceedings, with him in that silly golden miter he dusted off for holy nights and religious (never political) decrees—lifted her eyes and laughed in that harsh way that the General loved. "Hell no, I've never wanted part of that horseshit. Sir. Your Grace."

In a miraculous turn of events, this proved a rare moment when the courtiers had laughed before the Holy Father. While they tittered, he patted the girl's hand. "No wonder she loves our dear General—they have so much in common. Your friends," he pressed beneath the room's recovery. "Family members?"

"No," she said, firmly.

"Good. Because, when you are transformed, it will become apparent if you are a Lazarene."

"I'm not." Irritation brewed beneath her words. "What happens if a Lazarene is martyred?"

"They are damned to eternal hell and excommunicated from the Church. It seems an odd problem to have, but there have been instances of martyred Lazarenes. These, I have snuffed myself. The blood of the heretic Lazarus is poison for the soul; depraved humans force it upon their infants, being of the opinion that death is better for them than eternal life. Horrific, the things people will do to their children in the misguided name of protecting them."

Cassandra did not speak, or move, or even blink. Neither did he, until he said, "This is one of the many reasons why it is not in my custom to allow the martyring of adults without special permission."

"That's why Dominia brought me, Your Grace."

"Because she understands there can be so great a many…complications. Psychologically and"—the Hierophant studied her up and down—"physically." He drew nearer, his massive frame shading the human from lights that glowed bright in the ceiling to emulate sunlight without its dangerous effects. When Cassandra's head lowered and a few honey curls fell out of place, he lifted an eerie finger to push them away. "I wonder if you understand those complications. The ramifications of this choice."

"I do."

"Is it immortality you want, Cassandra? Or do you seek this transformation from the purity of your love? What I ask is: Do you think this is a selfish choice, or a selfless one? Of the body, or the soul?"

"I feel...called to it, Father."

With a few seconds' consideration, he patted her cheek, and said to Dominia, "You may martyr her as pleases you, though perhaps sooner than later. Can't have her aging too much before her preservation. Not that she is very old—you cradle robber, you."

Sweet relief washed over Dominia, who exchanged a smile with Cassandra while her Father guided her new fiancée on to the next painting of a tour that wouldn't be finished for at least another hour. Sort of the trouble with his approval: once he decided he wasn't going to kill you, it meant he was going to talk to you. Forever. Luckily, Cassandra was engaging, herself.

"This guy was in the painting of Regulus." The prospect now observed (with admirably unflinching eye, for a human) a painting called "The Castration of Saint Julius." Indeed, the torturer in question was identical, his red waistcoat and gleeful expression a trope in martyr paintings stretching further back into history than was recorded.

"That's San Valentino," explained Dominia. "Saint Valentinian. The fictional saint."

Cassandra made a noise of interest. "I guess I never really thought about how the city got its name."

"Saint Valentinian is the patron saint of death in many of our stories," said the approving Hierophant. "Death, prisoners, slaves—and painters, because he is the only martyr without an historical basis. I liked him so much after his first appearance that I insisted the following painters slip him into official works whenever possible. He is in every painting in this castle, albeit often hidden. One must have one's amusements if one is to live two thousand years."

Laughing in her good-natured way, Cassandra said, "I suppose so. But why pick a fictional martyr to be the patron saint of death?"

"Because, my girl, every martyr has died, and every martyr is responsible for death: every martyr alive or dead has a claim on the patronage of Death. Were it not a fictional martyr responsible for such matters, well, such patronage would become my burden. I've enough responsibilities as it is, don't you think?" Playfully, he nudged her, and though Cassandra restrained her wince, Dominia had been delighted to see that level of familiarity.

Oh! The joy of that night. The joy of sweeping Cassandra up in her arms and feeling for the first time that it was allowed. Now, in the shipping car, amid industrial-size crates of soaps and tea, Dominia tried to hold herself together: tried not to ask herself again and again why he had allowed it. Why hadn't he stopped them?

Not that she didn't, deep down, know the answer, but the asking of the question was somehow a comfort. As if, in the asking and in the refusal to comprehend his motives, she was somehow superior. The feeling was similar to the one she had at the Lamb's failure to intervene in her tragedy. His understanding of probability would have revealed her destiny. Both the gentler Lamb and the not-so-good Father had foreseen all this, and hadn't warned Dominia of anything. Hadn't warned her that, in spite of all her success, her strength, her glory, she would someday be crippled enough by circumstance to weep over the loss of a necklace.

The trick was staying calm. She had made it this far and stayed calm. Would she fall to pieces over some glittering rock? Of course, it was more than that (poor Cassandra's beautiful body, rendered to ashes), but she had to tell herself (in the clutches of some uncaring stranger who thought it a base, mined diamond), for the sake of reason (instead of the General's one chance to see her wife again), that it wasn't. Otherwise, Reason would find itself too poisoned by Emotion to do its work—to raise Dominia to her feet and allow her to ponder, as she dressed, why the woman who knocked her out and stole her diamond would also be kind enough to leave her a disguise. The DIOX-I, at her behest, scrolled through its most recent profile, and Dominia repeated the name out loud as she tucked the bun of her hair beneath the porter cap: "Miki Soto."

Real name? Fake name? Not a porter, whoever she was. Her profile listed no occupation, and no age or relationship, either; but there were self-taken photographs enough to indicate to Dominia that the girl was not a complete construct. It looked like she had spent time all over the world. The human parts of it, anyway. Most of her status updates (the name given by digital social networks of the era to doomed-to-remain-unread blurbs about the user's life) had to do with what bubble tea restaurant she'd visited or where she'd eaten in Hokkaido, and most text posts were high on the ratio of emotive icons to actual words. Dominia's IQ dropped to see such statuses, so she blinked the image of the page away while she tossed away the remnants of her broken watch and examined the dummy. A newer, less-abused device, it had survived the electrocution and would at least serve enough to get "Dominique" into her suite.

Damn good thing. Whoever Miki Soto was or wasn't, she was still on the train. She could be found, and had to be found, before she absconded with the diamond. That meant the General would have to leave her room far more than she'd anticipated. But, of course, before she worried about leaving her room, she had to find it. That was a challenge all its own, and she checked her ticket several times before wrapping her equipment in a parcel made from the paper covering of a crate. Their room was in the Satin Car, with each car of the train named for a kind of fabric as a nod to the Silk Road it traveled. This storage car was not open to the public and, according to the map upon the wall, was positioned behind the kitchen and dining cars. These let out to the Observation Car (the Cotton Car), the Silk Car, and then the Satin Car, with many others to follow until, near the Luggage Car at the front and past Coach, the Burlap trio of ultra-economy cars rushed along, packed with budget travelers.

Though Dominia kept her head down as she navigated through the diners, it was impossible to avoid awe when a room of such elegant design fit in a train car. It seemed not just a restaurant but one modeled after the European aesthetic preferred by martyrs. A great crystal chandelier irregularly swayed from the ceiling, and the frescoed walls were decorated with frosted molding like a well-iced cake. And all the flowing wine! It provoked a twinge of desire. She was thrust back into the Hierophant's parties, right down to the haughty glance of some woman who might have been a courtier had she not been a human on the train. Amid all the luscious fur stoles and tuxedos, Dominia couldn't help but feel out of place; yet, for that reason, she was invisible, the parcel in her hands and the uniform around her better than any cloaking device. A porter she may well have seemed, but the delivery in her hands marked her as unavailable for use, so she was free to cross the scarlet carpet of the Dining Car and emerge on the other side with a soft breath as she made her way across the gangway connector wubbing with the eerie whip of the tunnel outside. The short, glass-enclosed passageway, empty of all other bodies, just her and the dark vacuum outside: she shuddered and moved on.

The Observation Car was a strange affair. With nothing but the tunnel walls to observe, the large glass windows now bore holographic simulations of the vibrant fish and strange, giant creatures beneath and beside which the mega-train rushed. She suspected a similar effect had been installed in the Burlaps, as she had seen so many face-filled windows.

In the next car, a multilevel masterpiece in similar style to the Dining Car, a Japanese conductor emerged from one of the Silk Car's compartments; she strove not to hasten her step. He nodded at her, then did a double take when he did not recognize her face, but she was already on her way out of the car and looked so busy that, surely, she was a person who did what she was supposed to be doing. Yes, she looked busy, was busy. So busy, and in such a hurry, that it took her until halfway across the gangplank to recognize what her sensitive nose had smelled as she'd passed that cracked door. Lavender.

The temptation to turn around was enormous, but porters had special pass cards that allowed them to enter any room. Dominia, not being a real porter, had no such pass card, and had to settle for swiping the digital ticket on the face of her dummy watch at the (difficult-to-find) second floor door of their suite. This same false watch dropped from her hand in surprise as the door slid open to the greetings, not just of René, but a dog.

"Basil!" While the great beast looked up at her, tail still wagging, eyes still bright, coat still black and white and alive, Dominia lowered to her knees and let her parcel of things lay where they'd fallen with the ticket. The door shut behind them while the border collie accepted her embrace with a wagging tail and kisses for her jaw. "Did you smuggle him out somehow? I don't understand. I thought you must have made it in right before the gate closed."

"I wondered the same thing." René muted the television and sat up from where he reclined in the lower bunk. "It was weird, like magic. As soon as you stopped, I got out of the car and biked like a Tour racer—made it without getting shot even carrying my bag, no thanks to you. I slipped in right before the station gate closed. Then, it's a few shoves before I'm on the train, economy boarding, since all the other Satin passengers have been aboard for hours. I go to the economy bathroom to clean up, all well and fine; then, I'm making my way to the room, and I'm alone in the hallway, but all of the sudden I get the feeling that I'm being followed. I look, and bam!" The professor waved a hand at the dog in her arms, who assessed René with much less unconditional affection than he seemed to have for Dominia. "There's Basil, creeping along like he's been there the whole time!"

"What's your deal?" she asked Basil, almost too happy to argue with a being who couldn't argue back—almost. "I don't understand. How did you get out? I left you. I saw—"

No, she didn't. She realized while looking into skeptical dog eyes that she hadn't verified he was still in the T1-63 before she left it. She hadn't been able to look at the animal, so she had spoken to it without looking back, and assumed it was there. Who was to say it had been? Logic, of course, but…her mouth opened and closed. She frowned, squished the dog's fuzzy cheeks, and frowned harder still.

"Border collies have always been my favorite breed of dog," she said. As Basil's tail wagged, René turned up the volume on the television.

Her thoughts lost track as Theodore's whiny voice pierced her ears with the explanation that "the new Governor of the United Front will do everything in his power to protect the freedoms humanity enjoyed under Governess Dominia's rule."

"They're bringing back camps," translated Dominia, slipping her cap from her head. René scoffed.

"That could mean anything. Are they going to jump right to that?"

"Watch. First it's ghettos, then it's camps."

Theodore, who had continued droning under their voices, could be heard answering: "—best way to protect these most precious liberties is to band together in a group. Thus, we will be establishing new communities for the Abrahamian spiritualists, and for the descendants of the Risen Sun. It should be easy to migrate them, why, after all—San Valentino looks a bit like China, doesn't it."

His ignorant titter made Dominia say, "Oh, that idiot. Turn it off! I can't watch him anymore. I've had to deal with this simp for almost sixty-seven years. If Cassandra hadn't been enough to ruin my view of the Family, his existence might have done it by itself. Speaking of Cassandra"—she slipped out of the heels and cracked her toes with a sigh, then swept the lotus card from her bundle—"do you know about this?"

"Tsk! Naughty girl." After flipping the card all around, René laughed and stroked his goatee. "I suppose widowhood is lonely."

"What are you babbling about?"

"This is the Red Market! Their calling card." He gave it a waggle before reading its back. "'See you soon'? 'XO, XO'? What did you get up to while you were gone? No wonder it took you so long to show up."

She snatched the card from his hand. "How long have we been on the train?"

"Oh, two hours. Not too long. Lose track of time?"

"Lost track of consciousness." In brief, she told him what happened: the blur of gunfire, swinging her way onto the car before the train was sling-shot all the way into its tunnel, the foxy porter, her missing wife. "I think this Miki's in the Silk Car, but I can't get to her."

"She invited you, didn't she?"

"Don't be stupid. I'm surprised this place isn't on lockdown: I passed a conductor on my way over, and he looked tense. The more often I leave this car, the greater risk I run of bumping into a problem. Besides: I don't know what the hell I'm walking into."

"You'll have to get that diamond back somehow. You want me to go get her?"

"God no. You'll either never come back or repel Miki into keeping her."

While René tittered at her bad humor, Dominia swept up her real clothes. How they stank of sweat and dried blood! Her beloved leather jacket was as good as destroyed. Just as well; most humans along her journey would have been disgusted to realize they interacted with the General while she wore one of them. Examining René's new tie and white shirt, Dominia sucked the gap in her teeth she wished she'd had time to see replaced in Japan. "Did you happen to get me some fresh clothes while you shopped for yourself?"

"You know, I thought about it, but I didn't know your size. Those pants are leather, right? They wash."

With an annoyed look shared by Basil, Dominia strode to his bed-side, pulled his bag from beneath his bunk, and, over his shouts of irritation, obtained a shirt and pair of slacks. "I'm taking a tie, too. It'll help me blend if I have to go out."

"Oh, these fussy rich people wouldn't know you from Eve. They don't pay any attention. You want to know why the staff hasn't put the train on lockdown and turned over every car?" René ground his fingers and thumb as if rubbing coins. "Have to keep the people who paid a fortune unaware of danger, lest they never drop the cash again."

As René again turned up the volume, Dominia grimaced to find he had changed to a station reporting the incident in Kyoto. Though the broadcast was Japanese, her DIOX-I transformed hiragana, katakana, and kanji characters into English words. This allowed her to read the scroll beneath the stern reporter. Officials still seemed to be piecing together what happened, but the Hierophant himself was expected to comment on the incident, which leant weight to the international rumor of ties between this incident and the allegedly dead Dominia di Mephitoli.

Dead. She wasn't dead, but seeing news of her death continued to bother her. The urge to right the wrong perception was strong, but that was what they wanted. They wanted her to claim responsibility for her so-called crimes. Jaw clenched, Dominia slipped into the bathroom and sank into the tub.

At some point, she would have to deal with the woman, but not now. Theodore flitted up into her thoughts like a big-nosed moth bashing itself against a lightbulb. All those citizens of the Front were now in such peril that Dominia was sure her escape from the country would be but herald of others. The government would be prepared for it. It astonished her to see over her three hundred years of life how that vast country that she so loved seemed to dwell in a bizarre cycle of perpetual cognitive dissonance, alternately inviting and castigating (often downright imprisoning and killing) immigrants. The immigrants knew this, and yet they continued pouring in—why? Because of what the region had once been, she supposed, or because they had no choice. When, in one's home country, one was poor and famished, the Hierophant's lure—his universal basic income for the first five years of a human's legal citizenship, and his promises of land and dreams and futures—seemed of greater weight than his threat. This was nowhere truer than in the western UF, around that capital city of San Valentino.

The Western Front often felt its own country from the rest of the continent-spanning empire, and that was due in part to the large Asian population inhabiting the coast: their ancestors or lost relatives had come to the land many years before and joined a panoply of industries, and more immigrants continued enduring the risks with similar hopes of integration. Even though it had once been the cause of war and, ultimately, the ruin of Tokyo, the Empire of the Risen Sun remained protective of Western Front citizens. Martyr military intelligence stretching back to the late 1600s indicated Hunter cells based in Japan often infiltrated United Front lines. The Hierophant had never cared for that, and, after his many attempts to deport dissenters failed due to the wily nature of the human race, he'd turned to Dominia to keep both groups pacified. This had been her duty, lest they consume the Front, and the Empire of the Risen Sun come to believe they own the entire stretch of land, sea to shining sea: north to the Hierophant-controlled Canadian Winterlands, and south to the border of Latin America, filled with humans who sometimes got the idea to press north and contest his occupation of the Mexican Territory. In truth, since the United Front annexed Mexico around 1412 amid spurious mutters of "weapons of mass destruction" and "terrorist cells," it could be argued that the Front was never not at war. Hence its name. Mexico was, so far as the UF was concerned, its 64th Jurisdiction, after Puerto Rico, Washington D.C., the United Kingdom (a controversial single Jurisdiction), and those ten added in the Canadian Deal. Of course—try telling a Mexican that. The UF tried to tell all of them that for good around the turn of the century, and by 1906, it had culminated in the worst loss of the General's career.

Her promotion to Governess after the Reclamation of Mexico had paused a great deal of violence because, feared though the General was, she had also been known for her reasonability. Even before Cassandra's compassionate influence, Dominia had served the Hierophant as a leveling force, and was, one might argue, the most stable member of the Holy Family. Cicero was hungry to sweep up all humanity as though they were game pieces to be dumped in a box and taken out for his amusement. The Lamb was beaten down by years of his husband's abuse and a constant barrage of prayers. Theodore too often whined about his lack of opportunity, and the nebulous plans that he would never have the chance to see to fruition. And Lavinia wasn't even allowed to change her hair without their Father's permission, not after just shy of sixty-seven years of conscious life. Amid this ill assortment of dysfunction, Dominia the Governess had sat at the Hierophant's right hand whenever she slipped past Cicero, and advised Cassandra's routes of compassion: disguised as a General's practicality, of course. The Hierophant agreed to maintain his control of Mexico and descend no further into America once she pointed out how profoundly humans had damaged rain forests and sucked up natural resources before and during his rise to power, from 75 BL to 300 AL Since so many of their descendants worked to restore the environment, was it not sensible to wait, to let them do the fixing, and swoop in when Earth was healthy again?

Yes, that did make sense to him. He had agreed, no doubt knowing she delayed him to spare a few generations of human life. She nursed the hope that his desire to use America like a great, money-filled pitcher plant would depart him, as had many of his more bloodthirsty qualities. Funny though it was to say of the man who had torn out her eye, but the Hierophant had become gentler than he'd been when she was a girl. In those nights, he was more like Cicero, more desirous to claim everything the planet had to offer. That hunger had left him— or at least had relaxed in him—around the time Lavinia appeared.

Hard to explain, Lavinia. She was the Western world's idol, a pure and innocent dove cooped up in the castle for her own protection. Technically, she was the Duchess of Florence, and the owner of several palaces; but that was only as most rich human girls owned their own pony, kept in the stables of their father's summer house. The most troubling aspect of Lavinia's personality was that, in person, she was every bit as innocent and sheltered as that young, horse-loving inheritor—if a bit temperamental, as all spoiled children. She was a novelty in many ways, but the strange tale of her origin and that long coma made her a walking treasure: proof that the protein was a miraculous, life-giving gift from God. Not a burden from which too many martyrs someday sought or met some tragic escape, as had poor Cassandra. Dominia's hand landed upon her clavicle. That space where the diamond should have rested. Miki Soto.

Was it her real name? Probably not. The DIOX-I offered many details available about each translation, a list of virtual footnotes that unfurled when she concentrated on the dot at the corner of each translated phrase. Thus, it was that Dominia discovered the characters of the name "Miki" as it was written on the Halcyon account—美樹—meant "beautiful tree." "Soto" meant "outsider." This was fine, but raised doubt in Dominia's mind as to its veracity when she considered that "Soto"— in addition to being one letter off from "Sato," the "Smith" of Japanese surnames—meant "copse" (as in, "of trees") in Spanish. The eye was eager to give a lot of information about those two details; she could have fallen into a rabbit hole of speculation about more meanings, such as the complex cultural meaning of the word "soto," as she could have on a lazy Noctisdomin while browsing her wristwatch. But the most interesting thing to Dominia about the DIOX-I was the accessibility of—well, everything in Japan, so far as the Internet was concerned. In Europa and the United Front, the situation was different. Internet access—to books, in particular—was gated through various insidious means the people had come to accept as normal.

The first barrier was economic. If an individual did not have money to pay fees for the device of their choice and its monthly maintenance, they could count on limited to no Internet access depending on the resources in their neighborhood. This meant they had no Halcyon, which, as the standard profile for every global citizen, martyr or human, was the central network by means of which one accessed all of one's personal accounts, such as banking and electronic mail. Such a "ghost citizen" had no way to find and apply for work, housing, or even, in a cruel twist of irony that Dominia had fought hard to fix, welfare and health care above and beyond the Universal Basic Income—which, in the case of souls so impoverished they had no bank account, was paid into the rent and (government-purchased) food bills of the account-less recipient. Universal Basic Income, therefore, was an illusion. The mere existence of the Halcyon banking and social system made United Front poverty a cyclical trap. A third of the human population was thus disqualified from access to the Internet and to any knowledge that might save them. The second third of potential learners was knocked out by the pay gates for the websites of their choice: most people opted to spend their hard-earned money and precious free time on pornography, movies of a less explicit nature, and video games, rather than the high annual subscription fee of La Biblioteca. And then there was La Biblioteca, itself.

Every book ever created existed within the digital halls of La Biblioteca, in original and translated variations. Organized centuries before her birth, the sum of human knowledge, glorious and shining

and difficult to access. La Biblioteca was free to her, being the daughter of the Hierophant, but it was also censored of religious books, a fact
about which she'd neither know nor care until centuries later, when she
raised an army to turn back upon her Father. In those nights soon after
coming to live with her new Family, she was given a tablet: a square of
glass she'd heard discussed but never seen before that moment, which in
her case accessed La Biblioteca and nothing else. She could read whatever she pleased, whenever she pleased, and so she did. Books became
her most desperate means of escape from her strange new reality, that
terrible upside-down way of living, which grew, in a sadly observable
manner, more normal every day. Gradually, she stopped feeling bad as
she thought about the humans who had died for her meals; it wasn't
long before she saw one being killed without getting broken up about it,
so long as she remembered to detach herself and keep busy, keep reading, when she was later at risk of being alone with her thoughts.

Sometimes she read passive-aggressively, hoping to provoke him, but
he was unmovable. Once, at twelve, she lay under the moon in their
gardens and consumed Aldous Huxley. She'd just finished Orwell's
1984, and in Winston's tale found, in foreshadowing of the rebellious
teen into which she'd sour, many obvious connections to her Father's
regime. But the plight of Oceania only resembled in part the state of
affairs experienced by her Father's humans (and, of course, martyrs).
Indeed, when she moved to the logical follow-up, she found the truth
closer to Huxley's dystopia—even if the saucy text was, to her young
mind, quite embarrassing throughout. The more "adult" nature of the
text that her Father had negligently allowed her to access was perhaps
what inspired her to blurt as the Hierophant trimmed his roses, "I'm
reading *Brave New World*."

"Are you?" Far from displeased, he offered a playful shake of his
head. "Will you be inspired to whip our world into a frenzy, my little
freethinker?"

"I don't understand why you were allowed to get so far when books
like this exist."

This further delighted him. "That is the funny thing about such
books, my dear. Tired people, as Huxley will tell you, don't want to

think: and when they do want to think, they want to think of happy things. Not sad and dreadful things. They want their neighbors to do the thinking for them, and save them from what they must do themselves."

"But why don't you destroy all the books? Like in that Bradbury one."

"Oh, I love books! I would never, ever do that. I love books, and I love to see humans crave knowledge. Never would I deny anyone the right to learn. Instead, I have arranged the system so learning comes at cost; and so that only people of a certain age and a certain education and a certain situation even have the option of certain books. People are more understanding of being denied knowledge when they are told it is distributed based on income. Even location is an acceptable barrier! Many a member of the Front curious about political texts has seen the disappointing disclaimer, "This Book Is Only Available in Europa." And why would most of them read a book when they've instant access to any movie, any game, any television show once their eight hours of work are done?"

As he resumed clipping his roses, she realized he was right, and returned to *Brave New World* less keen for his approval. Behind her, he said, "We must get you reading Shakespeare, my girl, if you like dear old Aldous."

VIII

Miki Soto

What couldn't a person access from the Japanese Internet? The question inspired Dominia to get out of the bathtub for another look at the card. There was no address, whether web or physical, as there hadn't been an address on the ad floating across that billboard; instead, when she studied the lotus embossed upon the card, the DIOX-I highlighted it as though it were a link. How fascinating, this augmented reality! After fixing the device's settings back to manual control, she "clicked" on the link with an unsteady wink, and her right field of vision was covered by the floating window of a browser. Had she cochlear implants, she would have heard some sort of music, or even a voice accompanying the woman's writhing in and out of the browser's dark: less a whole person, and more a disembodied assortment of lips, fingers, lower backs, and thighs. At last, the vision disappeared to present her with the crimson words, "WELCOME TO THE RED MARKET."

A button appeared: "Connect Your Halcyon for Age Verification." The idea of giving the women of the international and highly loathed illegal organization any information might have stopped her in a simpler time, as it surely stopped 70 percent of potential Red Market customers—the ones able to access the site, anyway, inaccessible from Europa and the Front through traditional routes. That had been all the Hierophant could do to combat in any meaningful way the world's oldest profession-cum-cult. Far trickier than hampering Internet access was controlling in-person transactions in gold or silver, or the off-brand cryptocurrency, Redcoin; and because there were almost no freelance prostitutes left in the world, catching a working girl was difficult.

The Red Market took great pains to train its women, all de facto priestesses, on avoiding martyrs and questionable humans. One of their preventative measures was the Halcyon background check. Though used by almost every human being on Earth who could afford to keep a device and maintain an account, the social network was, in truth, her Father's project, going way back before she was born. It ground his gears to know it was used by the Market, but those very data-securing technologies that allowed the rise of digital currencies also made other forms of data more secure, and easier to spoof. Once the spoofing was discovered, however, it was always too easy for security agents employed by the Holy Father to lock down offending accounts. This was particularly devastating to a citizen of Europa or the Front. In an instant, alleged criminals lost access to everything: not just bank accounts and photographs, but access to other websites, e-mails, bus passes.

All the more reason to use the profile of Dominique LeBlanc: but with the DIOX-I already logged into her previously frozen Halcyon, she was as stuck as she was surprised to see her finances once again liquid. The bank account page showed its seven-digit number in cheerful cerulean, and her stocks were once more available for manipulation. The Holy Father was tracking her transactions, of course—but the mood she was in, let him see his money pour into the coffers of prostitutes. She didn't care anymore.

Dominia gave the website her consent and was approved within five seconds. While she marveled at the ease of access, the DIOX-I opened a new page. This looked more like a fashion website than an application by means of which one ordered a prostitute. A banner featuring a well-off, smiling pair of women rolled across her view, then panned up to reveal their "mission statement," which involved, "Celebrating the sexual liberty of the body," and "Connecting to the core of femininity." What any of that meant to somebody interested in getting laid, Dominia had no idea; but she had the feeling she was on a version of the website meant to appeal to her demographic. In this case, lonely rich women more interested in sexual experimentation or temporary companionship than the quick and dirty lay desired by someone like, say, René.

After selecting "Our Girls" from the site's navigation menu, she was confronted by a page of a great many charming—and clothed—animated images: each girl posing, laughing, clapping like a fashion model before a white background. A few of them waved as though they saw Dominia scrolling past, recalling Mimi Shin and her slipping cap. Each moving image was embossed with a lotus watermark, the girl's name, and a flag demarking her region. There were forty girls on each page, and at least 124 pages that were accessible to her. Rather than shuffling through them one page at a time, she tried the search function and found, relieved, a "GIRLS NEAR ME" feature. Better than sorting them by location, race, and age, as though they were a bunch of jackets. She tried it and watched the lotus cursor load until she was brought to a map that zoomed in to reveal they already neared Beijing. Three dots traveled at her rapid pace, though two were grayed out, meaning the girls in question were either booked up or weren't working. The third dot, however, nearest to the navy dot marking her location, was active tangerine. It resulted in yet another window: a new image of a waving model whose name, "MIKI SOTO," scrolled beneath her feet while she blew Dominia a mocking kiss.

The profile was filled to the brim with statistics, even more than her Halcyon: height, weight, bust, waist, hips; eye and hair color; blood type and birthday horoscopes; education; favorite films; favorite foods; favorite kinks. At the bottom a status read, "Miki is: OCCUPIED" with a frowny face emotive icon, which meant she wasn't open for video chat. The "Book an Appointment" button, however, was promising and bright as candy. When she blinked past it, the appointment page opened with a same-day booking highlighted on its calendar. Even more promising. Though skeptical as to whether it was as easy as making an appointment, Dominia couldn't come up with a better plan. At least, not a more straightforward one. Since she wasn't willing to engage in an unnecessary conflict after suffering through so many already, this seemed the best choice. As her Father had taught her, the courteous path was the correct one. If information could be acquired without violence or tedious espionage, was that not the preferable path? She hoped as she booked the appointment that gentility was even an option, and that Miki was reasonable. When reason failed, violence was all that was left, and the General had wearied of that.

With the request for an appointment one hour out pending in the corner of her vision, Dominia dressed. Undershirt on, she was stopped short by her reflection, and the realization that she now saw herself for the first time since her procedure. Good as new, that eye, and yet it was somehow—wrong. Flatter, perhaps, in its coloring? Not quite the periwinkle of its predecessor and more a soft seawater aqua that depended on ambient lighting to give its colors life. How strange, like a new scar to which she needed adapt. The DIOX-I was already adapting to its new home (according to that peppy anime girl) and, within a few weeks, would be comfortable as if it had always been there. Reliable as her old organic model. Nothing to it, except for all those psychological ramifications.

The eye looked so different to her, was so much a symbol of irrevocable loss, that she could not imagine how, to the outside, it looked normal. To the outside, she looked herself. Dangerously herself. With a frown for the long hair to which she'd been attached all of her life, she shuffled through the drawers until a pair of scissors emerged. With these, she clipped away her still-damp locks. It was as though she heard the Hierophant—and Cicero, for that matter—tsking over her shoulder between every snip, insisting her new hair was, "Fine, if that was how she wanted to look."

"Androgynous stockbroker" was not the look she wanted on a regular basis, strictly speaking, but it was what she needed if she meant to meet a high-paying escort in the Dining Car. It was also going to be necessary at one point or another in the Middle States. Dressing as a man sent a simpler message to Abrahamians than being a strong woman. Of course, try being gay! Most of them understood better now, but there were a few pocket regions of extremists, like the Hunters, who eschewed all homosexual behavior and considered it a sign of degeneracy in human beings: unnatural activity made acceptable by the Hierophant because it was evil. However, as the Hierophant had explained to Dominia, he did not do things because they were evil. He did things because they were sensible. It got the rational people on his side when it seemed he did the opposite of what all history's other dictators had thought to do. So women in history were reviled at worst and, at best, subjugated by means of disenfranchisement or dress code? Good. When the Hierophant came, he loved them and they loved him in return. It was human women and sensitive California liberals who formed the early basis of his political power in the UF and the barren land once known as Russia, before he got the conservatives into his pockets. Abortions? Yes. Homosexuality? Yes. Female priests? Yes, yes, yes. But coveting thy neighbor's wife, or murder? Of course not. The Hierophant was a man of law and order: a higher order. The order of God that escaped the minds of primitives such as the Hunters, who had been relegated to the status of terrorist organization even within their home territories. She would have to deal with them, too, and soon. Dominia might have shattered a mirror for frustration were it not for René outside.

Of course, when she emerged, hacked hair pomaded down with gunk from René's toiletry bag, the professor was already off gambling. She sucked the gaps in her teeth while Basil, ears pinned, assessed her with displeasure. After standing up and sitting down in place a few times, the dog whined.

"You sure you're not mad at me?" She patted the border collie's head while it sighed. "You're a really great dog, you know. I just don't understand how you got out. The timing doesn't make sense. Even if the cops got the *tanque* open…"

Dominia frowned, rolling off into the fog of her thoughts. As the dog tilted its head, a small exclamation point leapt in the corner of her vision. She started as if having perceived a fly dart into her visual field before the notification resolved: the sort of thing she'd see on her watch, if more alarming. Her traumatized brain was ready to flood her body with adrenaline at a second's notice, so as she read a box that said,

"Congratulations! Miki has confirmed your appointment," she had to steady her trembling hands by resting them upon the dog.

"It seems like every time I try to ask myself what's going on with you"—she laughed to the wag of his tail—"I get busy with something else. Try to behave, okay?" Then, already nearing that hour to which she'd set the appointment and wishing she'd set it out (as if it mattered, as if this were really an appointment, a "date"!), Dominia glanced into the bathroom, and back to Basil. "You seem like a smart dog. I assume you can figure out the toilet, right? Or something? Tell me?"

To her bizarre relief, the dog pranced into the bathroom. "So well trained," she marveled, trying to tell herself that was the explanation, because any other was too weird. Safe to leave the animal alone, Dominia gathered her wits, her gun, and her pounding pulse, then left the room behind.

The normally comforting revolver concealed in her slacks gave her an odd feeling as she walked down the gold-carpeted hallway of the Satin Car; Dominia smiled lips-closed to herself, rearranging the letters into the "Stain" Car, and, of course, the "Satan" Car. She had to keep herself amused. Had to keep a sense of humor. If she lost it now after all those harrowing and horrific years, well—that was a bad sign. Moreover, she had to look like she was having fun on a train that cost between three thousand and fifty thousand American dollars a ticket. Otherwise, she'd be liable to attract the attention of one of the many helpful conductors and porters nodding and bowing as she passed, eager to see her pleased because she resembled money.

She did have money, a small amount of gold cashed out for the trip and a large amount in her thawed Halcyon; but outside of spending the latter on Miki Soto to rub it in her Father's face, she daren't use a penny. It killed her that René was off spending his cash in the Dragon Car, which merited a non-fabric name because they wanted to draw attention to the casino. Not that Dominia could criticize the professor. She was about to spend a large portion of her finances on a prostitute, whether it was Dominique LeBlanc or Dominia di Mephitoli about to do the spending. The privacy damage would be somewhat mitigated by the purchase of Redcoins for the transaction (the Red

Market's legal defense for their activities, since their clients were not paying for sex, but rather an unrecognized form of cryptocurrency not legally exchangeable for goods or services and therefore useless in reimbursing prostitutes). She had to hope René had taken the extra step of acquiring his own off-market cryptocurrency before they set out on their trip, especially if he used those electronic slot machines.

The soft piano and murmur of conversation that filled the Dining Car didn't so much as miss a beat as she entered, her appearance garnering no more than a few glances of acknowledgment. Thank the Lamb. The host, smiling with bright-white teeth and not saying anything at all lest he mis-presume his guest's native language, marked that she expected company and took her to a quiet corner of the gilded car. The man clearly had his job due to a sixth sense for what people needed; or maybe it was the shifty look in her eyes, the anxiety winding tight her jaw, that made him want to get her out of sight. Either way, she was glad to be alone in a quiet, civilized corner of existence with a bottle of wine that was soon to arrive and better, for some reason, than any she'd had in years. Its rich oak fragrance and stinging taste honed her senses to a dagger point so that, when the door opened and Miki stepped in, the General was ready to get some work done.

Much as had Dominia, Miki had made a stark transformation, though less long-term. The escort's dress was scarlet and silver, as fit for a red carpet as the makeup that transformed her shrewd face into that of a porcelain geisha; her lower lip curved like a rose petal and made Dominia remember its taste, made her anticipate the scent of lavender that rolled down to her table. The scent accompanied Miki along with, to Dominia's mild displeasure, a stranger. No doubt for Miki's protection: a body to throw in front of the martyr if things got ugly. Some meek, blushing businessman whose lowered eyes avoided all others in the car as Miki zeroed in on Dominia with complete disregard for the poor host who tried to seat her.

"I wasn't expecting you to bring company," said the General, who, for the benefit of the surrounding passengers, kissed Miki's hand before helping her into the booth. She regarded the businessman, who studied her in nervous return. "Who is this?"

"He's nothing, don't worry about it. Some stupid client. He can't even speak English. *Sōdeshou ka? Kisama wa baka desu.*" The man winced and then, in a way both apologetic and creepy, smiled.

"Does he have to be here?" asked Dominia. Miki laughed.

"No, but then, neither do I." The host arrived with two empty wineglasses; on his leaving, Miki removed a cigarette holder from her embroidered clutch. Now that she was still, it appeared the fabric bunched at her shoulder was the sole non-makeup decoration near the human's neck. No diamond.

"Where is she?"

"You're not in a position to be making demands, Mephitoli-sama." As Dominia tried to hiss her volume down, Miki giggled again, then stomped on the man's foot and snarled something in Japanese. He responded by filling her drink. "Annoying pricks like him like to get lazy, so they'll be punished for their laziness. I don't care for it. If they're going to pay me to dominate them, I'm going to be the one in charge of the whens and the wheres and the whats. Right? Anyway—don't worry so much! No one is listening to us. They're all too obsessed with themselves. I could climb under this table and go down on you"—the blanching martyr scrutinized the lovely fleur-de-lis wallpaper, gold and malachite—"without them noticing a thing."

"How about you return my wife and we'll call it good, before I make this ugly."

"If you want your wife back, you have to play along." Miki had gotten her cigarette lit—by the slave, probably, Dominia hadn't seen—and blew a smoke ring across the table. "Trust me. You'll thank me for all this later."

"Thank you for what? Stealing my wife? The small amount of brain damage I'm still healing from your stunt?"

"Saving you, of course. And your wife."

Somehow able to suppress the roll of her eyes, Dominia refilled her glass and hid her lips behind it. "I hope somebody's able to save you from me."

Giggling, Miki shook her head, and Dominia was amazed that none of the elaborately piled locks fell from the places where they'd been pinned with plum blossoms. "You're not a threat to me, Mephitoli-sama. If you kill me, you will never see your wife again: whether as a diamond, or in the flesh. And that's enough to take the wind right out of your sails, isn't it."

"Maybe you'll explain to me how you know all of this?"

"My boss briefed me on you. She said, 'You'll meet her in the shipping cars of the Light Rail before it embarks on its journey.' Of course, I gave up when it started moving—but wouldn't you know." Catlike, she smiled, and ashed her cigarette into the empty glass of the man. He regarded it with reluctance until she deigned to splash some wine overtop. As he drank it and Dominia tried not to be disgusted, Miki carried on. "I hooked up with idiot over here to get a free ticket and earn us cash for the trip."

"The trip."

"Uh-huh."

"What trip is this?"

"Our trip, of course."

"Of course," she repeated as Miki perched her chin upon the palm of her hand. This action did not smudge her meticulous white makeup, or the vermillion petal of her lip.

"Did you cut your hair since last I saw you? You have to let me fix it. Sort of cute." The laughing prostitute reached across the table and, amid the batting of Dominia's hand, tugged an embarrassing chunk from behind her ear. While the martyr smoothed it back, the human sipped her wine. "I liked your long hair better, though."

"Me, too, but it's conspicuous. I'm conspicuous. People will recognize me." She ran a hand over her forehead. "Stop getting me off the point, please. Everybody's doing that. I can barely think. I'm already on a trip, you may or may not know."

"Of course, but you'll need a companion on your journey. Someone to keep you safe while you sleep. What are they called? Renfields?"

Dominia snorted. "So pejorative. Wouldn't you rather call yourself a 'footman' or something? Anyway, I already have one."

"You want to keep around a weirdo like René Ichigawa? I saw that guy's file. I don't like him."

"Want to explain how your boss has so much information on who I'm with and what I'm doing?"

"And where you're going. I don't think even you know where you're going."

"To Kabul, in the Middle States."

"Yeah, and then? You're going to walk into the Hunters' lodge and say, 'Send me to Lazarus?'"

"That's more or less the plan."

Lifting her eyebrows in a patronizing way, the geisha demanded, "And what will happen when you get Lazarus? You think the Hunters are going to let you walk away with a man they've tried to acquire for the last two thousand years? With your wife? Hunters hate lesbians almost as much as they hate martyrs. They'll let you keep Lazarus busy while they sweep in to get their hands on his blood."

This notion had crossed her mind more than once in both the planning and escape stages of this mission, but she'd been in a one-thing-at-a-time frame of thought. Now here was someone as concerned about the issue as she, despite René's many protests that she need not worry. "How much more do you know?"

"I know more than you know. More than you're willing to admit, at any rate."

"And how does your boss know this?"

"My boss knows everything."

"Does your boss have a name?"

"The Lady's names are taboo to martyrs." Miki snuffed her cigarette with a smile that was sly, or smug—hard to tell with the makeup. "You should know that by now."

The General's eyebrows lifted. Oh, sure, she understood that the Lady was the legendary head of the Red Market; but, much as she once thought of Lazarus, she had always believed the woman a human myth. The stuff cults were made of, not anybody's direct supervisor. This was a notorious enemy of the Hierophant, with many names taboo to martyrs because the words themselves were believed to possess corrupting influence on the soul. This, of course, had bolstered young Dominia's research on this subject—a fruitless effort, since the

Hierophant had wisely censored all those religious texts. When he had found out about it by reviewing her tablet's search history, snooping in his Family's private business being his number-one hobby, he had once more disappointed her with his calm desire to educate. He had even told her a particular name of the Lady that she had not found in her cursory research, explaining that it was not the Lady's real name, or even Her oldest one, but that it was still very old and one of her favorites. He loved to mock her pursuits of knowledge by flaunting the depths of his own. "The Lady is your boss," skeptical Dominia repeated to Miki. "I mean to say, your direct—manager?"

"Yeah, she is. She is now, at any rate, since my promotion! She called me to me and said, 'You will be the one to bring her to me. If you do this for me, I'll make you live forever.' The chance of a lifetime."

A likely story. "Because She's a martyr, I'm sure. To have lived since the dawn of time? I mean, She has to be."

This earned a scornful look from the glittering geisha, and while she snapped something in Japanese, the man hurried up to skitter away. Alone, Miki slid to Dominia's side of the table. She pressed the martyr into the corner of the booth where they were shielded by the high seats and the discretion-friendly drapes hung between each set of guests.

"The Lady is no martyr," murmured Miki, lips parted against Dominia's ear to release a voice light as a wisp of cotton. "She controls life and death; She is the seer who gazes into the mirror of the world."

"That sort of nonsense is why the Hierophant calls the Red Market a cult."

"The Lady is a religious leader, whether or not you men will accept it."

Laughing, Dominia began to say, "I'm not a—" but considered her tie—René's tie—with a frown.

"You've spent your whole life controlled by men: losing your eye to men, losing your wife to men, losing your hair"—she tickled long fingernails across the back of Dominia's scalp—"to men. And now you'll go to the Hunter's lodge and expect them to help you? Now you travel with René Ichigawa, and expect him to help you?"

"What do you know about René Ichigawa?"

"I know that someone like you should never trust someone who comes to you of their own volition."

"Didn't you?"

"Of course not. I came because I was told—and because you booked an appointment, remember?"

She supposed Miki was right. Nothing good came of trusting people who came to her. The Hierophant had come to her. So had Cassandra, and look how that had turned out. Now René had come to her, and she expected him to be different? What Miki suggested was not a new idea. This was why she had trust issues, why she'd never settled into her friendship with the professor. It was all so convenient that he should come to her with this story of resurrection, no matter what rescue organizations with which he worked, or which groups had him in their pockets. Not that those groups didn't have good reason to seek her out in a time of need if they thought they might use her, but...

Was she being paranoid? Were these feelings of mistrust the result of being in a situation where, more than ever before in her unstable life, she was surrounded by strangers possessing their own malicious agendas? Were these feelings because she had lost the last good thing in her life and now floated around, clinging to absurd dreams and waiting to die?

As Dominia drifted into thought, Miki lowered her eyes. "I see you're a woman who needs more convincing than logical persuasion. Some evidence of treachery will be necessary before you see the truth, won't it? Well, don't worry: it won't take long, I'm sure."

From her clutch, she removed a business card that on one side featured an embossed lotus. Another link, Dominia observed, to Miki's profile. The prostitute's name and private number were printed on the reverse. "If you want to make another appointment," she said, a coy smile on her lips as she scribbled a four-number code with a pen from her purse, "or, if you just want to come by my suite, this is the guest pass code."

"You aren't afraid I'll break in and kill you in your sleep? We have at least ten more hours on this train. That's plenty of time for something to happen."

"Too messy, too much attention. Besides, you know I have my own friend with me: he might not be good for much, but he'll take bullets enough for me to run screaming down the hall."

Smirking, Dominia accepted the card and memorized its 7162 code. As she looked back up, Miki snapped shut her purse and slid out of the seat. "Think about my offer of friendship."

"You'll take me to Lazarus, will you?"

"We'll find him together, if you promise to come with me to see the Lady after."

"What does the Lady want with me?"

Sporting that sly expression, Miki bent and gave Dominia a glimpse into the plunging depths of her décolletage. "If you want to know that, I suppose you'll have to come to your senses about me."

Those lips pressed to hers once more, along with that insidious tongue. Dominia could not relax as last time but all the same accepted, her eyes falling closed to fool her brain into believing it was Cassandra on the other side of their shut lids. "Hail Amaterasu," crooned Miki, who pulled away to breathe the illegal word. "I'd have thought a martyr's lips to feel cold, like stone."

"I'd have thought your makeup to taste like paste, but I guess we're both wrong. Don't do that again."

With a laugh in her voice and a wiggle in her step, Miki left the Dining Car; Dominia, alone with her thoughts, finished her wine under a cloud of paranoia. Why did she need to believe in René? Dominia had no attachment to the man himself, but in what he represented. Miki put her finger on it with her troubling insight into Dominia's trust issues. The martyr wanted to prove to herself that not everyone who came to her did so with poisonous hearts. With a great wall of lies erected to mitigate the chance of true connection. The kind of wall Cassandra had erected in secret before they'd ever met.

That wasn't fair, of course. Or maybe it was—when their relationship was founded on false pretenses, how could Dominia but grapple with betrayal? Even close to a century after their meeting, it still stung. But there wasn't anything to be done. She hadn't been about to end their marriage—not once they'd eloped and Cassandra was martyred—and the illness had claimed her in three days, which came a mere eight weeks after their meeting. So stupid! But it had seemed more romantic than stupid at the time. The woman had thrown away her whole life for Dominia, to be with Dominia: or so Dominia had thought. Too soon, she learned she could never trust the motivations of others to be quite so pure as her own.

A few nights after being martyred, Cassandra started getting sick again. That wasn't right. Once a martyr's transformation was complete, they should have felt healthier than ever. Stronger, faster, smarter. Instead, on night three, Dominia awoke from their brief state of matrimonial bliss to fine their honeymoon aborted. Cassandra shivered in the bathroom, her body around the porcelain toilet like it was the first hour of the illness over again.

Dominia forever remembered that conversation in fragmented images: the cold tile floor; the strand of hair sticking to her wife's damp cheek; her own voice saying over and over, "Are you okay? Are you okay? Oh, Cassandra, oh, sweetheart, oh, honey, are you okay?"

Cassandra's terrible red vomit. The sticky sensation of her forehead and shoulders; the acid stench of the bathroom as the new martyr's quivering body recoiled against the sink. Her great doe eyes, lined with sleepless shadows, landing fearfully on Dominia's.

"I should have told you. Oh, I should have told you— I'm so sorry."

Her hand on her stomach. The pallid skin of her face. Cassandra lurched to vomit again, gasping for air between horrible wretches, while a million tiny things clicked into place for Dominia. The powder-soft fragrance of her bride's skin, the perfect glow of her face, the comforting pillow of her body. A perfect kind of softness found in the swells of maternal breasts and thighs thickened just so. The thunder of terrible understanding propelled Dominia from the room until she came to her senses at the door.

"You can't be pregnant. How can you be pregnant?" Dominia's brain tried to make sense of this and found perfect sense in their whirlwind romance that had felt so destined, so beautiful and pure and true. She knew the truth without having to be told as Cassandra lifted her gasping head and from behind shaking shoulders wept, "I'm sorry, I'm sorry: I was pregnant when I came to you. I wanted to save my baby. It was all I had left— He was shipped off to the war, Dominia—"

"You lied to me."

"I never lied to you! I just never knew how to tell you. I knew after I told you, nothing could be the same."

"Because you knew I never would have let this happen! I would have made you—wait, at least."

"That's why I couldn't tell you."

Dominia had ground the heels of her palms into her eyes as if she then wished to hasten her future blindness along. Oh, Lamb, the *pain*. To discover their love artificial! "No wonder we rushed. No wonder it was so serendipitous and urgent. That was how you wanted it."

"I'm sorry." Cassandra uttered a sob that was muted by the back of the hand she pressed to her mouth. "I'm so sorry. I'm so in love with you: I would never lie about that."

Like a broken automaton, the General paced the hall. "Why would you do this? Why would you do this to me? I thought you loved me."

"Please, I do love you. Dominia—" But more vomiting came, and with it, more weeping. Even in memory, Dominia's ribs ached to see Cassandra suffering so. In seconds, she was by her wife's side, hands on her shoulders as Cassandra righted herself. Carefully, the new martyr said, "I do love you. It's true that I came to you at first because of who and what you were. But I didn't expect—feeling the way I do. Loving you the way I do. I didn't want to tell you. I didn't want to hurt you. I wanted to hide it, to have the baby in secret, and then…I don't know. Find some place for it to go. I didn't realize it would be like this, that I would feel like this."

"Of course! Do you understand why? Do you understand what's happening? Your baby is eating you from the inside. Your body is feeding itself to your baby. You know why pregnant women aren't martyred? Because they *die*, Cassandra. The mothers and their babies, they both die." Dominia took a sharp breath and, fire in her watering eyes, gasped, "But I won't let you."

"Even though I hid this?"

"No. Because you've made this my baby, too. And I—I have to handle this."

The delirium of that moment. She had put Cassandra back to sleep and excused herself to get a bottle of wine; her wife still slept when she returned. Then, as now, her lips trembled to think that their happy synchronicity, that beautiful and romantic moment on the beach, was some lure to trap her forever: But what good had been her feelings when her wife suffered? At any rate, she believed Cassandra. When she said that she loved Dominia, it was true. The General felt it then, and felt it still almost a full century later as she let herself into the empty Satin Car room. She felt it, much as she felt the weight of her failed responsibility to keep her good wife, her kind wife, safe from the world's many harms. She was glad René hadn't returned, because only Basil saw her cry.

IX

The Dog and the Rat

René's extended absence would not be cause for Dominia's concern until almost too late. Without Basil, the professor might well have maintained his tenuous control of the situation. Frankly, without Basil, her journey would have been shorter and messier, but she wouldn't realize that for several nights; and it would take far longer before she came to understand why this was. For the moment, she was occupied with a storm of distressing problems, like the absence of Cassandra's diamond, and the thought of what happened in the United Front, which rose back every so often. All those suffering people. Or people who were, at any rate, about to suffer. She lay catatonic in the top bunk, Basil asleep on the floor and the television the solitary glow of a room, which, lacking open windows or active lights, recalled a mausoleum. The Light Rail raced the sun and always lost, but it made an impressive effort, and was a cause of major disorientation in most travelers. She would hurtle through about four time zones and emerge in Kabul before the city saw dawn. When that happened, in what condition would she be? How many eyes would she have? From minute to minute, her life was a tahgmahr such that she couldn't keep up. The distractions of media were, for her, no more distracting from her problems than newspapers for a schizophrenic: every headline, pregnant with a threat. This was a more objective situation, however, as she watched the Hierophant's statement on the events in Japan. The man on the old-fashioned two-dimensional set absolutely addressed her. He was thin with lack of food, had probably eschewed sleep to make himself look extra haggard. His hair looked whiter than usual, lacked sheen, and reminded her that Basil needed to eat something proper.

"My children," began the sorrowful Holy Father, "it has come to my attention that Kyoto has been the site of a tragic terrorist attack." While Dominia suppressed her annoyance, the Hierophant heaved a sigh. "An error was made in my most recent press conference: Dominia di Mephitoli, thought dead, is alive and well. I am sorry to say I have proof. If you have children, please remove them from the room."

There followed footage already overplayed by the Japanese news: Dominia cringed to see herself sweeping out of the fog of war. The guns, the blades, the blood, the horror. Her hand rested against her forehead as she endured the scene. Why did this feel so much worse than all those military nights? Not to say those nights didn't plague her—there was a reason she, with three-quarters of a bottle of wine in her system, already thought of ordering another while she still had the luxury. Those nights did plague her. Had plagued her. They had driven her out to the seaside to meet Cassandra that day.

It was her wife's softening influence that had made the vicious General into such a compassionate Governess. It wasn't hard to appear kinder than the previous governor, Dominia's late (very late) second cousin, Trimalchio of California, who was assassinated by a South American Hunter cell early in the twenty-year conflict. In this war's aftermath, her Father had placed her on the North American throne; the Family then began to prod her into reinstating Trimalchio's camp system, which had, in their estimate, streamlined both labor and food production processes.

Dominia disagreed. She saw the Front as a model for how martyrs and humans might live together. The notion inspired her all the more now, nursing as she did memories of that month in which she and Cassandra were happiest. Happiest as human and martyr, prey and predator. All the problems started when Cassandra became a martyr. Yet, being martyred never changed Dominia's wife: her heart was, in the end, the greatest burden the poor woman was forced to endure. Martyred as an adult, she had retained intact her conscience, morals, and ethics; she had struggled to eat; and she had begged Dominia, from the instant the General was appointed Governess, to rule kindly, if only to ease Cassandra's mind.

"Imagine all those humans are me," she would plead.

Impossible. No other human being could be such a unique combination of heart-wrenching and heartbreaking, of inflaming and infuriating. But all those pleas over time had worked, and Dominia had been able, with her wife's support, to stay strong on the issue of camps, of labor laws, of human health care and a real brand of universal income, which, in the General's experience, did an excellent job of attracting large swathes of free, mobile immigrants to allow a more sporting, hunt-based system of food acquisition. The game was fairer when humans knew they'd ought not to be out at night. They were defenseless without the government streamlining undesirables into grocery stores.

Of course, not all humans were defenseless. On the train, Dominia was drawn back to reality not by the words of her Father but by the whine of the dog. Basil sat by the door with his big eyes turned to Dominia, sometimes easing up on hindquarters as though reaching for the handle.

"I was just thinking about how hungry you must be."

As the Hierophant went on to say, "Even now, I am taking extreme measures to ensure the hasty capture and extradition of my daughter," she rifled through René's bag in pursuit of a necktie, the best option for a leash in a place that would never abide an unrestrained dog. All the while, Basil's whines grew more urgent, and rose to such a frequency that they almost drowned out her Father. "Though her whereabouts are yet uncertain, I have some intelligence regarding her destination, and her means of transportation. And my instincts inform me she watches this broadcast even now."

"I'm working on it, buddy, just a minute. I don't know how this is going to work out...that's a pretty nice Dining Car. Are you sure you want to— Hey!"

Incredibly, she'd caught him stretching on his hind legs, every ounce of his canine weight used to force the handle with both paws to trigger the door. The second it slid open, he was out. Teeth clenched, Dominia tossed the tie away and darted in pursuit rather than remaining to hear the words of her Father. She didn't have to: they followed her into the hall. "If you are indeed watching this, Dominia, I beg you: please, come home. No more killing. The time in which we live is already so fraught with misunderstanding between martyr and mankind. Add not to fear, but come back home. All will be forgiven."

The car outside was empty. Considering the hour, most people digested in the simulated beauty of the Observation Car. The rest whiled away their boredom in front of televisions, playing on phones, or gambling in the Dragon Car. Thank the Lamb for that—nobody to disturb. The dog was in a panic about something, barking as he pawed at the automatic door to the Silk Car. Though she almost caught him, he sprang like he knew where he was headed. Dominia suffered a twinge of maternal anxiety as the door slid open and they emerged upon the gangway with the transparent walls of the giant pneumatic tube all around them. Wouldn't most animals be terrified? But Basil seemed more competent than even her. Not scared at all. What a strange animal—and stranger still because he went not after the source of distant food smell but straight to Miki Soto's door. He gave one urgent, muted bark, then danced from leg to leg while hopping to indicate the keypad.

"Stuck in a well, is she? You're not even pretending anymore." With a shake of her head, the General tapped the code that allowed them into a foyer with a marble floor, a small chandelier, and an artificial ivory-lined telephone table. As if she had stepped into a scaled-down mansion. The dog, without Dominia's amazement, charged through, and she snapped from her momentary befuddlement to follow that which Basil pursued: sounds of violence.

Through the door to the left and past the tiny dining room, a miniature living area stood in terrible disarray. A coffee table covered in takeout had been upended, but it hardly obscured the dead businessman who'd just wanted to suffer at the hands of a beautiful woman. Poor guy. Who didn't? While Dominia tutted in sympathy, she turned her attention to the struggling humans and might have felt more like an adult breaking up a couple of children if she weren't so pissed at René, the apparent assailant, who was on top of—and throttling—Miki. For her part, the smaller human appeared as if her brain was about to go out of commission. While the dog barked in a panic, René looked up in time to see himself yanked off of Miki. He made another grab for her, but too late: blood flooded back into her brain as oxygen rushed back to her lungs, leaving the escort to gasp and cough back to consciousness while Dominia shook René by the collar.

"What the fuck is wrong with you? You lying bastard, what is this? Who sent you?"

"It's not what it looks like, Dominia," he said, but the prostitute spoke, or tried: wheezing words, over and over. They sounded like "hiss size" or "his sighs" until, with a great cough and a clearing breath that came as Dominia worked it out on her own, Miki bellowed, "His eyes!"

The martyr's mouth opened and shut in terrible comprehension. For the first time, she really looked into René's eyes: and, perhaps because Dominia knew what to look for after having seen her own (a porcelain, creamy flatness), she realized Miki was right. René's eyes, all this time, had been cyborgans made to upload video streams to the Hierophant.

The human in her grip winced when asked, "How could you?"

Whatever explanation he had drifted away. He tried being pathetic instead of making excuses. "You don't understand, Dominia. He came to me. He forced me."

"Of course he did. You would have to be stupid to go to him on your own. I'm not saying you aren't stupid, of course. But anybody with half a survival instinct is going to stay far, far away from the Hierophant—and from me."

"Not the Hierophant," breathed René. "Cicero. You think what your old man did to you was bad? My eyes were normal before I met him—before I was busted for involvement with the refugees and the

Hunters. The Hierophant was apologetic. He promised me that he would see me taken care of if I did this favor, but I—I didn't want to do it, Dominia. You understand, don't you? Like you said, no person would choose to do this. I was a good man, once. I *ran* a rescue operation, risked myself in a double life funneling refugees out of the country. But he found me. He threatened my whole operation. Threatened me. Please, Dominia, please! You're a good woman. I hoped—I wanted to get you to Lazarus."

"That's what the Hierophant wants, too." Miki clambered to her feet and smoothed the silk of her disheveled gown. Her hair, beyond repair, fell in velvet curtains as she loosed pin on hidden pin. "The Hierophant, and the Hunters. Poor Dominia's not a tool to scoop up Mr. Popularity."

"But I wanted to help her from the goodness of my heart." The pleading man turned those recording eyes again upon the General "It's true. Once I met you and learned about you, I wanted to bring you to Lazarus. To find a way to…" His expression strained. "I am sorry about your wife. I think it's sad."

Barely breathing, Dominia stepped away from René and half tossed him toward the door. "Did you kill that man?" She jerked her head in the body's direction.

"It was self-defense."

"Because he broke in," Miki explained. "The Hierophant probably gave him access to your DIOX-I's stream; I'm sure he's had ready access to it the whole time that thing's been in your head. Both he and René must have watched us while we were in the Dining Car. At least, I'd bet that's how he got my pass code. Then, while I visited the Dragon Car, he killed my man and waited for me. If I weren't quick as I am, I wouldn't have escaped with my life."

"If I decide I need to kill you," Dominia told him while he backed to the door, "I know where to find you. And if I decide I need to kill everyone on this train—"

"I won't say a word to any of the staff, Dominia, believe me. I'm turning my eyes off right now, I promise!" The eerie phrase bothered her, but not as much as the notion that she had no way to verify he'd turned them off. "Oh, thank you, thank you for leaving me alive. I don't deserve it."

"You're a thousand times more repulsive than him," said Miki, nudging the corpse, then hurling a sharp-looking hair comb in René's direction. "Get out of here if she's not going to kill you."

Before Basil snapped his ankle, René tried saying, "I wouldn't have done anything to you if you hadn't—"

A yelp—and not by any means the dog's yelp—interrupted him, and the professor hurried out the door while Miki turned furious eyes to Dominia.

"Why are you letting him go? You really are stupid."

"He's harmless."

The human, much shorter without her heels, raised her chin to show the bruises. "You've got to be kidding. Talk about damaging the merchandise! This is why beautiful vases are put behind glass."

Dominia used an index finger to steer Miki's chin back and forth under the light. Yeah, it was bad, but she had seen plenty worse; and from the look of it, René hadn't known that the goal of strangulation was to cut off blood, rather than oxygen. Any progress was incidental. "You'll be fine."

"Easy for you to say, martyr. Get away from my neck." With a slap for Dominia's hand, Miki lowered her jaw, looked around in a huff, and began to straighten. "I don't mean to be rude, or prejudiced"—a certain pleased pup pranced back into the room and received a pat from Dominia—"but I'm on edge at the moment."

"I'm sure you are. Tell me again what happened?"

As the women slipped the body upon a tablecloth to be whisked into the suite bathroom, she did. After her appointment with Dominia, Miki had taken the Redcoins automatically deducted from the General's virtual wallet once the appointed time had been met and, after exchanging the fake currency for a standard one, laundered their finances in the casino by buying chips, gambling for a few minutes, then cashing out. "Gambling for a few minutes," however, apparently meant "spending an hour playing cards and another hour getting blitzed at the bar," the latter being evident in the flush across her cheeks and the brusque way she scoffed, "What's it to you if I did? Do you judge everyone you meet, Preachy?" in response to Dominia's innocent query about whether she had gambled away the money.

"I ask because, if you're going to travel with me, we might need it. They've thawed my account for the moment but might freeze it again anytime. That means René and the dummy account he gave me made up most of my wallet." Now that the professor was revealed as a servant of the Hierophant, though, didn't that make Dominique LeBlanc's account as suspect as her own? She frowned while Miki went on.

"Not anymore. As a matter of fact, I *made* money in the Dragon today. Ten thousand yen—that's almost a hundred bucks, UF—and furthermore, what are you? My husband?"

"You're a pretty mean drunk," observed Dominia, cheerful as she stood before the bathtub-cradled body with her hands on her hips. Despite the betrayal, she felt lighter. Perhaps on some level, she had known René was a traitor who needed to be expelled like an ingrown hair.

"You're in a pretty good mood," rebutted Miki, observing this lightness.

"Well, I'm sorry that this guy died, but— Hey"—she assessed the fellow's features again—"you know, the eye doesn't pick up on his face." Nor had it on René's.

"He must pay a privacy fee to Halcyon. Keeps you out of search engines and facial recognition databases." Not too bent out of shape over the corpse, herself, Miki turned away to wash her hands, then removed a bottle of golden oil from the drawer of the ivory-inlaid sink whose dead-eyed cherubs made Dominia a little homesick. While Miki wiped the makeup off her face and scrubbed it with some comically bubbling wash, Dominia watched her in the mirror.

"You mean to say that you, a prostitute, don't value privacy enough to pay the privacy subscription?"

"On the contrary, it's in my interest to maintain an accessible public profile. Especially—well, I haven't for some time, but I used to work in hostess clubs after I got out of being a geisha."

"You were a real geisha." Dominia laughed.

"Are you surprised? Please, nobody spends hours doing this makeup on a regular basis if they aren't trained to endure it. You need, like, therapy and shit."

"You seem more…crass than I would expect from a geisha, I guess. And I didn't think they existed much anymore."

"Well, we're rare. I was. I'm not one anymore. Anyway, the hostess clubs were less involved, but similar, in a way. Sort of like being a geisha, you know, where I would come to a table and be their hostess, get them to spend money on drinks and all. But there's no art to it. Mindless work, stupid and boring. So"—she turned her now-bare face and big, bright, organic eyes to Dominia—"I promoted myself."

"You mean, you became a prostitute."

"I don't feel there is much difference between promotion and prostitution. Not when you're a geisha. When I was young and stuffy, of course I did. I used to think that the pure and icy living dolls only bought in pressing circumstances by top-dollar lovers were the epitome of the divine feminine. Anyone easier was classless to me. But I sort of told you before. A woman came to me one day." Miki slipped past Dominia to right the upended table, then busied herself in the pouring of wine, an act that highlighted the delicate beauty of her hands. "A beautiful woman. She asked me to come with her, to serve Ishtar"—that most popular appellation of the Lady—"with her. And what woman wouldn't take an opportunity to meet the creator of the Red Market?"

"Quite a few. Most." Dominia lowered into the couch and Miki flopped beside her. "Most people don't want to meet the queen of prostitutes."

"She's not the queen of prostitutes!" Miki's tone was as sharp as her clout of Dominia's head. "She's the mother of the world. And that's capital: the Mother of the World. She's also the Queen of Springtime, of Youth and—cows. Bees." The already-drunk prostitute made herself drunker between objects, and the General wondered if that wasn't how she had gotten through most of her life. Not that Dominia couldn't relate. "Lots of other things, too, but it's pearls before swine, talking to you about it. Oh…pearls are sacred to her, too, I think."

"And swine?"

"No, that's your Father." Miki laughed at her own joke until she snorted, looking like a schoolgirl. Most humans looked somehow fresh, childlike to ancient martyr eyes (or, depressingly, eye). Even without the sacred protein, they modified themselves to hell, and experienced a pretty extended shelf life given money and diligence. Miki was probably in reality more of a late thirty-, early fortysomething, but Dominia looked at her and saw, at best, a twenty-year-old when she wasn't burdened by makeup. Her age became visible when her eyes narrowed and she got a stern, serious look. "Have you turned off that DIOX-I? Its recording capabilities, I mean. He's for sure watching us right now, you realize—you think it's just René's data he's got?"

"I hadn't had a chance to think about it until now. I've been trying not to."

With a curse, Miki threw back the contents of her glass, wiped her lips with the back of her hand, and leaned toward Dominia's right eye, her lips over-forming the words to allow easy lip-reading. "Then I'll take this opportunity to say, 'Fuck you, you snooping pieces of shit. And your rat, René.'"

"Which, for the record—"

"No more talking. First, go into your eye's settings and turn off its data transmission to all places—storage clouds, DIOX error teams, anything."

Dominia blinked. "What?"

"It's a front-line precaution at best, if you know what I mean. There's probably software still embedded in the eye that's inaccessible to the user: something that streams data to the Hierophant's offices no matter what we do, especially if the eye was originally leased to him. But we can keep DIOX from delivering it over the table. You don't know how to shut it off? Don't you care about computer security?"

Still startled by the woman's chiding, Dominia tried to find some excuse, but was forced to admit, "Computers and—anything more than a cell isn't popular with my people. Even fancy phones and watches aren't popular. They're frowned upon. E-readers are about as high-tech as we get."

"What? Why the hell are you guys such Luddites?"

"It's the blue light. The blue light of the sun is what causes our reaction to it; the blue light of electronics isn't as bad, but studies have indicated it impacts a martyr's motivation and, in some cases, digestion." Never mind that she and Cassandra had once made frequent fun of goofy martyr housewives who claimed to have any number of nebulous issues thanks to the glow of their neighbor's holo-corner as seen through a curtained window. Miki, as though sensing this, snorted, and forced Dominia to struggle on. "I think my Father has a point when he says that people don't learn anything when they rely on computers." That justification seemed ironclad to the General, as it was one of the few "common sense" beliefs she had always thought exceptions to the rule of her Family's backward evil. Nevertheless, Miki laughed.

"How do you have room to create anything when you're wasting your mental space remembering junk you could store on a computer? Doesn't a computer run faster when it isn't bogged down by nonsense? Of course it's important to learn, but it's more important to discern."

"Was that a poster on the wall of some depressing school of yours? No wonder you humans are in the shape you are."

"Sassy. But I mean what I said. And for the record"—Miki's eyes blazed bright—"humans will always come out on top. That's *because* we're willing to rely on tools outside ourselves. You can tell an animal over a human because the animal has too much pride in its physical traits to condescend to the use of a tool."

Dominia blustered without meaning before stringing together a wounded conclusion of their debate. "You're a fine one to speak of condescension. Just help me with this stupid eye, okay?"

Rather than taking offense, Miki laughed, and proceeded to walk her through the process of turning off things like forced software updates and data backups from her eye to the cloud. "The cloud" was a term for data virtually stored in (often insecure) servers, rather than more controllable personal hardware. Somewhere along the line, her Father had helped convince everybody this was a good idea, like Halcyon; it might have continued to seem like a good idea until martyrs showed up, and even for a while after, when people still believed there was no way he could access their private information. But, long before Dominia's birth, the digital line between "personal" data and "government" data became blurry. Privacy meant keeping one's data in one's personal possession, which meant scouring a new device for any sign of uploading software, malicious or otherwise. Basil, bored, wandered off, and Dominia admitted during their work, "I suppose it is pretty stupid to refuse to use something out of pride. That's probably why I got stuck with this eye now. Karma, right?"

"That's almost how karma works," agreed Miki, impressed. "Is it off?"

"All off, I think."

"Good. You should still be able to use the Internet, but—hasn't he frozen your Halcyon account, yet?"

"Well—no. The eye nabbed my real information from my brain before I could stop it, and everything was frozen at first, but by the time I was on the train, it seemed to have been released again. I'm going to toss the dummy watch René gave me—not like I need the ticket anymore." Despite this sensibility, annoyance tensed the human's face.

"You need to delete your should-be-frozen account, if you still can. He's for sure using that to track you, too. Accessing your brain— Ugh! Stuff is evil these days. All these details!" The prostitute raised her hands from where they'd rested on her hips. "You have to take care of them."

"I will. But, as far as details are concerned, there's one I'm worried a...bout." Dominia's thoughts trailed off as she became aware of the horrific, wet sounds of a dog eating. The women shared a sidelong look of disgust before they peeked into the cramped bathroom with its undefended corpse. Basil, tail wagging, lifted his head to smile with a gory muzzle, eyes brighter and coat shinier by the minute.

Eating him had crossed her mind, but it was hard to prepare such a large body in such a small space. She had to admit she was a little jealous. Dominia's mouth opened and shut in silence before she found her question, at which Miki scoffed. "Is this dog a martyr?"

"What? No, stupid, of course not. Dogs eat flesh all the time. This one's been eating poorly, running around with you. No wonder he's hungry. *Sukuramu, sukuramu.*" The human waved the dog away so that it scrambled between their legs and out of the room like a more innocently mischievous hound caught in garbage.

"Right," cautioned Dominia, but Basil's innocent look stayed her from further discourse. Right, of course. Dogs ate flesh all the time. That was what her Father had suggested to her, right? That she leave the door open so the dog wouldn't starve once he'd eaten his humans. And their own dogs in Europa: some of them were trained to eat human flesh, too. The hunting hounds, and all. Of course, dogs ate flesh. It was just— Basil was so...*intelligent.* So...

"So, what are we going to do about him, huh? You're daydreaming." Miki snapped her fingers in front of Dominia's face while standing between the General and the dog; the pup behind her appeared oblivious to the dollop of blood gathering at his lip, about to drop upon the spiraling pattern of the lilac-moss carpet. "I can't take care of all this by myself. It's your man who did this, so it's you who should clean it up."

"There's only so much I can do."

"You need to at least keep him out of sight of the porters for the next few hours. And keep the smell down, too."

"It won't be that bad that fast," said Dominia, observing the gaping stomach wound carved by Basil's hungry jaws. "But you're right. We have to keep this from getting out, and we have to keep other people from getting in. For all we know, René could make a noise complaint. Maybe somebody's already lodged one."

"Too impolite. These people mind their business to a fault. It's a matter of keeping our volume polite and quiet between here and Kabul. Easier said than done"—the human rolled her shoulders in a shrug—"but all we can do is try."

The prostitute wove past Dominia, past the bloody dog, and tumbled into her bed: not a bunk like the arrangement in Dominia's room, but not near as wide as most would wish and barely comfortable for two. Alone for the space of a second, she studied the corpse and wondered if her Father watched through her eye even with its backup features disabled. If it was true what Miki said about programs for some reason delivering information to the Family, wasn't it possible that the Hierophant had potential access to every pair of DIOX-Is available? That was paranoid thinking, but if anyone was capable of such a thing, it was him. How? He couldn't manage it. He owned Halcyon, but DIOX and their cyborgans were an enterprise of mostly human clientele. Why would he fund their medical technology?

She had to hope he wouldn't. If that was the case, it didn't matter if she had a DIOX-I of her own. Walking down the street, she would be exposed to thousands of streams recorded by passing strangers, and the Hierophant could observe any or all. Horrible. This thought lulled the General into a trance from which Miki drew her with the pluck of a shamisen string.

"That's a pretty old-fashioned instrument," said the martyr, coming to sit in the awkward, armless white chair in the corner. "I've always liked it."

"You martyrs love human culture. You just hate humans. At least, you don't think that we're as good as you." While Miki's slender fingers produced twangs that filled the air like incense, she talked away. "He's convinced himself—and everybody else—that you're all so much better than us. That you're different from us, at all. How is a martyr different from a genetically engineered human?"

For an ugly second, she was back on McLintock farm. "I've begun to ask that, myself. I always asked that. I…ignored it." Dominia frowned at her hands, at her hungry stomach. Soon she needed to eat, and she regretted letting the dog get dibs on the businessman. "You have to ignore things to survive sometimes."

"When your nervous system tells you a situation is bad, you should listen."

"Of course, but what's a kid supposed to do?"

Miki's lips twisted in the shred of a sympathetic frown as her face lowered to her instrument. "That is the tragic part about this. Things would be different if martyrs were not so convinced of their own righteous nature. But your Father is good with children. Give him an infant, and blue will be red in a few centuries."

Too true. The martyr rested her face against the cool wood of the door and listened to the instrument, let it quiver into her while she said, "I wanted to protest. I did, often, but I was afraid to take action."

"What changed? Why have you taken action now? Not because some rat came to you. Not because your wife died."

"But it *was* Cassandra. Cassandra changed me." In the back of Dominia's head, she saw her, pale at the table, the adult version of the girl that the General had once been. So reluctant—so terrified—to exchange humanity for immortality. Every bite of food Cassandra consumed for the next six months were for her child; after the birth, they were for Dominia. Now, Dominia regretted that fact more than any. "She never let anyone make her forget that what she did was wrong. That shame kept her human, but it also kept her apart from us. It kept her so unhappy."

"Better to be unhappy and repentant than an ignorant sinner," said Miki. Dominia laughed.

"You believe in sin?"

"I might not worship your Father, but I'm a very religious person."

"Ishtar, the Lady?" At Dominia's question, the human's dark eyes fluttered in surprise. The General smiled. "I'm not concerned anymore with the illegality of— It's just a word."

"Nothing is 'just' a word. Nothing is a word. Words have power; words bind, conceal, illuminate, and curse. So, too, can they free. The Lady is older than the word that is Her name; older than the word 'Lady,' older than the concept of 'man' and 'woman.' Older than the world."

Over the plucking of the shamisen, against the closed lids of her eyes, great imaginings of near-psychedelic variety played out against the warm madder backdrop—some formless Lady with the world in her arms. Miki went on. "The world has been created many times over: so believe the Lady's priestesses, those in the marketplace who have been initiated into its higher echelons of truth. But we are not the only ones who believe that. Many religions—all of them, if you pay attention—say the world has been created again and again. All of this has happened again and again."

"That's a depressing thought."

"Then let that be motivation to live a pure life. That way, you can minimize the amount of pain you endure for eternity." While Miki chuckled cheerlessly, the shamisen carried Dominia away with the sound of the human's low voice. "The Lady is the one who creates the world each time it is destroyed. She was not present in the universe when it first began. Rather, She was created by the first destruction."

"What destroys it?"

"The death of Lazarus. Lazarus is the sun around which the Earth of the Lady rotates, and when his light is snuffed, She has no means by which to see, so he must be made again. But, to make him again, She has to make the universe."

"Lazarus is really a person?" asked Dominia, unable to open her eyes against her fatigue, but conscious enough to be distressed by the fleeting notion that maybe René had lied to her about everything. Maybe all the old murmured human legends were the stories she'd believed them to be. Miki, however, soothed her.

"Lazarus is a person, yes: but he is also a pillar for the world. It is said he was only human once, the first time the universe was created. It is said that your Father stole the protein from him and used it to his own, unholy ends. That Lazarus is the Protomartyr, and the one to whom the people should have always looked. He has not been a human since the first time the world was new. Created a martyr, he dies a martyr, too; and when he dies, the world begins again. It is why he stays so far from mainstream humanity—why he is capable of such great miracles but has allowed his name to slip into obscurity, echoed on the sidelines of the Abrahamic books and worshiped by the cult of the Lazerenes."

"But why? Why is Lazarus tied to the death of the universe?"

"Lazarus is a miracle worker. This Lazarus of whom we speak is a great man, but humble, and so he took his name from one who was saved by a messiah, rather than one who did the saving. The miracle of Lazarus is that he saved even himself from death: saved himself through Her. The first time he died, the Lady emerged from his blood to revive him, and She seeks to make from him Her King. She seeks to purify the world of martyrs and set all things right again. For, much as he was responsible for the release of martyrdom upon the world, so, too, must he be the one to end it."

"Then why hasn't he ended it already?"

"That, I cannot answer. Perhaps because he has seen it all before, and knows that the Lady's way is not the true solution to the problem."

"Because it will all happen again, the next time he dies and the universe is created?"

"Aren't you a wise woman." The shamisen's twanging stopped and a light flickered off; Dominia, too tired to lift her head from the wall, accepted the blanket that Miki draped over her. "Only Lazarus knows why he does what he does; only the Lady knows why She does what She does; only you know, Dominia, why you do what you do. Worry about yourself, and let the gods handle themselves."

X

Mass Hysteria

Dominia must have been tired: that night was the first time in over a month she managed to sleep longer than three or four hours. And that included those spells of unconsciousness. Best, it was a concrete block of sleep that hosted no bad dreams. Almost strange to come to under the comforter feeling refreshed, instead of panicked. No traumatic memories unfolded themselves in a rapid fractal of pain. Yet, a weird shame lurked in that. Half of her wished to never think of Cassandra at all, ever again; the other half was desperate to keep her alive or re-invoke her being through sheer willpower, however impossible this might have been. But it was all impossible, wasn't it? Even the dog, who twitched in his sleep, was impossible. Miki snored on her bed, tangled in her sheets and sweaty with the alcohol processed by her human body. There was Cassandra's far sweatier forehead, her sweaty palms, as she waited in the Family doctor office— the Family doctor, of course, being Cicero, as partial to playing doctor as to playing priest.

"A rather naughty girl, aren't you." He checked Cassandra's pulse under Dominia's hawkish scrutiny.

"Has anybody ever told you how creepy you are?" the new martyr asked. Cicero laughed, the spitting image, sight and sound, of the Hierophant.

"Try not to take offense. I think of you as a child, of sorts. You would do well to think of yourself as such, too."

As Cassandra shot Dominia's amused expression a far more rueful look, Cicero selected a tube of gel for the ultrasound. "You are, though, quite ill-behaved to have brought an unwitting party for the ride. Lie back, there we are." While Cassandra obeyed, her hand stretched out, and Dominia realized belatedly that her wife wanted her to hold it. Many long days the General had been up, dealing with Cassandra's sickness and talking about the circumstances that had brought them to that point. Cassandra's lover had been killed by a martyr, and she then learned (through the miracles of that same over-the-counter pregnancy test that had informed her of the bittersweet conception) that the baby had a genetic defect: a particularly unfriendly one that would leave the child dead in utero and threaten the mother's life without unaffordable genetic treatments. Even with those treatments, no amount of money would have guaranteed the infant. The baby was all she had left of her lover—all she had in her life—and she had nothing to lose in martyrdom. Everything to gain.

Cicero swept up the small wireless wand of the portable ultrasound device. "How has your nausea been?"

"Violent," answered Cassandra; Dominia added, "She can't keep anything down."

"Well, she will need to try. She is, as they say, 'eating for two.'"

In one sweet second, Cassandra's eyes lit, her head lifted, and she asked, "It's alive?"

Even Cicero's smile was genuine enough to crinkle his features. "Yes, she's fine."

"Oh, 'she'! A girl." Those beautiful eyes welled up in tears, and Cassandra shone with a smile that inspired a matching one in Dominia. As though it were her child. "I'm so glad she's okay. Thank God, thank God—alive."

"Yes, the blood test showed her to be a girl; physical differences should just be developing. Your instinct to turn toward martyrdom rather than flee east for refugee medical care, as so many women do, is quite interesting. Has Dominia told you the true history"—he glanced from the screen—"of the sacred protein? We keep it at the 'gift from

God' level for the common man. Humans and martyrs who only go to Church to receive the stabilizing blood of the Lamb."

Cassandra shook her head, and Cicero spoke without looking up from the laptop with which he printed pictures. "Quite a long time ago, there was no such thing as genetic modification. This was when I and my brother, Elijah, were mere humans. As men of science, we saw the world's problems and wished to solve them. Foremost among these problems were mortality, cancer, genetic defects—all those things handled in the medical field, which, it became apparent in time, could be fought with a combination gene editing and various other therapies. He and I studied a protein that compares the DNA of foreign bacteria to stored RNA to better identify and eliminate biological threats—a miracle of a thing, a genetic pair of scissors still used to treat humans unwilling to take the steps to immortality. But it was mortality that we sought to cure through the protein. There were, after all, animals in the natural world that went without aging. Animals that survived in the vacuum of space. There was a cure for everything, given the protein and the correct RNA. We were on the cusp of something most grand; and then, one day, the Hierophant came knocking on our door. He looked frighteningly like me, and explained he had come from Acetia, a world far away, to bring us the answer for which my brother and I, of the whole human race, had most feverishly searched. He martyred us that day. Humans prefer to teach that the protein was developed in some lab, and it is true that my brother and I never would have become the first martyrs of Earth without our scientific background; but, you see, we had to rely on the grace of God for the answer we required."

"I had always heard that the Hierophant brought the protein from his alien world," said skeptical Cassandra, accepting her first—and only—baby pictures with a soft smile. "I guess I thought it sounded kind of...odd."

"He was attracted by our discovery. The martyrs of his world knew Earth was ready for the protein, and may have discovered it alone if not for the intervention of the Lord's highest servants. The Hierophant, His high priest on Acetia, was sent to instruct us in its use. That is why the blood of Lazarenes is forbidden; his protein was synthesized in a lab. It is not a gift from God but a base creation of the world."

"And—you, and Elijah—you thought this was worthwhile when the Hierophant told you that you'd need to resort to cannibalism?"

"Oh, I seldom *resort* to it, as I am always within my brother's comforting proximity. But I choose to engage in it, because it is the highest pleasure that our Father's world may offer." While Cassandra shuddered at the merriment in his black eyes, he added, "Most martyrs, as we did at that time, consider it a small price to pay for salvation. You must also agree, Cassandra, or I would not find you thus."

"You weren't put off by the alien business?"

"Certainly not. How thrilling! What vindication it was to meet him, evidence that our paths were divinely inspired! Like having a child who stood up right away, walking and talking on day one. We had never considered the existence of aliens, let alone that they should be servants of the divine; but it only makes sense that higher intelligence should have a higher standing of Eternity."

While Dominia's wife frowned at the images of her baby, Cicero patted her arm. "I think you should be proud, and excited. Two thousand years is a long time, and this has never been allowed to happen. The occasions that almost slipped through the cracks have not started this well."

Dominia, irritated, slipped in with, "She's puking day and night. You call that 'starting well'?"

"Pregnancy is a difficult time. I recommend eating a lot of crackers, drinking something carbonated, staying off your feet. Aren't you lucky to have such a doting wife!"

"I am— So, the protein is fixing my baby?"

"Editing her as we speak: clipping here, rearranging there, adding this and that."

The mother-to-be found, after brief struggle, a way to phrase a difficult question. "Will she still be my baby?"

"Your baby, a dead man's baby, and the Lord's baby." Cicero crossed himself, chuckling, on his way out of the office.

Yes. A dead man's baby. Now, having lost her, Dominia understood why Cassandra had been so desperate to hold on to one thing—anything—that contained part of the person she'd loved. It was why she now stood in Miki's tiny suite and quietly shifted the lid of some luggage in hopes of finding the diamond. Somehow, though Dominia's sigh on waking, her stretch on standing, and her footsteps across the room had not been enough to awaken the prostitute, the rustle of her clothes in foreign hands proved better than an alarm. Miki bolted upright and shoved away the blanket without a thought for her modesty, then recognized the General.

"Oh, it's you." She fell once more and yanked her coverings back while tucking her drool-soaked pillow into the crook of her neck. "You're not going to find it."

"'Her.'" The General grimaced at her reflexive correction, but doubled down. "You don't even know what I'm looking for. I might be trying to rob you. Maybe I already found it."

"Of course you're trying to rob me, but you won't find it, and you haven't found it already because the diamond hasn't even been in this room."

"Where is she?"

"Beats me." Her rear wiggled for an emphasis lost on the fuming martyr.

"You mean you don't even know where she is?"

"Actually"—she smacked dry lips and cracked her arid eyes open enough to look at the clock—"I don't think she's even on this train anymore."

A chill whipped over Dominia at the skipping of her heart. "Did you sell her?"

"No, no, of course not. I sent her somewhere for safekeeping. She's on her way to the Lady."

Impotent adrenaline flooded her trembling limbs, but that may have been the protein going to town on her DNA as her body entered starvation mode. Whatever it was, Dominia barely heard Miki's words over the intrusive images of Cassandra's remains in the negligent hands of some stranger, headed someplace Dominia didn't even know, for purposes occult in every definition of the word. She remembered the unavailable prostitutes she had seen near her location when making the appointment with Miki. Cassandra was with one or both; the inactive dots would be gone if she looked now. Losing grip on her temper, the martyr strode to the bedside of the human and gave her shoulders such a shake that Basil awoke with a soft bark. "Why would you do that? What the fuck were you thinking?"

"It's the only way to guarantee you'll bring Lazarus to the Lady. She's being treated with the utmost respect, don't worry. Do you think remains belong swinging around your neck while you run all over creation?"

"Now's not the time to develop a sense of moral decency. Who's to say I don't just kill you?" She examined the bruises developed on Miki's throat and narrowed her eyes. "Finish the job René started. I'm a fool to trade him for you, anyway: the Hunters don't deal with women. René's intimacy with them was integral to finding Lazarus."

"We'll find him."

"How?"

"You just *think* the Hunters don't deal with women. The truth is, they're more than a secret club of jihadists sitting in a bunch of tents outside of Jerusalem, in the jungles of Brazil, and working with yakuza. They're *everywhere*. Why do you think you were headed to Kabul in the first place? There are less-extreme extremists who are part of their stupid brigade, and those less-extreme extremists are more flexible when it comes to talking like a civilized human...or putting down money to get laid." As Dominia relaxed her hold, Miki stumbled up in search of her robe. "I know a guy who can tell us where Lazarus is. At the least, he has the resources to find out."

"And he'll do this because..."

"As I said, his bosses are way more extremist than he is. You think it would sail with them if they found out he'd solicited a prostitute? You're half right about that sort and women. To the Hunters, Red Market workers are as bad as a martyr." With a scoff of derision, Miki lifted her arms and sent her hair pluming in great jet-colored streams from the maroon cotton of her *yukata*. "It's like, the tiny penis club, or something. Look at René! Whining like that to save himself. Makes me sick. I'm sure he's going to tattle to the Hunters—We need to find Lazarus as soon as possible."

The General felt almost bad, but Miki was right: René was, for lack of a more eloquent phrase, a little shit. Responsible for the flight of a great many refugees or no, he could only be considered so noble when associating with even the lowest echelons of a terrorist organization. It wasn't so much that he deserved was he got; it was that what he got was such a straight-line consequence of his spineless nature that an excess of empathy for him was out of the question. "Maybe you were right, and we should have put him out of his misery. If they buy into the story that I'm a rogue terrorist responsible for the atrocities on the ship and in the hospital, some loose martyr mass-murdering humans across the globe, any agreement we might have had to peacefully exchange information is as good as ruined. If they don't, well—there was nothing in the first place to stop them from betraying me, and there isn't anything now."

"But, with the power of technology, anything is possible! Like I said, my guy's a better solution than risking a conversation with the Hunters' higher-ups. Kahlil's okay, you'll see. A bit misogynistic, but all Hunters are. He doesn't mean it; I'm reeducating him. Anyway, if he's going to keep my mouth shut"—she shrugged slim shoulders as Basil scrambled up and, apropos of apparently nothing, wandered into the hall—"he's going to have to do me a favor. We should be there in an hour: I told him we'd take a cab from the station."

"What's he do?"

"Oh, he helped found one of the biggest tech start-ups in Kabul—for whatever that's worth, fast as that industry moves!—but a couple years ago— Sh." The human lifted a hand almost pale as her face while the front door of the suite slid open. Her dark eyes highlighted by alertness, Miki glanced into Dominia's face, then let her gaze slide toward the bathroom—and the corpse inside. Dominia's brain churned. Was the dog's face clean? She hadn't paid attention since waking up. Why had a porter ignored the "Do Not Disturb" light? Had some complaint been lodged? If so, why hadn't they called over the intercom and asked to be let in? Why did her heart beat with the fast insistence that it was someone she knew and didn't want to see? Not Cicero, please. But Basil barked a happy note, and the familiar, carefully cultivated chime of an airy voice sang, "Oh, aren't you a handsome boy!" And Dominia felt a deep kind of horror.

It seemed ever more that the General lived in the worst possible scenario. She almost would have preferred Cicero. Saint Valentinian, himself. Anyone, really, but Lavinia.

With a grim expression designed to anchor Miki in place, Dominia edged down the short hall. Its tiny length increased to an incomprehensible stretch that revealed, second by Zeno's subdivided second, the tip of Basil's curling tail; then it unveiled his fuzzy black haunch, which was matched, by pure chance, to the lace of the elaborate gown worn by the woman who petted him. The smile on her pearly face and the unyielding gold of her hair seemed bright as those portions of the border collie's fur that were white, and the DIOX-I's box resembled less a digital affectation than a halo. Dear Lavinia—now was not the time.

"Oh, Dominia, I'm very happy you're alive, but I'm just as pleased to meet this handsome chap! Yes, hello, yes, hello, aren't you sweet, how are you." While the dog's tail beat a delighted rhythm against the marble floor and once or twice threatened to upend the telephone stand, Lavinia turned her Marianas eyes toward her older sister and hugged him to her breast. "But, oh, Dominia, I *am* so happy you're alive."

"So am I, mostly. Did he send you here?"

"Yes and no. I've *begged* Daddy to tell me where you were! I pestered him and pestered him ever since that ship ran aground in the Port of Kyoto, and finally he told me you were on the Light Rail, and I've never *been* on the Light Rail before!" Her vast child's eyes sparkled bright with her breathless delight as she released the dog to spread her hands. "It's so *beautiful*, isn't it, Dominia? Like a big gold snake popping in and out of its tunnel. And it's funny to see how the foreigners think we dress and act."

"They've got it pretty close. Have you seen the Dining Car?"

"No, not yet—I came straight here! I wanted to see you. Oh, Ninny, Daddy told me about your eye, and I'm *sorry*. Does it hurt?"

"No, it doesn't hurt, it's fine. Look—you want to go to the Dining Car with me? Maybe we can have a bite to eat? Nothing real, but—"

"I can't, Ninny. I've come to deliver an important message and then hurry off posthaste: I don't have much time to dally."

Snorting, Dominia glanced down at Basil. "Can't let you out for too long; you might start getting ideas."

"Ideas like yours! But Daddy sent me to say that he wants you to come home, Ninny. And so do I." Lavinia threw the pout of a twelve-year-old, rather than the solemn expression of a near-centennial Princess as worn for official broadcasts. "I miss you. I was so scared when I thought something had happened to you. And whatever's gone on with your *hair*?"

"People were going to recognize me."

"Well, yes, but you wouldn't have to worry about people recognizing you if you'd come home. I've never seen you without your long hair, how funny! You'd make a pretty boy, if you were a boy."

Trying not to cast any anxious glances down the hall where Miki was blessedly silent, Dominia laughed in as normal a manner as she managed. "Thanks, I guess. I kind of like it. But I can't go home. Not after what he did to Cassandra."

"Daddy didn't do anything to her! Why would you say that?"

"You don't know what happened."

"She was such a dreary lady." Lavinia sighed at the thought, as oblivious to the sting as any child. "I always heard she made an awful fuss about being a martyr, even though she chose it! She was nice enough, I suppose, but since her baby died, after all, I mean—the whole thing was pointless, wasn't it? Holding on to that for ninety years…weren't you enough for her? And now she's causing you so much grief. Why don't you meet a nice, new girl? A proper martyr?"

She wasn't going to get angry. She had to maintain reason. The girl didn't understand. How could the Eternal Virgin of Europa understand anything about love? "It wasn't pointless, Lavinia." A thousand kisses and sighs and touches and smiles and lazy evenings and good nights and bad nights and seeing her there, asleep. "There's so much I would never trade, even for all the pain. The pain was worth it."

"If the pain was worth it, you wouldn't have run away clinging to the false hope some liar put into your head."

Was it worth trying to convince her that the Hierophant had sent René, and had therefore been the one to tempt her into running away? "If the hope is false, then what does the Hierophant want with Lazarus? He could have killed René and me in the Front—but he didn't."

"Of course he didn't. Did you see his broadcast? He's been so sad, Dominia, he barely eats or sleeps. He looks so tired. I hate everyone *fighting* like this. Aren't we supposed to get along? We're a family."

"Families fight."

"They don't have to!" Optimistic Lavinia's perception of family life had always been half what the Hierophant told her and half what she selectively gleaned from books, preferring ancient works like the exhausting *Anne of Green Gables* while ignoring *Anna Karenina*. "Families can be happy."

"Or deeply unhappy."

Frowning, an unpracticed expression on her gentle face, Lavinia looked like she was beginning to understand something long hidden. "Are you unhappy, Ninny? Don't you love us?"

Dangerous territory. "I love *you*, Lavinia. Isn't that enough? Look: part of the reason I left is because of the way he treats you."

"What—Daddy? He spoils me! I don't know what you mean, 'the way he treats me.'"

"Keeping you like…this." Dominia waved a helpless hand without finding a word gentle enough. Nonetheless, Lavinia's face fell further. "Not that there's anything wrong with you! You're a sweet girl, but it's the way he—shelters you, and denies you so much of your own life. You must see that sometimes."

"If I wanted to go into the world, I'd go. I don't because our cities"—she lowered her voice—"well, a place like Denmark, Old Elsinore—it's *safe* for me, isn't it? Instead of doing something like this."

"I didn't say you had to take the fu—fudging Light Rail your first time out on your own. Just, you know, try living your own life. Away from him, and Cicero. You like our cities, so get an apartment in

New Elsinore in the Front and live like one of the young poets there;
Brooklyn's a nice neighborhood. Or hang out in your duchy! I lived
an anonymous life in Canada for about twenty years…didn't talk to
anybody from the Family until the final years of the South American
Conflict." She relished the thought. "What a nice vacation."

"I couldn't do that! I love Daddy and Cicero. And what about the
Lamb? Why do you act like they're such horrible people? All they've
done for you! Given you!" It was like listening to a feminine clone
of the Hierophant. Dominia shut off in a way so visceral that Lavinia
noticed; she changed tack, and her features softened. "I know you're
sad for Cassandra, but—"

"Please: I think you've done enough damage there. I'm not coming
home."

The girl's tone dropped to a note of warning. "You really want
more people to die?"

"It's them or me," she said with a pathetic attempt at a smile. Her
little sister didn't find that funny, from the looks of it, and official
worry vibrated in Dominia's skull. There were other reasons why the
Hierophant kept Lavinia away from the world—why she was a walking, talking, singing argument against unregistered martyrings and the
martyring of adults, the latter being ironic since she was found as
a baby. But because she awoke as an adult, and had, in a vague and
technical way, the right to an adult's agency, she served as paradoxical
warning for both cases in one person. Dominia glanced at Miki, who
briefly appeared down the hall, now dressed in a chic suit and looking as mundane a professional as anybody else on the train. Though
Lavinia's head turned with the sound of movement, Dominia stepped
closer to distract her sister by taking up her hand.

"I don't want anyone to die, Lavinia. I don't want to be doing this.
You think I wanted to upend my life? Lose my position and power,
everything I had? I wrestled with the choice to leave. But the best
choice for me—the healthiest choice—was to leave."

"Daddy said some scummy human offered you a deal."

"Because the Hierophant *sent* him," insisted Dominia at last, in
fruitless—and fatal—agitation. As predicted, Lavinia looked offended

by the notion. Once, she stomped her foot. Twice, she tapped it. Horror filled Dominia and she scrambled to placate the girl. "But he only sent René because—because—"

"Daddy would never send some gross creep to trick you." The tapping of her foot became the beat of a metronome. Miki, who had continued peeking (with what she must have thought to be subtlety) from the bedroom, began to move her foot to the rhythm. Everything was lost if Dominia didn't calm her sister down. Was it possible to escape from a train in a hyperloop tunnel alive? How about with a dog under one arm and a prostitute under the other? That was, assuming said possessed prostitute survived. Lavinia insisted something about the Hierophant's integrity, and Dominia, fear-deafened, forced herself to tune back in as Lavinia said, "And that's why Daddy sent me. Because he was worried about you, and sad that you let some human tempt you off the righteous path."

"I don't think there is a righteous path," the General suggested. Her sister sniffed.

"I'm sorry you're depressed, Ninny. But when we get you home, you can see a doctor! Cicero will help you. He gives me pills to help me sleep all the time!"

Gritting her teeth, Dominia let slip, "If I never see Cicero again, it will be too soon," which darkened Lavinia's face more than even aspersions against the Hierophant.

"I guess you'd rather hang out with your garbage friends like René and the prostitute. Is she here?" Now graceless as a bossy toddler, Lavinia shoved Dominia aside with a shocking amount of force. Before the dog even barked, the martyr strolled around the corner, her steps marching to the beat she'd tapped: the beat that possessed Miki, whose knee and hip now wiggled with the pace, and whose expression brightened without regard for the threat represented as Lavinia appeared, cheery as ever, her own body moving to a silent dance.

"There you are! Do you know who I am?"

"Lavinia di Forenzzi," said Miki, unable to stop smiling or, for that matter, dial back the way her legs moved her into the hall. "The Duchess of Florence and the Princess of Europa and like twenty other things, too, right? Do you know what humans call you? Satan's Pet."

"Daddy's not Satan." Lavinia cheesily mimed tossing a lasso to the inaudible beat, which caused Miki to mime being pulled toward the martyr. "What's your name?"

"Miki Soto." The prostituted came to a stop in which she danced, hips and shoulders and chest wiggling in time with the moves of the martyr.

"Do you like to dance, Miki?"

"When I choose."

Giggling in that soft, condescending way, Lavinia said, "Nobody chooses to do anything, Miki! You didn't choose to be born. You didn't choose the life you've lived. And you don't get to choose how you die, either."

"I'll never die." Miki laughed, inappropriately gay, given the circumstances, but unable to help herself when her extremities forced her to do the hustle. "Ishtar will protect me."

Lavinia's pupils shrank with alarming speed while Dominia asked the dog, "Can't you do something?"

"That's a dirty word." Lavinia's dancing stopped, but her foot-tapping continued as Miki wiggled past, bent to the martyr's will. "You shouldn't say words like that. If you do, your tongue will fall out."

"Ishtar, Ishtar, Ishtar," repeated the prostitute, singing it to the sound of the beat until Lavinia gave a murderous banshee cry of distaste. After a few more inaudible bars, Miki lifted her hand to her own wide-eyed mouth and stuck out her tongue while saying around it, "No, wait!"

Before Miki began yanking out her own tongue, Dominia was upon her, martyr hands clamping down on delicate wrists and then, with profanity, dropping away to hold the human's jaw as it shut to gnaw the organ off.

"I don't ever want to hear you say that word again." Lavinia's face was a mask of porcelain fury. "I don't ever want to hear you *speak* again! Ninny, what dirty friends you keep!"

While Miki and Dominia wrestled with Miki's body and Lavinia ranted over the whining of the dog, the General tried to think of a way to solve the problem. The high priority of keeping mass hysteria under control struck Dominia when the front door slid open. An oblivious porter, reading off his paperwork, stepped into the foyer.

"So sorry to disturb, but I was sent to tell you that we are almost to—"

He had looked up: his eyes landed on the struggling women, then on the one who watched. Dominia could only cry, "No!" as Lavinia, with her sunshiny grin, kept up the tapping of her heels and lifted her hands to clap in time. The porter, weaker than Miki and requiring much less exposure to fall under Lavinia's so-called spell, dropped his papers to clap with her.

"This is going to be so fun! I wish we had music— I'll call Cicero! He should be in the engineer's cab by now, I bet he can do it!"

This month was getting worse all the time. The porter danced back to the train car's hallway and Dominia knew what happened out there. It had happened a few times before, albeit in isolated human villages, and mostly when Lavinia, just awoken, dealt with emotions in a (partially) conscious way for the first time. The effects of her powers had been reported as "outbreaks of mass hysteria, delusion, and paranoia," and cited as examples of the human brain's capacity to be controlled by others. More alarmingly, some (Cicero) interpreted it as evidence of the human's implicit desire for relief from self-control. An almost fair assessment, as the effects of Lavinia's powers always seemed at first glance to be fun.

Laughter was a common effect. A whole village, starting with one person, would burst into hilarious uproar. The first man's neighbor would catch it; and that neighbor's kids and wife would crack up at that; that wife inevitably laughed all the way to the market; and in a matter of no time, every man, woman, and child in town rolled on the floor, asphyxiated by guffaws of sourceless amusement. Dominia and her Family pieced together the cause not that first time, when Lavinia had herself first descended into hysterics as an amazed messenger fell from his bicycle and into the mud on seeing the Holy Family. Rather, it was the second instance that had clarified Lavinia's influence over the human nervous system. As now, she had caused a different village of humans to forego their jobs and lives for the pleasure of a spontaneous, seemingly choreographed dance, which did not stop until everyone in town dropped dead of exhaustion several days later.

Those were the charming instances. The zany, wacky ones that made every girl on Earth think Lavinia's life was a fairy-tale adventure. When Dominia thought about the sheer number of sharp objects in the Dining Car, let alone all the candles for mood lighting, electrical outlets, and countless other means of death...she grimaced as Miki's body tried gnawing off the General's fingers to get to the tongue that was its target.

"Don't bite me! If you swallow my blood, you'll end up one of us."

Incoherent with her mouth full, Miki insisted something to the effect of, "I'm not trying to," then gagged as the suite loudspeakers crackled with a catchy human pop song. Lavinia bounced in place and clapped her hands the way most ill-informed children might on seeing her.

"He heard me, Cicero heard me! Yay!"

Caught up in her own excitement at the possibility of seeing a dance number just for her, Lavinia charged through the front door of the suite and made an immediate right for the Dining Car.

Was it appropriate to thank Cicero for anything, let alone this? She was tempted. Dominia took a breath and, with a free hand, slipped off the belt stolen from René. Through a quick apology and a bevy of protests, the martyr gagged Miki—not to keep her quiet, though that was sort of a bonus. Rather, with the belt angled between her teeth and buckled in the back of her head, she couldn't bite off her tongue. When her hands lifted to undo Dominia's work, the General took the human's wrists, dragged her down the hall, and searched her massive collection of luggage for the handcuffs the prostitute was sure to have. As they clicked in place, Miki demonstrated control of her faculties enough to offer a lascivious eyebrow waggle. Dominia pulled her out of the room, insisting, "Now's not the time," then paused at the great fuss the woman kicked up. "What? What's wrong?"

Her great dark eyes waggled toward her bag, then down the hall, and Dominia took her meaning after a few seconds but shook her head. Her voice raised over the thundering music. "You want us to haul that massive thing with us? There's no time." Fleeting panic that Miki had lied about Cassandra's diamond being off the train filled her, but she saw in the prostitute's urgent and angry look that the concern was not for the sake of her duty but for her attachment to the many dresses, makeup pots, and Lamb-knew-what sex toys she'd (for some reason) brought along with her. "All that stuff had its purpose," consoled the martyr as she hauled the whining, dancing human down the hall, "but that purpose has been served. Look, I need new clothes, too! We can get clothes when we get to Kabul. If," she added, frowning, "we get to Kabul."

The porter had come to alert them to the half hour, it seemed, and she had to assume for the sake of her sanity that Cicero was either not planning to conduct the train at all, or was not conducting it yet. If he was, they were in trouble, because it was likely he wouldn't stop at Kabul and would instead keep going on to wherever it was he was supposed to drop his victims off. And where was the Lamb? Never far from Cicero: his brother, his husband, and his keeper. She daren't think too much on him, either. And if Lavinia was here, then the Hierophant...

One thing at a time. Before the Holy Family killed them, everyone aboard would die in a choreographed frenzy of self-mutilation. There was precious little she could do about the latter; even diverting Lavinia's conscious attention would do no good once the proverbial party ramped up. After a certain point, the memetic infection was a self-perpetuating mechanism. A poisonous thought-virus that would sweep every car and compartment it touched. It would not guarantee death, but if Lavinia felt evil enough, it might. Even martyrs could, under some circumstances, become subject to it. This meant Dominia was going the opposite way, which meant dragging a squealing, kicking, gagged, possessed, and angry Miki Soto to the front car with her; making damn sure the train stopped in Kabul; and keeping everybody, if possible, from dying.

Except Cicero. She was almost fine with that fatality. But if she made it up there without any others—any human ones—that would be appreciated. This was possible if she capitalized on her infamy. A great many things were possible thanks to her reputation. Thanks to the Hierophant. She'd might as well take advantage of what he'd done to her already dark name.

"Look"—she glanced between the human and the dog—"this is going to look bad. I've accepted that. Sometimes you have to dirty your hands. But that doesn't mean I feel good about it. Try to remember: I'm a good person, okay? I actually really like people."

Three minutes later, Dominia stood on a table in the red-carpeted Dragon Car, her revolver having been fired through several rows of machines to keep from puncturing the precious hull of the far larger bullet within which they hurtled. Attention gathered, she brandished Miki like a hostage while the world's least menacing dog barked and the whole room of people screamed themselves to hushed silence. Amid all the faces, the Disgraced Governess of the United Front roared, "Listen to me, you stuck-up pieces of shit. My name is Dominia di Mephitoli. Yes"—she pointed the gun in the direction of the gasp—"by now some of you have heard rumors that I'm on this train. Yet, you're still surprised. Do you know why?"

The car was still. Miki did her best to resemble a helpless pinup model while Dominia pointed the gun at her head. "It's because half of you didn't think I was real, and the other half of you have been praying I'm not. I'm sorry to say that I am real, and in possession of what I imagine to be one of the only guns on the Light Rail—if not *the* only. I am not, however, needlessly cruel. With that in mind, will all passengers class C or lower please leave the casino."

A few people tarried to say the name of the God they worshiped; a handful of others dashed, mostly shabby, tired-looking people but one or two better-dressed, probable class Bs smart enough to get while the getting was good. She let them go, because those who were smart enough deserved to be rewarded, and those who stayed behind had opted the route of donation. "The rest of you"—she took the oversize purse of some wealthy lady wearing a fox-fur hat, who gasped as if she had been slighted at a party rather than robbed of her possession—"hand over your cash, your rings, necklaces, and watches."

A thrill passed through Dominia, who found herself the sort of figure she'd admired in spirited stories of the Front's ancient Old West days. Only the tiniest thrill, understand. As much as she dared. She had always dreamed herself more the lawman-hero type, but beggars couldn't be choosers when living on the fringes of normalcy—if this was still a shade of normalcy at all. One brave (stupid) porter released a childish war cry and charged for her. She let him run his nose into the butt of her gun and land, crying, on the floor.

"Any more questions?" she asked.

The queue which formed was more orderly than any she'd seen. She had to temper thrill with a healthy, quasi-religious sense of naughtiness. Otherwise, there was too much temptation to dive into the abyss of amorality and come out the other side a warlord of esteem more terrible than that of her preexisting reputation. Better to stay Robin Hood than Genghis Khan: but, if the Sheriff of Nottingham pinned her with false accusations, he deserved something to blame her for.

Not five minutes later, the bag was full of riches enough to make Miki's eyes bug when Dominia, having dragged her from the car, showed her the contents. "There. Feel better?"

The girl shrugged, and through teeth that sought to gnaw the belt to get her tongue, made a noise resembling, "Well..." Her hands had stopped clutching a tongue they could not reach and now seemed to be struggling to enact a choreography in which they could not engage; Dominia was relieved to see Lavinia wasn't feeling very homicidal.

Behind them, Basil's tail wagged, accompaniment to his joyful bark. The trio marched onward with Dominia's gun leading the way, aimed (playfully) at Miki while they beat their long and ragged path through the many cars of coach. In a kind break, they were beset by no more heroic porters or passengers, and were left to their own devices by people who quite rightly did not want to risk their lives. It was relief enough that no passengers from the Dining Car had made their way up, but that did make perfect sense, since they were busy dancing along to the beat that pumped through the cars like some sort of stupid music video. Grating, that. It was almost a relief when they reached the first of the Burlap Economy cars and the music paused with a bing-bong electronic chime to set the stage for Cicero's announcement.

"Good morning! This is your emergency engineer speaking. As most of you are by now aware, we have a special guest on our train today: the terrorist Dominia di Mephitoli." Dominia clenched her teeth so hard she thought the remaining ones might shatter; she hauled the human at a faster pace. "You may all remember the Disgraced Governess for such battlefield exploits as the Reclamation of Mexico"—many around her gave a cry of terror or sob of recognition, with some hissing as though she were a theater villain—"that infamous, single-handed sweep through a sleeping barracks known as the Nogales Rampage; and her integral part in what humans refer to as 'the Black Night.' But you know, I believe I once heard Dominia call it"—"No," she shouted at the intercom, but Cicero had already said—"Garbage Day."

The martyr winced. English speakers and those with cochlear implants translating for them screamed in outrage; even Miki gave Dominia a hard look from the corner of her eye. She was almost through the door by the time the first shoe hit the back of her head. Then came another, and then, because she had to shelter Miki with her body, she took quite a few other strange objects. Nothing expensive like a book or a leather bag, but a lot of garbage like phones and tablets, cheap in the East where such devices were plentiful. The hard amalgamations of metal and glass bounced off her head and back to skid across the floor in a clatter almost sufficient to drown Cicero's words. "You know the one. All those poor people in Trimalchio's camps! Just because the old man was killed—which worked out for her in the end, anyway! No amount of gentle governance makes up for that war crime. She'd like you to think she's changed, but she hasn't. Not in almost a hundred years. That's right—this is only what she did in the last hundred years, to your friends and relatives in the Front...I don't need to remind my Japanese passengers of what she did to Tokyo, since your classrooms have reminded you since infancy. If any of you would like to shake the hand of such a famous military figure, I recommend you take the opportunity now, as she makes her way through Burlap Economy–class Cars C through A. And"— his tone, which had already been bright, cheered further—"those passengers interested in having a good time on the way to their destination are encouraged to visit the Dining Car, where I can assure you, you won't be disappointed. If you like dancing, good music, and fast friends, be sure to drop by. We are now five minutes from Kabul. As always: thank you for choosing the LRT."

Between the cars, Dominia tried to catch her breath, but Basil surged forward with purpose. This automatic door slid open to a far more savage booing and throwing of objects. Car B, having had time to coordinate their effort, assaulted her with wads of paper, phones, shoes, and once an old lady's umbrella. Their hate had been given time to boil like a teapot; now it whistled out at her, and she could only hurry along and take it, to her shame. It was all true. If she was honest, she deserved this, and worse. When Trimalchio was assassinated by South American Hunters for what he'd done by encamping those vast swaths of humans, the vengeful General Dominia's knee-jerk suggestion to her Father had been the mass slaughter of every last human in those camps. It wasn't so much that she cared about Trimalchio; she barely knew the man. But she had made the suggestion because it was what she thought her Father wanted to hear. They had not been real people to her at the time, those souls in the camps. There was no point in her life other than violence; therefore, the lives of others deserved to have the mere possibility of point violently wrenched from them. The awful, awful things she had done—the awful person she had been. After Nogales, she was forced to face it. And the day she started to face it, Cassandra showed up.

Did Cassandra change her? Or was her love of Cassandra mere man-ifestation of her own desire to change? Maybe she was still that same awful person she had been all those years before. The same shameful person who had enacted genocide with the flippant disrespect of a child kicking through a sibling's army men. She was ashamed, and that shame turned into fear to imagine what the last batch of humans would do to her.

Of course, as trepidation for the anger of the class A passengers melted into horror when the door opened to a terrible stillness, she considered that, for as bad as she was, she was far from the worst member of the Holy Family. Miki let out a terrible cry but couldn't shut her eyes against the gory sight because, of course, what proper dancer kept their eyes closed? All Dominia could do was shield the human's head against her shoulder while the dog went ahead, sniffing the blood dripping from the hands of slumped passengers and, once or twice, giving it a lick. The windows with their digital images flickered and buzzed, some of them broken and at least one passenger's skull attended by holographic birds that skipped forever between the same three positions. Grimacing, Dominia nudged Basil along with her boot, pushed him through to the baggage car, and walked the gangway suspended across the stacks of bags. Miki trembled, silent tears rolling down her cheeks at the horror of so much death. More death than the poor human had ever seen at once.

The door to the engineer's cabin was unlocked. In United Front trains, these areas were different, and the job of the engineer was more involved. The LRT required less effort in some ways and more effort in others: timing was the most urgent concern of a Light Rail engineer, followed by the watching of a great many scales, monitors, dials, and the Lamb knew what else. Dominia would have taken more time to look around were it not for the engineer slumped in the corner, and the sight of Cicero wearing the dead man's hat. While El Sacerdote looked over the dials in his stead, Dominia tried to lay Miki down and found her body yet moved with too much strength to be stilled, even bound and exhausted. Cicero spoke without looking from the security camera footage on the screen below the map.

"You know, sister, I didn't think they'd have the gumption to take me up on my offer. Now I think it rather a pity Lavinia and I exterminated Car A: they would have thrilled for a chance to detest you to your face! Ah, humans. They get so excited to be part of a mob."

"Why would you kill all those people, Cicero?" Annoyed, Dominia freed one of Miki's hands and slapped the empty cuff around a rail welded to the wall—presumably for when the engineer had to pull the brakes on a giant train traveling excess of six hundred miles per hour. While the human protested and her now-free arm began to engage in a series of choreographed gestures resembling semaphore, Dominia continued, "This is unnecessary. Bringing Lavinia…you could have just found me."

"Yes, well, no one planned to bother you on your train adventure, but unfortunately your…companion"—he offered a sneer in the direction of the prostitute—"was too canny when it came to René Ichigawa's sight. It became apparent that the whole Family needed to get involved. Lavinia will be collapsed with exhaustion by the end of this! Do you know the poor girl was shipped by jet to Almaty just to get on the train to Kabul! She didn't even have a look around. A fine first trip to the Middle States—and for such a pitiful reason. I must say, Dominia, I'm disappointed you would turn on a friend over something so simple as his being blackmailed by Father. That rules out a quarter of the adult martyr population from your pool of potential friends. Anyone in politics, for certain."

She barely listened, too busy rolling up her sleeves and emptying her gun of bullets. "I guess it wouldn't have been a concern if this particular blackmail didn't put me at risk. Sort of funny how that works."

"You always have been sensitive."

Before the butt of her Remington made contact with the back of Cicero's head, his hand caught hers with such speed that it seemed it had always been there, crushing her wrist. By this wrist, Cicero whipped her around to slam her head against the glass with an audible thud, but wasted time trying to aim her unloaded gun at her own head. When he'd made it click, she had managed to twist her knee hard up into his groin while her free hand landed a nasty jab to his throat. Hat askew, Cicero wheeled back with a noise that was as much a laugh as a wheeze; Dominia righted herself, then her fists.

"Trying to keep me from Kabul? From meeting Lazarus?" A few swift jabs were ducked by Cicero, who fought with as jolly an attitude as if the scene had occurred two hundred, three hundred, years before. Back when he still seemed Family. "You thought if you brought Lavinia on board, I'd be faced with a moral dilemma."

"I thought you would try to 'rescue' her," admitted Cicero with a laugh. He took a wide hook in the jaw but managed to fend off the trailing uppercut. While his hand lifted to his cheek, then came away in a fist that jabbed (almost) quick as the Hierophant's, he tutted. "Terrible shame you'll let those people in the Dining Car meet their ends. Such a terrible way, too. Although I may suggest Lavinia draw it out for them, give them time to disembark in Kabul, assuming we stop at all. Have you ever seen an entire *city* overtaken by mass hysteria? I mean, one the size of San Valentino?"

Once, twice, thrice, she tried to punch the smug light out of his eyes. Each time, she missed. Cicero glanced behind her with a smile while he countered her strikes, landing a few sharp jabs in her sternum while he said, "At last, here we are! But what a pity that it seems we'll overshoot it. I do so hope you weren't planning on meeting anyone—"

Was as much as Cicero got out before he was interrupted by the bark of a dog: the boxers paused to look in the direction of the noise. Basil, tail wagging, stood on his hind legs in all his canine glory. To Dominia's astonishment—and Cicero's humiliation—the border collie made defiant eye contact with El Sacerdote while, with a paw too deliberate to be accidental, he applied sufficient pressure to drag the brake lever down into gear.

"Did that dog"—was as much more as Cicero managed before Miki (sweet Miki!) used her one free hand, some understanding of the pattern of her dance, and the butt of Dominia's fumbled gun to crack the Holy Family member twice in the back of the skull. To the General's profound relief, Cicero fell, unconscious, to the floor.

"I could kiss both of you," said Dominia. Amid a great deal of squealing and grinding, the train sought for purchase, found it in the bottom of its translucent tunnel, and slowed as they emerged from their belowground track to the distant silver pool of Kabul's elaborate buildings. Even with the brakes on, the sweet vision grew larger, building itself out of the desert to swallow them in welcome. "But we don't have time."

She didn't have time because Cicero, as usual, was right. All they needed was for one dancer to disembark at Kabul. Then there could be a real problem on her hands, as well as the hands of the human officials running the city. She had to hurry: but the train offered a real advantage in distributing a cure. The intercom system. She was quick to find and activate its fuchsia button, which banished the stupid music by its happy chime. On air, as it were, Dominia cleared her throat. Outside, the buildings whipping by did so at an incrementally slowing pace. Through a great deal of research, the Holy Family had discovered one way to consistently cure the effects of Lavinia's hysteria, and enacting said cure made Dominia self-conscious. However, now was not the time to doubt her capacity for recitation.

"Shall I compare thee to a summer's day?" While Miki arched a skeptical brow that waggled in time with her dance, Dominia tried not to smile and stared out the windshield. "Thou are more lovely and more temperate. Rough winds do shake the darling buds of May, and summer's lease hath all too short a date."

It always seemed like magic. Lavinia's memetic virus could be definitively cured in even the weakest minds given sufficient exposure to quality art. To thinking art. The experience of reading or hearing Shakespeare was always effective, but afflicted humans had been given tours of the Louvre or, in less time-sensitive cases, brought to a Wagner opera to equal success. As Dominia recited sonnet eighteen, Miki's eyes brightened, and her body's movements stopped; as Dominia recited the second piece which popped into her head, Cassandra's favorite, which began, "When I do count the clock that tells the time, and see the brave day sunk in hideous night," the train slowed past an industrial district and cruised home into the shopping center that was its station. Miki's dancing and gnawing had stopped, and instead she laughed with joy. Basil, tail a-wag, put his forepaws upon the nearest window to bark at the people passing. Miki was her gauge for how the Dining Car looked without bothering to flip through the security feed, and by the time sonnet twelve was over, that living gauge was still. As their bodies swayed with the slowing train, Dominia unbuckled the belt around Miki's mouth and winced at the deep indents at the corners of her lips, about to apologize when the human exclaimed, "That is *bitchin'*, dude!"

"I don't mean to sound like a preachy three-hundred-year-old, but if more humans read Shakespeare rather than playing with their phones, Lavinia wouldn't have so much power." After accepting the gun from her friend, Dominia frowned at her brother. What was that about Cicero and fatalities?

"You should kill him now and save us trouble later," said Miki, but Dominia shook her head.

"I can't do it. If I did, I'd be everything they said I am. A terrorist. Then he'd really be a martyr"—she smirked—"and I would have no hope. They'd throw everything they have at me. The Hierophant loves Cicero too much." As did the Lamb, who was surely on the train. A shot into Cicero's head would cause the gun to backfire; or she would discover the remaining bullets were somehow blanks; or another improbable event would be elicited. El Sacerdote would live to fight another day.

"Who loves such a creep?"

"More people than you'd expect."

"Well"—Miki snatched the plundered bag to assess its contents with a petulant sigh—"I can't believe I'm saying this, but you were right to leave that luggage behind. All those years of clothes, though! Oh, my shamisen. My mother gave me that."

"I'm sorry, Miki, but—"

"It's fine." The girl shook her head before straightening her power suit and smoothing the bun of her hair. "Once we pawn all this stuff, there'll be enough money for twenty shamisen, and I know just the guy."

"And how will we get there?"

"The same way anybody gets anywhere," said Miki, laughing while she ducked back through the baggage car. "We'll get a cab."

XI

Welcome to Kabul

After all they'd endured, Dominia had not expected getting a taxi to be simple, but they were soon well away from the train thanks to a driver who didn't look twice at the disheveled, suitcaseless women and their dog. He had seen weirder tourists—probably ones more criminal, too, since he didn't bat an eye as Miki guided him, in brisk Arabic, to her choice pawnshop. Dominia, still buzzing with adrenaline, barely registered the city outside; yet, even to her distracted eye, how it resembled San Valentino as it was when she was young! The San Valentino with which she'd fallen in love, before she'd fallen in love with Cassandra. All the tight-clustered shops: so many shops that even the DIOX-I could not comprehend the many passing signs. There was the market district, disrupting like a cock's crow the sleepy morn with vendors shouting a chant to hypnotize listeners into purchase. (This, perhaps, was the meaning of "enchantment." No wonder she didn't trust Mass anymore!) There were the glittering spires and massive towers and all-over busyness of construction, of doing, of being and seeing. Kabul had stolen the achievement once held by San Valentino, and did so in a manner somehow more glorious. The sunlit mirage of a megacity glittered its defiance against the martyrs in a collective cry of humankind: *We are still here, we will never leave, we will never die.*

Something soft rested on her hand; the dog had lowered his chin.

"You are such a good boy," she said. Though the animal's tail wagged, the praise felt condescending for a creature so intelligent. This wasn't like shaking hands or rolling over. How did you thank a dog for stopping a train? How did a dog know to stop a train, and with such precision? *Was* Basil even a dog?

Now, that was a weird thought. She recalled the game show aboard the ship: its well-trained Shiba Inu, conditioned to press a random button. Basic Pavlov. But Basil seemed a mite more advanced. Her head hurt as she considered it and she stoked memories of cell phones thrown at her skull, the hisses of the angry people, and the horrible thought that, if Miki was right, she was, in a way, having that experience eternally. Not that she didn't deserve it. Dominia glanced at the human, who had lapsed into silence with the driver to count the cash and coins in their bag.

Dominia licked her lips. "What he said about the Black Night—"

"I don't want to talk about it here." Soto didn't look up from her count.

"Does he speak English?"

"I don't think so, but, to be honest, I don't want to talk about it anywhere. 'Garbage Day'?"

The General could only bear to face the city. "It was a different time, I was a different person. When I believed—"

"That humans are trash? That Asian people don't deserve to live in the United Front?"

"That my Father was right," said Dominia helplessly. "That my Father was right, that he was close to God, and that if I did something like this, I could finally get his real approval. Maybe for five seconds of my life I would feel like I was better than my brothers and that I hadn't been martyred to be the black sheep of a dysfunctional Family."

Miki paused her counting with a sigh and a look not lacking in sympathy.

"Look"—the human folded the cash over and tucked it into her blouse—"all kids believe stupid things because of their parents. That's part of growing up: realizing half of what they taught you is flat-out contrary to the person you are. I already told you my old beliefs on sex. That was my mother's doing. She implanted those beliefs in me. The wronger and harsher our parents, the more powerful and pure we'll be when we overcome the beliefs they've ground into our souls. But that doesn't mean people around us now have to accept the people we were then."

That didn't make her feel any better. "What does the Lady teach about forgiveness?"

"Depends. Usually, that it comes from within. Have you forgiven yourself?"

"Not entirely."

"Then you can't expect me to forgive you, right?" At Dominia's frown, Miki patted her hand. "But I'll tell you: I had a great-great-great-uncle or something who was exterminated in the Black Night, and my mother talked about it like she'd been there to watch him die. She said that we could never forgive the martyrs for what they did to our family—so, based on her track record, I'm bound to forgive you, right?"

The General smiled as much as she allowed herself, though it was true. She hadn't forgiven herself for what she had come to view in recent years as crimes against humanity—no more than she forgave herself for her crimes against Cassandra. That, however, was a dangerous line of thought. After all, she couldn't see how she could ever forgive herself for Cassandra—but that was because grief for Cassandra provided a focus for the otherwise free-floating grief over her own existence, having killed so many.

A swinging pendulum of violence and shame, her thoughts. She shielded her face against the atomic dawn growing across the city and longed for shelter. Above the traffic noises sang birds who met the sun with greater cheer. There were ravens in Kabul, just like home. Just like everywhere she traveled in the world. Always ravens, and tidy onyx crows. A few sat upon a lamppost, flew off with that dawn. The skipping record of her mind produced the final lines of a poem she once loved, read a hundred thousand times, memorized with an eagerness surpassing even that for the Bard. The lines—to a little girl, so intriguing and beautiful—were, to Dominia, harrowing reminders of loss represented, for the ancient poem's protagonist, by its eponymous black bird.

And the Raven, never flitting, still is sitting, still is sitting
On the pallid bust of Pallas just above my chamber door;
And his eyes have all the seeming of a demon's that is dreaming,
And the lamp-light o'er him streaming throws his shadow on the
floor;
And my soul from out that shadow that lies floating on the floor
Shall be lifted—nevermore!

The last time she'd heard that poem, during Cicero's annual Walpurgisnacht recitation, Cassandra had burst into tears well before the end, and Dominia had been forced to pursue her. The next night, she was dead. The silken, sad, uncertain rustling of each purple curtain that had once thrilled Dominia was now forever linked with Cassandra's pain, and her own. Well now did she understand that deep crest of loss attached to the word "nevermore." Behind her hand, she closed her eyes, and Cassandra's face, beautiful and pale, emerged: pale as the walls of the hospital room in those early nights of their romance. Cassandra had been in-patient since month five because her body fed itself to her baby too quickly to maintain her health without constant nutrients and supervision. She had to be given drips for fluids and for pain, but nothing stopped her nausea. In response to this, she was given blood transfusions from healthy martyrs—largely, her wife—and put on a steady diet of bland soups.

Her room, meanwhile, overflowed with Dominia's flowers as though it were a garden: a place of life and life's beginnings, rather than a place where most healed from illness or died trying. The hospital was in the mystical city of Venezia, the star of Mephitoli that had once been drowned by man-made climate change and that, resuscitated by the Hierophant's bottomless bank account, was a territory under control of the woman not yet promoted to Governess. Until giving up her Mephitolian territory on her promotion, she had an exquisite palazzo there: a paradisiacal Roman villa. She had not once visited it since coming into town. Instead, she would sit and talk to Cassandra, hold her hand, and droop to sleep in her chair while her lover watched some benign sitcom whose formulaic nature was designed to inspire maximum comfort (and, consequently, limitless boredom). Themes focused on family; Dominia always winced at that, because if she were in Cassandra's position, that subject would be the least desirable locus of thought. But Cassandra wanted to dream, and often Dominia awoke to find her wife still glued to the old television, shadowed eyes bright with better humor than the General could have felt. With one hand, she would hold Dominia's right, while her other clutched one of the many stuffed animals that littered the room, supposedly for the baby.

Then, one morning, something small but beautiful happened. Dozing Dominia, who had gotten a chance to slip off for a moment, awoke to Cassandra pulling on her arm with those eyes big and beautiful and wide and wet while her mouth cried the words, "She's alive, she's kicking, she really *is* alive!"

The General's hand leapt upon the ballooned stomach Cassandra couldn't have hidden had her pregnancy gone well enough for her to remain home. Yes, there she was. The kick of tiny feet, like someone thudding the opposite side of a great drum. Dominia was more awake then than she'd been for any battle. She stood with wild-eyed laughter: first, to listen to the sound with an ear to that soft stomach; then, to kiss her weeping wife. Her sobs indistinguishable from hiccupping laughs, Cassandra shut her eyes, leaned her head against Dominia's breast, and listened to the sound of her heart.

Then, as now, the General's eyes welled in silent tears. Then, she had been able to weep into Cassandra's hair. Now, she had nobody. She had a dog, who gazed at her with melancholy eyes. As if he knew her every thought. Basil wagged his tail at that silent supposition, or seemed to.

Let that be coincidence!

The absurdity of a telepathic—certainly sapient—dog distracted her enough that she lifted herself from out that shadow. Fine timing, too, for the cab driver pulled in front of a pawnshop. The district in which it was located seemed…less than kosher, given its general uncleanliness, multiplied by the density of wig shops and adult arcades to actual businesses. Her guess was this was spurred by the presence of the corner theater. Everybody who attended the Elsinore Theater

Festival knew theaters attracted a strange group: in testament to this, the distant lampposts marking entry to the borough were enlivened by red flags, each dotted by a black lotus.

"Isn't that the Red Market symbol?" asked Dominia.

Miki, with reluctance, removed the cash wad from her bosom and slipped a few bills free for the cabbie. He doffed his hat while his passengers piled out and the prostitute said, "I guess it would seem pretty remarkable to you, that we have locations friendly to us. You— your Family is so stuck-up." They both had to dance around the word "martyrs" in public. Some English words were universal.

With a grimace for the slow-rising sting beneath the growing light of dawn, Dominia took shelter within the entrance of the shop. Miki made sure the cab door had shut itself and hurried to the store's security gate while the cabbie squealed off for his next mark. Though the prostitute's hand dipped into her purse, she stopped with a furious gasp of displeasure.

"That's right! Since you insisted on leaving my stuff there, I'm missing my key. God dammit." On instinct, Miki lifted her hand to lay a slap on the back of Dominia's head, but the General had been getting enough of that action and caught the human's wrist. Though startled, Miki whipped up a lascivious grin. "Learn to pick a better moment. People are going to start filling this street!"

"I'm not messing around." Dominia released the human, who slipped with a laugh down the alley on the building's west side.

"Neither am I. Come on!"

As the geisha mounted the shadowed fire escape with annoyance, Dominia and the dog followed along. The martyr asked, "Are you allowed to operate here?"

"Here? Technically, no, but the Market…exists, at least, as an entity. There are some Middle States even worse than your Father when it comes to prostitution; I've never even visited New Persia, which is too bad, since it looks like a beautiful country and I'd love to see Mecca. But we're fortunate that Kabul has gotten even to this point—like, Red Market girls can go to doctors and stuff and legally can't be turned away because of their profession."

"What a privilege," said the General, her tone dry as the air. Miki snorted.

"Right? Even toleration here isn't like where we'll be going."

"Which is?"

"Cairo—the real Babylon. At least, where the Lady's center of operations moved after Babylon's fall."

More words that would have made Lavinia wince but gave Dominia a twinge of naughty pleasure to remember murmuring to Cassandra that she was a hot little Babylonian harlot, which was some pretty filthy talk by martyr standards. To hide her flush, or at least reroute it, she gave a huff as though from exertion. "So it's still a real place? I thought it was just a legend that the Lady had a city."

"Of course it's a legend"—Miki glanced west as they emerged atop the roof—"as much as Jerusalem. But that's the difference between legends and myths. Legends have historical basis. The Lady has to live somewhere, man. She's real. And She keeps Her city a lot nicer than the Abrahamians' deadbeat dad."

Dominia always had a weird time with references to God, because the Triune was still so tied to her Father's mythos that she barely separated the original intentions of the deity from his corrupted variant. She compromised in her conversation with something nonconfrontational: "That's nice. I don't care how great whose city is, unless we'll find Lazarus there. Cairo, Jerusalem. Doesn't matter."

"You wouldn't find him anywhere near that garbage dump. It's controlled by the Hunters—they're its skeleton, at any rate, and the skeleton can't help but pollute the whole body when it's full of poison." Miki frowned at the shabby padlock sealing the rooftop door. After a glance at the martyr, the human stepped away and let the General's foot shatter the rusted knob. Miki sighed and shook her head.

"Why Kahlil spends as much as he does on girlfriends like me without paying a lick for security…"

They descended down the grimy stairs, the flat, unwashed oil smell that came with stores dealing in used goods so plaguing Dominia's sensitive martyr nose that she bumped into Miki when the human stopped at the first landing to rap upon the door. The reason for the lack of security was that Kahlil thought he had enough in the form of the assault rifle that he thrust in their faces on answering; but the tremble to the gun's barrel and the softness to the face behind his glasses, which somehow escaped the masculinity beards afforded other men, indicated the General had nothing to fear. Indeed, on recognizing Miki's scornful face, Kahlil lowered his gun with an exhalation of surprise, relief, and mild humiliation.

"Miki, what the fuck!" It came out in English; the boy glanced toward the martyr with one hand atop his taqiyah as if surprise's aftermath might blow it off. "I thought you said you'd call me. And come in through the front."

"It's a long story. And, I'm going to need money. Real, digital currency: none of this useless paper shit. What a pain it is to convert it to Redcoins! You do it for me. It'll make me look like I'm the saleswoman of the month when you transfer it all into my account."

As she spoke, she dumped the contents of the bag on the undusted coffee table askew in the center of the room. In an instant, Kahlil looked torn between blocking the martyr's way and attending to the wealth of objects awaiting his attention. After a careful glance past the man's head for the dusty bookshelves within, Dominia studied the nervous fellow and tried to make him comfortable. "Kahlil? Like Kahlil Gibran, right? Are you Lebanese?"

"No." His frown deepened as he was forced to make an intellectual connection with the martyr. "My mom liked his poetry. Come in, I guess, but if I see you move funny—"

"Why are you so hostile?" Miki collapsed into the couch and kicked off her business flats in a way that made both Dominia and their host give a tsk. "You knew I was bringing her! I told you. You probably saved the chat, even though it's supposed to self-destruct."

"I save everything you send me." The chestnut of his face further colored as he stooped to collect her shoes; Dominia's brow knit to see telltale signs of some poor schmo in love with a working girl, then smoothed it over when he righted himself. "I'm not sure I'm comfortable hosting her after what they've reported!"

"You're the last person who should be listening to rumors." Miki rubbed her palm over her left eye and snuggled in against the couch cushions, yawning as she spoke, worn out by her dance recital. "What are they saying she did? Because what she did was save a whole train of people, and possibly all of Kabul. That's pretty great, no matter what she did before." It was gratifying, that glance from Miki.

Outside the room, Basil politely wagged his tail. Kahlil, annoyed, said, "Well! Come on, bring him in. Look at the place, it's haram as it is. A prostitute and a martyr, what am I doing to myself…"

As he spoke, Dominia shut the door behind Basil, and Kahlil lowered his voice with a shifty look around. "I've got a couple of tenants downstairs, so keep quiet. They heard on the news that she massacred an entire car of people and were already up here talking about it— I haven't even had breakfast."

Miki, bless her, did the talking. "Car A? Cicero did that. I saw— well, I didn't see him do it, but Dominia couldn't have done it. Mostly because she was with me the whole time, and I was occupied."

"They said Cicero was sent by Iblis," said Kahlil, who spat in the corner at his use of the Hierophant's epithet. (Small wonder about his bachelorhood, if that was his custom.) "That he was to retrieve ad-Dajjal"—this was a new term to her, but it made Miki roll her eyes as he went on—"and was defeated by her sheer strength."

While deigning to stand, Miki crossed her arms and exclaimed, "Really, 'ad-Dajjal'? I thought that was what they called the Lamb."

Now Dominia spoke up, curiosity piqued. "What does it mean?"

"It's the anti-Christ in some branches of Abrahamian faith." Miki rubbed the bridge of her nose while triumphant Kahlil declared, "Everybody is saying it's her. The prophet Muhammad, peace be upon him, said ad-Dajjal would be blind in his right eye."

But that amplified Miki to full blast, the girl being versed enough in this particular branch of Abrahamianism to correct on her fingers, "'His' right eye, *and* it's a metaphor, *and* didn't your Prophet (*peacebeuponhim*) *also* say something about eyes that bulged like grapes? And all kinds of stuff about miracles, and whatever ridiculous nonsense? I haven't seen her do a miracle. As far as I've been able to tell, her greatest power is poetry recitation—and running Family therapy sessions, based on her conversation with Lavinia."

"Hey," tried Dominia, but Miki waved a dismissive hand. "You know you sounded like a social worker. Anyway, her special—skill, or whatever, is her ability in combat. She's not one of these crazy people like the rest of the un-Holy Family and other powerful martyrs who can do messed-up stuff to your head. I don't know why everybody acts like martyrs are so much better because they have talents. Humans have individual talents, too. Like you have a talent for being a real pain in my ass."

Dominia fell silent while Kahlil rebutted, "Me, in *your* ass!"

A sly smirk crossed Miki's face and Kahlil looked horrified, as if he had made a terrible mistake. Instead of making a joke that she was visibly pained to resist, Miki tapped her foot. "Yeah, a pain in my ass: since I brought you a whole bunch of new stock for your pawnshop, and you're also getting plenty of favors in exchange for the imposition."

Did she need to cover the dog's ears? Was this inappropriate for Basil? His fuzzy mouth opened in a canine grin that turned into a yawn, and she was unconvinced that the yawn was not put in place to cover his reaction to her thoughts. Lamb! She'd become so paranoid! Dogs, reading her thoughts, hell. Sapient dogs, hell. She was starving from the trip, or tired from the fight, or both.

Dominia wandered to the cramped and unclean kitchen while the humans quarreled. In the dirty refrigerator, she discovered the pleasant surprise of several pints of blood. Miki had thought of everything—or maybe Kahlil had. Either way, the dog left the living room to prance down the hall once she turned around. She followed, blood bag in her hand like a juice box, and found Basil circling a spot on the floor of a guest bedroom crammed with two sorry twin beds and a lot of crap. A vanity with a broken, inexcusably dusty mirror once very nice; a nightstand with a crooked drawer she wasn't interested in trying to fix. As she fell into one of the mattresses, the dog sneezed at the dust kicked up from the bedclothes, and Dominia noted that the singular window was sealed against police raids.

She had a feeling it had been like this before they were on their way. The Hunters, who were also known in this area as the Caliphate, al-Siyadun, and al-Saalihin, (or, to their opponents, al-Mawta), posed huge political and legal danger to the states they inhabited. It wasn't enough for them to act as vigilantes who killed any stray martyr wandering into the area. The official position of the Hunters was that the only acceptable course of action, from a moral standpoint, was for human governments to wage total war upon all martyrs until one side or the other was destroyed to the man. Any government not fighting active war against the species was opposed to the human race and worthy of overthrow. Their presence in South Africa rendered that entire continent highly unstable, and although areas farther north were at greater risk of playing host to the odd tourist martyr (or even, in the Hierophant's friskier years, an invading army from Europa), living there was still a safer bet than anyplace south or east. The Hunters were scattered across Africa and the Middle States, and though they elicited much turmoil in the region, they also struggled to maintain reasonable foothold. Consensus was that it was better for a human to risk being eaten by somebody on vacation to see the Fertile Crescent than to allow the Hunters power. Martyr tourists were far more reasonable and predictable than the Caliphate.

All this made Dominia wonder again what she was doing there: terrorist organizations aside, every human city held for her limitless danger. It was true that the presence of the Hunters in the Middle States put the region at risk, but since signing the Constitution in 1260, the union had held strong against both martyrs and extremists. The States, though independent and often in disagreement, were able to maintain order enough to serve as stronghold for generations of Abrahamians driven from Europa. This harmony was a defense to support spiritual humans as much as a move against the Hierophant, who had bloodlessly claimed the former human state of Italy, and changed its name, a mere ten years before. Often, he had tried the boundaries of the Middle States, and even after they had banded together, he still sometimes sidled up against them. He forever awaited the time he might penetrate their boundaries. One thing that kept him out was the sun, but if he had means to blacken it, no pocket of civilization would be free of martyr control. Then, the humans would have no choice but to turn to the Hunters for help.

That assumed, of course, there could still be a world after the sun went black. Did the blackening of the sun not mean the death of Earth? She had once, long ago, read the story of an unwilling man, a torturer, who journeyed to renew the sun of his world, and became a man of God: but there could be no renewal here. Not of this world. Further, if Miki was right, and the blackening of the sun meant the death of Lazarus, and the creation of a new iteration of the universe, did it matter if it, everyone, everything, died? Hadn't they all done it before? Hadn't Cassandra died before? Hadn't her baby, also, died before? Died twice over each iteration: once with her mother's martyring, and once on her own, not long after those delayed first kicks. Not long after Dominia, in equal maternal joy at tangible evidence of life, rushed to furnish a former guest apartment in the palazzo with a gilded crib, and a real ivory changing table, and sweet little cashmere socks, and far more stuffed animals than even comforted the sick mother through each day's restless sleep. The kicking continued, night by night, and Cassandra's nausea worsened: but then, at the apex of that sickness, the kicking stopped. Cicero was on a plane from Europa that same night. The next, he sat at Cassandra's bedside in the midst of another ultrasound, lips narrowed in a frown behind his mustache while the expectant mothers asked in stereo, "What, what is it, what's wrong?"

"Cassandra"—the words rolled from his lips after an agonizing moment of thought—"I am sorry, but this is one of a great many reasons why this sort of thing is ill-advised."

Pale Cassandra began to sit up, only to be pinned by Dominia. The General demanded, "What are you talking about?"

"The baby's heart has stopped."

The silence carried its own sound: a ringing experienced by both openmouthed women. Cassandra, of course, felt the weight of the words more intensely than Dominia ever could. Cicero went on explaining, "It is too early to tell, of course, but I would suspect it to be a result of the protein's interaction with her particular anomaly."

"What do you mean, 'it's too early to tell'?" Numbed by the notion that her wife's pain had been for nothing, Dominia realized the question had come from her own lips once Cicero looked at her.

"I mean—unpleasant as this may be—your wife shall have to carry the fetus to term."

"Oh, no, please," Cassandra now forced herself upright, tears filling her eyes. "Please, can't something be done? Oh, God, if she's dead, I can't—I can't, I can't, I can't." She was unable to vocalize the words "carry her to term," her lips and cheeks wet with the tears of a rising panic attack. Dominia pushed onto the bed and folded heaving Cassandra into her arms.

"Can't you induce and let her deliver it early? Won't it calcify?"

"We are on the barest cusp of eight months now, Dominia." As her brother slid away and packed his equipment, wailing Cassandra was forced to bury her face in Dominia's breast if anyone was to hear. Cicero continued as if deaf. "Blood clots would be the biggest risk facing your wife, but the protein would never allow that to occur in a martyr. These situations clear up after two weeks, but if she requires the full four to come to term, we should not be alarmed."

In the end, of course, it took five weeks. Five miserable, painful weeks of Cassandra knowing each evening, each morning, that her baby was dead inside of her. That she would have to give birth like it lived. When the day arrived, there was a strange, almost complete disinterest on the part of the staff in seeing to her, as if she had disappointed the nurses by her failure to keep the baby alive. It was far from her responsibility, of course. Neither would Cicero arrive in time for the labor; a replacement doctor had to oversee, and in the midst of all the disinterest and confusion, despite repeated pleas from both Cassandra and Dominia, by the time said replacement arrived, he announced it was too late to give an epidural. Cassandra had to deliver the corpse naturally.

All the screaming, and the blood, and the joyless, alien silence of the staff. The silence of the baby. The silence of Cassandra when her screaming stopped and she slipped into unconsciousness, a blissful break for which Dominia was glad when she saw the infant. She had always been skeptical, when people—usually humans—referred to sleeping children as "perfect" or "angelic." Yet, in that second, she understood. A perfect porcelain cherub: wrapped in a pink blanket, then shipped away. Oh, Cassandra's face when she learned she wouldn't be able to see her baby, that she was already being prepped for burial. How she cried, and cried, and carried on with her crying while her breasts wept, also, with gifts for an unreceiving baby.

"I keep feeling like she's alive," repeated Cassandra, sobbing into her hand, into Dominia's neck, into the pillows of her recovery bed. "I keep forgetting. Oh, God, I wish I could hold her."

Once, Dominia thought she could never comprehend her wife's heartbreak; now, she only hoped hers would not take ninety years to fade.

XII

Filling in the Gaps

Wherever Dominia went, she seemed to end up in the hands of medical professionals. Funny, in an unfunny way. Twenty-four hours after arriving in Kabul, she lay in the chair of a dentist with a booming laugh, a Nigerian accent, and a face that filled her vision like a great blob rendered square by the lines of that same DIOX-I that tagged him "Doctor Tobias Akachi." The dark flesh of his face left his perfect smile all the whiter, and Dominia found herself thinking of the man as a talking set of disembodied teeth. "You know, I've never worked on a martyr before! What a crazy world we live in. But people's mouths are all the same, no matter who they are."

When was the last time she'd been to the dentist for more than a cleaning? When she got her artificial teeth, she supposed. She barely remembered the occasion, since, at the time, she'd been put under anesthetic and had woken up with a pair of fangs. Her Father had done her a favor by yanking them out; she increasingly felt toward them what a fortysomething businessperson felt toward a regrettable lower back tattoo. Since they were gone, the step of removing them was saved. She'd ought to write a thank-you note.

"I'm surprised you were willing to see me at all," she admitted when the man swiveled to examine the x-rays of her mouth, fine aside from absent cuspids.

"You mean after the train? Miki told me you saved those people!"

"And the destroyed hospital in Japan, and the ship, and…"

"I know bullshit when I hear it." The man chortled in a booming bass while he rolled from her vision to root through a tray of tools. "Even if you were a terrorist, I mean…the whole hospital? Come on."

"That's what I've been saying." She felt motivated to talk by the vague sense of dread instilled upon finding herself at the mercy of anyone, no matter how friendly; Cicero's fault, to be sure. "It's so over the top. Don't people think it's absurd?"

"Always easier to assume the other person is wrong and that our own opinions are right—that there is no conspiracy and that mankind is fighting a battle against itself, instead of playing a game for God."

Beyond the window, Kabul glowed in a neon rainbow by even those earliest hours of the evening. "I thought 'God' was 'Allah' in these parts."

He rolled back, now holding a device resembling a mechanical pencil, mouth hidden behind a blue mask. "Only when my patients discuss Him. I am an English-speaking Christian, myself."

These Abrahamians! Jewish, Christian, Muslim. You couldn't tell them apart for trying—at least, martyrs couldn't—yet they were touchy about getting mixed up. Their petty distinctions made little sense to her, and this must have been communicated by the near roll of her eyes as the dentist opened her jaw and began using the small water drill. Though less cruel than its prehistoric metal counterparts, it still made her wince deeper into the uncomfortable chair. As he cleaned, the dentist continued above the whine of water, maybe imagining her responses.

"You probably don't know much of our faiths, soldier as you are, but we Abrahamians are quite different from one another. Even Christians are different from one another! You know that, don't you?" She tried to nod, but he carried on, using another implement to vacuum spittle from her gums while he lectured. "As it happens, none of us used to get along. Even before your Father showed up, and for many generations after, there was much struggle about 'the right faith.' That was what helped him rise to power. But, as he took control of North America, we realized we all fought the same enemy; and when we were abandoned in the Rapture by the wealthy and the elite, a new era of cooperation began on Earth."

Ah, yes. Dominia had been so young those nights: not quite hopeful for the future anymore, but not as bleak a woman as she would become. Martyrs had been open about their presence for almost seventeen thousand years at the time of Dominia's human birth as Morgan, but the species had begun to close their iron grip decades before that fateful day in which the wealthy fled. This had mostly to do with the failed attempt to conquer Japan, regarded as a victorious maintenance of the boundaries of the UF in much the same way that the harrowing destruction of Moscow and the inhabitability of much of Russia was forever regarded as an opportunity to experiment with terraformation technology—and further evidence that martyrs were a cruelly maligned, unfairly detested people.

He had given society so much, the Hierophant: by the time Russia's terrain was at all recovered, he donated the many technologies estab-lished in its healing alongside tech developed for asteroid miners to support the first living colonies of Mars. These were quick to die, of course, but every generation after died slower; and while humans on Earth were busy fighting among themselves and keeping their heads down to avoid Hierophant attention, Martian humans slaved to make their planet habitable. By the time 1700 rolled around, it was in impres-sive shape; come 1744, the wealthy multitudes, whose human life spans shielded them from the knowledge that the Hierophant had begun the terraforming effort in the first place, were ready to flee to the stars. Her Father had gladly let them go: more land for him. The impoverished of Earth, however, hardly realized they had been abandoned until too late. They seldom realized anything until too late. As Dr. Akachi pointed out, this was because they had been under the thumb of the Devil.

"You Father would like nothing more than for us to continue the old ways—persecuting one another while crying over our own persecution. So, we have done the opposite, and brought ourselves together!"

When Dominia gagged at her ill-advised attempt to speak, the den-tist removed his hands enough to let her sputter, "Except the Hunters," before he dove back to work.

"Well, I can tell *you*, miss, that their mouths look like yours. Maybe they would like their mouths to look different! But no. The same. Only"—he dropped his voice to a conspiratorial whisper—"they are bad about brushing. And try getting one to floss. Gum disease! It's rampant with that sort. Which reminds me—are you being sure to brush your gums? You'd ought to take your time. I notice you haven't been in the habit lately."

"I've been busy," she said, her tone sufficient to tan a hide. The man laughed.

"So I understand. This process takes a few weeks, but Miki told me we do not have that luxury. I can see why she insists it needs doing. Rather indiscreet, eh? If one of the Caliphate saw your missing teeth, you would be good as dead. We'll have to install both your titanium implants and the crowns that lock into them, all four in the same appointment. I don't care for that, even if it can be done on a martyr, but we have no choice. I'll still need a day to prepare the crowns; those, I can print at my apartment. Are you comfortable waiting that long?"

"Do I have a choice?"

With a hearty chuckle, he lowered his mask and offered a cup of pink mouthwash. "Of course! You have many choices. You could go running in the street and get hit by a car. Fine a choice as any. You could go home. Or, you could choose to carry on. And since it seems to me like you're making that last choice, I have to say, I am pretty impressed."

"Thanks," said Dominia, who fell silent as the dentist carried on.

"We'll put you under light anesthetic, and when you come out of it, you'll be good as new!"

At this statement, her brain replayed the cartoon nurse's assurance that her eye installation would be, "Just like going to the dentist." As Tobias turned away, she snatched his arm. His understandable wince passing by, the man met Dominia's blazing eyes with curiosity.

"Can you remove DIOX-Is? Or—uninstall them, I guess."

The dentist regarded her face, his own a cautious mask in the wake of his fright. "I could, but I hardly see why you would want such a thing. After going to all the trouble of having it installed...isn't that why you were in the hospital?"

"Yes, but"—she considered how unwise it was to confess to the man, whose face was labeled by an azure box, that the Hierophant may have watched her every movement because he owned her eye—"it's a terrible distraction. The features are outweighed by—everything. The ads, for example."

"You would rather be blind in one eye than see a few targeted commercials!" The earnestness in her expression faltered the humor in his. With gravity, he pressed, "Have you given this much thought?"

"Well, no...this idea came to me right now. But I hate having this thing in my head. And I hate how I got it. I hate how I look in the mirror, and it looks like my old eye, but I know that it's not my old eye. It's not even *my* eye. I didn't buy it. The refugee operation provided it pro bono. Best case, it's the company's. Worst, Cicero's, or the Hierophant's. I don't know; I'm not sure how they manage to get into my device's software if it's not somehow leased to them. It was awful when he installed it, and"—she took a sharp breath and loosened her grip on the dentist—"I want it taken out."

Brows knit in sympathy, Tobias removed his gloves to pat her hand. "Please give it more consideration," he said while rising from his seat. "I do not know how comfortable I am with this idea, but we can decide when you return for your implants. It is possible. I have done it before, for patients with ill-functioning, jailbroken DIOX-Is or small cyborgans who could not afford to go to a real clinic. But when there are so many who would kill for such sight, Miss Mephitoli, would you throw it away?"

It was a question she'd asked herself for a few nights, since before the train, or before Kabul. The DIOX-I was invaluable for purposes of battle, but the merest possibility that her Father might use it to record her comings and goings made her ill. What she had said about the ads was true, too. As she emerged into Kabul's yet-warm evening with Miki, who had been slouched over a dented magazine e-reader in the waiting room chair, the right side of Dominia's vision populated buildings with digital billboards not present in her sinister eye. Wholesale liquor, cheap (virus-loaded) pornography, cigarettes, fitness tips, new books, plus more weird spam about weight loss and digitally altered pictures than she absorbed. And try to tell the digital ones from those *actually* there! It made her crazy. She focused on the dentist, and asked Miki, "Where did you find that guy?"

"Oh, he's an old client. Actually, I met him through Kahlil when we were having a sandwich one day with this super-hard bread, and—long story, anyway I needed a fake tooth, and 'Bias hooked it up. No money down."

"Is there anyone in Kabul—in the world—you haven't fucked?"

In response to that, Miki gave her ass a shake, brandishing like a weapon the short-shorts purchased while Dominia had slept that day. "Only you, *senpai*."

"I thought a *senpai* was supposed to be a kind of mentor." The martyr lifted her blushing face to the light-polluted sky.

"Well, aren't you? You're my upperclassman in the school of life, *oba-san*."

Dominia cleared her throat as Miki wandered in the direction of a food stand. "You're going to blow our cover if you keep calling me things like that."

"And you're going to blow our cover if you don't try to look like you're having fun. Come on! So serious." After jabbering in Arabic with the huge man running the food stand, both laughed, and he assembled a falafel for Dominia while Miki said, "Eat that, you'll lighten up."

To her credit, the falafel was damn fine: even though it lacked the basic nutritional components which Dominia's body required, it didn't lack the taste requirements. She found herself overjoyed to eat after her procedure, since taste was the final sensory frontier when it came to DIOX corporation's replacements. Taste was still pure. Taste, unlike sight and sound and even touch, was not yet marketable by their standards. But once the first super-tongue or digital nose was on the market, rest assured, everyone would be a gourmand in the way everybody was trilingual thanks to audio implants.

She was crotchety, Dominia. Another reason she so missed Cassandra. Her wife had been there to soften her, to make the General seem kinder than she was. But there was also something to be said for the leveling influence of her new friend. Miki wasn't interested in soothing Dominia's ego or making her feel like a good person. Miki was interested in…being Miki, the martyr supposed. Even now the girl bopped down the street while savaging the sandwich whose cardboard tray she had already trashed.

"Hey," said Miki through her full mouth, as if confirming Dominia's thoughts while, with a free, un-sauced hand, she gestured to something down the block. "It's the Hie-Race! I didn't even think about it."

Squinting and then troubled (and disoriented into closing her good eye) to find the DIOX-I zoomed in for her, Dominia watched a crew of yellow-geared workers setting up barriers and signs that translated to state that the street would be closed the next morning. "The what?"

"It's a thing they do here. Like a special marathon where people dress up in costumes and stuff to make fun of—uh." Miki coughed as she almost choked on her bite. "Your folks."

At seeing that Dominia's expression was not offended so much as flabbergasted, Miki felt free to continue. "It's super fun! We have to lighten the mood somehow, right? And this city can be so uptight— it's like, half serious tech businessmen and a quarter religious families. It's up to the last quarter, people like us, to cheer them up, so we do it with fun things like this!"

"'People like us,'" repeated Dominia. Miki giggled.

"Yeah, 'us'! Weirdos! Anyway"—the human turned away as Dominia caught a chilling glimpse of chrome upon a rooftop overseeing the preparations—"we should head back. I'm—"

"You go." The General pushed her trash into Miki's hand, oblivious to the girl's noise of protest. "I'll meet you there."

"Hey"—the human waved after her—"where are you going?"

There was no delaying. She knew the Lamb when she saw him; it didn't matter how far away. Those horns were distinct. Always the first things she saw of him. Often, the only things that stuck in her memory after a conversation with him. Warm words and loving reassurances all got lost in his horns. Or in the arrival of Cicero. But until then, those times when, sent to her room for inability to adapt to her new reality, she had wished her windows unbarred to accommodate suicide— Ah, how often he appeared in her doorway! He'd sit at the edge of her bed, his knee a pillow to her tear-stained face, as she struggled to make verbal sense of the new and violent shift in moral expectation. She would try to explain how it made her feel every time she was forced to eat human flesh, struggling to articulate how awful it was that she wasn't allowed to treat humans like people; more often, she burst into a new crest of tears and explained that what hurt her most was the loss of her parents, and the thought that they were in the world without her.

"I'm sure they think the same about you," the Lamb told her, gentle, patient. Or: "Just because you can't be friends with the humans working around the castle doesn't mean you have to be cruel to them the way Cicero is." And: "Nobody reasonable likes eating human, sweetheart."

"Daddy does," she would sometimes accuse. "And Cicero, and the people who follow them around at parties."

"True; but they're exceptions. I don't like eating human. Thankfully, I don't have to."

"Then why do I have to do it?"

"Because that's the way your Father and Cicero decided the world would be when they released the protein to the public. It's important for you to be able to eat if you can't receive my blood some week, for some reason; and you'll be miserable if all you're having is my blood at services. Trust me."

"But we could make fake people, in labs, the way they make beef and poultry? I read in school—real school—"

"Martyr school is real school."

She hadn't been in the mood to argue that point. "People used to eat cows and chickens, too. Then they were rescued because people developed fake meat that was like the real thing. Why can't we do that with people?"

"They tried that with people," explained Elijah, "which is something you'll learn in fake school during next year's history class, but I digress…it didn't work, is my point. Eating lab-grown people was good as starving."

"But why? Why does it have to be this way? Why does everything have to be so violent and ugly?"

"Because that's the way the world is. This physical world."

"It doesn't have to be," she insisted at the time, eliciting a wan smile from the Lamb.

"Please, don't ever think otherwise."

"But why didn't you stop them from releasing the protein? You were there."

"And so was your Father. But even if he hadn't been there..."

"You'd still let Cicero push you around." The flippant accusation gave way to immediate guilt, but she refused to take it back, and he didn't make her. The hand petting through her hair never even stilled.

"I didn't stop them because, once they infected me with the protein, I saw all things. All possible things. Not in a way I could control as much as I can now, which isn't much. I saw that if we didn't release the protein, someone would, and I wouldn't be able to do anything about it that time. But, most of all, I saw you."

"You did?"

"Yes. And I couldn't find it in me to stop him when he would someday give me a daughter like you, right?"

What a stupid reason. She knew at the time he had only been trying to comfort her. In the unit that was her Family, the Lamb may well have been the good cop: but he was still a cop. And wherever the Lamb was, Cicero was never far behind, possessive as any psychopathic husband. Between that quality, and the Lamb's duty to be carted from church to church throughout martyr territories and symbolically sacrificed every Noctisdomin—rather close to a literal sacrifice, which, given a martyr's healing abilities, always recovered itself by Noctismartin—the brothers rarely separated in body or in mind. If the Lamb was given the courtesy of time with his daughter, or the privilege to comfort her without interruption, it was because Cicero willed it.

Cicero, or the Hierophant. This last notion arose as, atop the fire escape of the building whereupon she'd seen the glitter of his horn, her stomach lurched to see not just the Lamb but, pleased and dapper as ever, her Father. Beetle eyes glittering, he assessed her head to toe and crowed, "My girl! At last! Here you are. How happy I am. I do so love your new hair. Did you do it yourself?"

"Here I thought you'd hate it. And"—she recalled the broadcast watched aboard the train a few nights before—"that you were back in Kronborg."

"Oh, for a jot—but I had to catch up to the Family at some point. I can't leave your welfare in their hands, or vice versa. A man has to be responsible for his child; any parent is responsible for their child. Cassandra knew that very well."

Lamb, keep her temper in check. "Starting early, are we? I thought you'd try soft-balling before you riled me up."

"I'm sure you know well as I do that the time for soft-balling passed—if there ever was such a time for you, my hard-hearted daughter. What trouble you make of yourself! As if you did not spend nearly a hundred happy years as Governess of the Front."

"I wouldn't say 'happy.'"

"Neither would Cassandra."

"You don't know anything about our lives."

"I know enough. Its rocky start and questionable end, and quite a few moments in between. Or are you forgetting that I was as devoted to Cassandra, my spiritual daughter, as you were to Cassandra, your wife?"

How sick she was of his childish jabs in her open wound. Her eyes narrowed at the silent Lamb, whose expression remained placid as ever. "And here you are as usual, letting him say whatever comes into his head while you look sorry for yourself."

"Sorry for you," corrected unflappable Elijah.

"We are not here to abuse your emotions." The Hierophant crossed to lay a hand upon the Lamb's shoulder. "We are here to plead that you come home."

"I won't. You would do anything for Cicero, wouldn't you?" This, to Elijah, who did not respond as Dominia placed an instinctive hand upon a diamond not there. "I would do anything for Cassandra. I would die to see her live again, to make up for the mistakes I made. Letting these awful things happen to her. Letting her die."

"You didn't let her die," the Lamb assured her, but her eyes welled up in furious tears.

"I did. I failed her."

"You are failing yourself, my girl," said the Hierophant, not unkindly. "You would throw away your whole existence—three hundred years of a well-built life—to spend time with humans of the worst sort, in pursuit of a false hope."

"Lazarus is not a false hope." The General was weak in her conviction on this matter but unwilling to admit that she was even potentially wrong. "I've already been brought back from the dead once. So have you both. Probably," she added, with respect to her Father. "Is it that insane to think it can happen again?"

The Hierophant's tone remained oh-so gentle. "All things are as God made them in this world, my daughter; the river of time will never flow backward. The protein is the gift of eternal life, and those who would reject that are rejecting God and life, as did Cassandra."

"Cassandra rejected you," Dominia insisted. "You and your hideous world."

"It breaks my heart to see you so wounded by her cruelty that you cannot admit who is to blame for your poor wife's death. Will you fight me to the end over mistakes you made? Over your own choice to hand your heart to a stranger who abused your good nature?"

"Why don't you kill me here? It would be quicker for all of us. Cleaner, too."

With his thinnest smile, the Hierophant lifted his eyebrows. "And force you to miss the marathon? That would be a shame. We intend to meet you there; there, you'll deliver Lazarus."

Oh! Now, that was funny. Laughing, the General covered her mouth at her own surprise on the abrupt noise, and exclaimed, "Give you Lazarus? And why would I do something like that?"

With a sympathetic glance to the Lamb, the Hierophant shook his head. "Perhaps, my dear, you had ought to tell her why we have come by; we will argue ourselves in circles, trying to reason without getting to the bottom line. You know how she can be."

"Your Father brought me here to tell you the probabilities, Dominia."

"He brought you to scare me back home."

"He brought me to tell you that, no matter how long this continues, or what direction events flow, the ending is the same. Your death. I have seen that this is true." Bracing herself against his words as though against a physical onslaught of truth, the General let him carry on. "Cassandra won't come back. She can't. Even if she weren't cremated, it wouldn't be possible. You're throwing your life away."

"It's a lie." Dominia covered her eyes, then shifted to her ears. "It's a lie, and I won't hear it."

"You will die, my child," assured the Hierophant, his expression solemn. "You will die, and I will be the one to kill you. I do not want that."

"Can't dirty your holy hands."

In the thud of a single heartbeat, the Hierophant appeared centimeters before Dominia: she had not seen him move. He did that now and again. Uncanny every time, as though he teleported through the air so the object of his prey might spend their last seconds in terror. As this terror passed and the General was in the process of stepping away, he caught with a stonelike hand the fist raised in self-defense; but, rather than tossing her to the ground to initiate a boxing match as might have been Cicero's aim, the Hierophant pulled her into his arms and crushed her with the force of his embrace.

"Please think on this, my girl." He relaxed his hold enough to take her shocked face in his hands and tilt it toward his, so she was forced to see his earnest expression. "We have brought this offer out of love. It will not come a second time. If you continue down this path, you shall be an enemy, not just to man- and martyr-kind alike, but to your own immortal soul. I could not bear to see you throw that away."

Every word she spoke caused an unnerving tension of her face against the grip of his hands. "You can already see me doing everything, anyway. I'm surprised it matters to you what I do when you can see through my eye. I'm getting the thing taken out. Not that that's news to you."

"So I have seen, I do admit. But I wouldn't worry about that. Don't you understand, my daughter? I run Halcyon, I provided the technology for the terraforming of Mars—I *am* the DIOX corporation."

Startled, she at last managed to yank her face out of his hands. "The CEO?"

"Answers to me. I would never publicly reveal my position at the top of the corporation, my dear; not without good reason. What trouble it would have caused me if you knew that going in! But now, you understand the futility of all of this. The *pain* it causes me! So many people in this city have augmentations—praise God, for, to lay eyes upon my dear daughter, I must steal their sight! To hear you speak, I must invade their ears!" As her mind raced, the Hierophant made a pained noise, and covered his shutting eyes. "Oh, my child. If you knew the agony this causes me! Your soul—your poor soul."

As those manipulative tears sprang in skyward-turning eyes, the General was able to dart to the fire escape. When she turned to see if he pursued, her Father had disappeared without so much as the scrape of his shoe upon the rooftop. The Lamb, still there, lingered but a few seconds to study his daughter's expression; then he, too, abandoned Dominia by exiting through the building's door with a harsh metallic slam.

XIII

Trust / Issues

What a fool she'd been! The owner of the DIOX Corporation. Of course. Wasn't he everywhere? Dominia's stomach remained rancid all the way back to pawnshop, a path she couldn't have recalled if the DIOX-I didn't light the way with a floating aureolin line that plunged ahead to decapitate passersby. So, the Family was traveling together. Good to know. Also good to know that Cicero was at greater length than arm's reach from the Lamb, which put a skip into every third or fourth step. Had Miki made it home? Dominia couldn't risk trying a call. Who knew how much data was always being transmitted to the Hierophant at a given moment? Who knew what she would find when she returned to Kahlil's? Maybe Soto was already dead, along with their host.

Even after all these years, her Family terrified her. That was why the idea of a marathon designed to poke fun at them didn't stir her offense: she needed it more than any human did. Her Father, in particular, was always popping up to startle her. What had just happened was such a common occurrence that she should have grown to anticipate it.

Take, for instance, the day the Hierophant visited Cassandra after the disastrous birth of her child. Dominia would never forget the jolt when, tray of food and coffee cautiously balanced in her hands, she nudged open the door of her wife's hospital room to find the

Hierophant holding her Cassandra's delicate hand in his big, spidery own. The yet-new martyr choked on her tears.

"I was so hopeful. I believed so much— I believed, I believed."

"I know, my dear. I know. But there are times when belief is not enough. Times when the will of God, mysterious as it is, must be accepted. All tragedies that arise do so to strengthen the faith of Man."

"My faith is so shaken. My faith—"

She hiccupped and stopped herself to follow the Hierophant's eyes as he acknowledged Dominia's presence. Grieving Cassandra looked right through her, released a sob, and ducked her head to study the Holy Father's hands. "I wish I had never done this. I love Dominia, but for this? For all of this…"

The sting! It was natural to be hurt, Dominia told herself, as natural as it was for Cassandra to think such a thing. Her gentle eyes, after all, had skipped over the lunch tray. While she put away the offending human-based meal and lowered upon her wife's bedside, the Hierophant tutted.

"That is no way to think. The Lord called you to His service for a purpose. No martyr is expendable. No martyr is without value. Your baby"—the Hierophant bent to kiss the back of Cassandra's hands as she burst into tears on the words; she had to be consoled by both the Holy Father and her wife before she was able to accept his repetition of the phrase—"your baby did not suffer, although you did. But through her absence, and your suffering, how close you've come to God! How blessed you are with a loyal wife, a loving Family, a wealth and privilege unheard of by any but those few I call my true children."

"But I want my baby." Cassandra's lips trembled with the same suppressed sobs wracking her shoulders. "I just want her to be alive. I wanted to name her 'Lucy.' Is that a stupid name? It was his mom's name." Her eyes met Dominia's red-ringed own with guilt, but the General stroked her hair.

"It would have been cute," the future widow assured her grieving wife. "A sweet name, for a sweet girl."

Something in this paused Cassandra's tears. Dominia felt exposed until the woman shut her eyes and said through trembling lips, "I wish you would hate me."

Alarm plunged from the top of her skull to the base of her spine. How was she to feel on such words? At her (perhaps sharp) demand to know why Cassandra would say such a thing, the woman lamented, "Because then I'd have no reason to live, and I could die. I could be at peace, alone, with him."

"What was his name?" asked the Hierophant.

The query calmed Cassandra by its tone enough to say, "Ben— Benedict. He was also—he—" Cassandra trailed off, unable to bear the look on the General's face as poisonous recognition flowed in. "He was in the military, too."

Yes. Benedict Miller, with a mother named Lucy. She remembered that name like all the names of the remembered dead (easier before the DIOX-I revealed so many). But Benedict, she remembered better than the others. The Battle for the Reclamation of Mexico was a fresh wound in those nights; her time spent as a POW still stuck in her teeth like the grit of Nogales.

If the suspicion that she had killed Cassandra's lover had ever crossed her mind before, it was tucked beneath more relevant thoughts. Confronted plainly, the Holy Father's black eyes drilling into her from Cassandra's other side in that cramped hospital room, Dominia understood at last the depth of her responsibility. The nature of her bond with her wife. What strength of spirit it took for Cassandra to love her at all, even if, at first, she'd but pretended! Ben Miller: the young, impromptu soldier and even more impromptu jailer she had befriended, then used like a doorway by murdering and escaping in the midst of a momentary lapse of the human's judgment. His death had bothered her more than the average because he was a young guy shipped from home to serve as backup, and because she had discovered on his person a photo of his mother. Humans had an ugly habit of sending kids to war: especially in emergency situations, which the Reclamation had been. It had been a dark fortnight for Dominia, and for many others. When the dust was washed from her scalp, the battle remained.

That damned spot. A symbol of how bad things were. Its memories drove her day after day to the seaside, unaware that Cassandra had learned of her travels on news stations that (in the most literal sense) religiously announced the comings and goings of the Family across the globe. Cassandra turned her hatred for Dominia into a doorway of her own. One which was exit only.

"I think I meant to kill you," her wife confessed, lips twisted with wet despair. "But the way you looked at me the first time you saw me...oh, Dominia."

"I'm so sorry," was all the General could say; Cassandra shut her eyes.

"I didn't want to tell you because I didn't want to hear you lie. You're not sorry. He was any other dead man to you. He's only important to you now because he was important to me. And if you hadn't killed him, you would have been killed, yourself. So, you don't regret it. I'm the only one here who has anything to regret."

"But"—the Hierophant stroked her hand—"you have everything to gain."

Her lips were back to trembling again. "All I ever wanted was a family."

Magnanimous as ever, the Holy Father lifted his eyebrows. "My girl, be glad: you have one."

Afterward, he took the General aside in the hall and asked how she would like to be Governess of the United Front. Fine time to ask. Finer time to accept. No doubt his ability to pull a stunt like that and still get an affirmative response was the reason he showed up now, his presence a threat not just to Dominia and her friends, but all Kabul. Kabul, which was supposedly protected by the Hunters. In a world where cameras were everywhere, even in the eyes of passersby, was Dominia to believe her Father was the only one with omnipotent access to every device? That the Hunters didn't know her Father was there? That she was there?

That they didn't know Kahlil abetted them?

As her legs pumped with the pace of her run, she couldn't help but think something here was wrong—and not, necessarily, Miki. All the major players—at least, her Father and the Lamb—seemed in on the game; why wouldn't the Hunters be? That was what all this seemed more and more, in truth. What Tobias had said. A game. She wished she could flip the board, but she supposed that meant suicide in this context, so she wiped the metaphor from her mind as she stood before the pawnshop. Miki's back door was still open; the General's entrance was silent, but that silence proved needless when she arrived at Kahlil's apartment to find the prostitute and the Hunter already having a too-loud fight.

"I think you could have warned us!" Miki's sharp tone resolved when Dominia pushed open the front door and laid eyes on the man who, beneath his beard and olive skin, nonetheless paled to macabre slate. Somehow, Miki had discovered the news of the day, and agreed that her friend should have been wise to it. Never a good sign. The martyr was upon Kahlil before he so much as moved, holding the human foot above the floor to be shaken in one brisk whip of his head. Amid the uproar, Basil barked for joy.

"Is there something you'd like to tell us, Kahlil?"

"I didn't know your Family was here! I swear, I swear, I didn't know, oh, Allah. You think I sit around switching between security feeds all day long? Huh? You think al-Saalihin would actually tell me anything?" While trying to extricate himself from the martyr's fists with one hand, he used the other to straighten his crooked glasses. "They can't stand my guts! I'm their tech support. I run their Halcyon accounts. I'm PR! They used to bully guys like me—well, not in *school*, but in the crappy neighborhoods where they grew up."

"Then you'd better start doing your job and spin your story."

"You tell 'im, boss." Miki, arms crossed and foot propped against the wall, did not look as belligerent as intended due to her short-shorts. "I have a hard time believing your bosses didn't send out some kind of high-priority emergency alert as soon as the Hierophant set foot on Kabul's soil. You let us walk out of this place knowing those creeps are out there wandering around!"

"I swear, Miki, I didn't. I'm their cleanup crew! They don't tell me anything. Do you remember—remember when they tried that coup in Iran a couple of years ago? That was my first year on the job! How do you think I felt, having to handle the social-media backlash?"

"How do you think *they* felt?" asked Dominia, rattling him once more for good measure. "The people who lost their lives, their families—how did they feel? How do you think they *will* feel when whatever violent conflict brought to this city spends more lives today? You're responsible by failing to tell me these important details."

Fear vanished from Kahlil's face, and his expression hardened to a steel mask that came from somewhere else. Some divine source, she thought in ironic tone. "How about all the people you killed, huh? All the humans killed in all the wars you've fought, all the things you've done. War crimes."

"War crimes," scoffed Dominia. The man sneered.

"Yeah, war crimes. Torture, genocide, enslavement, who knows what else. And then there's your so-called legitimate battles."

"All my battles are, by definition, legitimate battles. Battles with soldiers who signed up to be there."

"I guess those people murdered in the Black Night volunteered for camp?"

Miki averted her gaze. Nostrils flaring, the martyr lowered the human to the floor. After he had put the couch between himself and the General, Kahlil cleared his throat, straightened his shirt, and said, "Every human being is a soldier in the war against you, your Father, and your so-called people."

"So why didn't you tell me he was here?"

"I haven't been debriefed yet."

"Miki"—eyes blazing, Dominia turned to assess the prostitute— "why are we wasting our time with this idiot?"

"Because he's going to have information on the Lazarenes. *Right*, Kahlil?" The prostitute stared the man down with a devilish look.

"When my computer has finished decrypting his location for the week." The man stepped toward the humming collection of screens and towers so old as to practically be artifacts. Somehow, these constituted one device, though said "one device" took up a quarter of his living room. "It's not instantaneous. This is how he protects himself, and why the Hunters and your Family get only a slim window of opportunity to acquire him. Every Friday night at nine o'clock, wherever he is, he releases a message in a few secret digital channels—mostly via direct messages to his priests, but also in one of two Lazarene chat rooms with forever-changing addresses. This message is encrypted, and the instructions for the computer on how to derive the key are also encrypted, but known to those who use the chat rooms, and to worshipers. It's not dissimilar to blockchain, the basis for most digital currencies, but it's lighter, and instead of crunching problems to mine for digital coins, computers are crunching problems to mine Lazarus's encryption. Like digging out of a cave, instead of mining."

"Reminds me of the protein somehow," mused the martyr, glancing into the bright eyes of the dog. "If everybody in the world is trying to get ahold of him for one reason or another, why is he releasing information on his location?"

Miki, annoyed by Dominia's ignorance, said, "Because he's got people to save."

This was a controversial topic. Ask her Father and the Church, and Lazarus's blood was a one-way ticket to permanent excommunication— the condemnation of the soul to eternal hell. Miki, however, was one of a great many people who seemed to believe the opposite, the subject of Lazarus being the point where the common cultist joined with the Red Market priestess. Indeed, they sometimes seemed part of the same faith. This was so well veiled from Dominia for over three hundred years that, seeing so now, she hardly understood. "So Lazarus travels the world like Cicero and the Lamb, distributing his location of the week to humans who believe in him. The Abrahamian Hunters intercept these codes in hopes of capturing him, and using him to…what?"

"What do *you* want him for?" asked Kahlil with a shrug and an adjustment of his glasses. "Whether or not he's a martyr, he's a useful one if he can resurrect the dead."

For her own benefit, the General pressed, "Do you believe he can?"

The young man turned his back on the martyr to study his computer's progress. "Why does it matter? Like I said. I'm tech support at worst, PR at best."

"I guess I wanted you to clap your hands for Tinkerbell." From behind the human's shoulder, the muttering General studied the screen. She had to admit, the eye's translation of Arabic to English was useful. "Get me the second this is done. How much longer?"

"Even the fastest computers can only manage to decrypt the code by Saturday night, and mine's the fastest in Kabul. It's been at it for twenty hours already. Any minute now, it will be finished."

After translating "Saturday night" to "Noctisatur" in her head, she nodded. "And the rest of the Hunters will lag behind us?"

"Better," insisted Miki, her grin ear to ear. "Kahlil is the one who gets them the information every week! He's going to have a computer problem tonight, right?" This, with a cheesy wink to her friend, who rolled eyes that landed on the General.

"Yeah. I'm willing to hold the information back for Miki's sake because, well…my career is ruined either way." His annoyance was directed to the prostitute. "But this way, there's a chance I can salvage it by making it seem like a computer problem. It's not the end of the world to them if they miss one Lazarene ceremony, since even if they're able to interrupt it, they're not going to catch him."

"Why not?"

At Dominia's question, Kahlil offered an answer that reminded her chillingly of her Father's uncanny movements earlier that evening. "I don't know. I've heard he just disappears."

Shaking her head, the General made her way down the cluttered hall and let herself into the cramped guest bathroom. Miki was not more than a few steps behind as the martyr washed her face in the sooty-looking sink. After flipping on a single lightbulb whose pale fluorescence amplified the depressing state of the broken tile floor, the human rustled through all visible drawers. Dominia watched her shameless snooping with fond relief.

"I'm glad I made you stay behind."

As Miki straightened with a pair of tarnished scissors in hand, the human exclaimed, "What *was* that with you? You see something, or what?"

"Not just the Lamb, but the Hierophant." The General allowed herself steered to a seat upon the toilet lid.

"I gathered from what you said in there…are you all right?"

"Fine. I was surprised. He tried to convince me to come home." Memories of her discussion with her Father reminded her that she had walked in on Kahlil and Miki having an argument, which she had thought to be about her Family—but perhaps she'd been wrong. "What were you and Kahlil fighting about when I came back?"

"Oh"—Miki turned to close the door but for a crack—"I was pissed because he wouldn't try to find you on a camera feed. I didn't know where you were! What if I needed to help you?"

She was a good kid. "You're a kinder friend than I deserve. When I talk to my Father, I always walk away feeling like there is no real way to change. Like I'll always be the same evil person he taught me to be."

"You're being too harsh on yourself! Look, hey!" When her eyes remained lowered, the scissors tapped Dominia's ear, and the cold contact sent them springing up. "I mean it. I already told you that nobody has to forgive or accept what you were before, but the worthy will be able to see that who you are now is different. You have to see yourself as different. But, if you can't forgive yourself, at least try to learn. Look"—she glanced slyly toward the cracked door, with the dog waiting outside and the unbreaking flow of distant keystrokes—"if I tell you something to make you feel better, will you keep it secret? It's bad for business. Well…this business. Sometimes it's *great* for business, you wouldn't believe."

Embarrassing how quickly Dominia's self-pity morphed into burning curiosity: she waited, the picture of childlike impatience as Miki leaned in and whispered, clipping the air with her scissors. "I was born with a penis."

"Really!" Astonished, Dominia found herself reacting in the stupidest way possible: a way that made her think of blushing, flustered Tenchi sticking his foot in his mouth on the *Jun'yō* only after she realized she'd said, "But you're so hot!"

Luckily, Miki had a good enough sense of humor to raise her head in a cackle. As she resumed snipping the stray hairs of twice-embarrassed Dominia's 'do, she exclaimed, "I know, right? Modern medicine, it's a miracle! All thanks to gene therapy, hormones, and one great surgeon." Like an all-business hair stylist, Miki directed

Dominia's head this way and that. "But none of that matters, see? I mean, look at me."

Before Dominia said, "No," Miki slipped down shorts and skivvies, and grinned to see Dominia's furious blush. "See? A sputtering lesbian is praise from Caesar."

"It's—very organic looking."

"You want to touch it?" asked the leering human while Dominia averted her gaze.

"Um, no! Not—"

"You're right, this bathroom is gross, and that dope will be back before we get anywhere. When we're alone, *senpai*." To Dominia's relief, she slipped her bottoms back up, and Dominia looked down to make eye contact with Basil, whose tail wagged through the crack of the door. *Pervert*, she told him in her head, and his mouth opened in a big doggie grin that made her smirk. Miki, redressed and back to clipping, missed this.

"Anyway, who we really are is living consciousness. Light on the inside and out. What do our bodies matter? I wanted to be a girl since I was little! I was a regular hoodlum, getting into my mother's gowns and makeup. So many beautiful kimono, smeared with white paste…it makes me want to die to think about them. Sigh"—she said the word "sigh" out loud, and the martyr laughed, earning a nick on the ear that instantly healed—"I could have inherited those someday. Theoretically."

"Was she mad?"

"About the dresses? You should have seen my ass!"

"No, about—"

"Oh, no way. Are you kidding? She was always disappointed that I was born a boy! I was almost eight when I admitted to her that I was a girl, and it was like, we were at the doctor two days later." She told the story laughing, but Dominia couldn't help sadness for the small child forced to endure eight years of life in tortured secrecy. At least young Morgan had been granted a sweet sliver of Eden before life unveiled its unjust face and delivered her to her fate among the Holy Family. "Part of the reason I look so good now is because we were able to make small adjustments while I was young. You can at least feel *these*!" No boundaries, the woman: she snatched up Dominia's hands and settled them on the warm breasts beneath her shirt. For her part, the General tried to maintain the objective and studious look of someone, say, at an art gallery, or perhaps a doctor looking for lumps. She even threw in a bit of, "Oh, mm-hmm? Ah, I see," which cracked Miki up.

"You're so *shy*! This is hilarious. I always heard you martyrs were super-depraved S and M freaks. Anyway, yeah, these are real, see? The doctors couldn't do anything at first, of course, because I was small, so Mom overhauled my wardrobe, started treating me like a human being, and taught me how to be a proper woman. Then, when I hit puberty, the hormonal therapies started. It was a long road, but I was cured by the time I was in my early twenties. No better way to take it all for a ride than to leave work as a geisha and apply my talents elsewhere! Hah, she was way more pissed off about that! But, see?" She caught Dominia's chin. "It doesn't matter who we were before. None of who I was would have mattered if I hadn't told you. None of what you've done matters now that you have this chance to free yourself through change."

"Thank you," said the martyr as Miki clipped and arranged one last lock that was allowed by the stylist to hang upon the General's pale forehead.

"Any time, cutie. Come to me first, next time you need a haircut." Kahlil appeared in the doorway and drew her attention. "There are a few chunks I wasn't able to save...what's up?"

"You guys are going to want to take a look at this."

Always fatal words. Sensing the weight of what she was about to observe, Dominia followed Miki, Basil, and their maligned host to the proverbial command center. There, a paused video buffered. She recognized it before he said anything at all, because she had seen it, quite literally, with her own eye.

"You wanted it, you got it. This stream was obtained by a friend of mine in Jerusalem, a guy who has access to some serious martyr information. They've had this stream's link for the past couple of days."

That fucking DIOX-I. The fucking Hierophant. There it was, her conversation with her Father on the rooftop of Kabul, recorded in perfect silence. Everything she had done, everything she had seen: watched not just by her Father, but by the Hunters, and every human government in the world. She would have gouged it out right there if she wasn't sure it would try to cram itself back in.

Calmly, she asked, "The stream was leaked by whom?"

"A confidential source."

Still reeling from before, she almost speculated aloud, "the Hierophant," but refrained as he went on. "If they don't already know you're here with me, they will when they've caught up. And that's assuming they aren't getting live reports from its GPS, anyway."

Oh, yeah. This thing was coming out of her skull. In retrospect, of course it tracked her location: it had a map feature, didn't it? What was the world coming to!

"Do you happen to have an eye patch lying around?"

Kahlil offered the kind of expression that made even Dominia feel stupid. "Do I look like a pirate?"

"A little," said Miki, earning an irritated look she exchanged for a grin. "With the beard, and all. A software pirate, at least."

Muttering something in Arabic that got him slapped in the head, Kahlil minimized the video stream with a tap of his touch screen. "Look, Miki…I've got a lot of equipment here to interfere with recording devices and unauthorized uploads while people are in my house, but this…you can't stay here. I'm sorry. I broke the encryption, but I can't help you beyond that. The Lazarene ceremony is in the basement of a music store, at"—he paused, looked at Dominia in irritation, and covered his mouth to prevent lip-reading efforts while he shared the address.

"This is bullshit," said the prostitute; their host rose from his seat to defend himself.

"What do you want me to do, Miki? I'm stupid. I'm stupid to have taken your money. With the Caliphate—and probably the government—aware that you're here, I'm as good as dead."

"This is a risk you knew when you agreed to put us up," Miki began, but Dominia shook her head.

"He's right. He's done enough for us. There's no reason another human has to die because I'm here."

"They'll be dying because the Hierophant came," said Miki.

"And he came because I did." She thought of the lifelong suffering of the patient Lamb, who never wished for anything but to be with his brother. How she struggled against the urge to admit defeat against suffering; how she grappled with inevitability! The calm, rational General forced herself to say, "We can go elsewhere."

"Thank you." The man's voice relaxed with a heave of gratitude. "I'm sorry. I wouldn't be this inhospitable. But—"

"We understand. At least, I do. Thank you for keeping us this long. I hope"—she frowned and decided not to carry on with that particular line of thought, opting instead to say—"I hope we'll meet again, in better circumstances."

Then, with a glance down the hall, the sighing General added, "At least we don't have a lot of luggage."

They did, however, have a dog. A dog who was found in the bedroom with his head upon his paws, ears pinning back and forth upon his tuxedoed head like fuzzy satellite dishes. A dog who, when called, "Basil, we have to go," decided he was now as stupid as all other dogs in the world. He got up in place, dashed in fast circles, then settled back down with a pre-nap huff.

Somehow, this action gave Dominia the idea that she'd done something wrong.

"Come on." Miki pushed the mongrel with her toe while the dog peeped up at her from one eye. "We'll get you some bacon or—oh, wrong town. Do dogs like falafel?"

"Lamb," the martyr profaned, stooping to the level of the dog. "I'm missing something, aren't I? There's something…something I'm not doing. Or maybe…"

"Are you seriously talking to the dog?"

"Thinking out loud to it," she tried, which was blatantly false, because the border collie deigned to lift his head and wag his tail in some kind of indicator. She was, in fact, talking to the dog. Miki's tongue expressed her displeasure with a click against the roof of her mouth.

"Primitive man—I mean, before the primary Western calendar flipped from CE to AL—used to just, like, murder each other for fun. You know that, right? Not only gladiators in Roman times, I mean, but serial killers—and this *one* dude talked to his dog. Or his neighbor's dog. I don't remember."

"And Caligula promoted his horse. Why do you know this?"

"It's a requirement for Red Market women to learn the savage nature of mankind because now the savage, murder-for-fun types are you. I just mean to say, when I see you talking to a dog, my palms start to sweat."

"That's a kind of profiling I don't appreciate." Dominia struggled to keep a straight face and failed when she turned her attention back to Basil. He stared intently at the gun concealed in her waistband: that emergency-only device that seemed ever more chain than tool. "But maybe you're right. I mean, it looks like he's staring at my gun right now."

"Hey," said Miki, "it kind of does."

At the time, what Dominia did next seemed to be a small mistake: as an experiment, she removed the gun and held it out to see if it was the dog's focal point. His gaze remained plastered to the weapon. The General was about to comment on the strangeness of it, amused that in all her years of working with military dogs she had never seen an animal interested in guns; Miki appeared on the verge of a similar conclusion; but none of that happened, because Kahlil opened the door without knocking, saying as he entered, "Look, guys, I feel bad about turning you out, and—"

No dog had moved faster; no martyr, slower. It was the sheer surprise of having the dog move in a way so sudden and directed. Not for her hand or her arm or her body or even Kahlil, but for the gun. The next five seconds abstracted: sheer surprise, the scramble of movement, black-and-white blur, the clatter of metal, and the urgent *no-no-no* of thought followed by the inevitable crack of the gun. All this chaos released into a new kind of order, which took the form of the scream of their unfortunate host and his string of Arabic profanity. While the man clutched his hip and cried, "What the fuck, what did you shoot me for," Dominia exchanged with Miki a startled look. Both women turned this incredulity down upon the dog; Basil, for his part, wagged his tail, laid the big, sweet doggie eyes on extra thick, and stepped away from the weapon.

Feeling somehow apart from this tableau as much as she felt a part of it, Dominia considered that this was what her Father must have felt all the time: vague amusement. That, or the palpable sense of being the butt of some intangible joke. She cracked a smile that let show the gaps the Hierophant had made in her teeth.

"Well…we do know one medical professional in Kabul."

XIV

Communication Skills

In many ways, Tobias Akachi seemed too good to be true. Dominia first thought this was because she had not known many humans in anything other than a bureaucratic sense, as when they came into her San Valentino office to appeal to her for grants, favors, stays of execution, etc. Humans, therefore, seemed increasingly to be an otherwise defenseless group in need of a compassionate hand—though she had always felt that way, even while slaying them. The bloody course of her final war arose from a deep admixture of love and hate, in which love found but recent consideration. Somehow, love was more painful for the General. Was that a symptom of evil? Humans, after all, seemed to express love with ease. Not having seen them in their own environment since her aborted childhood, she had not recognized how their kindness, their prevailing belief in the basic decency of conscious individuals, drove some to help even martyrs. And martyrs, well…perhaps it was wrong to call her kind inherently selfish, but what else could be said of a cannibal race? Her Father had, since before their human births, drilled the message of martyr superiority: How could humanity but believe it? How could martyrs but act with those beliefs lodged in their hearts? If, in the martyr world, Dominia had called a friend for help at a strange hour, would she have received any friendship? Any help? Martyrs were to be hospitable to other martyrs, of course. But they were also taught it was understandable to refuse the phone call of an absurd hour, and acceptable to find a solution other than inviting a general, a prostitute, a wounded man, and a dog over for unlicensed emergency surgery. Dr. Akachi had a different approach, about which he discoursed while tending the thrashing patient.

"One should leap at the opportunity to help one's fellow man." The dentist used one great hand to hold Kahlil while the other manipulated a pair of silver tweezers in a way topical anesthetic and slow-acting opiates wouldn't help. "And, with love in the heart! If you do not have love in your heart, you'd might as well do nothing at all."

"I don't know." Miki pinned Kahlil's shoulders to the silver surface of the dentist's chic dining room table, sometimes grimacing through her friend's struggles. "A lot of great charities were founded from a sense of obligation. Lots of old people have been helped. My country has a whole system of elder care—and why? Because old people are so good at guilt!"

"Obligation breeds mutual resentment. I help because I am happy to! Because I was put on God's Earth to help my fellow man. To help you, Kahlil, get this nasty fellow out of you!"

With a glance for the martyr, then the dog, who observed from the living room couch, Miki said, "This is a great argument for ID-locking all guns."

"This is an antique," protested Dominia, who lifted the hem of her shirt to show the handle. Kahlil hissed.

"Put it away! Didn't you learn your lesson? That stupid dog— Ow!"

While lifting into the light a bloodied bullet that made Miki wince, Tobias laughed. "Relax. You won't die! Maybe limp a bit. Some long-term aches. You'll get a good idea of when it's going to rain!"

"You should be grateful." Dominia adjusted with a snap the band of her drugstore eye patch, procured at a clerkless convenience store to blind the DIOX-I to their conversations. "That dog saved your life by forcing you to leave your house. You think your Caliphate would have been understanding?"

"Oh, Allah." Kahlil tried to sit up until Miki shoved him back. "Do you need to mention my—affiliations?"

"I do not care. Much." The winking dentist brandished a hooked suture needle intended for stitches in gums. "After all, I have a martyr who can testify to my impartiality! That is high praise, I think."

"You should have destroyed her brain while she was in your office," said Kahlil, who swore as Miki slammed him down into the table. "Shit— Well? Can you blame me?"

"Yeah, asshole, I can blame you. It's your own fault you got shot, the way you barged in." Sniffing, Miki looked over at the dog. "Poor boy was startled. Weren't you, boy? Who's a good boy?"

"He *shot* me!"

"He doesn't know that!"

Dominia wasn't so sure, but there was no point in arguing. Better to play along, to smirk and say, "Holding a grudge against a dog is kind of petty, Kahlil."

"So maybe I hold one against you."

As Dominia pointed to her own chest in a *who, me?* way, Tobias rinsed the closed wound with distilled water and daubed on some hiss-provoking antibiotic cream. "Good as new!"

"Great. Can I go home, now?"

Dominia's hand on his chest rendered his effort to sit up humorously futile.

"Actually," she said, "since we have you here, maybe you could do us a favor. I've been thinking…two can play this hacker game, right?"

"What do you mean?"

"I'm not the only one who's been blinded by the Family."

Miki took her meaning right away. "Yeah—yeah, that's a great idea! That idiot, René…he's probably making the mistake of appealing to the Hunters as we speak! About to lose his life, too."

"Then what are you hoping to gain?" Kahlil's voice reached a high pitch of annoyance. "He'll be dead soon! All of us— *I'm* going to be dead soon! You have to let me get back to my apartment."

Eye narrowing, Dominia demanded, "What's so urgent?"

"You heard me before. In spite of my security efforts, your stream is going to lead the Hunters—even the government—straight to my house."

"Then you should make yourself scarce," said Miki, but he didn't agree.

"They'll think I'm colluding with you. If I was in my apartment, I'd have a chance to explain myself and protect my possessions. Now they're going to rifle through everything, and they're going to find Miki's information, and that will be that. Either the government realizes I'm part of the Hunters, or the Hunters realize I've been running around with a woman of ill repute."

"Looks like you're going to have to find a new business," suggested the aforementioned working girl, who looked amused as anybody might in the given circumstances. "I'm sure we could use someone like you for our own tech stuff. Ever thought about joining the Red Market?"

"And join a bunch of heathen prostitutes?"

"Whom you *solicit*," Miki emphasized, much to the visible chagrin of Kahlil. Clear on the source of his offense, she waved a hand. "Oh, nobody here cares. Hell, you introduced Tobias to me."

"To fix your *teeth*."

"And, of course, I did." Akachi remained shameless and jolly as he'd be for any other subject. "She is a very fine woman! Perhaps an exception among the usual Red Market sort. The Bible says, my brother, that the sin in prostitution is upon the shoulders of the customer—not upon the prostitute, as such."

"And the Prophet said that the finances made through prostitution are as haram as that made from soothsaying. And the sale of dogs. No fucking wonder! All this is happening to me because I've been a bad Muslim."

Rolling her eyes, Miki said, "I love how men are all happy to stick their dicks into a whore, and then judge their character as soon as their boners are gone...be as stupid about this as you want, Kahlil, but you're going to end up dead if you stay in this city. Look"—she made sure Dominia's eye remained covered—"we're going to Cairo after we meet up with Lazarus. It's safe there. At least, the Red Market isn't going to kill you in cold blood because you hosted us. They might even reward you for it. And if it's religion you're worried about, nobody cares! You won't be forced to worship, or even meet the Lady. But I'm telling you, Kahlil…you stay here, you're dead."

"Fuck," said Kahlil; then, in a higher and more tearful pitch: "Fuck! Miki, why would you do this to me? You've ruined my life!"

"Oh, buddy"—the prostitute patted his shoulder—"I didn't ruin your life. I saved it. Sometimes your old life has to be ruined before you can start the next. Like bankruptcy!"

Looking between the two of them, Dominia was in the process of asking, "Now I have to take two humans to Cairo—" when Kahlil, not in the rightest of minds, made an angry, stupid, and sluggish lurch for the gun in the General's waistband. She got to it long before him and used its handle to crack him on the back of the skull much as Miki had Cicero, whereupon the human dropped against the table with a theatrical clang.

"Shit," cried Miki while the much-startled dentist, who had retreated against the midnight marble of his kitchen counter, now hurried to study the young man's well-being. Dominia lifted her free hand to her good eye—to rub it, its brow, the bridge of her nose.

"Sorry. It was instinctive."

With a look of disapproval, Akachi said, "Resorting to violence is never the right choice…he will live, as you did not break the skin, but I would be concerned about a concussion."

Miki nodded. "All the more reason to get him to Cairo as soon as possible. Red Market medical care is top notch."

The subject of Cairo was what had agitated the General, and was, in retrospect, a contributing factor to poor Kahlil's head wound. That, and her starvation. Four bags of donated blood over the course of her stay did not a full stomach make—no more than it helped her recover from the fast of her train journey. Among her problems, tremors were somehow both the least and the greatest of her worries. While Miki continued Tobias's conversation in Arabic, Dominia tried to reduce her trembling through sheer force of will. That wasn't successful with the adrenaline of conflict flowing through her limbs. It was Kahlil's own fault for trying something so stupid on a rattled martyr who was ready for many things: for a meal; for a bed; for a therapist; but, most of all, for somebody to do something stupid. And because she was so ready for the latter, she had "resorted" to violence. So? So what. Violence was her art form, wasn't it? Violence was her life.

But that was her Father's influence. She tamped it away, cleansed herself of the notion that he had permeated even the human world. Dominia hid the gun once more on her person while Miki said in English, "What the fuck are we going to do about René now, wise guy? That was an important detail you thought of, and you fucked it up, yourself! We're blind. *And*, if we're going to get him checked out, we don't have time to wait around for your teeth."

Tobias looked up in an offer that seemed, at the time, altruistic. "I can work through the night, if necessary. The most difficult portions of creating the implants are already complete."

"I would be in your debt." To Miki, the General said, "It'll take my body all of thirty minutes to recover from the procedure. The Lazarene ceremony starts before dawn?" At Miki's single nod, Dominia said, "We'll be cutting it close."

"A good day for it. Everybody will be busy with the marathon." The prostitute's statement reminded the almost-grimacing martyr of her Father's promise. She would deliver Lazarus to him during the race. Dominia tuned out as her friend continued, "The odds of police raids, or even Hunter interference, are pretty low."

"Even so…" The General studied the unconscious man, whose head Akachi supported with his hand. "I don't think it's safe for you guys to come with me. Especially if he's in need of recovery."

"Remember I have your diamond," sang Miki, wearing that sly expression. "At least, the Lady does."

"I'm not trying to get out of going to Cairo. But I'm going to have to meet you there. When I saw my Father"—Tobias's gaze flickered up in brief attention—"he made a threat about Lazarus, and about the marathon. About meeting me during the race."

"Did he say where?" When the General shook her head, the prostitute crossed her arms. "Probably near the start, in front of that big hotel. At least, that's the most logical spot. That or the end, out by

Hashmat Khan Lake. Otherwise, it runs through the whole city, so I can't imagine where you'd find him."

"Staying in the hotel's penthouse," speculated the General with a snort before turning away from the humans. "Can you handle the car situation, Miki?"

"For me, or for you?"

"For yourself, and Kahlil."

"Yeah, I can do that. We have enough 'Coins from our stunt on the train that it won't be a problem. But how will *you* get to Cairo?"

She hadn't stopped to think about it. After all, her next step was emergency surgery. While a simple procedure would not normally bother her, the idea now stuck in her craw after her experience with Cicero. Her mild preoccupation with the forthcoming removal of her eye and replacement of her teeth was more irritating than the actual event would prove to be. But perhaps it was the principle. Could there never be a moment of peace? A moment when the tide of her thoughts didn't turn to crush her beneath their loathsome waves?

If she went home, perhaps. Perhaps, given time, she'd get over her pain and her moments of doubt. With enough effort, she could return to that numb half-life in which she dwelled before Cassandra's arrival. That security of unfeeling. The more Dominia observed herself, the more she recognized an upsetting pattern of dichotomy. Perhaps she had created it. The world was more complex than a binary of goodness and badness; yet, she could no longer use that complexity to justify evil acts. Now she was forced to admit that evil—the truest evil—would be a knowing return into the bosom of evil out of sheer, pitiful fear.

But how easy it would be, going home! How safe. How comfortable. Normal. Not like this, her life destroyed, her body displaced in some human's (admittedly classy) high-rise apartment, where she washed her face and tried to convince herself she wasn't a complete fool.

This inner division traced to the issue of her parentage. The discovery of a parent's imperfection was a natural (indeed, pivotal) point in a child's development so far as the General observed, but that opportunity was swept from her—she thought—when the Hierophant stole her away. That made the initial divide neat and tidy. Morgan's parents remained forever pure and good and helpless. A couple deprived of their only daughter, into whom they had poured no small amount of love and care, by the wickedest man in all the land. It sounded like a fairy tale, because Dominia insisted on a child's way of thinking about the matter for almost ten years; until, at sixteen, the ever-surly girl and all-the-surlier teenager spotted, by total happenstance, a quartet of out-of-towners gone for a day trip to the Vatican. Two of the tourists, she recognized in an instant: beside their grief-grayed hairs, her parents could never be that changed. Ah, that second of joy! Of thrill! What small odds that they should both visit Rome at once! Her Father rarely brought her back to Mephitoli in those teen years. Yet, this week he had surprised her. She had been optimistic that, for once, the trip might be pleasant—and then, this vision.

This was a sign from the God her Father was always babbling about. Her heart raced as she pulled away from the Hierophant with whom she walked. She took two steps forward, and stupidly called out (if she had but waited a few strides, until there was no escape for them!), "Mamma! Papá!"

Words she had thought that would never use again. Words she would forever wish she had never used again when her father's head lifted, and terror filled his eyes. Terror, or sorrow. Whatever they contained, he tapped his wife on the shoulder. Morgan's mother looked at Dominia with a kind of coldness that made the girl think the human looked at the Hierophant.

No. This woman, turning away, gripped the hand of the little girl with whom she walked, and yanked her along so fast that the child's pigtails snapped in the wind. While Dominia stood, dumbfounded and making excuses (they hadn't recognized her; or were afraid of the Hierophant; or, the saddest excuse of all, they were too busy to speak to her), Morgan's father lowered his shamed eyes and tugged attention out of his son's shirt collar. Then, with another pained flicker toward his lost child, and what might have been something akin to the subtle wave of his left hand, he and the boy he guided disappeared into the crowd.

The Hierophant appeared at pale Dominia's elbow.

"What is it, princess?" His great hand lay on her shoulder. "What did you see?"

Nothing, of course. She had seen nothing. Eating was easier after that moment because before she had held out secret hope that some-day, somehow, her condition would be cured, and her parents would be her parents again. How silly she'd been. What a child. In that moment, she understood that the emptiness of a martyr would be with her forever. The one thing to do was to try to fill it with flesh.

That abject emptiness that plagued her at the thought of family was what made it so easy to be home with Cassandra while her mourning wife reclined upon the favored couch of their new San Valentino estate. She looked like a painting from the Holy Father's galleries. Sometimes she would lay, unspeaking, for hours; Dominia spent that time reading, sipping wine. Just looking at her. An hour seemed much shorter to the Governess, who'd lived far longer than Cassandra. In the scale of her life, an hour was good as a minute, or less. Yet, those hours with Cassandra had seemed an exquisite eternity in which Dominia forever watched sleet waves of the Pacific in the picture window behind her wife's head, the image framed by gauzy curtains that, sail-like, bloomed with wind creeping through the patio door. That same wind stroked Cassandra's hair until, as the starry night gave way to the viscous fog of coastal morning, Dominia, jealous of that wind, kissed her wife, and coaxed her off to bed, and gave her the opportunity for the smallness and safety that came with being in a lover's arms. That same safety Dominia felt in holding her. She refused to believe she would never feel that safety again—perhaps with the same stupidity by which she once believed her parents would return. But she had to cling to something. The notion that memory was now her only respite weighed too much to bear.

Even in that respite, after all, she had no real peace. Emerging from the bathroom to find Miki flinging herself upon the guest bed, Dominia adjusted the awkward band of her eye patch and studied, with her organic orb, the tasteful decoration of the slick room. A palace beside Kahlil's, with a lot of in-built storage and bookshelves curiously empty of books, but ornamented with a few fake orchids. "I'm surprised Dr. Akachi is so accommodating."

"That's why I brought you to him! He's been my client for about two years. Pretty good guy. Does good cleanings. Lets me pay him in—"

"Okay," interrupted Dominia. "But, I mean, I'm a martyr. You think that would stop him."

"You're not going to bite him when he sticks his fingers in your mouth, for Lady's sake. He's a good, Christian man, but he's not—well, of course he's an idiot. All people are idiots. But he's not a *complete* idiot."

"You can't think all people are idiots."

"I'm an idiot! You're an idiot. Even—especially—Basil here." Finished unpeeling her socks from her feet, she tossed one over the dog's nose, then sprang to squish his fuzzy face. "Yes! Yes, especially Basil, you're so cute and stupid."

As Miki sang to the dog, Dominia made smirking eye contact with the animal that, despite its tail wags, strove to communicate something with its hilariously dry expression. The General laughed, then turned to study their view of Kabul when she recognized the distinct shape jutting inside the duffel bag to which Miki went when done harassing the hound. One patched eye meant she couldn't watch the human from her periphery, and had to wait: had to listen for the sound of the zipper when Miki, sure the martyr wasn't watching, opened the duffel bag to reveal the shamisen within.

Thoughts whipped at rapid clip across Dominia's consciousness, a chain unfolding in the order of shamisen, train, Cicero: by the time her brother's smug face entered her mind, she was already upon the human, who emitted a shocked cry as the martyr pinned her to the wall with a hand to her mouth.

"That was your mother's shamisen. It was special, you said." The licorice lacquer, the cherry blossoms: yes, it was the same. "Where'd this new one come from, Miki? The pawnshop? I thought it was strange you were already fighting with Kahlil by the time I got back from seeing my fathers, but you managed to keep me occupied until something else came up. You were angry with him for the same reason as me. Just like he didn't tell me they were in town, he didn't tell you, either, and you met one on your way back to the pawnshop."

As the martyr lowered her hand for the human to speak, Miki said, "Shit, dude, listen, I wanted to tell you, but we've been—busy. You need to relax."

"Where'd you get the instrument?"

"You said it yourself. When you ran off, I made my way back to the shop, but on the way, I—"The prostitute laughed, a high-pitched noise that indicated high levels of anxiety enfolded within her comic layers of brazen self-defense. "I thought I was dead, for sure!"

"Cicero."

After glancing at the eye patch blinding Dominia's DIOX-I, she uttered the word, "Yes."

Dominia swore through the broad window that overlooked the glowing city, perhaps more active for sake of tomorrow's race. "I guess you'll betray me, too, huh? He returned your shamisen as a bribe? Or did he give you something else?"

"This was why I didn't tell you. I knew you wouldn't trust me to be better than that!" At the martyr's skeptical look, the human's temper reached such a pitch that Dominia grew more inclined to believe her. "Of course he tried to get information out of me, to get me to spy on you or whatever. But they only have chump shit to offer me. Cicero, the Hierophant—none of your Family can give me what I want."

"What will it take to get you to betray me?"

Here came a slap, which caused the martyr to study with new, ringing perception the scowling human. "You bitch! I'm not some rat, and I don't appreciate your assumption that I am. Did I bump into Cicero? Yes. Did he offer me money to report to him because he was 'concerned'"—the girl made air quotes—"about you? Yes. But I didn't take it. I'd be getting in my own way. Ishtar's way."

Miki then went on to describe their interaction, but Dominia didn't need her story, because she could picture it. How deferential Cicero was, how quick to assure Miki need not worry about the crack in the head. He'd tell her he was fine and just impressed that she'd force of will enough to pick up the gun, with her state at the time. Well

Dominia saw how he'd have gotten into Miki's personal space while handing her the instrument. After draping an arm around her, he'd start walking her back to the pawnshop to show her he knew where they stayed. All the while, he'd say something to the effect of, "My poor sister has lost control of herself in the wake of her wife's death. We've discussed paying a caretaker. Would you be interested?"

And when Miki, politely as she could, refused his offer, he listened to her with that frigid priest's air, patted her shoulder, and said, "If that's how you insist things must be."

"Then he left me, and I was already at the pawnshop. Creep." Miki frowned down at the shamisen. "I had time to put it away and get into an argument with Kahlil before you showed up. Sorry I didn't mention it sooner, but, like I said...we've all been busy."

"Did you check the shamisen for recording devices? Tracking devices?"

"Of course. There's nothing, it's unmolested."

Naturally. Cicero would never hurt an instrument. "And did you remember to thank him? For bringing you the instrument, I mean."

"Yes, of course. I'm not stupid, Dominia. I've seen the public service announcements since I was a toddler."

Ah, the PSAs: ads in television and magazines and Internet videos that explained to humans how they should behave if they ever met a martyr. Most humans went their whole lifetimes without needing the information—those who lived in Asia might never see a martyr at all, let alone merit one's attention—but, much as all people knew from early on that, in the event of immolation, they were to "stop, drop, and roll," so, too, did they know that being alone with a martyr meant staying calm, friendly, and respectful. Particular emphasis was placed on the last directive, as certain subsets of martyr populations were arrogant and prone to quick offense. Cicero, as it happened, was often cited as the textbook example of this quality, for El Sacerdote made it clear that the world owed him reverence for his position in the Church, and that humans were totally subservient animals beside the martyr race. He was also well-known as the most violent Family member, and in any poll would have been recognized as the one most likely to take liberties with local laws. It was that temper of his. For instance, had Miki forgotten to thank him, he might have cited this as a form of entitlement on the girl's part; worse, he might have seen it as a deliberate slight. The Lamb's company helped, in large part, to keep him relaxed, his love of his brother being the single thing that might be said to humanize him. They were never apart for long. It should not have surprised Dominia that the entire Family had stopped at Kabul together.

"Isn't it a nice Family vacation," said the General to herself, calculating with relative certainty that Cicero and the Lamb had gotten on the Light Rail in Kyoto and been on the train the entire time. Lavinia and the Hierophant only joined them at martyr-ambivalent Almaty, as the girl was no more allowed to travel alone than was the Lamb. Now all of them were here. Waiting for her.

Let them. They could wait until the sun came up. In a few hours, she would be in possession of what seemed to all the world a full, normal set of human teeth. And the General would be missing an eye, but if that sacrifice was what it took to shake herself free of her Family's influence, she gave it with a glad heart. Especially if she could meet Lazarus without interference.

Now the question was whether Lazarus wanted to meet her.

XV

The Blood of Lazarus

Miki, like most children, possessed the miraculous ability to expunge all
recent trauma when given a toy. Thus, upon her early-morning airport
acquisition of the rental car while Akachi spent an hour replacing
Dominia's teeth, the human returned to collect the General and the
semiconscious (former) IT whiz with an attitude that indicated she
had put her frightful meeting with Cicero—along with Dominia's
reaction—from her mind.

"I can buy songs straight from this thing's dashboard! Did you know
all vehicles have access to J-Sing? What a wild world!" She wiggled to
the beat in the driver's seat of the cherry-colored, human-operated
coupé; in the General's opinion, not the most discrete getaway vehicle
around these parts. "I haven't ever owned a car, you know. They're so
expensive! All the licenses and taxes and insurance—give me a break.
I let other people drive me around."

"I'm sure there's no shortage," muttered Kahlil from the back seat,
one wary eye always on the dog that, happy for a car ride, panted away
while the city passed.

"Are you jealous?" Miki asked with a wrinkled nose. Dominia,
trying not to be annoyed, checked her face in the mirror of the sun
visor. The swelling beneath her eye patch had reduced to mild irritation. And her mouth, well—that was already healed, and had been
since moments before they left Akachi's. The dentist had marveled over

the speed with which the martyr body recovered. Such recovery was commonplace to the General, but she had to admit she was particularly grateful for the enhancement at a time like this, in a place like this, where there was no safety or sanity to be had.

Her regret was that her recovery speed meant she had no reason to linger and thank Akachi as profusely as she'd have preferred. The world as wide as it was, she would surely never see him again.

Too bad.

After folding up the visor, Dominia contorted in the passenger's seat to don the black niqab that would hide her face from Kabul's early risers along with its most bright and punctual one. Moving through the city on her own was bound to be challenging anytime, but it was set to be a downright tahgmahr in the sun. Her only advantage was that marathon, which would, she'd been told, tie up most of the city.

It was always good to see serious people coming together for fun. Too bad it had to be against her Family, though she appreciated that aspect now. She could use a bit of levity, knowing that the Hierophant floated around the city, haunting the start of the race. Waiting for her. As if she would bring him Lazarus! She supposed it had been worth a try—nothing ventured, nothing gained, as they said—but he had to understand that she was in no mood to be subservient to him. He had to know he wasted his time.

Yet—if it was absurd, why was she so bothered?

"You're awfully quiet over there, dude." Miki glanced at the hooded General. "You okay?"

"Thinking. Is there a password or something, Kahlil?"

"No. He knows who's acceptable and who isn't. If you're supposed to be let into a Lazarene ceremony, he'll let you in."

Annoyed to hear that, Dominia demanded, "Then he has to consent to seeing me at all, let alone coming with me?"

"Better hope he wants to see you." The Hunter lifted his eyebrows with a certain theatrical disdain. "I don't know why this is hard for you to grasp. The Hunters have operated in various forms for almost two thousand years: if it were possible for anyone on Earth to catch

Lazarus, my people would have him by now. You don't stand any more chance than they do. Far less. You're going to have to hope he wants to see you as much as you want to see him."

"I'm sure he will," said optimistic Miki, who never missed an opportunity to cheerlead. "He's got to! That's how the world gets saved. Lazarus comes to Cairo and together he and the Lady lead an army that brings about the final battle with the Hierophant."

To think, martyrs thought of the Abrahamians as a cult! Though, as cults went, Abrahamians were considered the most charming. An infantile permutation of the martyrs' own "true" faith, which the Hierophant brought with him from that (certainly fictional) planet called Acetia where martyrs ruled the land. She had, sometime in her centuries, been in frequent contact with all manner of human contraband for various roles in the military police; during this time, she discovered a positively ancient (positively filthy, positively illegal) United Front comic book series about a female vampire in scant clothes who came from a similar planet. Glancing through that by accident (because who read such trash, ha-ha), she had felt certain that this particular bit of his backstory was a myth; but even her skepticism about her Father's origin could not spur her into questioning his many opinions about God, and about other religions. It was as if something in his mythos had to be provably false to assure her the rest of it was true. That was the power of the Hierophant. He could wave a truth—a horrific truth—before the eyes of anyone, and in so doing render them silent by complicity. All martyrs were cannibals. Therefore, it was in the martyr interest to believe what the Holy Father said when he explained martyrs were the true master race, made in the image of God.

In fairness, their prejudice was more interesting than most human standards. It was not the color or the creed or even the moral character of a person that counted to the divine: it was possession of the sacred protein, which had raised them from the dead. The already metaphorical Bible was rendered in the martyr Church a massive series of metaphors for the protein, whose arrival was embodied in the second coming of Christ. This second coming was never outright stated to be the Lamb, for no true second coming would announce Himself, of course. But it was implied to the point that certain disdained human cults that had once been called Christian turned their prayers, instead, to the Lamb; and even some less-devout fringe Muslims and Jews confused the martyr Elijah with his namesake. These sects, appearing across the United Front and Europa, were not just left unmolested by the martyr government but held to the rest of the human world as shining examples of proper attitude. Subservience to martyrs was key to a long, semi-safe life.

Other, real Abrahamians despised this sort, whether they distinguished themselves as Jewish, Christian, or Muslim. Dominia had never cared for such groveling humans, preferring those Abrahamians such as Kahlil and Tobias. They insisted on maintaining a certain purity of their faith, keeping it all as martyr free as it had always been—except to acknowledge the obvious fact that, if there could be said to be an earthly embodiment of the figure of Satan, the Hierophant was he. The martyrs were hardly more than demons: real devil worshipers who needed, from the popular perspective, extermination. This was where the Hunters came in. This was also where Dominia sometimes came in, because—not always, but sometimes—Abrahamian houses of worship, whether church or mosque or synagogue, became hubs of anti-martyr terrorist activity. These needed shutting down. Most attendants of such places were good citizens. These, the General sought to protect while Governess; but she had long since learned how to tell the difference between the two groups of humans, based on a lifetime spent campaigning against their violent variations. She had broken up more than a few Hunter cells attempting to operate across her Father's territories, but never during an Abrahamian service.

Lazarene services, however, were a different matter. Dominia had never been privy to Lazarus's coming and goings and had always considered him as fictional a character as the Lady, or her Father's martyr planet. However, she now knew that after Lazarus visited an area, his followers kept the ceremonies running in secret: so Miki explained to Dominia on the way to the actual, physical music storefront (a rarity in those nights) where the ceremony was to be hosted. The whole thing was not dissimilar to the Lamb, who bled out every Noctisdomin; the local priests would collect every drop, for Elijah's blood was as sacred as it was physiologically vital to martyrs who were not engaging in nightly cannibalism. Such martyrs had no choice but attend Mass, yet houses were always packed with irregular worshippers when El Sacerdote and his sacred brother rolled on through.

Those Lazarene ceremonies that the General had broken up over the years were almost certainly not ones at which the man himself had been present; all the same, they always seemed outrageously crowded to her. He had probably passed through some years before and left his message, along with some of his blood, with a person he trusted to keep the ceremonies going in private until he could risk coming through the area again. Nobody knew which ceremony would be blessed by a personal appearance until the encryption was broken, at which time it was usually impossible for anyone nefarious to mobilize in sufficient time to reach him. There was no detectable pattern. He seemed to travel miles in the blink of an eye. Today he was in Kabul; last week, he had appeared in some obscure corner of South America after manifesting nowhere for a fortnight, which sometimes happened. Where would he end up next, if Dominia didn't lure him to Cairo?

"If he's supposed to be the Lady's partner, why doesn't he present himself to Her? I'm sure he knows where She is."

"He can't just waltz into Her house without bothering to help humanity! You're pretty selfish sometimes." As the martyr blushed, Miki laughed at her. "Humans can't be saved from martyrs and your Father's world without the blood of Lazarus."

"No wonder Christians can't play nice with you guys." The General checked her gun as Miki pulled the car to a stop along a line of shops tucked beneath a broad overpass, the sort of architectural feature that made her pine for San Valentino. "They must get offended when you talk about it."

"Some of them. Christian-identifying Hunters, especially. But it's true! Watch, you'll see. You'll drink his blood and something crazy will happen."

"I'm not going to drink his blood," scoffed the General, while Miki rolled her eyes and slid open the passenger door with the press of a button.

"Still stuck in your freaky-deaky martyr ways? Whatever. You have to get over it soon. You've spent all this time acting like we're a bunch of cults with messed-up beliefs, but why don't you look at yourself? If it weren't for Tobias, you'd have leftover skin cells in your teeth."

At Dominia's humbled silence, Miki sighed, released her seat belt, and leaned over to hug her martyr friend. "Look, I'm sorry."

"Don't be. You're right. I have to admit that my Father and my people are wrong. I have to change deep down inside—not what I'm doing, but what I believe. I just don't know if I can. Or if I'll be able to live with myself once I do."

"You have to live, idiot! I don't think we'll manage to save the world without you. We need an inside man, right? Somebody with knowledge of your Father's world. You can help us. And we can give you Cassandra."

Those words rolled over her with such cool promise that Dominia closed her eye, exhaling against the fabric of her veil. "Yes," she said as Miki patted her cheek and released her from the embrace.

"You'll be fine! Remember: if the legends are true, Lazarus has done all this before. Listen to him, and you'll end up at Cairo in no time."

"I will. Kahlil"—into the back seat, she thought to say—"I'm sorry."

"Don't worry about it." He lifted a hand to wave her away, along with her concerns. "It was time for a change in career, anyway. People who know too much can be dangerous to the Hunters...I'm sure you know how it is."

Did she ever. Basil had edged forward in his seat and now wagged his tail expectantly. "I suppose you want to come?"

The animal sprang over the center console, across her lap, and upon the pavement of the city.

"What *is* the deal with that dog?" asked Kahlil. Dominia slipped out of the car to shrug as the door shut.

"I'll let you know if I figure it out. See you around." With a pang of sorrow, the General waved to Miki through the window, and the woman who had become her friend waved back with a purse of her lips and a furrow of her glassy brow. Then, boldly, the Red Market priestess turned up her radio and hit the electric. The car whizzed off, destined for Cairo.

Alone with the dog before a storefront whose Arabic letters she could no longer read, Dominia squinted at the time of a distant clock-tower: 0400 hours, almost on the dot. The ceremony was supposed to start at four thirty, but she'd secretly hoped (selfishly hoped, according to Miki) to lure him away before it began. They could somehow acquire a vehicle of their own and get out of the sun before it rose. The marathon had already started, and the racers would be weaving through the city for several hours. Running until the dawn, and after. Something martyrs could never do. Attention would be focused on said race, so it wouldn't be impossible to steal a car, or…

The dog looked at her. She sighed, caught. "Why is my first thought always a criminal one?"

You know why, Basil's face seemed to say. Free to stop pretending he was ordinary, he shut his happy mouth and pranced in the direction of the store. To Dominia's surprise, the front door was open, and the pair emerged in the dusty store of antique and new records to find it empty. Aside from her footsteps upon the carpeted floor, she was most keenly aware of music. The choice of song was an old Front one, more popular with humans than with martyrs for the obvious reason that the theme of the song was the love of the singer's eponymous "Lady." Even so, it got the occasional cover in the Americas; therefore, she recognized it, but not this version, or this accent. It might well have been the original. Had it been a new version, one of the heavily mixed, grinding bass modern songs, she might not have heard the soft drone of a familiar voice before she noticed the blue light of the holo-vision emitting in the otherwise unbroken dark. That nasal tone made her skin crawl with irritation no matter where she heard it: but to hear Theodore here? Her baby brother was in the middle of saying: "—times, we must come together as one nation: one people beneath the brilliant banner of the United Front, and the Hierophant."

She cringed. There he was, floating behind the counter, no doubt left on for her. Lo and behold, his doll-size hologram sat behind the desk of her office. She would never adjust to seeing that simp sitting there.

"But there are those who do not believe in the cause: who wish to divide our great nation amid this tenuous transition of power. This is why I am tightening border security in and out of the Front, and am issuing a temporary stay of applications for travel visas. Those of you who had legitimate reasons to leave the country on business or even pleasure, I'm sorry to say a certain former Governess and her terrorist organization ruined it for the rest of us. As for said terrorist organization"—he must have meant René's refugee ring and the Hunters behind it—"we are doing all we can within our borders to detain and punish every member for his or her part in this sordid effort to undermine our nation's unity."

Theodore was, by far, the newest addition to the Holy Family. In his human life, he had been a doctor of some small acclaim who had, in a turn of apparent luck, been selected to watch over young Lavinia, whose first twenty-four years of existence resembled death in all ways, including lack of pulse or organ function, but for one: she grew. When she was around ten, Theodore graduated medical school, and a few years later, he had kissed enough asses to catch the attention of the wrongest right people one could hope to know. Thus, he found himself overseer of a sleeping princess for over ten years, and when she awoke, his service was rewarded by martyrdom, and, the greatest honor possible, adoption into the Family. He had been there when she awoke, and that miracle of all miracles that a once-tiny body should have grown while dead was overshadowed by the greater miracle: that twenty-four years of clinical death might end in sudden life. Why Theodore reaped the reward for this achievement of the protein, Dominia would never understand. As he exclaimed with joy, "With that in mind, I'm pleased to announce the initiation of our long-term space reallocation program!" she could not help but think his reward should have been the ending of his life.

Ghettos were the first step to genocide. She had known them to be coming but had not anticipated them so soon and could not stand to hear of them now. She kept up with snatches of Theodore's babbling explanation but found her mind drifted off; she turned off the holo-vision, because she didn't need to hear him to know what he would say. The rationalizations would be the same as they'd ever been: something about how the most recent wave of immigrant humans represented a dangerous trend in immigration, where, rather than good, hardworking human families coming to contribute to civilized society or labor as the servants of martyrs, people flooding through the borders came to incite rebellion amid their human compatriots. Yet, now that they were there, they could not leave. Ones already in the country needed to be contained, though this was a concept always delivered in terms as whitewashed as possible. People were sensitive.

Dominia, however, was not sensitive. She knew what would happen and recited it in the silence of the shop as Basil led her around the counter to the poster-hidden door that revealed the basement stairs. Humans would be herded like chattel into ghettos, then camps, with healthier ones slaughtered and distributed for food to United Front population centers where martyrs thrived in happy neighborhoods the way humans once had. Many immigrant humans had worked hard amid their neighbors to earn and maintain their homes, their lives, and their families; martyrs hungered to steal that away. Those nice houses would be redistributed to more deserving hands by Theodore as he played favorites in his term as UF governor; those lives would be ended and used to sustain the lives of so-called higher beings; and those pretty, talented children who had once been the future of humanity in the Front (a flicker of hope that Dominia had inspired by the notion that things could change, and humans and martyrs could both work together to meet the future in an optimistic way) would become martyr children. Martyr children who, like Dominia, would grow up to hate the parents they felt abandoned them, either by getting themselves murdered, or by accepting their child's fate and moving on. To a developing and confused mind, a crime nonpareil.

This life was unsustainable. Small wonder she had snapped, albeit slowly, with the death of her wife. After all, it was not so much the death of her wife that had crippled her. Rather, in the midst of that hurricane of absolute emptiness, after René had approached her with promises of Lazarus, she had been invited to a military conference hosted by her Father. The military conference wherein he had announced Project Black Sun.

"Can you remember warmth on your face," he had asked the room packed with high-ranking generals, seeming, as ever, to ask Dominia in particular. "Remember what it was to live and move in the world without fear of the sun? We may be the children of God, but that is why we are hampered by His greatest creation. Without the danger the sun presents, we would be gods, ourselves."

There was a way, he claimed. A way martyrs could walk in the sun. "It seems like a fantasy from where we stand, but the means exist. Humans are in possession of it, and do not even know! Over the next two years, Cicero and I will roll out a plan to acquire these means: and the fine men and women in this room will help me. The world is ours. We need to take it."

A whole world of ghettos. A planet, at constant risk of people like her. The horrors humans endured in the Front paled beside those the world would see if martyrs moved freely. The thought terrified even the General. It had driven her here, and it found her now, along with a dog, knocking at the heavy locked door into which the hidden stairs terminated. A peephole was revealed, then snapped shut. She was close to annoyed when the door opened and there, exactly as she had pictured him, stood Lazarus: a resemblance to imagination so unexpected that she almost fell back against the narrow steps while Basil bolted past her, into the room.

"There you are, Dominia," said the man, a stranger she nonetheless knew. His eyes, pale blue as Basil's, crinkled despite his crabby tone. "Take that damn thing off. You're not fooling anybody."

"I—" Faltering to find he had already turned away, the General removed the niqab and bundled it beneath her arm. The room into which she followed him looked more like an addiction support group than a church. Sweet incense was replaced by humid mold, and pews were nowhere to be seen. Folding chairs had been arranged in the tight space, and a rickety podium served for a pulpit upon which the thickly bearded man resumed arranging a bowl, a dagger, and some napkins. "Do you know me?" she asked, and he said without looking, "Of course I do."

Though she studied his face and felt the familiarity of imagination in his features, she no more truly recognized him than she could divine what race he might have been while human, or his age. For a martyr to achieve grayed hair was an impressive feat: accomplished, to the General's knowledge, only by her Father. But Lazarus looked older than even he, face lined with deep furrows doubtless caused by centuries of nomadic living and, if Miki's stories were true, infinite lifetimes' worth of knowledge. However, old or no, no one lived forever, and she had a hard time buying the story that the world ran itself on repeat. If he did know her, it was from the news.

"If you know me, do you know why I'm here?"

"I know why you think you're here, and I know you're going to be disappointed. Do *you* know why you're *actually* here?"

At her blank look, he lifted the dagger and said, "You're going to help me," while slitting the forearm beneath his robe. Even the battle-hardened General winced to see such an abrupt spray of blood. Basil, who had been sniffing all around the room, bounded to the holy man's side. "Hey, kiddo," he said to the dog, and Dominia asked, "Do you know him, too?"

"Of course I know my good-for-nothing son." He bled into the bowl with a casual expression, unmoved by the bafflement that bloomed in Dominia's voice.

"Your *son*," she clarified, as if it would make any more sense coming from her own mouth. It did not. As the holy man grunted the affirmative, she studied Basil with a kind of grim clarity.

It shouldn't surprise her the old man was crazy, she supposed. It was just—well, it made her job more difficult, didn't it? She already saw herself trying to drag a lunatic to Cairo and wondered if it wouldn't be better (certainly easier) to drop him off with her Father after all. But, before she followed that train of thought to its depressing station, he had tied off his arm and dabbed at the blood with the napkins. "You need a daub of this blood before you can join the ceremony, or they'll never accept your being here."

Almost laughing, brows lifting above her remaining eye, she asked, "Can't we tell them that we did?"

"Sure we can, but you can't tell me." As her laughter faded, she realized he stared at her mouth. "Show me your teeth."

"What—"

He was around the podium and reaching for her with hands almost certainly unwashed. Grimacing, Dominia leaned away until Basil leapt behind her and, paws against her back, shoved her into Lazarus's path. Like he checked a horse, the mystic lifted her upper lip, then shoved her away with a sigh of agitation and a flurry of motion from his hands. The meaning was apparent after a few repetitions.

You know sign language, don't you? For slaves, right?

Yeah, she signed, as displeased to acknowledge that as she was to have had her gums probed by some homeless guy's grubby finger. *Don't you sign at me like I'm the one who decided to start muting and deafening uppity gossips.*

I'm not. I know that was Cicero, and way before your time. Anyway—his hands fluttered together in a dismissive wave and he edged back to the podium—*sorry. I saw the eye patch and forgot for a few minutes that just because you've made one good decision doesn't mean you've made two. Sometimes I get sentimental when I see you again.*

"I've never seen you in my life," she exclaimed aloud, echoing her sentiments with hand gestures and a roll of her eye at the severity of his look. *Never in my life.*

Not in this one, he agreed. *You never remember anything. Consider yourself lucky.*

And you?

Every time I'm martyred, I remember everything again. It's my blood.

The blood you want me to drink, she signed with an arched brow of skepticism for the rust-stained basin. *The blood that my Father says is a sin. The blood that humans sometimes kill each other for, that we kill humans for even speaking about. The blood that works miracles.*

Yeah. Imagine being full of it.

Unable to resist her wry smirk, she signed, *Oh, I imagine you're full of it, all right*, and Lazarus cracked something of a grin beneath that unkempt beard. *So why aren't we speaking?* she asked as another knock rang against the door. Her muscles tensed. Before responding to it, Lazarus lingered to deliver a disturbing explanation.

It's Dr. Akachi, he signed before indicating they word-shorten the man's name to a gesture that indicated either the sign for an elephant, or somebody who spent a lot of time ingesting parts of male anatomy. *He's listening through those nice, new teeth of yours.*

Oh, yeah.

This Lazarus guy was certifiable.

Right?

She still reeled from this schizophrenic accusation when the old man opened the door and the first worshiper, the store owner, stepped into the room, chatting in Arabic, then crying out when he saw the General. Before he got too deep into what universally read as a plea for them to escape with their lives, Lazarus stopped him and said something that left his host's expression, at best, dubious. While the men had a conversation, Dominia turned to lay Basil with an annoyed look. Did the dog sign, too?

What is this shit about Akachi? Can't you see this guy is nuts? You're not his son, you're a dog. Why don't you do something?

With those too-cute eyes turned up at her, Basil's tail gave just one wag. The animal was too polite to point out that she was as crazy as Lazarus, signing at a border collie as though it understood. Yet, it was too obvious that it *did* understand. Wasn't it?

Oh, she needed real help. Cassandra's death had done something to her, that was for sure. Miki was right to be worried; she'd started to feel concerned, herself.

"Hey." Lazarus caught her attention once more. *Mehrang here wants proof that you mean to join the Lazarenes for good. It's been almost a thousand years since the last martyr converted. Can't say I blame him for his concern. Looks like you're going to have to do something to prove you're trustworthy, huh?*

Lamb, she signed, glancing over at the bowl.

Lazarus, he corrected on his way to the podium. *It's painless, I prom-ise. Get over the taboos of your culture. If you're going to hell, it won't be because you drank my blood.*

Is *there a hell?* she asked, reluctantly edging toward the podium, as anxious as she'd been when, at fifteen, she was first forced to take full part in a martyr service and have the blood of the Lamb.

If there is a hell, it's almost certainly this world. Calling in Arabic, Lazarus waved the man over to witness Dominia's conversion. The human was as uncomfortable standing near the martyr as the mar-tyr was uncomfortable with what was about to happen. Would she experience something tangible? Would she feel a shift in her own spirit? Surely no. Surely she was just repulsed because, well—it was an intimate thing between martyrs, the sharing of blood. She wasn't eager to taste this random man's. But even the dog studied her. The General pursed her lips.

What was she doing, hesitating like this meant anything at all? There was no point. It was a tiny gesture to make them trust her. Take a dot of blood and talk Lazarus into Cairo. Simple enough. Bracing herself, she dipped a fingertip into the crimson meniscus, and lifted it, stained, to her lips.

Not even the taste was extraordinary! An average martyr's blood, the same as any other. Intriguingly impotent, which was why so many humans ingested it without being martyred—but, aside from that, the same as any man's.

There, signed Lazarus, gesturing toward Dominia. After the human expressed something in Arabic, Lazarus nodded: Mehrang did, too, and offered Dominia his hand.

What did he say? asked the General. Lazarus smiled.

He asked if you would be assisting me today. I told him "of course."

Of course, signed Dominia with irritation. The next knock resounded upon the door.

To what had she agreed?

XVI

Prisoners' Mass

An hour later, Dominia was no longer clear on what she'd expected from the Lazarene ceremony. Some great miracle, she supposed. Some sign of power. Yet, in a way, she had expected this, too: this grinding hour of an old man using sign language to preach to his ramshackle parishioners while in her former periphery. She was forced to turn her head if she wished to see him sign, but he had assigned her the task of holding the bowl of his blood and greeting those (understandably reluctant but incredibly bold) men and women who, in the hurry to kiss Lazarus and taste his blood, looked past all the horrors the General had committed—or had, of late, been accused of committing. Therefore, her understanding of the sermon's start was limited to those glances she stole, but not limited by language. Universal Sign Language had been taught in almost all human schools regardless of nationality since 1200 AL or so, right alongside arithmetic, history, and all the others. Some of these people, she suspected, had not gone to school, and some were children too young to keep up with his words. All told, about thirty followers were in attendance, and those who were not rapt to the motions of the old fellow were riveted by the interpretive whispers of their companions. They watched from the line that led to the bowl, then from their seats, hands folded and faces eager with hope. Those listeners not interpreting were so silent they might have been dead. A few kids too small for even the explanations of their parents had accepted with distaste the bitter substance, then been allowed to gather around the happy dog in the corner; even they seemed to sense the need for silence. Perhaps Basil told them so himself, the General thought as the last worshiper tapped a fingertip of blood upon their tongue and hurried to the edges of the insufficient seats.

Now, Dominia was free to turn her attention to the service. She had caught pieces: the theme, she'd discerned, was forgiveness.

If there's a singular, personal, almighty sentience to the divine forces running the cosmos, I don't think I've met Him: but I know I've met all of you tonight. And when I look into the eyes of the people in this room, I see walking, talking, conscious fragments of the divine, because nature is divine. You are divine. And nature that has evolved to the point of consciousness is true divinity. It is a god that has emerged from a tree, or a statue that has sprung to life. When that emerged consciousness becomes conscious of its own divinity, that consciousness may heal itself, and its body, and its world. When that soul emerges, it is immortal: and that which is immortal is so eternally. I am called a martyr, but my blood will not martyr you. If it did, it would offer a false immortality. An extension on your prison sentence in this world. But prison should not be a place of punishment: it should be a place of reformation. And a prison does not contain prisoners, alone. It has guards, and wardens; janitors, cooks, and nurses. It has holy men to save the battered souls of the living prisoners, and to placate the ghosts of the victims that have followed them to their cells—for the prison also needs the victims of crimes, without which it would have no prisoners. The building of the prison takes much time and planning and many hands, and all those employed for the purpose have been given wealth and good lives in return. They have since died, for a prison requires many generations if it is to be established long-term.

He looked at Dominia. *And a prison also has visitors. Those who stay, even for a short time, to comfort the condemned. They do this generous act through a combination of circumstance, free will, and love; after all, they would never visit such a place if their loved ones were not within. When their visit is terminated, it causes the prisoner great pain. But we martyred prisoners carry their company with us forever.*

Cassandra flashed through the General's mind in such a painful manner that her eye filled with hot tears, and she was forced to weep in front of a room full of humans if she wanted to see what this ragged bastard rambled about. And, oh, *what* a bastard! Making her cry. His mission accomplished, he focused on the crowd again.

Humans are not prisoners. Martyrs are. You all agreed to be here, though you do not remember it. Even the martyrs agreed to be here. Even I, tired as I am, agreed to be here. I am here for you. I am here, not because my blood is a key to your prison cell, but because my blood will reveal that never will you be prisoner unless or until you make the choice to become one. When you choose a life of misery and violence, when you inflict pain on others, when you take from their mouths or bodies to satiate yourself, it is you who will suffer most. You will be made a prisoner of this world and blinded to all that is higher. You will seek and seek and never find, like thirsty, starving Tantalus. But when you choose a life of joy and love, and heal your brothers, and allow the world to feed you, you will never starve or thirst. You will never die. You will be free: and you will see upon your passage to a higher state someday that you have never not been free, and never not been divine.

The sun is a blessing, he summarized. *It is a gift that brings all life and all things. But a prisoner never sees the sun. Not without good behavior, and the help of a guard.* His hand landed on Dominia's shoulder. She started, even though she'd seen him reach for her. With one hand, in common Arabic, in dying Farsi, in universal English, he said, "Never forget. Though they be terrifying, though they may rape the nurses who heal them and stab the guards who protect them from themselves: none in the prison suffer more than the prisoner."

This was nothing like a martyr ceremony. Where was the unfeeling pomp? The prayer-bruised knees? The acrid incense? The gilded icons and bright stained glass? Where were those moments for her to get lost in her own thoughts and feel nothing? That was what she missed. Where was the emptiness that came with a martyr service? Where was the freedom from looking so closely at her own inner substance that she had to cover her eye, lest her weeping be observed more than it already had? The hand Lazarus still rested upon her shoulder patted, then lifted to her head to draw it to his heart.

"It has been over three hundred years since Dominia has seen the sun without fear," said the old man in English, signing around her for those Arabic speakers who did not understand. "But the sun gives life. The sun gives power. It has always given us power—it has always given us everything. What you have now is the ability to access this power, though it is harder for humans to see without willful practice, meditation, and prayer. When you are in duress, you may well understand. You, all of you, have within you now that substance that allows the body to transcend this place as much as the soul. You possess that which has protected me from danger all this time." He released Dominia and stared hard into her eye.

"If you follow me, and are a careful student, you will learn how to achieve this bodily escape. Even the prisoners among you will bask in the glory of the sun. I will show you how it is I've come to do all this."

She might have asked him what "this" was, if it did not become self-evident the second he disappeared.

Dominia's gasp was but one of a chorus that rose soon rose into climactic clamor. As heads whipped toward those of neighbors to ask what happened in tones no longer hushed, a flurry of movement drew the General's attention. Basil bounded through his circle of admirers, past the shocked worshipers, and to the door at which he pawed. He was unable to work the round knob, but he was able to demonstrate urgency. Her motions swift as those of the animal, she rushed down the makeshift aisle and regretted how a few humans uncomfortable with the martyr's company winced away. No time to linger for apologies: she threw open the door, and the border collie sprang four stairs at a time, confident that Dominia scrambled behind. She had not exchanged a word with the dog, yet was positive of its intentions. Could a dog be the son of a martyr? Lazarus's blood was impotent for means of martyring, or so she'd heard over the years. It was not a metaphor for the dog's suspected martyred condition. What did it mean?

Upstairs, the storefront remained empty, with the front door still locked from within: but raucous sounds pervaded the room as though a thousand marchers streamed through its aisles— caused, Dominia thought, by the holo-vision. It had been turned on again, and switched from Theodore's smarmy face to a far more graphic scene. An Arabic broadcaster, safe in his station, spoke with hurried gravity in words

Dominia did not understand, but the gruesome models of light did the translating for her. Before her eye, and those of the cameras, a river of joyous runners ran through Kabul's streets. The first group of "serious" racers had already finished, and now a great mass stumbled through, looking better fit for Halloween than a marathon. Cow costumes, mermaid costumes, bee costumes, djinn and ghost and zombie costumes, naked runners: but, most especially, runners dressed up as parodies of the Hierophant who, in their oversize suits and various states of decomposition, sparked an age-old, ingrained sense of sacrilegious offense until she remembered she could laugh. The Hierophant probably also viewed it with a good sense of humor—superficially, anyway. Every action he took was formulated for its ambiguity, and his doings were so consistently patient, good-natured, and generous that, when it came to complaining about him, no one who knew him could vocalize the distinct root of their mistrust. By the time they had a clear reason, it was too late—as late as it had been for Cassandra. Oh! Opening the door that night: that night after ninety years of love. Ninety years, unable to prevent or expunge one moment's tragedy.

Yet, the images before her cleared her spell of self-pity, for they were perhaps worse than even that odious discovery. The runners, shots of whom were absent any journalists, smiled, laughed, and were frequently joined by those who stood watching the race on the sidelines: people in casual clothes, sometimes even business clothes, despite the weekend, ran in dozens between their costumed fellows. They ran, and ran, and the camera feed cut to their destination, Hashmat Kahn Lake, where floated the bodies of all those winners who had drowned themselves in waters ankle deep. Smiling followers pursued with merry laughter, floating the bodies of serious runners off to the center of the lake so as to kneel facedown in the shallows. A few intrepid marathoners sprinted through the water, to its center, in search of a deeper patch in which to drown effectively.

Her brain almost failed to comprehend the scene. Then, a racer in a curly blonde wig hefted a rock from the water to crush her own skull in particular savagery. Lavinia's doing. Dominia turned toward a noise at the door and found Lazarus standing before it.

"We have twenty minutes to sunrise," said the mystic over the drumbeat of feet amplified hundreds of times by the open door. The marathon's route (perhaps thanks to Lavinia) included the overpass under which the music store was tucked. "Do you understand? That means we have fifteen minutes to save Kabul from your Family."

"They'll be forced inside by the sun, too. Whatever we start can be finished in their hotel."

"We won't be going inside when the sun comes today. At least, you won't."

"Where will I go?"

"Same place the dog's going." The old man stepped out of the store, and once more disappeared when Dominia pursued him onto the noisy street. Cursing, she studied the riotous overpass, then turned around to ask Basil—herself, she supposed—what she'd ought to do—

But the dog, too, was gone.

"Basil," she called in the silence of the shop. "Here, boy, we don't have...Lamb." The title crossed her lips in the wind of a heavy sigh that marked the moment she turned heel and ran as fast as she could in the direction opposite the marathon.

To be fair, marathons were rather less impressive when one was a martyr. Everything from increased reflexes, to improved metabolic efficiency, to simple muscle mass differences, meant that martyr was to man what cougar was to house cat. Consequently, humans tended to favor athletics as a hobby more than martyrs did. It was more impressive and more vital that a human maintain their endurance. As active as she was, Dominia had always resided among that niche of martyrs partial to watching the human Olympics. This made her something of a nerd in her culture, but she had never been ashamed to like what she liked, and she had always been interested to see the physical development of mankind as chronicled in their Olympic statistics. Even in her life, the time it took the best of the best trained human Olympiads to run a mile had shaved off so many seconds that it had begun to approach the three-minute mark, hovering somewhere around 3:34.89, if she recalled the women's record—men had pushed their number down into the two-minute-something region.

A martyr's physical capabilities, meanwhile, were in excess of even those top Olympiads (which meant that they were unwelcome at the games, much to the General's profound dismay as a young girl). Of these, Dominia's physical capabilities were within the top percentile. Most acknowledged that the only martyrs capable of besting her in a brawl or match of wits were Cicero and, of course, the Holy Father. But a race? The General could outrace them any day. At her absolute physical peak, she could clear a mile in one minute and fifteen seconds; she was forever aggravated that she couldn't get it down to a clean minute, to render herself good as a low-speed self-driving buggy of the sort in gated communities established by those rare wealthy human families remaining in martyr territories. Granted, when she was running more than one mile, there was a significant drop-off with each subsequent. Add to that the fact that, though she was far from out of shape, neither had her third century of governance left her quite so honed as she'd been in her dual centuries.

This was all to say that she had to hope she was no more than five miles from the start of the race, if Lazarus's cryptic declaration was to be believed; if she was to have sufficient time to handle her Family and cure the racers before sunrise, it would be best if she had less than five miles. On top of her aggrieved emotional and physical condition, she was forced to run upstream, against that happy crowd so eager for her to join that sometimes they tried to turn her by the shoulders to get her going in the right direction. Well-meaning folks, these hypnotized sorts.

Another problem: she paused at the corner of one block when she recognized a storefront from the broadcast, feeling obligated to destroy a holo-camera set long since abandoned by its infected crew. The more sets she destroyed, the better. The memetic virus was much stronger in person than over a medium like television or radio—so far as the Family's experiments on the matter had discerned—but that did not mean it was without effect. People rushed down the street to join the race, having seen it on television in their apartments. These infected were obliged to take part in a happy mass suicide, motivated by Lavinia's fury. The General was ashamed she had failed to predict this result the instant Miki had explained the marathon's premise. Of course saintly Lavinia would react this way after one look at all these sacrilegious racers: these gross humans mocking her beloved "Daddy" and good uncles and poor, corrupted older sister. Of course this was the result of their presence in Kabul.

Of course this was the result of her running away.

A nearby electronics store, across a panoply of screens and holographic figures, demonstrated that the bodies had begun to pile up. Above her, even the light poisoning of the dense city could not hide the intensifying blue tint of the coming sun. She fancied her skin already burned, for mere knowledge that the blue wavelength of sunlight had such profound effects seemed sufficient to sicken her. It may have seemed silly that the tiny amount of light from electronics—enough to impact a human's sleep—could do a martyr harm, but that small amount of artificial blue wavelengths were good as shade compared to those belched by the unforgiving sun. Enough to kill a martyr frighteningly quick, especially with UV involved; even these predawn minutes were known to be dangerous. When Dominia had reached the cove in which she was destined to meet Cassandra, she'd already felt the gentle sting of spotty sunburn avoided. Now she was as concerned about her ability to endure the path to the marathon's origin as she was about how seared she'd be. All Cicero would have to do was slap her in the face, she mused, trying to make herself laugh amid her deep duress, and failing. As she paused to destroy another camera set, Lazarus appeared from the depths of the crowd and grabbed her arm.

"We don't have time for that." As he drew her forward, he urged, "Come on," and flung her through a space that didn't exist.

What a strange lurch! The world flickered. For a skipped beat, not a racer remained in sight. In the second during which she stumbled, it was through a strange velvet place whose darkness was not so much interrupted or overlaid by light, as it was embossed by vast bands of bent colors that emanated from the slats between her ribs and from elsewhere, too. They tugged her forward by the solar plexus, yet showed her so many other ways that she might go. She only recognized the tug as a sense of direction—and only recognized they weren't alone—when pulled out of that strange space by Lazarus, who ran, as normal, through the marathoners that made themselves once again present.

"What was that?" cried the General.

"Patience, please."

Hindsight exhibited hints of what her mind had experienced but not perceived: a carmine waistcoat, and the bitter scent of cigarettes. "I saw a man there."

"Right," he said. "My son."

Dominia could not find words to articulate her questions—*concepts* to articulate her questions. Her mind now struggled to parse from the ground great obstructions between which the racers were funneled, and she was shocked to recognize the grandstands rising at the head of the race. In that eerie flicker of reality, Lazarus had drawn her steps sufficient to take her several miles. She trembled in his grasp, so overwhelmed by her comprehension and her added confusion that, at best, she half saw the Family. They had assembled themselves to watch the chaos of a race that was now infinite, surpassing the boundaries of its starting line and stretching as far through Kabul as there lived people to be infected. Yet, she paid the tragedy no mind: she asked, voice hoarse, "How powerful are you, Your Holiness?"

"Don't get weird and religious on me! No titles, please. I'm a fraction as powerful as you. Now, get out there."

With one, sharp shove, Lazarus pushed her through the crowd and left her exposed beside the grandstand opposite that of her Family. Her eye met Cicero's; he rose in those same seconds in which she snatched the gun from her waistband. While veiled Lavinia cried out from beneath the Hierophant's parasol, Dominia expended bullets, but the effort was futile when the Lamb, also, rose from his seat. The first one missed El Sacerdote's shoe, polished for the occasion and matched to a suit that, still collared, was less garish than the Father's but by no means one of his typical cumbersome religious uniform; as he stripped off his jacket in preparation for the fist fight, a marathoner, by some stroke of the Lamb's ill luck, tripped over an untied shoelace and knocked the General's firing arm askance with such force that she did not just waste the bullet she had been aiming, but also its follower.

The next shot, by likewise remarkable luck when she decided to shift her target, ricocheted from the Hierophant's fat golden ring, and he uttered a noise of distaste audible even over Lavinia's shriek.

"Are you finished," called Cicero while the Lamb accepted his jacket and waded with him into the crowd. "Put down that gun! It's the weapon of the craven and the lazy. Fight me like a real woman and the Lamb won't need to be involved."

"I'll fight you whatever way it takes to kill you if you won't stop while you're alive."

"All for these?" The Family's priest waved about him, and in so doing, avoided taking a shot to the shoulder. "For these weak-willed fools manipulated into suicide with the words of a livid child in a grown woman's body? You would abandon your Family for *these*?"

"This was never about you! This was never about the Family, or treason, or terrorism. It was about Cassandra."

Sneering, Cicero thrust aside a few racers. While Dominia gritted her teeth and flipped her gun to use as a cudgel, the priest asked, "You would return her to life; is that right? Depend on the madness of pagans to accomplish what you know to be impossible? The protein is the only route by which we may have eternal life in this world. If that is scorned—"

"Cassandra didn't scorn the protein. She scorned this way of life." The handle of the pistol was meant to whip across Cicero's face, but with his most beloved brother there, he was close to unstoppable: he ducked with a full second to spare and tackled Dominia with such force that her head slammed against the metal bleachers. Garnet sparks burst in the eye still there. As she thought, with sympathy, of Kahlil, the priest forced her to the ground and slammed her skull once more—this time, against the concrete.

"Ninety years she lived this life, my sister, without complaint. You mean to say that you are free of sin in this? You don't think you had the slightest hand in how she died?"

"It was this Family." The words were hissed through a jaw clenched by Cicero's hand until he caught her fist. "It was this way of life, this Family, this whole fucking world! It was Father!"

"It was *you*, Dominia," snarled Cicero, as his free hand caught her gun in effort to break her fingers against it. "A healthy woman, satisfied with ninety years of marriage—"

"You don't know anything about our lives."

"Do you think such a woman would commit suicide?"

The word made Dominia ill. She had succeeded in not thinking on Cassandra's exact method of death so long that it came on her like it had the first time. That brutal surprise as the sound of the door's opening gave way to the discharge of her own gun.

All the shame in Cassandra's regretful eyes, locked forever on hers.

"It was Father." She had to say it through a layer of misting tears. "What he said to her that night, at Lavinia's party—I know that it was about."

"And you know"—he relaxed his grip on her hands—"Father is far from the only one culpable."

A third voice interrupted from across the clamor of madness. "Maybe not; but he deserves a lot of credit."

It was not the voice of the Lamb, but the voice of Lazarus. Heads turned to the source; in the distance, the Hierophant's eyes lit. The holy man stood with his ceremonial dagger poised against the throat of the Lamb.

"Sorry, Elijah," said Lazarus, tone causal, "but you should be used to this by now, right?"

The Lamb did not speak. Cicero showed his teeth, perfect and white and free of augmentation, but nonetheless sharp enough to elicit a lupine aspect. "So, Father was right. You brought your heretic to play."

"I brought her. Let the General go, or this dagger goes in his heart, and not his throat."

"You wouldn't." Cicero's pitch rose to that of uncharacteristic fear, and his body, in instinct's mistake, lifted toward his brother enough that the thrashing General freed the empty hand that he held by the wrist. As he looked back to her, his face written in layers of rage, the General clenched her teeth and, with the satisfying pop-and-splatter of gore, put out her brother's right eye.

Cicero's scream pierced the eardrums of those around, such that a few racers, even through their hypnosis, thrust hands over their ears with deep grimaces. A plethora of cameras formed a perimeter, all intended to capture the race, all transmitting a virus across Kabul, and now, all transmitting more evidence of Dominia's terrorism to the world at large. The Hierophant, wearing that same look of disgust worn when Dominia had shot Murph McLintock, handed Lavinia the parasol. Lazarus, meanwhile, seemed to have disappeared, leaving the Lamb standing there as calm as—

Well.

With her Father coming down the grandstand stairs, now was hardly the time to think in clichés. But what time was it? When was sunrise? Was this to be the moment of her death? What would it feel like? A thousand thoughts rushed through her mind as the Hierophant blipped out of existence (in a manner identical to Lazarus, it was worth noting) and appeared before her as if he'd been there the whole time. All those harried questions were laden with terror, and froze in that terror on his appearance; but, rather than tear out Dominia's remaining eye in return for Cicero's, or take her gun, or strike her in any way, he picked up his gasping son and slung the man, a few inches shorter than he, over his massive shoulder.

"It's always the same with you two, isn't it, Dominia? You and your brother have never gotten along."

"I always thought of him as more of an uncle."

"A matter of perspective, I suppose. Uncle, or brother: I will need your help to get him out of peril. And I shall require your help in protecting Lavinia."

The question was so strange, in this place, in this circumstance, that the General could not understand the words. "My help?"

Before he answered, the blast wrenched a hole through reality and responded for him.

XVII

Saint Valentinian

Until that moment, Dominia was sure she'd heard her life's loudest sound. A gunshot might not seem that loud. But it could be. One single discharge, looping in her mind in the world's most painful eternal recursion, blocking out all other noise, blowing out the world. That was loud.

How loud had Cassandra perceived that sound to be? Dominia pondered this when masochistic, and made herself sick in wondering. From within her wife's mouth, the discharge of the antique barrel's slender phallus must have sounded as loud as the explosion in Kabul, which, sufficient to rattle the ground for several blocks, shattered the street the way the gun had devastated the back of Cassandra's skull. But she never imagined what happened after that moment of death— that moment around which her mind swirled ever closer if she drifted too near the vortex of her sorrow. She did not contemplate any notion of eternity, for better or worse. It seemed from the General's jaded perspective that Cassandra's entire existence ended in that moment, when Dominia opened the door too late. Always a second too late.

There had been nothing in this physical world for Cassandra after that awful second of sonic disruption that marked the destruction of her brain. Martyrs had two irrecoverable organs: the heart, and the brain. Everything else grew back, or could be replaced with a cyborgan. But nothing could be done about those two physical main-stays of martyrs. A basic biological fact known the world around.

This had not been a cry for help. This had been a calculated decision that left Dominia as disoriented as now. Both times, she survived the tahgmahrish noise, and now, in Kabul, stood amid the screams of this *massa confusa* that might have been, for all she knew, her own charging back from the past. They must have been, at least partially: the screams of the humans were loud; yet, muted like a socked phonograph amid her Father's collection of antiques, they could have been miles away. It was the motion of the Hierophant's lips that drew her attention back to the present, and that helped her keen senses pierce the dense ringing to compile the meaning of his sounds. "We have a car," he was saying. She struggled to divine what he was getting at in the haze of the explosion; when it clicked as he said, "Come with us," she laughed.

"You want me to help you? I have to save these people from Lavinia's virus."

"You claimed before your quarrel was not with us; then, it cannot be with Lavinia." The spray of a semiautomatic weapon in the distance did not deter unharmed (even wounded) racers from resuming their run as if nothing had happened, with more ignoring the debilitated amid the rubble of the blast zone by the distant podium and most prominent camera set. The Hierophant placed a compatriot's hand upon her shoulder. "Will you help us?"

Before she spoke, the feedback of a microphone echoed through Kabul: the city's emergency alert system had been co-opted to announce the marathon. Now, it had been co-opted again, by a familiar voice whose inappropriate jolliness exceeded even that of the Hierophant.

"Ladies and gentlemen, there is no need to fear." Tobias Akachi didn't even bother to switch to Arabic, the prick. "The Hunters have heard your call of alarm. While your police waste their time at Lake Hashmat and the martyr terrorist runs rampant in your city, the source of the problem has presented itself for the slaughter! Miss Mephitoli? May I see you for a moment?"

Dominia leaned around the grandstand that had sheltered her from debris. Tobias lowered the microphone from where he stood surrounded by a bunch of armed and armored soldiers. With those perfect white teeth, he smiled, then called across the rubble- (and body-) filled pit that smoked with energy from the explosion. "I am sorry to see you have not secured Lazarus for us, but I am pleased, as I said, to see the bad teeth making up your Family are all here for the extraction. Even infamous Miss Lavinia! I suppose it is no use asking her to come along with us."

"What do you want with Lavinia," asked the General as the Hierophant set Cicero on his feet and rendered him, as usual, the responsibility of the Lamb, upon whom he leaned his bloodied face and caught his staggered breath. The drama queen.

Akachi, as though they were not present, enthused, "What does anyone want with Lavinia? As powerful as your sister is, a man could control the world. But I have so many questions—perhaps you could answer them for me."

"Go to hell." Dominia ducked back around the grandstand for a safe place to reload her gun. At that, the Hierophant spread his arms in a show of helplessness.

"How sorry I am to say, Tobias, that my daughter may be a troubled girl, but she is not a fool."

"You two know each other?" asked the aggrieved General. Her Father chuckled.

"I know him better than he does me, but we have some small association in this life, I admit. We have quite a lot in common, so far as I can tell."

"Then"—Tobias drew a gun from the tan fabric of his cloak—"perhaps it is a pity this will be the moment our association ends."

She had seen many people disappear that morning, but it was still uncanny to see the Hierophant blink out of existence and back into it five centimeters behind Tobias. As the dentist registered the event, he winked out of existence to the sounds of open fire.

Through clenched teeth—two of which were, indeed, designed to listen in on her private conversations—the General swore. She swore, not just for the observation that Akachi, head of the Hunters in Kabul and maybe all the Middle States, was also in possession of that same power as Lazarus and her Father. No: she swore because, after all the pain he had caused her, all the disgrace to her name and his responsibility in pushing Cassandra to suicide, she would greet dawn fighting by her Father's side.

The tone of the sky and the singe of her cheeks alerted her that they had, at best, five minutes. Darting around the corner, the General unloaded (by luck of the Lamb) three rounds and killed four men while the Hierophant snapped the neck of one, acquired his weapon, and put down three more. This much gunfire hadn't filled the air around her since Nogales, and it sent her into a conditioned response so efficient in open terrain that the DIOX-I couldn't have kept up. Before, she had needed the influence of the Lamb to clear the building due to problems of tight quarters and a clear outmatch in numbers and equipment: here, she was free. Here, she sang, first acquiring the ceremonial dagger that Lazarus had let tumble at the feet of the Lamb. With this, she meant to charge into the fray, but her Father called, "No," and, "Your sister."

The densely skirted girl crouched in a panic against the shelter of the grandstand. After ending the lives of some Hunters who charged around a corner, Dominia dashed to the side of her sister and caught her by the arm.

"Are you all right?"

The girl, paler than Dominia had ever seen her, shook with such violence that her older sister ached beneath the immensity of guilt. "I wanted to see the world with Daddy," Lavinia said, her pupils pinpoints. "I wanted to bring you home."

The poor girl. A soft heart was clay to the Hierophant. "Stay close to me and I'll keep you safe, all right?"

"Yes, Ninny, please."

Tearful, the Family's alleged superweapon clutched Dominia's forearm, and the General shifted her to reload. "Why would you do that to these people, Lavinia?"

"Didn't you see their awful costumes? It was terrible! They're disrespecting Daddy, and because they're disrespecting Daddy, they're disrespecting God."

"Our Father is not God."

"Of course not, Ninny. But he's closest to God on the whole Earth. He knows God."

"Your Father"—Tobias appeared in a blink before them and provoked a shriek from Lavinia—"is a liar."

"Why don't you join the race," hissed the girl, but the dentist laughed.

"I have taken the blood of Lazarus, thank you, and while I do not go in for the sacrilegious nature of his efforts to explain the phenomenon of his blood, the effects upon the body and the mind are undeniable. Your filthy pagan magic means nothing to me, witch."

While Lavinia squawked in indignation, Dominia leveled her gun with his face. "Why don't you show me how fast you can disappear."

The answer was "faster than a bullet." In her blind periphery, he reappeared, and she whipped right on Lavinia's scream to find him already pointing a gun at the General's face.

"Do you martyrs have time to drag this battle out? Dawn is minutes from breaking over the city's horizon. When the sun shows his golden face, where will your sister be? We can offer her immediate shelter if you'll send her with us. And if you hand her over, General, I am sure you and I can meet at some reasonable compromise."

"My daughters belong at home with their Family, Akachi." The Hierophant appeared behind him and pressed a rifle into the back of his head, for whatever good that might do. "Let them be."

"You are making a mistake by going with him." Tobias once more flickered out of existence; Lavinia, with a cry of relief, flung herself into her Father's arms to weep.

"There, there, princess, we'll have you home soon enough."

"I wish I'd never left," she lamented as he swept her off, the General racing alongside them and picking off scattered insurgents before accepting the assault rifle from her Father to act as their proper escort. While she continued mowing down anyone with a gun, keeping her bursts of fire short and even to prevent civilian casualties among the runners, the Hierophant did not seem inclined to stop shaming her to Lavinia.

"In all fairness to the big, bad world from which I have shielded you, it *is* often bad—but not often this bad. It takes a character wild as our dear Dominia to bring about this level of chaos."

"It's not my fault you followed me! And it's not my fault that Lavinia infected these people."

Their protector nailed a few snipers poised on fire escapes while the trio darted down an alley in pursuit of the Lamb and Cicero, who were already about to emerge on the other side; nonetheless, Lavinia insisted, "They deserved it!"

Dominia could have screamed, and almost had to over the battle. "No one deserves this! These are good people!"

With a pettish noise of disgust, the Hierophant ducked a spray of gunfire from behind and hurried Lavinia before him to hasten their escape. "Yes: humans are such good people, my girl! That is why they are trying to kill us because we are martyrs. Why they maligned us with the insulting marathon to which your sister took offense."

The alley's exit was close, but behind them it had filled with Hunters. Dominia wheeled about to dash backward amid her wild firing while she shouted, "That doesn't mean they all deserve to die."

"And they will not," answered the Hierophant, as, in a moment that seemed choreographed, the emergency alert system again booted up with the sound of feedback. No longer the voice of Tobias Akachi: to Dominia's relief, it was the voice of Lazarus, who'd taken advantage of a podium emptied by Hunters in pursuit of the escaping Family.

"To be, or not to be," his voice announced, "that is the question."

"You see," asked the Hierophant, smiling over his shoulder. "No harm done."

Throughout the city of Kabul rang the melancholy speech of Prince Hamlet, its English words capable of curing even those who knew no English. The effects were the same with reading the Japanese *Tale of Genji* to Spanish speakers, or even, in one remarkable instance, forcing an ailing human to look at a QR code that would have decrypted into an image of the "Mona Lisa" for a computer or digital implant—to a normal eye, was the same as any bar code, but it had some effect. The format in which the information of the fine art was represented did not seem to matter when it came to curing the memetic virus; so long as the information was presented to the ailing mind in any form, for any sufficient length of time, the will would be restored. A brain desperate for a cultural palette cleanse seemed to take what coherent information it got; or perhaps there was a deeper reason at work on another level, as Dominia would someday suppose.

As Lazarus continued on, "Whether 'tis nobler in the mind to suffer the slings and arrows of outrageous fortune, or to take arms against a sea of troubles and by opposing end them… To die," and Dominia shot down men, those many running citizens of Kabul began to slow, and stop; those watching from other countries who had felt compelled to drive or even fly to Kabul now found themselves in their cars or at the airport, baffled as to their own intent; and those earliest to heal, those quickest to regain consciousness, responded to the realization of what had happened with a citywide wail louder than any siren.

As the speech slipped into the subject of dreams, Dominia, Lavinia, and their Father emerged from the alley. Time was up. Sunrise stretched across Kabul, and as the *tanque* driven by the Lamb snarled to a halt before the ragged trio, the Hierophant turned to his former Governess. Studying the gun and deciding that forcing her into their car was not a valid option, he settled on his usual weapon: reason.

"Come with us, my girl. Come home now, and spare us this heartache. Are your false hopes worth this? Don't you see none of this would have happened—no one would have died—if you would have stayed at home? Come back, Dominia. Leave with us now, and it will be like nothing ever happened."

Lavinia's tear-stained, debris-smudged face gazing up at her, her Father's expectant, all-knowing black eyes barreling into her.

The empty spot upon her breast where Cassandra's diamond should have been.

"I can't." Her words were hoarse as she stepped away. "I'm sorry."

"You would rather meet the sun than admit you were wrong," shouted Cicero from within the vehicle, even as the Holy Father stuffed protesting, crying, and pleading Lavinia into the *tanque*. All the while, the girl screamed, "But Ninny! She'll die!"

"It is her choice," said the Hierophant, pulling the door shut behind him. "Drive."

Her Family peeled through the streets of Kabul; stomach in knots, Dominia faced the alley down which she'd come.

Save for corpses, it was empty. The remaining insurgents had seen they walked into a death trap and turned tail, either to run, or to try and acquire Lazarus, whose words came to their abrupt end with the phrase "Thus conscience does make cowards of us all," and another, swift-to-end hail of gunfire.

The General dropped her stolen gun and hovered in the shadow of the building as dawn glowed across the cured—but not yet near healed—city. What was she to do? Where was she to go? How was she to find Lazarus?

"Follow me," he had urged her.

She would see the sun, he had promised her.

She studied her own body with a wretched feeling and wondered, again, what it was like to die. "And thus the native hue of resolution is sicklied o'er with the pale cast of thought"—her voice was tight and humorless as her soft laughter—"and enterprises of great pitch and moment with this regard their currents, turn awry, and lose the name of action."

Although she laughed, laughed at herself and the (in)appropriate-ness of the soliloquy amid the citywide grief of Kabul, she could not make herself step into the sun. She could not believe that she was not reading into his words, that it was not all wishful thinking on her part. Yet, as Tobias Akachi appeared before her while his men called from the distance, she could not deny her eye.

"Alone at last, eh, Miss Mephitoli?" She no more bothered to level her revolver at him than she usually would have at her Father, and he smiled at that. "I am sorry to see you were abandoned by so many: first, Miki and Kahlil; then, Lazarus and your dog; now, your Family."

"I'll be meeting at least one of the pairs you mentioned elsewhere. For the others…I don't know what to say about them."

"You do not need to defend the actions of those who have abused you, General. We all must reach our breaking points, and rise against our traitors and slavers. If we do not, we are as good as dead!"

"I'm already as good as dead, whatever I do." She studied the hardening edge of the building's shadow and pressed against the clay bricks behind her. "You and your men seemed pretty comfortable with the idea of killing me a few minutes ago."

"When you tried to kill us, we needed to defend ourselves! It was your Father who began the fight, remember." She made no comment. "I see you are cross about the teeth."

"You're the most stunning hypocrite I've ever met. The Hunters are terrorists."

"To your people, perhaps."

"And yours. Don't play games. Your organization has killed more humans than martyrs over the years."

"All in the name of higher justice. The most important thing is that your species is wiped off the map. The cost required to achieve this goal does not matter to God."

"Met Him, have you?"

"I know nothing more of God than any other Christian man; but I will say that I know more than your blasphemous Father, who profanes the Word at every turn he may. He has so profaned the Word of God that he has dropped a veil before your eyes, and the eyes of all your people."

"My eyes are—" She fought back an expression of annoyance. "My eye is open." Although, it was rather obvious she did not believe it, and she was not at all surprised by Tobias's look of distaste down the death-filled alley behind her.

"Then perhaps you had better put it to use, General. Do you suppose those men you killed to be nothing more than dreams? Is that how you won your thousand battles?"

This blistered her, and had she not been restrained both by the increasingly spectacular sunlight and Akachi's supernatural capacity to blink out of sight, she would have killed him then and there to show him how she'd made so many victories. But that was what he wanted, wasn't it? Wanted to goad her into striking him so he could mock her. She almost hoped so; because, if she was just projecting her own expectations upon him, well, maybe Miki was right. Dominia needed to adjust her attitude toward herself before she learned to get along with anyone else. With forceful calm, she shaped the words. "I remember the men and women I've killed. If not their names, then their faces. How many faces do you remember?"

The son of a bitch laughed at her. "Why do you bother, Miss Mephitoli? Do you think that your remembering them makes up for what you have done? Think of all their mothers."

"Did you come here to shame me, Tobias?"

"No, my friend. I came to speak reason to you. I am concerned about what will happen if you will not be reasonable." Around the corner of a distant mosque flooded a troop of Tobias's men; Dominia rolled her eye along with her shoulders. "We cannot afford to let you die at this juncture—and it will cost a great many men, I suspect, to take you alive."

Her lips curled into a spray of her own bitter laughter. "So you need me for something? Want to find out about my Father's Project Black Sun?"

"My friend, I know all about your Father's project." This shocked her, until he went on with a pleased lift of his brows: "Monsieur Ichigawa was compliant."

"I didn't tell him anything of value."

"You didn't have to. You told him that your Father had a plan to allow martyrs to walk in the sun. That was all I needed to hear to know his intentions."

"Know him that well, do you?"

"No." The dentist's glasses, which had darkened with the rising of the sun, did not hide the way his eyebrows lifted to the top of his glittering bald head. "But I do know Lazarus that well. At least, better than you."

Dominia glanced into a cyan sky that her eye, blinded by that glare, collaged with great shards of noncolor. "You mean to say that Lazarus is going to help my Father?" She heard, as she spoke, the echo of her Father's commandment—declaration, prophecy—that she would bring Lazarus to him during the marathon. It had been the other way around, in the end—but Akachi's next supposition provided a particle of relief.

"No, Dominia. I do not proclaim to know the future as does your profane Father, for only God may know that. I do know that Lazarus is not the type to help your Father. You, however, may be."

"So why not kill me?"

His men assembled behind him, awaiting his word to attack or subdue her. "Because without you, there will be no one to kill your Father. If you are not alive, the magician will depart to a world where you yet live, and the martyr stranglehold on this world will never find relief."

"'Magician,'" repeated the baffled General while he ignored her and barreled on. "I cannot seem to discern the exact nature of his role. But he has made it most clear to me—as I have always believed—that this era in which we find ourselves is a tipping point. The mass panic in Kabul today is but a symbol for the state of this world: and when the chaos calms, either martyrs will have closed their stranglehold on the planet, or humans will shrug them off and rise to dominance once more. The cowards of humanity's past valued an uncertain future in an uncertain world above solving a problem that has grown worse by the year. But we have a duty to this world, Miss Mephitoli. We humans, that is."

"I'm a martyr," she admitted, "but I'm not like the rest."

"No: you are not like the rest. You are much more important. If the magician is to be believed, we would all do well to keep you alive. Your death, he has insisted to me, shall mean the end of the human world. Even if you live, you may yet choose to bring it on. A true apocalypse."

She tried to laugh in the face of his superstition, but she found she could not when she thought of the Red Market and the Lazarene belief in the cyclical nature of time in the universe. "I would never help my Father with his designs against humanity." Best to play it dumb. "I've changed."

"You have not changed, General. Had you changed, you would have apprehended your Father and come with us without spilling human blood. You are the same mass murderer you were before."

"You don't know anything about me. It's not up to you to say whether I've changed."

"Until you can admit that you are no better"—Tobias drew his gun, and the General readied hers—"you are a liability. I understand you lost your wife? That she killed herself." She did not speak, for she could not untense her jaw, and the dentist went on to explain, "She did that because she retained her conscience. If more martyrs would but follow her example! This world would be a safer, holier place."

Nostrils flaring, Dominia glanced at the ground, then in the direction of a dog's short bark. From the shadows of an alley, Basil made eye contact with her, stepped into the sunlight, and appeared to dissolve on its contact. While seeing this, Dominia admitted for the first time in months, "That wasn't why she killed herself."

"You know, do you? Yet here you are, trying to resurrect her—not only against the will of God but also her own will. Do you expect you shall flee to Cairo, reproduce her body, and live happily ever after in your Father's world? In the human world? If she took her own life and you give it back, will she be anything but resentful?"

"We'll make our own world. Wherever we go, whatever we do: it won't matter, because we'll be together."

"When all this is said and done, Miss Mephitoli, and you have helped us to kill your Father, I promise"—his men moved forward on some subtle signal of his head—"I will see to it that you and your wife are reunited forever."

"I'd rather see her right now than look at you another minute," said the General. As the insurgents closed in, she holstered her gun and dashed, not into battle with the men, but into that one thing that might save her: the risen sun.

Much as with the Lazarene ceremony, she had not known what to expect—but what she expected was, nevertheless, not quite this. In the instant that her body hit the sun and she expected her skin to burn under the intensity of its unhampered blue light, time appeared to freeze. Tobias and his moving men jolted to a halt, and so did the morning pigeons in the air, and so did the General's own body, which was frozen for seconds in the act of stepping until it seemed that all of this, like some vast shell, shattered away, then compressed into a pinpoint within her solar plexus that stole her breath and imploded every limb. This implosion, which she thought meant her death that first time, dissolved her body and left her ears ringing. Those great colored bands she had glimpsed during the race presented themselves once more, expanding from her core and meeting others that bent from the cardinal directions. Electromagnetic fields, she somehow knew. Behind her, the world altered: there was no more city but a vast ebony landscape with distant mountains, a sky the violet of a contusion, and a sun that burned like an outraged obsidian. But, most fascinating of all, this strange black sun did not sear her skin.

Mouth agape, the General touched her chest to find it there yet somehow different: but it was the sway of long hair before her face that shocked her more, perhaps, than even her environment. As she reached up to touch it, feeling in a dream, the ringing in her ears gave way to the sounds of a distant argument in a dialect she recognized as old, old English. She did not recognize the language until picking out her own name led to the picking out of the words "fucking dentist," although "dentist" was a much flatter and stranger sound than she was used to hearing in English as it was in 1997 AL. Much of the rest of the conversation was lost on her.

She turned in its direction, amazed to find the fields emanating from her center to be weighted in a direction she presumed north. In the distance, two figures were in the midst of a complex argument. One, she recognized; one, she did not. Not until her steps, uneasy and somehow broader in this echoing place, brought her close enough to make out a red waistcoat amid the starlike magnetic ribbons that flexed and parted for her vision as she drew nearer. This red waistcoat triggered memories of the glimpse she'd gotten before, yes, but more than that. Astonishment struck the General: she was not thrust back to Kronborg with Cassandra while the Hierophant finished his tour of the throne room paintings. Rather, she was thrust to that moment's diametric opposite. Still at Kronborg, where she had flown for Cassandra's memorial, her Father called her to his office. As a girl sitting across his great oak desk and wingback chair, amid all those books and portraits, she always felt so small. At that moment as an adult, she felt nonexistent, and had not so much studied the covered painting in the corner as absorbed it, unconsciously, along with the rest of the room.

"I thought about having your wife's cremains inurned in the Family catacombs of Rome," he began. Dominia listened numbly, having wanted nothing to do with the arrangements and having asked him to take care of them, but not to tell her about them until she had been given a year or two of relief. Typical of him to ignore that wish. "But Rome was not her home, even if the name she took from you marked her as Mephitolian. Nor could it be said that San Valentino was ever her home, no matter how many children she taught there, or how many good works the both of you did in the Front."

"Did you call me here to remind me I could never make her happy?" Her voice brittle from private weeping, the Governess's impudent words elicited an expression that, from the Hierophant, recalled a kind of sympathy. He reached out to hold her hand and pressed something cold into her palm.

"No, my girl. I mean to say that her real home—the only home that could give her any joy—was in your heart."

His hand lifted away, and there she was: a beautiful diamond, lying in the Governess's palm. Though she had expected to, she did not weep. Not in that moment, although she would often weep over the diamond later, day on day while other martyrs slept, Dominia edging ever closer toward contacting the René Ichigawa who had not yet come to her with promises of resurrection by the time she sat, there, in her Father's office.

In that moment, she perceived nothing except a chill in her cheeks, and a brief contemplation as to how much this amounted to desecration of Cassandra's corpse. But she had left the choice to him. She had to live with it now.

"Thank you." Her eyes passed his many books to land on that

covered painting. She raised her chin in its direction. "Is that her martyring painting?"

"She will be the patron saint of childbirth—of grief and suicides."

"May I see it." Not a request, but a resignation.

"Are you sure?"

After staring into her exhausted eyes, awaiting some protest, he rose. Centimeter by centimeter, the sheet of burgundy velvet drew away.

Reproduced in a richness of oil work like few had the privilege of viewing up close, was Cassandra: not with that gun in her mouth and her eyes full of fear, but kneeling down to pray at the bedside of their UF mansion while Dominia's gun rested upon the nightstand. The red of the painting was not of the blood and brain matter that had shattered, chunked with skull and matted with scalp, across their marriage bed. The red of the painting marked the waistcoat of the fictional saint who, with a most sorrowful expression, touched Cassandra's shoulder with one hand and, with the other, gestured off frame to indicate the time had come for their departure. It would be some weeks before Dominia awoke from a dead sleep with the epiphany that the painting's oil medium indicated it must have been commissioned months before the suicide. At the time, she did not think on it.

At the time, the Governess wept.

"You're Saint Valentinian," marveled the General now, interrupting his argument with Lazarus so that both men turned with a look of relief at the sound of her voice. As her approach ended before them, the bands marking fields that appeared as one with the two of them standing close flexed to accept her like a larger water droplet accepting a smaller one. While she overcame the brief vertigo this inspired, her vision cleared of color to allow both men to be easily seen. "I thought you weren't real. Am I dead?"

"Please, just 'Valentinian.' And you're not dead. Not right now. No more than anybody else here, anyway."

"Do you know each other?" she asked Lazarus. His taller companion laughed, then searched his waistcoat for a silver cigarette case.

"Some people! We've been halfway around the world together, and you don't even recognize me."

A few beats passed in which the General studied the tall man's pale-sapphire eyes. Somehow, she did know him. "*Basil?*" she asked in a tone almost accusatory.

"Woof." After bending to light his cigarette, the fictional martyr made to disappear the Tesla coil lighter that had emerged from his palm in sleight-of-hand demonstration. "It's more complicated than that, of course, but what isn't?"

A damn good question. The General's reeling mind raced through a thousand queries, almost all impossible to articulate. "Where *are* we, though?"

"That's not any less complicated than the dog question," said the useless saint. Dominia turned her agitated eye to Lazarus.

"I told you in the ceremony. You are liberated. Your Father's world? The material world? It's one way of viewing the information of the universe. And it's not the most accurate way."

"Your blood did this," she marveled.

The holy man nodded. "My blood does not deliver pseudo-im-mortality to the flesh. Rather, it gives the flesh—especially the flesh of martyrs—the opportunity to recognize it is already immortal. All things are already immortal."

"Welcome to Nirvana, kid," summarized Valentinian. "Rest assured, it's nothing like you dreamed."

XVIII

To Sleep

Whether Morgan or Dominia, General di Mephitoli had never done well with unanswered questions. Today, as she trudged through a desert dry without heat and visible without light save for colored bands warping her perception, she could not help but wonder how long her many, many questions had gone unanswered. One week? Two? Impossible—though she sensed it would be that long, or longer, before she had any measure of satisfaction. The black sun abuzz in the sky like a great, aching pit had not set during their journey, and not once had she hungered or even tired enough for rest, and never had those distant peaks drawn into greater detail than that of far-off thorns.

Yet something in her insisted no less than a week had passed since the men began their argument, which had been spurned by Dominia's simple observation. It had been an observation directed for the man who was, for his fictional nature, a source of exceeding curiosity to the General. To her mind, her observation was fair enough, though when it exited her lips, it sounded something more like an insult.

"You never seemed like a dog."

"I've never been a convincing liar," said Valentinian.

Lazarus spoke up: "You do it often enough."

"Still bent out of shape, are we?" asked the former dog with a bat of his eyes. She wasn't about to let them slip into a dialogue without her and cut in before Lazarus responded.

"Now, what's going on?" She tapped her hand as though a list of questions was written upon it. Of Valentinian, she asked, "Are you a martyr?"

"Yes, of course."

Dominia studied the icy-blue eyes he turned upon her single, resolute one. "But you've been in the sun." Old martyrs in particular began to leather in an instant under the sun's rays. The man arched a brow.

"Assuming it even matters once you have the blood of Lazarus: *Have* I been in the sun? Really? Even when you met us at the hotel, we were beneath an overhang."

The frowning General tried to sort her memory for an instance of this. She came up with nothing. It was true: the dog had been in the sun no longer than she. Basil had shown an almost exclusive appetite for human flesh, so much so that she had speculated herself that the dog was a martyr—but she had not speculated anything quite along these lines. Now, with a slap upon her own forehead, Dominia remembered, "The train! When René boarded the train and found you already there!"

"Now that's the ticket! You're so smart." Valentinian moved to pinch her cheek, but Dominia ducked away.

"You teleported then, the way my Father and Akachi and Lazarus…" Her thoughts trailed off and she pursed her lips. "All this time, you've been a man disguised as a dog so as to…what, exactly?"

"Nothing weird," promised the thin man, and the bearded nomad snorted from Dominia's good side.

"Yes, nothing weird. Not even of his own volition."

"It's a complicated story." Valentinian ran a hand over the eternal shadow of close stubble across his jaw. "I'll tell you sometime. At any rate, don't worry too much about me. We need to keep you focused, here."

"Where *is* 'here'?" she demanded again. Lazarus answered, beginning to turn away.

"Nowhere, really. It's sort of a pre-place. Not another dimension, so much. More a higher manifestation of the same universe. A higher frequency."

"So, another dimension," said Valentinian in a smart-assed way. Lazarus rolled his eyes.

"Different ways of saying the same thing. Some ways are better than others." After patting the invisible pockets of his ashen robe, which in this space seemed formless and shifting as everything else upon which Dominia tried to focus, the True Protomartyr withdrew from his pocket a white pebble. He had a whole palmful, and the one loaded in his thumb pinged like a bead from a slingshot into the distance. When she tried peering through the bubble of their collective magnetic field, the concept of depth had not seemed existent: not until the pebble indicated it. As the men began toward it, Dominia followed, and Lazarus carried on.

"This place is without static shape. It is where mind rules over matter: where imagination holds sway over the environment. Thoughts are information, like any material manifestation of energy. It's just that here, thought is given prevalence over matter."

"This can be a good thing," said Valentinian, slowing to match the General's pace. "It can also be a bad thing if you're, say, distressed, or dying, or if you arrive here without somebody to guide you or knowledge of what's going on."

Lazarus nodded. "In those cases, you're on a lower frequency instead of a higher one. But you don't have to worry about that much."

"We're moving within the electromagnetic spectrum," Dominia at last gathered.

"That's the axis along which we're traveling when we come here from Earth. Time is stripped away at higher and lower frequencies… the edges of matter become indistinct. This can be good or bad. Like Valentinian said, it can be bad if you drop to the lower, sub-radio frequencies. Or, if you're unfocused." They had reached the pebble and continued, though it drew Dominia's attention as they passed it; she was redirected by the sound of the second pebble skittering across the floor. "Focus is important here, because if your mind wanders, you can get lost."

"You can disappear," cautioned the waistcoated man. "But that's not likely to happen when somebody's there to observe you. One reason of many why we're here. Of course, I'm always here. Sort of."

The General's eye narrowed in scrutiny. "So you're not a dog? Really, all the time, you're a man?"

"Yes, and no. I'm here at the same time I'm there, of course—aren't we all—and this is arguably a higher truth of what I am. But the physical shadow I cast is mangled. I have lost my old one, the earthly one I had when the universe was first set into motion. All physical selves are mangled, in truth. Your physical self is mangled. Have you noticed your hair?"

She had, and once more reached up to touch the long locks shorn to make a fast disguise on the Light Rail. Still amazed to feel them again, she asked, "How is this so?"

"It's how you're used to thinking of yourself, isn't it? How you picture yourself in your mind, in your dreams. That's who you are all the time, but here it's visible."

"But my eye?" She realized she had not removed the patch, and began to reach for it. Valentinian stayed her hand.

"The damage incurred by your physical eye is symbolic of higher truth. You do have a sort of eye here, but the magnitude of its powers means it must be hidden. Leave it shut: when it opens, it'll end the world."

"You can't just be telling her these things." Lazarus, about to toss a third pebble into the distance, offered Valentinian a resentful glance which was bounced back to him in the form of an eyeroll.

"People have already started hinting stuff about her end-of-the-world responsibilities! It's worse to tell somebody a bit of something without telling them the hows and whys. Like keeping a gun around a kid and telling them not to touch it, but not specifying which end is dangerous." Dominia sickened at the metaphor, but Lazarus blustered off in immediate response, not noticing the expression, or the chill that wracked her to remember that odious moment in this place where thought was naked.

"It's *all* dangerous, which is why it's better the kid should know the gun is going to kill them if they touch it. Leave it at that."

Valentinian scoffed. "You're hardly an expert on child-rearing."

"And you are?" Lazarus laughed, his language shifting, then, to that old English variation. It had frustrated her the first time she'd heard it, like listening to characters in a dream babble in made-up languages only the unconscious understood: but, by the final time she would hear its words bandied between the two men, she would come to wonder if this was not how prelingual children perceived the chatter of adults. For now, trailing behind them, she observed by tone as the conversation escalated into argument. Though she knew a great many languages, Dominia found this one beyond her grasp; and she was used to being around many other people who spoke in foreign tongues, but she never appreciated when others had private conversations in front of her. This was how she began to assail her own brain, each thought punctuated by the irritating ping of a pebble as she came up with a great list of questions that seemed without number, and that were impossible to flesh out with the pinging of the pebbles separating each thought. By the time she managed to articulate a question, ping! Another pebble scurried across the textureless ground like the full stop at the end of a sentence, a period, a point audible with each stone flicked away. How long had they marched? Ping! Where were they? Ping! Who was Valentinian? Ping! How a dog, why a dog? Ping! What was beneath her eye patch now, and what did it have to do with the world, its end, anything at all?

Having thoughts in this place seemed futile as collecting water in one's cupped hand. Or perhaps it felt like sitting at the edge of a (pinging) fountain and trying to will it to collect itself into the form of a cup, without having a cup or a means by which to direct the liquid. Ping went a pebble, and Dominia was almost grateful for it, now. She became afraid of what might happen should she indeed follow a thought to the point of getting lost. The men chattered among themselves, their backs to her, and her body leadened at the absurd worry that they would forget her. Might she vanish while their backs were turned?

On the edge of quavering anxiety that felt it might be deadly, Dominia interrupted their conversation. "Are there other people here? Are we ever going to meet anybody else? What's going on?"

Their argument paused (for now), the men turned to look at her. While gentle relief flooded her mind to confirm that she, if nothing else, still existed, Valentinian said, "We'll meet some other people eventually. Lots of other people, but not for a while."

"We're going to Cairo," answered Lazarus. "It's a shortcut. Kind of. The walk won't be quite as bad as you're thinking."

"But we've been walking such a long time."

"It's been about"—Valentinian paused to check his pocket watch, and Dominia discerned a wing-cloaked tetramorph etched into the metal—"oh, six days or so."

"The sun will set soon." Lazarus gazed at the great mole that hadn't shown any signs, so far as Dominia had seen, of moving an inch, west or east, whatever good such directions did in a place like this, where she sensed—and where the fields around them seemed to indicate—that there were more than four cardinal directions. "We'll have to make a camp."

"We can go farther," insisted Valentinian, snapping shut his watch and studying Dominia with eyes that would be glacial were they not crinkled with cheer. "How's it going, kiddo? Can you keep it up? You're not tired, are you?"

"No, it's not that. I don't understand how we've traveled so long when the sun hasn't moved."

Lazarus seemed inclined to let the magician field these questions. "Time works differently here. Not only that, but the flow of time back on Earth—so far as our own perceptions are concerned, anyway—is more related to perceived distance traveled here than actual earthly time spent. If we spent three days hanging around the same place, like, say, a town, or a ship, or anything else one might find in this place, we wouldn't notice much of a difference when we came back, and we also wouldn't find ourselves having experienced a significant change in our relative space compared to that of other Earthlings.

"Think of it like a film strip." Valentinian rolled back his sleeves and from his empty hands produced an antique strip of movie film. As he ran it through his fingers, light projected from them to terminate in a moving image at an arbitrary point in space: a simple show, played upon a screen unobserved. "As the physical film moves in space, the images and sounds it's projecting carry forward in time and perceived space—though, of course, the film itself never leaves the boundaries of the projector, and the movie watched never leaves the screen on which it's being played. Unless it's stopped. But when the film stops moving, the image on the screen also stops. Strictly speaking, when we're at the movie and unaware of the film on which it's printed, we're still simultaneously viewing the physical print and the motion picture: but when we become aware of the prints, we're able to manipulate them, and our position in them, by operating solely on that level. Instead of being a viewer, we become a projectionist."

Somehow, perhaps because of the dreamscape the trio inhabited, the man's production of the film seemed so natural that she was not surprised by it. She decided he must be some sort of magician since he knew so much about the fabric of reality. It struck her then: Valentinian was that magician to which Akachi had referred. As she watched but did not see the image of a woman walking, the General asked, "Is it possible to run the film strip backward? If we walked back to the point where we started—assuming we even could—"

"Would time go backward? Well, yes and no. Think about the movie again. There's multiple perceptions at work: first, the character's in-world perception—that's everybody else, everybody we left behind, Miki Soto and René Ichigawa—all the people in the world. Everybody who hasn't entered this space. If I stop the movie and rewind"—he pulled the film backward through his fingers, so that the woman's wobbling stride reversed its motion as though she beat hasty retreat from some threat that left her expression bland—"what is this lady going to notice when I start it running again?"

"Nothing," said Dominia. "From her perspective, she never even got to the point from which you rewound it."

"Okay. How about from your perspective, as an audience member? That is to say, someone who knows the movie's a movie, but who also has the potential to walk up to the booth where the projectionist works? Now that you've seen the black sun once, you can call on it again any time that you need it, like how a person awakened to the existence of a projectionist can go knock on his door. What happens from your perspective when you're watching the movie and it rewinds, then starts again from a point not at the beginning?"

"Well, I get annoyed."

"Because you can't unknow what's already happened, and it's not going to change. It's filmed and already on a track, so your chances of having a new experience are reduced. In fact, you can't have a new experience. And since the present is nothing but new experiences, once you have crystalized reality by experiencing it—by rendering the abstract information around us the physical space of reality—it is impossible to go back. The projectionist can't rewind his film because the audience can't unsee what they've watched. He only rewinds it"—Valentinian let the film slip from his fingers, and the light vanished along with its walking woman—"when the whole thing's done, and it's time to show the movie over again."

"In other words, we can only really fast-forward."

"That's true when you've made contact with the material plane, or crossed paths with a visitor who isn't in your group; but when you're in this place, if you go too far or get lost and you haven't met any strangers to confuse your field, you can get back to your original position and no harm will be done. It will be like you never even left the spot where you stood in reality. All places you initially walk represent forward motion in time and space toward one of many potential ends, depending on which direction you pick and what intention you have; however, all places you backtrack represent backward motion along those same lines. Think of it like this: until you are forced to make up your mind by returning to Earth, you're free to change it as often or as much as you please. Like our projectionist searching the film strip, frame by frame—the movie can't start until he locks it into position."

"So I can do this any time? Come here?"

Lazarus said, "If a person, even a human, has had my blood once in their life, they can come here any time. Be here forever, if they wanted. But, please—don't do that."

"We need you too much," said Valentinian, laughing. "So, does that satisfy you?"

Enough, she supposed. There was no satisfying her in a situation like this, but there had not been any satisfying her since the Hierophant pulled out her eye, or before—since Cassandra died.

Cassandra. She had not thought of her wife in what was technically a week. The setting of the black sun banished the embroidery of their colored fields and Valentinian stood before the final pebble. As a fire blazed to life, seemingly sourced in the stone, she found herself thinking of her poor wife with stabs of sadness—and bitter disappointment that the vast space afforded no true backward motion. The darkness enclosing the circle of their fire, without benefit of their rays, was thick like tar. In day, the landscape had been already bleak under the dark un-light. Now, in this night that lacked a moon, the rest of existence had vanished, and Dominia failed to prove to herself that it had ever been there to start. Memories of Cassandra were her tether to reality, for they were the only memories of which Dominia could be sure.

There was something to be said for that place when it came to the subject of memories. Perhaps that was because, while lying beside the fire, she felt weightless. As if the ground upon which she lay was not ground, or even water, but a vacuum. Thus, with nothing to look at, nothing to feel, and nothing to contain her rampant memories, she dreamed. Hypnotized by the sound of shuffling cards Valentinian had produced from his pocket, it seemed to her the warmth of the fire now was the warmth of their estate's fire then, all those years ago, not that long after Cassandra had first appeared. Not all that long, either, after she had lost her baby. Night after night, her wife sat immobile by that fire.

At the time, Dominia feared Cassandra would never recover from her depression. She still felt that fear, ninety years later, and wondered if her wife ever did recover in a way that mattered. But, one night, in an effort to see some change in demeanor—and to prove it was possible to find moments of joy after a storm of loss—she took Cassandra to the zoo. San Valentino had many zoos, of course, but the San Diego Zoo was known as one of the best, and most compassionate—they subscribed to a strict anti-alteration policy when it came to the genetic code of cloned animals, and showed consistent preference for the acquisition and breeding of organic ones. Especially endangered species, which were legion, thanks to the long-lasting climate changes of industrialization. Most of the world's more fascinating animals, like its rhinos, its elephants, its tigers and its lions, would have only survived immortalized as weapons were it not for the noble cloning operations that had made their rebirth possible.

Cassandra had never seen a live elephant before—or a tiger, for that matter. Ocelots, parakeets, markhors: all were mythical animals to the twentysomething, who appeared a giddy girl dashing from cage to cage. The prohibitive cost of zoos meant they were predominantly attended by martyrs; humans who wished to see them often found the easiest way was to get a career as a keeper. That was a good, safe job for a human. No martyr was inclined to hurt a zookeeper.

Yet, as cherished an opportunity as this had been, and as bright as Cassandra had become in their hours wandering from exhibit to exhibit, the animals paled beside the moment her wife laid eyes on a trail of schoolchildren, aged eight to ten, forced to hold hands as they navigated the zoo. While Dominia had tried to turn down another path to save her wife's emotional state and to avoid wading through a crowd, Cassandra tugged her to a halt.

"Is that a school?"

"Bible school, I think." The Governess studied the uniforms, then tried to draw attention to the map. "Look—"

"Like Sunday school, you mean? Martyrs have that?"

"Sure we do. But remember, sweetheart, it's Noctisdomin."

While Cassandra substituted a bland stare for the eye rolls that she had learned were an insult to the Governess, she primly agreed, "Noctisdomin school. Cumbersome."

"Makes more sense than a bunch of nocturnal people talking about the *days* of the week. And, anyway, it sounds better in Mephitolian." At her wife's continued look, Dominia began to worry they would have a fight there, in the zoo, in front of the now-passing stream of kids; they'd been having a lot of fights around that time, weird fights, due to Cassandra's emotional state and—well, to be frank, the Governess's inability to empathize. She didn't want to be around kids, herself. That's why it amazed her so when Cassandra, with an abrupt flip to her bright expression again, strolled to the pretty Filipina martyr who seemed to be one of their three teachers, and asked for a moment of her time. Ten minutes later, she was back with a phone number written on her wrist, and—oh, Dominia's poor heart, just to remember it—a big, real smile on her face.

"She said I should call her sometime, and she can tell me more about how to get certified."

"You're going to teach Bible school?" Dominia laughed gently. "You haven't even been to Mass since we got married."

"It's creepy, that's why." Away from other people, they spoke of her Father's culture and their opinions on it. On everything. Together, they strolled hand in hand past aviaries of sleeping tropical birds. "If I taught Bible school, it would be *during* Mass. I wouldn't have to go."

"But you have to learn the material you're going to teach, is what I'm trying to say."

"I can learn it. You think I can, don't you?"

At her wife's anxious expression, Dominia's own had filled with pain. She had pulled Cassandra close, into a kiss. "I think you can do anything."

Oh, Cassandra! Ah, memory! But what was memory in this boundless place? There they were now, those lips, those soft lips, those hands, that—

"What are you doing," cried Valentinian above the scattering of fifty-two cards. Or, maybe the cry came as he shook her back to her senses: hard to tell, with half of her dreaming of Cassandra's mouth, from which she was unwilling to be torn away. "Hey, wake up, look at me!"

But she was with Cassandra, who said, so gently, "I love you, Dominia—oh, Dominia, I'm so glad I have you. Dominia, you're all that I have."

Those words! That woman who clutched her and looked up at her with such sweet, big eyes. That woman who needed her love and protection, who stood now by the fireside.

Yes, by the fireside, at its edge. Her form, dark in the unholy night, yet discernible as Cassandra's. But, oh, cruelty! The shouting men (Lazarus having awoken) would not let Dominia near the lover whose name she repeated in a chant. That name that rang across the thick night of formless space. "Come here," she cried, "come here, Cassandra, please— Oh, won't you *stop*! Let me see her!"

"It's not Cassandra," shouted Valentinian. Lazarus stooped for the king of hearts and ace of spades, which he caught in the fire. As the General tried to extricate herself from the magician's grip, the mystic tossed the flaming cards at the apparition. Light singed the shadow's face to reveal features much like Cassandra's—but not hers. Those eyes—bleak and flat rather than the great, emotional, haunted ones of her wife—awoke Dominia, who also found brassy hair to be a tarry lie. This entity was not her love.

"What is it?" Dominia asked. The shadow resumed its watch from the other side of the fire's circumference.

"Call it a thoughtform." Valentinian collected the rest of his cards. "It won't come into the light. It can't, without showing us how it looks. But that's the problem with this place, with remembering things too vividly here. There's a lot of…stuff…hanging around. Think of it as sentient negative thoughts: an active type of information that, given sufficient energy, looks for the best way to harvest more energy from you, for better or worse."

Cold, the General watched the odious thing. To think anything could be so sick, so cruel, as this which mocked her wife! "Why?"

The magician shrugged, tapped the incomplete deck of cards, snapped his fingers, and produced from the stack a new king of hearts, another ace of spades. "Why does anything do anything? It wants to eat. Biological viruses are the closest metaphor I have for you, but even that's not accurate."

"It's close." Lazarus lowered upon his haunches and warmed his hands by the fire, one eye upon the thoughtform's silhouette. "Viruses are programmed to evolve like anything else, and this thing is desperate to evolve. In this case, the evolution isn't genetic. It's an evolution from a state of near total abstraction, to physical representation. That's why we refrain from giving these things a real name or definition. Even calling it, say, '*tulpa*' like they do in Tibet, or '*egregore*' like they do in occult texts, gives it a preexisting form and eases its ability to manifest in reality. If it can collect enough energy, it might be able to manifest in real life—return attached to us, or attached to your energy—and that isn't a good thing for you."

"Not necessarily," cautioned Valentinian. "But there are good thoughtforms."

"Good thoughtforms don't need to drain you of psychic, emotional, or memory energy to manifest. They are parts of established patterns that exist in large varieties of information and help the person with whom they connect."

"Argumentative!"

"Just being specific. But do you get it?" Lazarus turned his attention to Dominia now, who touched her head, embarrassed.

"Yes, of course. As much as anybody can 'get' something like this, anyway…now that I'm awake, I know that's not Cassandra. Of course that's not Cassandra. But it was like I was almost…sleeping, before. Not here."

Valentinian nodded. "That's why you have to keep focused. I meant it when I said that, about getting lost in your thoughts. If you find yourself getting too deep into a memory here, you need to ground yourself—I mean, literally, make yourself aware of the ground." He patted it as he sat. "It'll put you in the present and keep you from attracting other…parasites."

"It'll be better if she gets something to do." Lazarus, upon his stomach, tucked his arm beneath his chin in lieu of pillow. "Give her your cards, '*Basil*.'"

"Why not give her your rocks?"

"Because she doesn't know how to keep time."

Dominia shivered under the stolen eyes of the thing wearing Cassandra's face. "How long do the nights last around here?"

"A while," answered the magician, handing his deck to Dominia. "It's better to sleep."

Bitterly, she laughed. "What if I dream while I sleep?"

"When the whole world is a state of dreaming"—Lazarus's voice was muffled by his half-curled position in the firelight—"sleep is the last place you should expect to dream."

"But how am I supposed to go to sleep without thinking of anything?" She clutched the cards in her right hand like an angular stuffed animal, and tucked the deck beneath her miserable arms. Lazarus's tone was less sympathetic than Valentinian's: largely because he was on the verge of sleep. "Ask yourself how a bluebird does it, and you'll fall right to sleep."

"Is he always like this," whispered the General to the magician. He patted her shoulder.

"It comes from a loving place."

His hand lingered with a brother's weight, his eyes no doubt the same place Dominia's singular orb found tense focus. That vacuous silhouette had edged along the light and now seemed all too near the General for comfort. The bands of color having vanished with the light, she had not even the psychological, imaginary barrier of their electromagnetic field. As Dominia ran her thumb back and forth along the edge of the cards, she murmured, "How am I supposed to sleep with that thing watching me?"

"It can't hurt you with the fire going. And it can't hurt you when I'm nearby." This sentiment was paired with a playful jostle that made her think of the dog she better knew. As though reading her thoughts—and she was certain, based on history, he could—the magician noted, "It's nice you trust me after the whole...you know, 'surprise person' thing."

The General laughed. "Out of everyone I've met this past two weeks, you've been the entity I've trusted the most, and even you've had a secret!"

"Yeah, but I tried to make it clear I was strange. I mean, all dogs are great, but stopping the train? Shooting Kahlil?"

"Thanks for that, by the way. The train, I mean, not Kahlil."

"Well, thanks for the food! And for the company, and for everything you've done for me in all those past attempts. Don't worry. This time, we get it right."

As strange as the world had become, she had somehow lost all doubt that existence was cyclical. She didn't bother asking how much he remembered about their lives before, or how he had survived, or what the future was like, because there would be no getting a straight answer out of him, and she was certain knowing all those things would prove a dreadful weight. The burden she held by virtue of being responsible for the world's destruction, whether proverbial or real, was dreadful enough. She had quite a few questions about that, but Lazarus would strangle her at this rate. Anyway, delirious as this place made the circles of her thoughts, she dared not spare much consideration for the suggestion. Instead, she turned back to see Valentinian staring down the silhouette, and caught his eye to ask, "How do you know we'll get it right?"

"I can feel it." He cast a twinkling glance into space, as though reading there the words of some invisible book. "And I can see it. There are a great many truths yet to be revealed, Dominia."

Was it the first time he'd said her name? Perhaps not—but for some reason, it felt as such, and she turned back to tuck her arm beneath her head in a fashion not dissimilar from that position into which Lazarus had curled. The magician continued speaking while he lifted his hand from her shoulder to reach into his waistcoat's pocket.

"Our success in ending this cycle is dependent on the number and proportion of truths revealed, in a way. The truth will set you free, or so says your Father's raggedy old book stolen from the humans, but I prefer, 'The amount and momentum of surprise information within the truth will help our consciousnesses achieve the escape velocity required to keep all this from ever having happened in the first place.'"

"But if none of this happened"—the General's throat tightened—"will I have existed?"

"You will have existed more than ever before!" He laughed, and leaned over her. Before she realized what he was doing, something—a dust or a powder or a sand—was scattered across her eye, and he murmured, "These are questions for reality, when they'll seem less oppressive. Now go to sleep, kiddo."

Magically compelled as she was, she did. For hours, it felt, Dominia plunged into a sleep in which one moment she lay upon her arm, and the next she did not exist: neither to dream a dream nor think a thought. It was like having her eye and spirit washed in the Lamb's blood, soothing a sleep as it was. So soothing, it induced brief delirium. When Dominia awoke, unsure of what had awoken her, she thought it to be morning by the profusion of light; then, she remembered the light of the sun here was not like any she'd known on Earth. It could not be day by any means.

As the tinkling of music reached her consciousness, she lifted her head and found Valentinian and Lazarus both sound asleep. During their inattention, it seemed the light of the fire had multiplied. Like trees instantly grown, torches had sprung in the darkened night. These thin rods of gold towered over the General, who was of no short height for a woman, and the blue-hearted fires atop them formed a chain through the darkness by the pools of light that licked the perimeters of their fellows. This light was clean, yet somehow false in comparison to the magician's. Her colored field still had not returned—would not, she sensed, until the day.

The most curious thing was not, however, the appearance of the torches, or the hue of the fire, or the late-noted disappearance of Cassandra's doppelgänger. It was Dominia's lack of fear. Not often a woman given to fear, she had of late been inundated; now, on being alone in this alien plane, with music streaming from an unknown source to tempt her down this new-laid path, Dominia looked back on those moments in reality where fear had visited her. She marveled that she had ever, in that place, been afraid. Reality had grown less real. Valentinian himself had said that this place was a dream, and now, without the thing watching her from the edges of the light, she remembered nothing could hurt her in dreams. Thus assured of her safety, she padded beneath the lights as if following a stream to its source.

A great many torches passed her by—she supposed she should have been counting in anticipation of her return—but, soon enough in comparison to that day's walk, she noted a far greater light in the distance. An island, amid all that watery darkness. The closer she drew, the better she discerned that the light formed a study with no walls:

only a door carved in an extraordinary forest tableau, and a few book-shelves lining the enclosures of a room that, like Valentinian's screen, was implied. The music increased in volume and clarity, and now she recognized it (an ancient composer named Berlioz), along with two chairs resting beside the orange-blue fireplace. The unanchored door obstructed her view of the filled armchair, but she knew what she would find well before she knocked—well before she heard the words, "It's open," and touched the knob. She knew what she would find well before that door yawned wide: yet, she did not stop herself from letting it swing open to reveal, wine in hand, the Hierophant.

"How glad I am you've accepted the invitation, my eternal General. Please: won't you come in?"

The men might tell her whatever they wanted to gloss the truth for her, but in that moment, Dominia confirmed her instincts had been right.

She was in for one long walk to Cairo.

[ed.: The following requests to Saint Valentinian, originally written in Modern Mephitolian circa 3670 CE, come from prayer cards said to belong to Dominia di Mephitoli in her childhood and first two centuries of life. As they began public circulation in Nogales, Arizona, this is a strong possibility.]

PRAYER TO
SAINT VALENTINIAN

For the Dying

Saint Valentinian! The Lord, in His wisdom, has seen you, above all His saints, fit to guide all souls, damned and righteous, to eternity. Through the Father's works, you know the trials through which beings strive. Pray now on the trials of *[the dying]* and relieve, somewhat, the burdens of their sins. You, who were too wise to be made real; for whom God has made home of eternity; who knew all things before Wisdom was revealed to mankind: your knowledge raised you high above all spheres and to the bosom of the Lord, into whose ear you speak. As pleasing as your wisdom is to Him, surely you will see to it that *[dying]* is granted that knowledge by means of which souls enter the next life not in fear, but peace and love of God. Amen.

PRAYER TO
SAINT VALENTINIAN

For the Success of a Creative Venture

O Saint Valentinian, master of all arts and wise attendant of the Lord, by your works of death you know the nature of Creation. See from your heavenly abode the struggles of the Father's beloved artists and pray they be delivered to greatness. Let their divinely granted gifts purify the world, and flood its land with the wonders of eternity. With your generous prayers, draw God's blessing upon all who would create in His name, and allow *[artist's]* works, models for that Greatest Work, to thrive as golden crops sewn beneath the shining sun. Amen.

A Timeline of Events

[ed.: As this document was transmitted non-temporally, concerns exist about the impact of foreknowledge upon future events. Therefore, certain names irrelevant to the story of General Dominia di Mephitoli have been redacted, in the hopes of preventing willful future atrocity. Names and events related to the Rise of the Hierophant or predating this book's first printing in CE 2019 (BL 25) have been left as is.]

CE 1974 / BL 70

American science-fiction author, Philip K. Dick, has a visionary experience with an entity that he calls VALIS: Vast Active Living Intelligence System

The Hierophant arrives on Earth

Paris radio station, France Inter, is subject to a break-in; the burglar is said to have carried off tapes waiting to be broadcast as part of a series about UFOs, with the missing recordings relating to the theory that UFOs are not extraterrestrial, but supra-physical

American neuroscientist, Dr. John C. Lilly, receives a warning about a nefarious entity called the SSI, or "Solid State Intelligence", delivered by an extraterrestrial organization that he calls ECCO: Earth Coincidence Control Office

While on tour in Detroit, alien-fascinated British superstar David Bowie happens to catch a local television report of a "verified" UFO landing; later reports deny the incident

US President Richard Nixon resigns in disgrace following the Watergate scandal

His replacement, President Gerald Ford, is quick to pardon him

American author and Playboy *magazine editor, Robert Anton Wilson, "enters into a belief system" concerning telepathic contact between himself entities residing on a planet of the double star, Sirius; Sirius A, the brightest star in the sky, is wildly known as "the Dog Star"*

CE 1976 / BL 68

The Man Who Fell to Earth, *a film starring and largely orchestrated by David Bowie, is released in theaters*

The film will provide vital contributions in Philip K. Dick's efforts to develop a frame of reference intellectualizing his VALIS experience

CE 1978 / BL 66

Pope John Paul I dies 33 days after election in the first Year of Three Popes since 1605 CE; his death proves the genesis of many conspiracy theories

CE 1980 / BL 64

An international cabal of prostitutes known as the Red Market is formally founded

American movie star, Ronald Wilson Reagan, is elected president; Robert Anton Wilson, among others, later notes this name to be an anagram for "Insane Anglo Warlord"

British musician and advocate for peace, John Lennon, is shot dead by Mark David Chapman as the result of a series of strange coincidences

CE 2005 / BL 39

Pope John Paul II dies and is succeeded by Pope Benedict XVI

CE 2011 / BL 33

The Hierophant reveals the sacred protein to researchers, Elijah, and Cicero

Lazarus goes into hiding after being martyred

CE 2013 / BL 31

DIOX Corporation is founded by Cicero and Elijah, with private funding from the Hierophant

Pope Benedict XVI announces his abrupt resignation and is succeeded by Pope Francis, 266th sovereign of the Vatican City State; Francis immediately proves a divisive authority among modern Catholics

CE 2020 / BL 24

The Hierophant works to quietly spread martyrdom to the hyper-elite of Russia

The Church of the Lamb is founded in California by a pair of eccentric brothers; it soon fails to maintain more than a small gathering, and will be reworked over the years into a proper organization

CE 2029 / BL 15

The newfound Holy Martyr Church is a more successful attempt than Cicero's previous effort, due in part to a number of fresh-martyred celebrities blackmailed into public support: ███████ *and* ███████

The organization's patriarch, the Hierophant, is thought to be a former politician due to those who begin joining the HMC, but he refuses to give his name and cannot be identified; until initiation into the Church is complete, most regard the Hierophant as a likely relative of Cicero's

However, official members also seem to transform into true believers overnight; many lose friends and family members to the strange group, which promotes, among other things, a nocturnal lifestyle resulting in isolation from one's former life

Due to the strange behavior, mild tremors, and pale countenance of many members, outsiders speculate their sacraments may involve the use of drugs; the Hierophant routinely decries these accusations and invites reporters to observe the services

These reporters eventually pervade the erroneous—and dangerous—conclusion that the Holy Martyr Church is merely an offshoot of the Catholic Church

The HMC's holy text is a book called The Post-Testament, *which the Hierophant claims to have recreated from a combination of memory and divine messages from his home world of Acetia*

Many outside the Church speculate that tales of extraterrestrial origin are mere fabrication, and the HMC is routinely mocked in pop culture

Nevertheless, by CE 2041, the organization boasts an impressive 10 Churches and 5000 worshippers in the United States: Elijah, now called the Lamb and thought by Churchgoers to be a prophet, travels between what is later identified as the fastest-growing cult in American history with the help of his brother and only priest, Cicero

CE 2045 / AL 1

Martyrs go public after one of the Church's celebrity supporters is indicted on murder charges

The species is considered the result of religious delusion until ▮▮▮▮▮▮▮ *dies in the custody of officers while forced to wait outside the courthouse for his transportation*

Blood tests volunteered by the Hierophant confirm that the proteins of martyrs are biologically different from those of humans, and that this trait is infectious

Many human beings refuse to believe in martyrs, but those that do fail to react well

CE 2046 / AL 2 – CE 2150 / AL 105

A dark time in martyr history where the species is relegated to the shadows, and many martyrs are killed on the discovery of their identity; some governments go so far as to render them "non-people"

Russia, home of the Hierophant and several martyr politicians for many years, extends itself as a safe haven of the "maligned" group suffering "religious" persecution

Defenders of martyrs point to the Lamb, the savior of the group; consumption of his blood makes it possible for a martyr to survive up to one week without consumption of human proteins

Detractors argue that the Lamb cannot be everywhere at once, and martyrdom is a disease which cannot be controlled

CE 2150 / AL 105

Senator ▮▮▮▮▮ *of Vermont is the first American politician to be outed as a martyr, sparking numerous gubernatorial debates about everything from the ability of martyrs to run for office to the number of terms they should be allowed*

For the first time in human history, a government recognizes the martyrs as a legitimate race: the United States of America

The American Registry of Martyrs is created in AL 120, which results in several decades of backlash wherein the list is used for discrimination, rather than to curb it

Martyrs are given the vote in AL 147, thanks in large part to the compassionate efforts of their human proponents

CE 2240 / AL 195

The Hierophant is formally elected president of the Russian Federation following the untimely death of his predecessor, ▮▮▮▮▮

In a terrible shock to the Russian people, ▉▉▉▉▉▉'s cause of death is listed as suicide; the Hierophant nobly swears to guide the people through this time of crisis

The Italian city of Venice is declared uninhabitable due to rising sea levels

CE 2310 / AL 265

British and Canadian martyrs win personage

Senator ▉▉▉▉▉▉ is arrested for murder after it is discovered he has not been subsisting exclusively on donated blood, as he has led the people to believe

While the United States has gone back and forth on the issue of martyr rights, the species has taken particular hold in Europe; China begins to demonstrate anxiety about its small martyr population

The Holy Martyr Church gains alarming claim to Apostolic Succession following the revelation that Bishop ▉▉▉▉▉▉ of Verona was martyred before his episcopal consecration; the bishop officially converts to the HMC soon after the public revelation

The Roman Catholic Church responds with the blanket excommunication of all martyrs, thus voiding the false claim to succession; the Holy Martyr Church claims, as ever, to be victims of persecution

CE 2400 / AL 355

When the slaughter of the Hierophant's second generation of children provokes dissent in Europe, China surreptitiously foments rebellion and funds the nascent Hunters

The Hierophant survives his sixth recorded assassination attempt, provoking World War III: Britain, Canada, Turkey, and Russia are soon awarded the support of the United States, which is increasingly regarded as a martyr nation; China manages to win the support of Japan, India, and small portions of Europe

CE 2401 / AL 356 – CE 2415 / AL 370

Over the course of fifteen years, World War III stretches global resources past their breaking point

Outside of densely populated countries, martyrs are at constant threat of hate crimes, which the Hierophant claims to be the result of war, religious bigotry, and racism

Russian annexes Poland during the war in what the country claims to be defensive action

High-tech drone warfare and the rapid speed at which information travels keeps the conflict limited to a series of skirmishes and intermittent bombings until Turkey joins Russia in an abrupt assault on Kazakhstan; it becomes apparent that the Hierophant's real goal in the war is to gain land

Desperate to end the conflict, the Chinese military makes the decision to drop an atomic bomb on the city of Moscow following a series of warnings to evacuate the city

For reasons unknown, the warnings fail to reach the populace in time; even those martyrs not killed in the blast die from radiation poisoning

Evidence later indicates a mass power outage gripped Moscow hours before the bomb was dropped

The Hierophant, in Rome for an unannounced business trip, is unharmed

Following the bombing, a vast swath of Russia is rendered uninhabitable; the Chinese government, having been provoked into a war crime, reluctantly admits defeat and pays reparations while firmly denying, now or ever, rights to martyrs in their country

CE 2545 / AL 500

After the war, the subject of martyrs and martyr rights becomes an important subject worldwide: in 50 years, 63 countries pass legislation either for or against their citizenship

Every country in Europe recognizes martyr citizens

Environmental repair of Russia begins in earnest

CE 2650 / AL 605

The Hierophant, on surviving yet another assassination attempt, appeals to the Pope; the official Catholic position soon becomes pro-martyr, an arguable contradiction of the Church's respect for all life

Despite amending their official position to assure their followers that martyrs deserve the dignity of life as much as any other living thing, the Catholic Church still believes members of the Holy Martyr Church to be heretical, and martyrs are still considered excommunicated upon their martyrdom

A series of small wars are fought between anti-martyr and pro-martyr European states; this loosely connected series of conflicts earns the name "the European Civil War" and stretches until 705 AL

CE 2770 / AL 725

The Second European Union is established; due to human majority leadership, the motion to conglomerate the separate nations into one country fails to pass

Nonetheless, the Hierophant is elected speaker of the Union, a position comparable to president of the United States

CE 2845 / AL 800 – CE 3045 / AL 1000

Russia, though considered once more habitable, is widely regarded as the most undesirable place in the planet, second only to the ultrahot island nation of Australia

Using technology created to save Russia, the drowned city of Venice is raised from the sea

The Hierophant turns his attention to the notion of a Martian colony

Hunter activities grow more prominent throughout South America and the Middle East, while the martyr population of the United States is deliberately grown; a terror attack in Washington, DC, leads not only to a change of capital city, but to war

American declares war on Afghanistan without sufficient proof that their citizens were involved in the attack; the European Union, now frequently shortened to Europa, provides military and fiscal support

CE 3060 / AL 1015

A series of wars with America rocks the Middle East while martyrs worldwide play the victim; every time a Hunter cell is disbanded, another pops up

America is eventually urged by its own people to end the conflicts and pay reparations; devastated, the Middle East struggles to rebuild

CE 3295 / AL 1250

After an escalating series of violent acts by Hunter cells advocating against martyr rights, Pope ▮▮▮▮▮▮ is assassinated; the Catholic world mourns, as do martyrs, who consider the Holy See to be a religious authority

In the wake of the violence, the Vatican offers a stunning response: Cardinal ▮▮▮▮▮ I is elected the first martyr Pope

The schism this creates in the Church is unprecedented

To celebrate this union of Catholics and martyrdom, Italy's name is changed to Mephitoli

CE 3305 / AL 1260

After much struggle, the constitution of the Middle States is ratified; those states ravaged by the Hierophant band together in the fashion of Europa and form a home for displaced humans

Supporters of the traditional Roman Catholic Church flood the new union's borders; Jerusalem is established as the new Holy See by the Council of Bathsheba in 1262

While the Vatican declares a merger of the RCC and the HMC, the congregation in Jerusalem formally denies the apostolic succession of the martyr church and expands the doctrine of excommunication to all martyrs, as well as human attendants of the martyr church

Millions of superficial Catholics, failing to understand the difference, continue attending their old churches and are, with varying degrees of awareness and concern, excommunicated

CE 3411 / AL 1366

After determining enough generations have passed since the merger of faiths, patriarchs call to order the Thirty-Third Ecumenical Council of the Catholic Church

Following the meeting, informally called Vatican III, Pope ▮▮▮▮▮▮ steps down, and martyr doctrine is seamlessly integrated into Church teachings

The Hierophant is formally elected Pope ad vitam aeternam *after the shortest conclave in history: 20 minutes*

CE 3445 / AL 1400

Following Vatican III, Asian countries begin rejecting martyr (and even Lazarene) influence more violently than before

By the year 3445, it is the official position of the Catholic Church that the Hierophant and his organization are the beings described in the Book of Revelations, heretofore considered symbolism: Jerusalem quietly calls its own Vatican III to establish the new position

In the United States of America, violence against humans proves on the rise; the Hierophant makes many special trips to advise the president on how to handle such trying times

Upon the release of a number of large-scale studies that indicate mankind's technological development has been drastically impacted by needless wars with the Hierophant, a coalition is formed between Japan, China, India, and the Middle States to develop the first global mass-transit system

Japanese Engineer, ▮▮▮▮▮▮▮ *, names this transit system "The Light Rail"; in celebration of this achievement, the Land of the Rising Sun becomes known as the Empire of the Risen Sun*

In AL 1412, a terrorist attack which military intelligence claims to be from Mexican soil leads to the annexation of Mexico: the world knows better than to respond to the Hierophant's attempts to provoke them into war, and Mexico's pleas for assistance go unanswered

CE 3495 / AL 1450

With more than 50 percent of the Senate and 30 percent of the House seats now held by openly martyr politicians in the United States, the first martyr president is elected

Two years later, the New Constitution is proposed, and the United States agrees to rejoin Britain due to "concerns" over expanding Eastern Hemisphere technology

CE 3517 / AL 1472

Through skillful tax maneuvering and no small amount of intimidation, the Hierophant acquires his dream castle of Kronborg, located in Elsinore, Denmark; the already martyr-heavy town becomes the political capital to the Vatican's religious one, and martyrs flood in, giving way to a new social structure that will spread out across most of Europa

New York's name is changed to New Elsinore to celebrate this achievement

CE 3560 / AL 1515

Most US citizens who were upset about America's rejoining have either been martyred, grown old, or died; the new generations raised with this reality accepts it as simple fact

They also accept as simple fact the notion that, as an extension of the British Empire, the Hierophant has complete sovereignty over their domain

Protests are launched when the term limits of American presidents are formally abolished; these same protests are soon squelched, and lifelong term limits for presidents become the norm for the next generation

Accusations of poor working conditions on the part of some humans in the employ of martyrs, especially the hyper-wealthy variety found in the Denmark city of Elsinore, echo accusations of slavery both in the European courts and in American factories and farms

Arguments about humans being murdered for food have long since become so rote that only a few countries, namely Japan, China, and a handful of African states, seem to care about the subject at all

CE 3609 / AL 1564

The Light Rail officially opens; one year later, the United States proposes unifications with Canada and Mexico, with the latter formally declared property of the United States

Mexico retaliates by declaring (civil) war on the United States in 1570

Turkey's president is outed as a martyr after a suspicious centennial term; he declares allegiance to the Holy Martyr Church, and to the Hierophant

After the death of US president ███████████ *of Virginia, Holy Family member Trimalchio is elected president*

He humbly signs a document formalizing Church powers over the government of the United Front, and grants the Hierophant the authority to install future presidents, hereafter to be referred to as "governors"

In a gesture almost certainly intended to be mocking, Trimalchio allows the measure to be submitted for a vote; the people pass it, even without the surreptitious influence of Hierophant-employed hackers over the electronic voting machines

CE 3666 / AL 1621

Under Trimalchio's controversial reign, new measures are put into place walking back the crimes of murder, assault, and kidnapping for martyrs in the Front

Many European countries follow suit, while increasing sentences for humans who commit the same crimes against martyrs

Humans lose the right to vote on anything more than local measures around 1650

Concerned about its citizens still flooding into America—lured by the universal basic income, which Trimalchio and the Hierophant work to establish in 1654—Japan begins to earnestly fund the terrorist organization known as the Hunters, and begins to engage in a series of sanctions against the Front, which inspires some countries to follow suit

The Hierophant's response to this is to encourage martyrs to vacation in or move to Japan, and to find a nice Japanese child to martyr

A small wave of martyr immigration in Japan is swiftly and violently halted, which provides the Hierophant a fine excuse to start another series of conflicts

Trimalchio isolates Asian and Mexican citizens into specialized neighborhoods, citing concerns of terrorism and spying; by 1658, proper concentration camps have been developed in Canadian Jurisdictions, Montana, and a few isolated spots in the Mexican desert

Horrible rumors about the treatment and slaughter of humans circulate quickly in an age where DIOX cyborgans equipped with Internet access and usable reality-augmentation features have begun to hit the market

By 1662, Japan and the martyrs are once more at war: the First Invasion of Japan leads to catastrophic loss of martyr life and the subsequent invasion of California

CE 3711 / AL 1666

The Hierophant martyrs an eight-year-old girl named Morgan in a small Mephitolian Jurisdiction; he changes her name, as is tradition

The child, Dominia di Mephitoli, will grow up to become the single most formidable—and frightening—general that the world has ever seen

CE 3731 / AL 1686

By the age of 28, Dominia has become well known for her particular capacity for violence and strategic warfare; after joining the military at 20 and being sent to the Southwestern theater to engage invaders in California and Mexico and achieving the rank of lieutenant colonel, the plight of the navy at the hands of the Japanese becomes woefully apparent

At the Hierophant's request, Dominia is transferred across military branches, and is forced to endure a brief stint in the navy; such transfers are common in the long-lived species of martyrs, but Lieutenant Colonel Mephitoli is personally unhappy in the new role, as well as disgusted to see so many of her comrades die

Believing a new, more serious strategy is needed than allowing the Japanese to play Battleship with them for the next twenty years, Dominia convinces her Father to stage a Second Invasion of Japan

Under Mephitoli's command, the operation proves so successful it leads to the Ruin of Tokyo, and her promotion to general; however, the deaths of many citizens means that Japan has formal evidence of war crimes

Strictly speaking, the Front loses the war, and is forced to dismantle its camps, pay reparations, and extradite Governor Trimalchio for trial in Japan

The Hierophant politely refuses this third demand, and Trimalchio will never leave the United Front again

Throughout the rest of her Earthly life, until her promotion to governess of the Front, the General will be shipped between wars, with any peacetime filled with an on-again, off-again career in the military police

CE 3845 / AL 1800

The increasingly paranoid governor, convinced humans are planning to murder him and that Japan is planning to invade just to capture him, has to be forced by the Hierophant to allow electric threshold technology in his country

The electric barriers only do so much good; human citizens are still at constant risk, and human immigrants are in particular danger

The Hunters are happy to oblige Trimalchio's paranoid fantasies and begin a long-term campaign of ideological subversion in the Front

Over the course of eighty years, multiple generations of Front citizens are warmed into dissent through subtle countercultural motifs worked into art, music, literature, and the platforms of those few human politicians still with money and security enough to run for office

The Internet makes this process, once practiced by the Hierophant for the sake of martyrs, very easy

CE 3905 / AL 1860

In response to an increase in violence against martyrs, a booming martyr population in need of ready food, and evidence indicating willful conspiracies of ideological subversion, Trimalchio quietly reinstates his camp policy; all humans may potentially be encamped for any number of crimes, and most city-dwelling humans receiving universal basic income are relocated into organized neighborhoods to allow for ease of their control

By 1875, the world is once more aware of what is happening in the Front, but the dangerous nation, having cut ties to every non-martyr country, refuses to yield in a folie à deux linked to the mental illness of its leader

Most humans agree that the removal of Trimalchio is the only way to make any progress in diplomatic relations with the Front

The Jurisdiction of Mexico, refusing to recognize his sovereignty, dismantles its camps and declares war on the United Front; it claims it has no need to secede, as it never accepted being made a Jurisdiction in the first place

Those freed from the Mexican camps form the first basis of the South American Resistance Army

Citizens all across the Front join secret local militias in support of SARA, which swiftly becomes associated with—and funded by—the Hunters

CE 3929 / AL 1884

UF governor and Holy Family member, Trimalchio of California, is assassinated by SARA extremists; the Hierophant becomes de facto governor until the war's conclusion

In retaliation, General Dominia di Mephitoli orchestrates the mass slaughter of encamped humans in an event which will come to be known as "the Black Night"

Soon after, the General enters seclusion in the Canadian Jurisdictions for 20 years; the reasons for this are broadly related to threats on her life following the Black Night, but the real reasons remain a mystery

CE 3948 / AL 1903

General di Mephitoli is ordered back from her sabbatical to engage in the ongoing South American Conflict, in hopes that her presence will end the thirty-year struggle

CE 3951 / AL 1906

The Battle for the Reclamation of Mexico, the final battle of the South American Conflict, begins as the bloodiest loss of the General's career; she is captured and spends six nights as a POW before making good her escape in what becomes known as "the Nogales Rampage"

The bloody path Cicero and his company carve to rendezvous with her in Tucson puts a brutal end one of the most horrific wars the planet has yet seen

On a Pacific Northwest beach following the war, the General meets her future wife, Cassandra

Six months later, General di Mephitoli is promoted to governess of the United Front

CE 3952 / AL 1907

A strange announcement is made: thanks to a tip from the Lamb, the Hierophant discovers an abandoned baby girl, which he claims to have been infected by tainted breast milk; however, through the mercy of God, the baby will rise again despite the fact that introduction of the protein into an infant body tends to kill the child permanently, rather than transmute it into a martyr

Therefore, although the baby dies soon after the Hierophant's discovery, he places the dead body under the care of a team of doctors

Incredibly, the abandoned child grows during death, and over the next twenty years, will develop into a physically normal adult; the reasons are unknown, and efforts to replicate the effect can lead only to permanent infant mortality

CE 3975 / AL 1930

Santa Lavinia di Firenze, Sacred Princess of Europa, Merciful Miracle of the Holy Father, and Blessed Virgin of the Holy Family, awakens after a twenty-four-year-long period of clinical death; a heartbeat begins in February and brain activity starts in March, leaving the girl in a comatose state until the year's end

She awakens for the first time in her life that December

For his efforts in maintaining watch for signs of vitals over the past decade, her doctor, Theodore, is martyred by the Hierophant, and awarded the title, "del Medico," as well as a large sum of land he tends to spurn in favor of following Lavinia's transportation between the Holy Father's many castles

CE 4036 / AL 1991

In an effort to increase the martyr population, which is still struggling to renew itself after the war, the Hierophant issues a blanket writ of permission: for the next twenty years, all martyrs looking to become parents may martyr any child under the age of 10 without an interview by a Holy Family member

Particularly in the Front cities of San Valentino and New Elsinore, martyring rates skyrocket

On a farm in the Jurisdiction of California, a border collie gives birth to a litter of puppies; one finds its way into a neighboring farmhouse, belonging to the McLintock family

CE 4041 / AL 1996

Santa Lavinia di Firenze celebrates her 66th Feast Day

CE 4042 / AL 1997

Cassandra di Mephitoli dies on the First of May, aged 113

The Governess of the United Front attempts to flee her post for reasons unknown to the public

She is branded a traitor, a terrorist, and the most wanted woman in the world

Don't Miss Book II of
The Disgraced Martyr Trilogy

THE GENERAL'S BRIDE

AUGUST 14TH, 2019

M. F. Sullivan is an author and playwright currently residing in the town of Ashland, Oregon. An avid student of the occult, Sullivan fills what little time she does not spend writing with reading, attending the local Shakespeare Festival, and the company of her significant other. With the trilogy finished and behind her, she is already hard at work on yet another novel. She loves cats, baking, psychedelic drugs, and 5-star Amazon.com reviews. Sign up for essays and book release updates on www.paintedblindpublishing.com, and consider leaving a nice note on Amazon while you're browsing the Internet. It would make her day.

ALSO BY THE AUTHOR

Delilah, My Woman
The Lightning Stenography Device